1983

Hamlet a sermon
of life.

spouses thats
gathering pauses.

DR. S. WEIR MITCHELL, AUTHOR OF "THE RED CITY."

D R. S. WEIR MITCHELL, physician, neurologist and author, in "The Red City" has produced an effective sequel to his good earlier story of "Hugh Wynne, Free Quaker." Dr. Mitchell, who finds in the writing of fiction relief and recreation from his arduous professional duties, enjoys a world-wide reputation alike as scientist and romancer. Since 1865 he has been a member of the National Academy of Sciences, with active and honorary membership and office in several renowned foreign medical and scientific bodies. His neurological researches and works also have earned him fame. Dr. Mitchell's home is in Philadelphia. The Century Company brings out "The Red City."

The mere fact that Dr. S. Weir Mitchell's new novel is a continuation of "Hugh Wynne," will be enough to pique universal interest, and I am glad to add that the book will not disappoint its readers. It is a historical romance of the second administration of President Washington and the title, "The Red City," refers to the red brick city of the Quakers, in which the scenes are laid. Though its love theme is well sustained, its most solid merit is found in its large and faithful picturing of Philadelphia life and people during the epoch of the French revolution.

Dr. Mitchell makes little use of mystery or of dramatic thrills. He tells his story in rippling narrative and natural conversation, seldom stirring the pulse, but steadfastly holding the interest and the heart of the reader. From beginning to end there is never a moment's doubt that the gallant Huguenot hero, Vicomte Rene de Courval, is going to win the sweet Quaker maid, Margaret Swanwick. But this young French refugee, who comes to Philadelphia with his widowed mother, has seen his beloved father murdered by the revolutionists at Avignon, and he has vowed to kill the man who is chiefly responsible for the deed. When this villain comes to Philadelphia on the staff of the French minister, Genet, the trouble begins.

The interest of the story is not in its rather simple plot, but in its admirably drawn characters and in the lively minor incidents by which their natures are revealed. Rene, impulsive, generous, passionate, sensitively honorable, is sufficient in himself to captivate feminine readers. He is the beau ideal of romantic fiction, and his Quaker Pearl is equally lovable. But there is something less trite and hence more noteworthy in the fine character of Rene's somewhat mysterious German friend, Schmidt, whose calm wisdom checks the younger man's fierce impulsiveness at the right moments. The friendship between these two men is one of Dr. Mitchell's finest achievements. Rene's proud, cold mother, too, is a superb literary cameo, and the scenes in which the girl melts her icy opposition are full of tenderness.

Of the characters that figured in the former novel, Aunt Gainor Wynne plays the largest and most amusing part. The view given of Washington is human and intimate, depicting him as a weary, kindly old man. Jefferson, Hamilton and Edward Randolph are less fully drawn. The whole story is woven upon a solid warp of history, especially Philadelphia history. The great plague that swept the city brings out the heroism of two of the characters, while the partisan strife over the French revolution contributes much to the plot There is no great climax at the end, but the story saunters serenely to its close, holding the reader with the quiet charm of an Indian summer day. The sense of quiet satisfaction that it leaves upon the mind is proof that Dr. Mitchell has given us of his best.

Books by

Dr. S. Weir Mitchell.

&

Fiction.

HUGH WYNNE.
CONSTANCE TRESCOT.
THE YOUTH OF WASHINGTON.
CIRCUMSTANCE.
THE ADVENTURES OF FRANÇOIS.
THE AUTOBIOGRAPHY OF A QUACK.
DR. NORTH AND HIS FRIENDS.
IN WAR TIME.
ROLAND BLAKE.
FAR IN THE FOREST.
CHARACTERISTICS.
WHEN ALL THE WOODS ARE GREEN.
A MADEIRA PARTY.
THE RED CITY.

Essays.

DOCTOR AND PATIENT.
WEAR AND TEAR — HINTS FOR THE
  OVERWORKED.

Poems.

COLLECTED POEMS.
THE WAGER, AND OTHER POEMS.

"She stood still, amazed"

THE RED CITY

A NOVEL OF THE
SECOND ADMINISTRATION OF
PRESIDENT WASHINGTON

BY

S. WEIR MITCHELL, M.D., LL.D.

WITH ILLUSTRATIONS
BY ARTHUR I. KELLER

NEW YORK
THE CENTURY CO.
1908

THE DE VINNE PRESS

TO

WM. D. HOWELLS

IN PAYMENT OF A DEBT LONG OWED
TO A MASTER OF FICTION AND TO
A FRIEND OF MANY YEARS

LIST OF ILLUSTRATIONS

THE RED CITY

THE RED CITY

A NOVEL OF THE SECOND ADMINISTRATION
OF WASHINGTON

I

ABOUT five in the afternoon on the 23d of May, 1792, the brig *Morning Star* of Bristol, John Maynard, master, with a topgallant breeze after her, ran into Delaware Bay in mid-channel between Cape May and Cape Henlopen. Here was the only sunshine they had seen in three weeks. The captain, liking the warmth on his broad back, glanced up approvingly at mast and rigging. "She 's a good one," he said, and noting the ship powdered white with her salt record of the sea's attentions, he lighted a pipe and said aloud, "She 's salted like Christmas pork." As he spoke, he cast an approving eye on a young fellow who sat at ease in the lower rigging, laughing as the brig rolled over and a deluge of water flushed the deck and made the skipper on the after-hatch lift his feet out of the way of the wash.

"Hi, there, Wicount," called the captain, "she 's enjoying of herself like a young duck in a pond."

De Courval called out a gay reply, lost, as the ship

rolled, in the rattle of storm-loosened stays and the clatter of flapping sails.

Toward sunset the wind lessened, the sea-born billows fell away, and De Courval dropped lightly on the deck, and, passing the master, went down to the cabin.

Near to dusk of this pleasant evening of May the captain anchored off Lewes, ordered a boat sent ashore, and a nip of rum all round for the crew. Then, with a glass for himself, he lighted his pipe and sat down on the cover of the companionway and drew the long breath of the victor in a six-weeks' fight with the Atlantic in its most vicious mood. For an hour he sat still, a well-contented man; then, aware of a curly head and bronzed young face rising out of the companionway beside him, he said, "You might find that coil of rope comfortable."

The young man, smiling as he sat down, accepted the offer of the captain's tobacco and said in easy English, with scarce a trace of accent to betray his French origin: "My mother thanks you, sir, for your constant care of her. I have no need to repeat my own thanks. We unhappy *émigrés* who have worn out the hospitality of England, and no wonder, find kindness such as yours as pleasant as it is rare. My mother fully realizes what you have given us amid all your cares for the ship—and—"

"Oh, that 's all right, Wicount," broke in the captain. "My time for needing help and a cheery word may come any day on land or sea. Some one will pay what seems to you a debt."

"Ah, well, here or hereafter," said the young man,

gravely, and putting out a hand, he wrung the broad, hairy paw of the sailor. "My mother will come on deck to-morrow and speak for herself. Now she must rest. Is that our boat?"

"Yes; I sent it ashore a while ago. There will be milk and eggs and fresh vegetables for madam."

"Thank you," said De Courval. A slight, full feeling in the throat, a little difficulty in controlling his features, betrayed the long strain of much recent peril and a sense of practical kindness the more grateful for memories of bitter days in England and of far-away tragic days in France. With some effort to suppress emotion, he touched the captain's knee, saying, "Ah, my mother will enjoy the fresh food." And then, "What land is that?"

"Lewes, sir, and the sand-dunes. With the flood and a fair wind, we shall be off Chester by evening to-morrow. No night sailing for me on this bay, with never a light beyond Henlopen, and that 's been there since '65. I know it all in daytime like I know my hand. Most usually we bide for the flood. I shall be right sorry to part with you. I 've had time and again—Frenchies; I never took to them greatly, —but you 're about half English. Why, you talk 'most as well as me. Where did you learn to be so handy with it?" De Courval smiled at this doubtful compliment.

"When my father was attached to our embassy in London,—that was when I was a lad,—I went to an English school, and then, too, we were some months in England, my mother and I, so I speak it fairly well. My mother never would learn it."

"Fairly well! Guess you do."

Then the talk fell away, and at last the younger man rose and said, "I shall go to bed early, for I want to be up at dawn to see this great river."

At morning, with a fair wind and the flood, the *Morning Star* moved up the stream, past the spire and houses of Newcastle. De Courval watched with a glass the green country, good for fruit, and the hedges in place of fences. He saw the low hills of Delaware, the flat sands of Jersey far to right, and toward sunset of a cloudless May day heard the clatter of the anchor chain as they came to off Chester Creek. The mother was better, and would be glad to take her supper on deck, as the captain desired. During the day young De Courval asked numberless questions of mates and men, happy in his mother's revival, and busy with the hopes and anxieties of a stranger about to accept life in a land altogether new to him, but troubled with unanswerable doubts as to how his mother would bear an existence under conditions of which as yet neither he nor she had any useful knowledge.

When at sunset he brought his mother on deck, she looked about her with pleasure. The ship rode motionless on a faintly rippled plain of orange light. They were alone on this great highway to the sea. To the left near by were the clustered houses on creek and shore where Dutch, Swede, and English had ruled in turn. There were lads in boats fishing, with cries of mock fear and laughter over the catch of crabs. It seemed to her a deliciously abrupt change from the dark cabin and the ship odors to a pretty, smiling coast, with the smoke pennons of hospitable welcome inviting to enter and share what God had so freely given.

A white-cloth-covered table was set out on deck with tea-things, strawberries, and red roses the mate had gathered. As she turned, to thank the captain who had come aft to meet her, he saw his passenger for the first time. At Bristol she had come aboard at evening and through a voyage of storms she had remained in her cabin, too ill to do more than think of a hapless past and of a future dark with she knew not what new disasters.

What he saw was a tall, slight woman whose snow-white hair made more noticeable the nearly complete black of her widow's dress, relieved only by a white collar, full white wrist ruffles, and a simple silver chatelaine from which hung a bunch of keys and a small enameled watch. At present she was sallow and pale, but, except for somewhat too notable regularity of rather pronounced features, the most observant student of expression could have seen no more in her face at the moment than an indefinable stamp of good breeding and perhaps, on larger opportunity, an unusual incapacity to exhibit emotional states, whether of grief, joy, or the lighter humors of every-day social relation.

The captain listened with a pleasure he could not have explained as her voice expressed in beautiful French the happiness of which her face reported no signal. The son gaily translated or laughed as now and then she tried at a phrase or two of the little English picked up during her stay in England.

When they had finished their supper, young De Courval asked if she were tired and would wish to go below. To his surprise she said: "No, René. We are to-morrow to be in a new country, and it is well that as far as may be we settle our accounts with the past."

"Well, mother, what is it? What do you wish?"

"Let us sit down together. Yes, here. I have something to ask. Since you came back to Normandy in the autumn of 1791 with the news of your father's murder, I have asked for no particulars."

"No, and I was glad that you did not."

"Later, my son, I was no more willing to hear, and even after our ruin and flight to England last January, my grief left me no desire to be doubly pained. But now—now, I have felt that even at much cost I should hear it all, and then forever, with God's help, put it away with the past, as you must try to do. His death was the more sad to me because all his sympathies were with the party bent on ruining our country. Ah, René, could he have guessed that he who had such hopeful belief in what those changes would effect should die by the hand of a Jacobin mob! I wish now to hear the whole story."

"All of it, mother?" He was deeply troubled.

"Yes, all—all without reserve."

She sat back in her chair, gazing up the darkening river, her hands lying supine on her knees. "Go on, my son, and do not make me question you."

"Yes, mother." There were things he had been glad to forget and some he had set himself never to forget. He knew, however, that now, on the whole, it was better to be frank. He sat still, thinking how best he could answer her. Understanding the reluctance his silence expressed, she said, "You will, René?"

"Yes, dear mother"; and so on the deck at fall of night, in an alien land, the young man told his story of one of the first of the minor tragedies which, as a Jacobin said, were useless except to give a good appetite for blood.

It was hard to begin. He had in perfection the memory of things seen, the visualizing capacity. He waited, thinking how to spare her that which at her summons was before him in all the distinctness of an hour of unequaled anguish.

She felt for him and knew the pain she was giving, comprehending him with a fullness rare to the mother mind. "This is not a time to spare me," she said, "nor yourself. Go on." She spoke sternly, not turning her head, but staring up the long stretch of solitary water.

"It shall be as you wish," he returned slowly. "In September of last year you were in Paris with our cousin, La Rochefoucauld, about our desperate money straits, when the assembly decreed the seizure of Avignon from the Pope's vice-legate. This news seemed to make possible the recovery of rents due us in that city. My father thought it well for me to go with him—"

"Yes, yes, I know; but go on."

"We found the town in confusion. The Swiss guard of the vice-legate had gone. A leader of the

Jacobin party, Lescuyer, had been murdered that morning before the altar of the Church of the Cordeliers. That was on the day we rode in. Of a sudden we were caught in a mob of peasants near the gate. A Jacobin, Jourdan, led them, and had collected under guard dozens of scared bourgeois and some women. Before we could draw or even understand, we were tumbled off our horses and hustled along. On the way the mob yelled, 'A bas les aristocrates!'

"As they went, others were seized—in fact, every decent-looking man. My father held me by the wrist, saying: 'Keep cool, René. We are not Catholics. It is the old trouble.' The crush at the Pope's palace was awful. We were torn apart. I was knocked down. Men went over me, and I was rolled off the great outer stair and fell, happily, neglected. An old woman cried to me to run. I got up and went in after the Jourdan mob with the people who were crowding in to see what would happen. You remember the great stairway. I was in among the first and was pushed forward close to the broad dais. Candles were brought. Jourdan— 'coupe tête' they called him—sat in the Pope's chair. The rest sat or stood on the steps. A young man brought in a table and sat by it. The rest of the great hall was in darkness, full of a ferocious crowd, men and women.

"Then Jourdan cried out: 'Silence! This is a court of the people. Fetch in the aristocrats!' Some threescore of scared men and a dozen women were huddled together at one side, the women crying.

Jourdan waited. One by one they were seized and set before him. There were wild cries of 'Kill! Kill!' Jourdan nodded, and two men seized them one after another, and at the door struck. The people in the hall were silent one moment as if appalled, and the next were frenzied and screaming horrible things. Near the end my father was set before Jourdan. He said, 'Who are you?'

"My father said, 'I am Citizen Courval, a stranger. I am of the religion, and here on business.' As he spoke, he looked around him and saw me. He made no sign."

"Ah," said Madame de Courval, "he did not say Vicomte."

"No. He was fighting for his life, for you, for me."

"Go on."

"His was the only case over which they hesitated even for a moment. One whom they called Tournal said: 'He is not of Avignon. Let him go.' The mob in the hall was for a moment quiet. Then the young man at the table, who seemed to be a mock secretary and wrote the names down, got up and cried out: 'He is lying. Who knows him?' He was, alas! too well known. A man far back of me called out, 'He is the Vicomte de Courval.' My father said: 'It is true. I am the Vicomte de Courval. What then?'

"The secretary shrieked: 'I said he lied. Death! Death to the *ci-devant!*'

"Jourdan said: 'Citizen Carteaux is right. Take him. We lose time.'

"On this my father turned again and saw me as I

cried out, 'Oh, my God! My father!' In the uproar no one heard me. At the door on the left, it
was, as they struck, he called out—oh, very loud:
'Yvonne! Yvonne! God keep thee!' Oh, mother,
I saw it—I saw it.'' For a moment he was unable
to go on.

"I got out of the place somehow. When safe
amid the thousands in the square I stood still and
got grip of myself. A woman beside me said, 'They
threw them down into the Tour de la Glacière.' ''

"Ah!'' exclaimed the Vicomtesse.

"It was dusk outside when all was over. I waited
long, but about nine they came out. The people
scattered. I went after the man Carteaux. He was
all night in cafés, never alone—never once alone. I
saw him again, at morning, near by on horseback;
then I lost him. Ah, my God! mother, why would
you make me tell it?''

"Because, René, it is often with you, and because
it is not well for a young man to keep before him
unendingly a sorrow of the past. I wanted you to
feel that now I share with you what I can see so
often has possession of you. Do not pity me because
I know all. Now you shall see how bravely I will
carry it.'' She took his hand. "It will be hard,
but wise to put it aside. Pray God, my son, this
night to help you not to forget, but not hurtfully to
remember.''

He said nothing, but looked up at the darkened
heavens under which the night-hawks were screaming in their circling flight.

"Is there more, my son?''

"As they struck, he called out 'Yvonne!'"

"Yes, but it is so hopeless. Let us leave it, mother."

"No. I said we must clear our souls. Leave nothing untold. What is it?"

"The man Carteaux! If it had not been for you, I should never have left France until I found that man."

"I thought as much. Had you told me, I should have stayed, or begged my bread in England while you were gone."

"I could not leave you then, and now—now the sea lies between me and him, and the craving that has been with me when I went to sleep and at waking I must put away. I will try." As he spoke, he took her hand.

A rigid Huguenot, she had it on her lips to speak of the forgiving of enemies. Generations of belief in the creed of the sword, her love, her sense of the insult of this death, of a sudden mocked her purpose. She was stirred as he was by a passion for vengeance. She flung his hand aside, rose, and walked swiftly about, getting back her self-command by physical action.

He had risen, but did not follow her. In a few minutes she came back through the darkness, and setting a hand on each of his shoulders said quietly: "I am sorry—the man is dead to you—I am sorry you ever knew his name."

"But I do know it. It is with me, and must ever be until I die. I am to try to forget—forget! That I cannot. The sea makes him as one dead to me; but if ever I return to France—"

"Hush! It must be as I have said. If he were within reach do you think I would talk as I do?"

The young man leaned over and kissed her. This was his last secret. "I am not fool enough to cry for what fate has swept beyond my reach. Let us drop it. I did not want to talk of it. We will let the dead past bury its hatred and think only of that one dear memory, mother. And now will you not go to bed, so as to be strong for to-morrow?"

"Not yet," she said. "Go and smoke your pipe with that good captain. I want to be alone." He kissed her forehead and went away.

The river was still; the stars came out one by one, and a great planet shone distinct on the mirroring plain. Upon the shore near by the young frogs croaked shrilly. Fireflies flashed over her, but heedless of this new world she sat thinking of the past, of their wrecked fortunes, of the ruin which made the great duke, her cousin, counsel emigration, a step he himself did not take until the Terror came. She recalled her refusal to let him help them in their flight, and how at last, with a few thousand livres, they had been counseled to follow the many who had gone to America.

Then at last she rose, one bitter feeling expressing itself over and over in her mind in words which were like an echo of ancestral belief, in the obligation old noblesse imposed, no matter what the cost. An overmastering thought broke from her into open speech as she cried aloud: "Ah, my God! why did he not say he was the Vicomte de Courval! Oh, why—"

"Did you call, mother?" said the son.

"No. I am going to the cabin, René. Good night, my son!"

He laid down the pipe he had learned to use in England and which he never smoked in her presence; caught up her cashmere shawl, a relic of better days, and carefully helped her down the companionway.

Then he returned to his pipe and the captain, and to talk of the new home and of the ship's owner, Mr. Hugh Wynne, and of those strange, good people who called themselves Friends, and who *tutoyéd* every one alike. He was eager to hear about the bitter strife of parties, of the statesmen in power, of the chances of work, gathering with intelligence such information as might be of service, until at last it struck eight bells and the captain declared that he must go to bed.

The young man thanked him and added, "I shall like it, oh, far better than England."

"I hope so, Wicount; but of this I am sure, men will like you and, by George, women, too!"

De Courval laughed merrily. "You flatter me, Captain."

"No. Being at sea six weeks with a man is as good as being married, for the knowing of him—the good and the bad of him."

"And my mother, will she like it?"

"Ah, now, that I cannot tell. Good night."

II

WHEN in a morning of brilliant sunshine again, with the flood and a favoring wind, the brig moved up-stream alone on the broad water, Madame de Courval came on deck for the midday meal. Her son hung over her as she ate, and saw with gladness the faint pink in her cheeks, and, well-pleased, translated her questions to the captain as he proudly pointed out the objects of interest when they neared the city of Penn. There was the fort at Red Bank where the Hessians failed, and that was the Swedes' church, and there the single spire of Christ Church rising high over the red brick city, as madam said, of the color of Amsterdam.

Off the mouth of Dock Creek they came to anchor, the captain advising them to wait on shipboard until he returned, and to be ready then to go ashore.

When their simple preparations were completed, De Courval came on deck, and, climbing the rigging, settled himself in the crosstrees to take counsel with his pipe, and to be for a time alone and away from the boat-loads of people eager for letters and for news from France and England.

The mile-wide river was almost without a sail. A few lazy fishers and the slowly moving vans of the mill on Wind Mill Island had little to interest. As

he saw it from his perch, the city front was busy
and represented the sudden prosperity which came
with the sense of permanence the administration of
Washington seemed to guarantee for the great bond
under which a nation was to grow. There was the
town stretching north and south along the Delaware,
and beyond it woodland. What did it hold for him?
The mood of reflection was no rare one for a man of
twenty-five who had lived through months of peril
in France, amid peasants hostile in creed, and who
had seen the fortunes of his house melt away, and at
last had aged suddenly into gravity beyond his years
when he beat his way heartsick out of the grim tragedy of Avignon.

His father's people were of the noblesse of the
robe, country gentles; his mother a cousin of the two
dukes Rochefoucauld. He drew qualities from a
long line of that remarkable judicature which
through all changes kept sacred and spotless the
ermine of the magistrate. From the mother's race
he had spirit, courage, and a reserve of violent pas-
sions, the inheritance of a line of warlike nobles
unused to recognize any law but their own will.

The quiet life of a lesser country gentleman, the
absence from court which pride and lessening means
alike enforced, and the puritan training of a house
which held tenaciously to the creed of Calvin, com-
bined to fit him better to earn his living in a new
land than was the case with the greater nobles who
had come to seek what contented their ambitions—
some means of living until they should regain their
lost estates. They drew their hopes from a ruined
2

past. De Courval looked forward with hope fed by youth, energy, and the simpler life.

It was four o'clock when the captain set them ashore with their boxes on the slip in front of the warehouse of Mr. Wynne, the ship's owner. He was absent at Merion, but his porters would care for their baggage, and a junior clerk would find for them an inn until they could look for a permanent home. When the captain landed them on the slip, the old clerk, Mr. Potts, made them welcome, and would have had madam wait in the warehouse until their affairs had been duly ordered. When her son translated the invitation, she said: "I like it here. I shall wait for you. The sun is pleasant." While he was gone, she stood alone, looking about her at the busy wharf, the many vessels, the floating wind-mills anchored on the river, and the long line of red brick warehouses along the river front.

On his return, De Courval, much troubled, explained that there was not a hackney-coach to be had, and that she had better wait in the counting-house until a chaise could be found. Seeing her son's distress, and learning that an inn could be reached near by, she declared it would be pleasant to walk and that every minute made her better.

There being no help for it, they set out with the clerk, who had but a mild interest in this addition to the French who were beginning to fly from France and the islands, and were taxing heavily the hospitality and the charity of the city. A barrow-man came on behind, with the baggage for their immediate needs, now and then crying, "Barrow! Barrow!" when his way was impeded.

De Courval, at first annoyed that his mother must walk, was silent, but soon, with unfailing curiosity, began to be interested and amused. When, reaching Second Street, they crossed the bridge over Dock Creek, they found as they moved northward a brisk business life, shops, and more varied costumes than are seen to-day. Here were Quakers, to madam's amazement; nun-like Quaker women in the monastic seclusion of what later was irreverently called the "coal-scuttle" bonnet; Germans of the Palatinate; men of another world in the familiar short-clothes, long, broidered waistcoat, and low beaver; a few negroes; and the gray-clad mechanic, with now and then a man from the islands, when suddenly a murmur of French startled the vicomtesse.

"What a busy life, *maman*," her son said; "not like that dark London, and no fog, and the sun—like the sun of home."

"We have no home," she replied, and for a moment he was silent. Then, still intent upon interesting her, he said:

"How strange! There is a sign of a likely black wench and two children for sale. 'Inquire within and see them. Sold for want of use.' And lotteries, *maman*. There is one for a canal between the Delaware and the Schuylkill rivers; and one to improve the Federal City. I wonder where that is." She paid little attention, and walked on, a tall, dark, somber woman, looking straight before her, with her thoughts far away.

The many taverns carried names which were echoes from the motherland, which men, long after the war, were still apt, as Washington wrote, to call "home." The Sign of the Cock, the Dusty Miller, the Pewter Plate, and—"Ah, *maman*," he cried, laughing, "The Inn of the Struggler. That should suit us."

The sullen clerk, stirred at last by the young fellow's gay interest, his eager questions, and his evident wish to distract and amuse a tired woman who stumbled over the loose bricks of the sidewalk, declared that was no place for them. Her tall figure in mourning won an occasional glance, but no more. It was a day of strange faces and varied costumes. "And, *maman*," said her son, "the streets are called for trees and the lanes for berries." Disappointed at two inns of the better class, there being no vacant rooms, they crossed High Street; the son amused at the market stands for fruit, fish, and "garden truck, too," the clerk said, with blacks crying, "Calamus! sweet calamus!" and "Pepper pot, smoking hot!" or "Hominy! samp! grits! hominy!" Then, of a sudden, as they paused on the farther corner, madam cried out, *"Mon dieu!"* and her son a half-suppressed *"Sacré!"* A heavy landau coming down Second Street bumped heavily into a deep rut and there was a liberal splash of muddy water across madam's dark gown and the young man's clothes. In an instant the owner of the landau had alighted, hat in hand, a middle-aged man in velvet coat and knee-breeches.

"Madam, I beg a thousand pardons."

"My mother does not speak English, sir. These things happen. It is they who made the street who should apologize. It is of small moment."

"I thank you for so complete an excuse, sir. You surely cannot be French. Permit me,"—and he turned to the woman, *"mille pardons,"* and went on in fairly fluent French to say how much he regretted, and would not madam accept his landau and drive home? She thanked him, but declined the offer in a voice which had a charm for all who heard it. He bowed low, not urging his offer, and said, "I am Mr. William Bingham. I trust to have the pleasure of meeting madam again and, too, this young gentleman, whose neat excuse for me would betray him if his perfect French did not. Can I further serve you?"

"No, sir," said De Courval, "except to tell me what inn near by might suit us. We are but just now landed. My guide seems in doubt. I should like one close at hand. My mother is, I fear, very tired."

"I think,"—and he turned to the clerk,—"yes, St. Tammany would serve. It is clean and well kept and near by." He was about to add, "Use my name," but, concluding not to do so, added: "It is at the corner of Chancery Lane. This young man will know." Then, with a further word of courtesy, he drove away, while madam stood for a moment sadly contemplating the additions to her toilet.

Mr. Bingham, senator for Pennsylvania, reflected with mild curiosity on the two people he had annoyed, and then murmured: "I was stupid. That is where the Federal Club meets and the English go. They will never take those poor French with their baggage in a barrow."

He had at least the outward manners of a day when there was leisure to be courteous, and, feeling pleased with himself, soon forgot the people he had unluckily inconvenienced. De Courval went on, ruefully glancing at his clothes, and far from dreaming that he was some day to be indebted to the gentleman they had left.

The little party, thus directed, turned into Mulberry Street, or, as men called it, Arch, and, with his mother, De Courval entered a cleanly front room under the sign of St. Tammany. There was a barred tap in one corner, maids in cap and apron moving about, many men seated at tables, with long pipes called churchwardens, drinking ale or port wine. Some looked up, and De Courval heard a man say, "More French beggars." He flushed, bit his lip, and turned to a portly man in a white jacket, who was, as it seemed, the landlord. The mother shrank from the rude looks and said a few words in French.

The host turned sharply as she spoke, and De Courval asked if he could have two rooms. The landlord had none.

"Then may my mother sit down while I inquire without?"

A man rose and offered his chair as he said civilly: "Oeller's Tavern might suit you. It is the French house—a hotel, they call it. You will get no welcome here."

"Thank you," said De Courval, hearing comments on their muddy garments and the damned French. He would have had a dozen quarrels on his hands had he been alone. His mother had declined the seat, and

as he followed her out, he lingered on the step to
speak to his guide. They were at once forgotten, but
he heard behind him scraps of talk, the freely used
oaths of the day, curses of the demagogue Jefferson
and the man Washington, who was neither for one
party nor for the other. He listened with amazement and restrained anger.

He had fallen in with a group of middle-class men,
Federalists in name, clamorous for war with Jacobin
France, and angry at their nominal leader, who
stood like a rock against the double storm of opinion
which was eager for him to side with our old ally
France or to conciliate England. It was long before
De Courval understood the strife of parties, felt most
in the cities, or knew that back of the mischievous
diversity of opinion in and out of the cabinet was our
one safeguard—the belief of the people in a single
man and in his absolute good sense and integrity.
Young De Courval could not have known that the
thoughtless violence of party classed all French together, and as yet did not realize that the *émigré* was
generally the most deadly foe of the present rule in
France.

Looking anxiously at his mother, they set out again
up Mulberry Street, past the meeting-house of
Friends and the simple grave of the great Franklin,
the man too troubled, and the mother too anxious, to
heed or question when they moved by the burial-
ground where Royalist and Whig lay in the peace of
death and where, at the other corner, Wetherill with
the free Quakers built the home of a short-lived
creed.

Oeller's Tavern—because of its French guests called a hotel—was on Chestnut Street, west of Fifth, facing the State House. A civil French servant asked them into a large room on the right of what was known as a double house. It was neat and clean, and the floor was sanded. Presently appeared Maxim Oeller. Yes, he had rooms. He hoped the citizen would like them, and the citizeness. De Courval was not altogether amused. He had spoken English, saying, however, that he was of France, and the landlord had used the patois of Alsace. The mother was worn out, and said wearily: "I can go no farther. It will do. It must do, until we can find a permanent lodging and one less costly."

Mr. Oeller was civil and madam well pleased. For supper in her room, on extra payment, were fair rolls and an omelet. De Courval got the mud off his clothes and at six went down-stairs for his supper.

At table, when he came in, were some twenty people, all men. Only two or three were of French birth and the young man, who could not conceive of Jacobin clubs out of France, sat down and began to eat with keen relish a well-cooked supper.

By and by his neighbors spoke to him. Had he just come over the seas, as the landlord had reported? What was doing in France? He replied, of course, in his very pure English. News in London had come of Mirabeau's death. Much interested, they plied him at once with questions. And the king had tried to leave Paris, and there had been mobs in the provinces, bloodshed, and an attack on Vincennes—which was not quite true. Here were Americans who talked like the Jacobins he had left at home. Their violence surprised him. Would he like to come to-morrow to the Jacobin Club? The king was to be dealt with. Between amusement and indignation the grave young vicomte felt as though he were among madmen. One man asked if the decree of death to all *émigrés* had been carried out. "No," he laughed; "not while they were wise enough to stay away." Another informed him that Washington and Hamilton were on the way to create a monarchy. "Yes, Citizen, you are in a land of titles—Your Excellency, Their Honors of the supreme court in gowns—scarlet gowns." His discreet silence excited them. "Who are you for? Speak out!"

"I am a stranger here, with as yet no opinions."

"A neutral, by Jove!" shouted one.

At last the young man lost patience and said: "I am not, gentlemen, a Jacobin. I am of that noblesse which of their own will gave up their titles. I am— or was—the Vicomte de Courval."

There was an uproar. "We are citizens, we would have you to know. Damn your titles! We are citizens, not gentlemen."

"That is my opinion," said De Courval, rising. Men hooted at him and shook fists in his face. "Take care!" he cried, backing away from the table. In the midst of it came the landlord. "He is a royalist," they cried; "he must go or we go."

The landlord hurried him out of the room. "Monsieur," he said—"Citizen, these are fools, but I have my living to think of. You must go. I am sorry, very sorry."

"I cannot go now," said De Courval. "I shall do so to-morrow at my leisure." It was so agreed. He talked quietly a while with his mother, saying nothing of this new trouble, and then, still hot with anger, he went to his room, astonished at his reception, and anxious that his mother should find a more peaceful home.

He slept the sleep of the healthy young, rose at early dawn, and was able to get milk and bread and thus to escape breakfast with the citizen-boarders, not yet arisen. Before he went out, he glanced at the book of guests. He had written Vicomte de Courval, with his mother's name beneath it, La Vicomtesse de Courval, without a thought on so casual a matter, and now, flushing, he read "Citizen" above his title with an erasure of de and Vicomte. Over his mother's title was written the last affectation of the Jacobins, "Citizeness" Courval. It was so absurd that, the moment's anger passing into mirth, he went out into the air, laughing and exclaiming: *"Mais qu'ils sont bêtes! Quelle enfantillage!* What childishness!" The servant, a man of middle age, who was sweeping the steps, said in French, "What a fine day, monsieur."

"Bon jour, Citizen," returned De Courval, laughing. The man laughed also, and said, *"Canailles, Monsieur,"* with a significant gesture of contempt. *"Bon jour, Monsieur le Vicomte,"* and then, hearing steps within, resumed his task with: "But one must live. My stomach has the opinions of my appetite." For a moment he watched the serious face and well-knit figure of the vicomte as he

turned westward, and then went into the house, remarking, *"Qu'il est beau"*—"What a handsome fellow!"

De Courval passed on. Independence Hall interested him for a moment. Many people went by
him, going to their work, although it was early. He
saw the wretched paving, the few houses high on
banks of earth beyond Sixth Street, and then, as he
walked westward on Chestnut Street, pastures,
cows, country, and the fine forest to the north
known as the Governor's Wood. At last, a mile
farther, he came upon the bank of a river flowing
slowly by. What it was he did not know. On the
farther shore were farms and all about him a thin-
ner forest. It was as yet early, and, glad of the
lonely freshness, he stood still a little while among
the trees, saw bees go by on early business bent, and
heard in the edge of the wood the love song of a
master singer, the cat-bird. Nature had taken him
in hand. He was already happier when, with shock
of joy he realized what she offered. No one was in
sight. He undressed in the edge of the wood and
stood a while in the open on the graveled strand,
the tide at full of flood. The morning breeze stirred
lightly the pale-green leaves of spring with shy
caress, so that little flashes of warm light from the
level sun-shafts coming through the thin leafage of
May flecked his white skin. He looked up, threw
out his arms with the naked man's instinctive happiness in the moment's sense of freedom from all
form of bondage, ran down the beach, and with a
shout of pure barbarian delight plunged into the

river. For an hour he was only a young animal alone with nature—diving, swimming, splashing the water, singing bits of love-songs or laughing in pure childlike enjoyment of the use of easy strength. At last he turned on his back and floated luxuriously. He pushed back his curly hair, swept the water from his eyes, and saw with a cry of pleasure that which is seen only from the level of the watery plain. On the far shore, a red gravel bank, taking the sun, was reflected a plain of gold on the river's breadth. The quickened wind rolled the water into little concave mirrors which, dancing on the gold surface, gathered the clear azure above him in cups of intense indigo blue. It was new and freshly wonderful. What a sweet world! How good to be alive!

When ashore he stood in a flood of sunshine, wringing the water from body and limbs and hair, and at last running up and down the beach until he was dry and could dress. Then, hat in hand, he walked away, feeling the wholesome languor of the practised swimmer and gaily singing a song of home:

> "Quand tout renait à l'espérance,
>   Et que l'hiver fuit loin de nous,
> Sous le beau ciel de notre France,
>   Quand le soleil revient plus doux;
> Quand la nature est reverdie,
>   Quand l'hirondelle est de retour,
> J'aime à revoir ma Normandie,
>   C'est le pays qui m'a donné le jour!"

The cares and doubts and worries of yesterday were gone—washed out of him, as it were, in nature's

baptismal regeneration of mind and body. All that
he himself recognized was a glad sense of the return
of competence and of some self-assurance of capacity to face the new world of men and things.

He wandered into the wood and said good morning to two men who, as they told him, were ''falling
a tree.'' He gathered flowers, white violets, the
star flower, offered tobacco for their pipes, which
they accepted, and asked them what flower was this.
''We call them Quaker ladies.'' He went away
wondering what poet had so named them. In the
town he bought two rolls and ate them as he walked,
like the great Benjamin. About nine o'clock, returning to the hotel, he threw the flowers in his
mother's lap as he kissed her. He saw to her breakfast, chatted hopefully, and when, about noon, she
insisted on going with him to seek for lodgings, he
was pleased at her revived strength. The landlord
regretted that they must leave, and gave addresses
near by. Unluckily, none suited their wants or
their sense of need for rigid economy; and, moreover, the vicomtesse was more difficult to please
than the young man thought quite reasonable.
They were pausing, perplexed, near the southwest
corner of Chestnut and Fifth streets when, having
passed two gentlemen standing at the door of a
brick building known as the Philosophical Society,
De Courval said, ''I will go back and ask where to
apply for information.'' He had been struck with
the unusual height of one of the speakers, and with
the animation of his face as he spoke, and had
caught as he went by a phrase or two; for the

stouter man spoke in a loud, strident voice, as if at a town meeting. "I hope, Citizen, you liked the last 'Gazette.' It is time to give men their true labels. Adams is a monarchist and Hamilton is an aristocrat."

The taller man, a long, lean figure, returned in a more refined voice: "Yes, yes; it is, I fear, only too true. I hope, Citizen, to live to see the end of the titles they love, even Mr.; for who is the master of a freeman?"

"How droll is that, *maman!*" said De Courval, half catching this singular interchange of sentiment.

"Why, René? What is droll?"

"Oh, nothing." He turned back, and addressing the taller man said: "Pardon me, sir, but we are strangers in search of some reasonable lodging-house. May I ask where we could go to find some one to direct us?"

The gentleman appealed to took off his hat, bowing to the woman, and then, answering the son, said, "My friend, Citizen Freneau, may know." The citizen had small interest in the matter. The taller man, suddenly struck by the woman's grave and moveless face and the patient dignity of her bearing, began to take an interest in this stranded couple, considering them with his clear hazel eyes. As he stood uncovered, he said: "Tell them, Freneau! Your paper must have notices—advertisements. Where shall they inquire?"

Freneau did not know, but quick to note his companion's interest, said presently: "Oh, yes, they

might learn at the library. They keep there a list
of lodging-houses."

"That will do," said the lean man. Madame, understanding that they were to be helped by this
somber-looking gentleman, said, "*Je vous remercie,
messieurs.*"

"My mother thanks you, sir."

Then there was of a sudden cordiality. Most of
the few French known to Freneau were Republicans and shared his extreme opinions. The greater
emigration from the islands and of the beggared
nobles was not as yet what it was to become.

"You are French?" said Freneau.

"Yes, we are French."

"I was myself about to go to the library," said
the taller man, and, being a courteous gentleman gone mad with "gallic fever," added in imperfect French, "If madame will permit me; it is near
by, and I shall have the honor to show the way."

Then Citizen Freneau of the new "National Gazette," a clerk in the Department of State, was too
abruptly eager to help; but at last saying "Good-by,
Citizen Jefferson," went his way as the statesman,
talking his best French to the handsome woman at
his side, went down Chestnut Street, while De Courval, relieved, followed them and reflected with interest—for he had learned many things on the voyage—that the tall man in front must be the former
minister to France, the idol of the Democratic
party, and the head of that amazing cabinet of di-
verse opinions which the great soldier president had
gathered about him. East of Fourth Street, Mr.

Jefferson turned into a court, and presently stood
for a moment on the front step of a two-story brick
building known as Carpenter's Hall, over which a
low spire still bore a forgotten crown. Not less forgotten were Jefferson's democratic manners. He was
at once the highly educated and well-loved Virginian of years ago.

He had made good use of his time, and the woman at his side, well aware of the value of being
agreeable, had in answer to a pleasant question
given her name, and presently had been told by the
ex-minister his own name, with which she was not
unfamiliar.

"Here, madame," he said, "the first Congress
met. I had the misfortune not to be of it."

"But later, monsieur—later, you can have had
nothing to regret."

"Certainly not to-day," said the Virginian. He
paused as a tall, powerfully built man, coming out
with a book in his hand, filled the doorway.

"Good morning, Mr. Wynne," said Jefferson.
"Is the librarian within?"

"Yes; in the library, up-stairs."

Hearing the name of the gentleman who thus replied, the young vicomte said:

"May I ask, sir, if you are Mr. Hugh Wynne?"

"Yes, I am; and, if I am not mistaken, you are
the Vicomte de Courval, and this, your mother.
Ah, madame," he said in French, far other than
that of the secretary, "I missed you at Oeller's, and
I am now at your service. What can I do for you?"

The vicomtesse replied that they had been guided

hither by Mr. Jefferson to find a list of lodging-houses.

"Then let us go and see about it."

"This way, Vicomte," said Jefferson. "It is up-stairs, madame." Ah, where now were the plain manners of democracy and the scorn of titles? A low, sweet voice had bewitched him, the charm of perfect French at its best.

The United States bank was on the first floor, and the clerks looked up with interest at the secretary and his companions as they passed the open door. De Courval lingered to talk with Wynne, both in their way silently amused at the capture by the vicomtesse of the gentleman with Jacobin principles.

The room up-stairs was surrounded with well-filled book-shelves. Midway, at a table, sat Zachariah Poulson, librarian, who was at once introduced, and who received them with the quiet good manners of his sect. A gentleman standing near the desk looked up from the book in his hand. While Mr. Poulson went in search of the desired list, Mr. Wynne said: "Good morning, James. I thought, Mr. Secretary, you knew Mr. Logan. Permit me to add agreeably to your acquaintance." The two gentlemen bowed, and Wynne added: "By the way, do you chance to know, Mr. Secretary, that Mr. Logan is hereditary librarian of the Loganian Library, and every Logan in turn if he pleases—our only inherited title."

"Not a very alarming title," said the Quaker gentleman, demurely.

"We can stand that much," said Jefferson, smil-

3

ing as he turned to Madame de Courval, while her son, a little aside, waited for the list and surveyed with interest the Quakers, the statesman, and the merchant who seemed so friendly.

At this moment came forward a woman of some forty years; rose-red her cheeks within the Quaker bonnet, and below all was sober gray, with a slight, pearl-colored silk shawl over her shoulders.

"Good morning, Friend Wynne. Excuse me, Friend Jefferson," she said. "May I be allowed a moment of thy time, James Logan?" The gentlemen drew back. She turned to the vicomtesse. "Thou wilt permit me. I must for home shortly. James Logan, there is a book William Bingham has praised to my daughter. I would first know if it be fitting for her to read. It is called, I believe, 'Thomas Jones.'"

Mr. Jefferson's brow rose a little, the hazel eyes confessed some merriment, and a faint smile went over the face of Hugh Wynne as Logan said: "I cannot recommend it to thee, Mary Swanwick."

"Thank thee," she said simply. "There is too much reading of vain books among Friends. I fear I am sometimes a sinner myself; but thy aunt, Mistress Gainor, Hugh, laughs at me, and spoils the girl with books—too many for her good, I fear."

"Ah, she taught me worse wickedness than books when I was young," said Wynne; "but your girl is less easy to lead astray. Oh, a word, Mary," and he lowered his voice. "Here are two French people I want you to take into your house."

"If it is thy wish, Hugh; but although there is

room and to spare, we live, of need, very simply, as
thou knowest.''

''That is not thy Uncle Langstroth's fault or
mine.''

''Yes, yes. Thou must know how wilful I am.
But Friend Schmidt is only too generous, and we
have what contents me, and should content Mar-
garet, if it were not for the vain worldliness Gainor
Wynne puts into the child's head. Will they like
Friend Schmidt?''

''He will like them, Mary Swanwick. You are a
fair French scholar yourself. Perhaps they may
teach you—they are pleasant people.'' He, too, had
been captured by the sweet French tongue he loved.

''They have some means,'' he added, ''and I shall
see about the young man. He seems more English
than French, a staid young fellow. You may make
a Quaker of him, Mary.''

''Thou art foolish, Hugh Wynne; but I will take
them.''

Then the perverted Secretary of State went away.
Mrs. Swanwick, still in search of literature, received
an innocent book called ''The Haunted Priory, or
the Fortunes of the House of Almy.'' There were
pleasant introductions, and, to De Courval's satisfaction, their baggage would be taken in charge, a
chaise sent in the afternoon for his mother and himself, and for terms—well, that might bide awhile
until they saw if all parties were suited. The
widow, pleased to oblige her old friend, had still her
reserve of doubt and some thought as to what might
be said by her permanent inmate, Mr. Johann
Schmidt.

III

ON reaching Mrs. Swanwick's home in the afternoon, the vicomtesse went at once to her room, where the cleanliness and perfect order met her tacit approval, and still more the appetizing meal which the hostess herself brought to the bedside of her tired guest.

Mr. Schmidt, the other boarder, was absent at supper, and the evening meal went by with little talk beyond what the simple needs of the meal required. De Courval excused himself early and, after a brief talk with his mother, was glad of a comfortable bed, where he found himself thinking with interest of the day's small events and of the thin, ruddy features, bright, hazel eyes and red hair, of the tall Virginia statesman, the leader of the party some of whose baser members had given the young vicomte unpleasant minutes at Oeller's Hotel.

When very early the next day De Courval awakened and looked eastward from his room in the second story of Mrs. Swanwick's home, he began to see in what pleasant places his lot was cast. The house, broad and roomy, had been a country home. Now commerce and the city's growth were contending for Front Street south of Cedar, but being as yet on the edge of the town, the spacious Georgian house, stand-

ing back from the street, was still set round with am-
ple gardens, on which just now fell the first sunshine
of the May morning. As De Courval saw, the ground
at the back of the house fell away to the Delaware
River. Between him and the shore were flowers, li-
lacs in bloom, and many fruit-trees. Among them,
quite near by, below the window, a tall, bareheaded
man in shirt-sleeves was busy gathering a basket of
the first roses. He seemed particular about their ar-
rangement, and while he thus pleased himself, he
talked aloud in a leisurely way, and with a strong
voice, now to a black cat on the wall above him, and
now as if to the flowers. De Courval was much
amused by this fresh contribution to the strange experiences of the last two days. The language of the
speaker was also odd.

As De Courval caught bits of the soliloquy under
his window, he thought of his mother's wonder at
this new and surprising country.

What would she write Rochefoucauld d'Entin?
She was apt to be on paper, as never in speech, emotional and tender, finding confession to white paper
easy and some expression of the humorous aspects of
life possible, when, as in writing, there needed no
gay comment of laughter. If she were only here,
thought the son. Will she tell the duke how she is
"thou" to these good, plain folk, and of the prim
welcomes, and of this German, who must be the
Friend Schmidt they spoke of,—no doubt a Quaker,
and whom he must presently remind of his audience?
But for a little who could resist so comic an opportunity? "Gute Himmel, but you are beautiful!"

said the voice below him. "Oh, not you," he cried to
the cat, "wanton of midnight! I would know if,
Madame Red Rose, you are jealous of the white-
bosomed rose maids. If all women were alike fair as
you, there would be wild times, for who would know
to choose? Off with you, Jezebel, daughter of darkness! 'Sh! I love not cats. Go!" and he cast a pebble at the sleepy grimalkin, which fled in fear. This
singular talk went on, and De Courval was about
to make some warning noise when the gardener, adding a rose to his basket, straightened himself, saying:
"Ach, Himmel! My back! How in the garden Adam
must have ached!"

Leaving his basket for a time, he was lost among
the trees, to reappear in a few minutes far below,
out on the water in a boat, where he undressed and
went overboard.

"A good example," thought De Courval. Taking
a towel, he slipped out noiselessly through the house
where no one was yet astir, and finding a little bath-
house open below the garden, was soon stripped, and,
wading out, began to swim. By this time the gardener was returning, swimming well and with the
ease of an expert when the two came near one another a couple of hundred yards from shore.

As they drew together, De Courval called out in
alarm: "Look out! Take care!"

Two small lads in a large Egg Harbor skiff, seeing
the swimmer in their way, made too late an effort to
avoid him. A strong west wind was blowing. The
boat was moving fast. De Courval saw the heavy
bow strike the head of the man, who was quite un-

aware of the nearness of the boat. He went under.
De Courval struck out for the stern of the boat,
and in its wake caught sight of a white
body near the surface. He seized it, and
easily got the man's head above water. The
boat came about, the boys scared and awkward.
With his left hand, De Courval caught the low gun-
wale and with his right held up the man's head.
Then he felt the long body stir. The great, laboring
chest coughed out water, and the man, merely
stunned and, as he said later, only quarter drowned,
drew deep breaths and gasped, "Let them pull to
shore." The boys put out oars in haste, and in a
few minutes De Courval felt the soft mud as he
dropped his feet and stood beside the German. In a
minute the two were on the beach, the one a young,
white figure with the chest muscles at relieving play;
the other a tall, gaunt, bronzed man, shaking and
still coughing as he cast himself on the bordering
grass without a word.

"Are you all right?" asked De Courval, anxiously.

For a moment the rescued man made no reply as
he lay looking up at the sky. Then he said: "Yes, or
will be presently. This sun is a good doctor and
sends in no bill. Go in and dress. I shall be well
presently. My boat! Ah, the boys bring it. Now
my clothes. Do not scold them. It was an accident."

"That is of the past," he said in a few moments as
De Courval rejoined him, "a contribution to experience. Thank you," and he put out a hand that told
of anything but the usage of toil as he added: "I was

wondering, as I dressed, which is the better for it, the helper or the helped. Ach, well, it is a good introduction. You are mein Herr de Courval, and I am Johann Schmidt, at your honorable service now and ever. Let us go in. I must rest a little before breakfast. I have known you,"—and he laughed,— "shall we say five years? We will not trouble the women with it."

"I? Surely not."

"Pardon me. I was thinking of my own tongue, which is apt to gabble, being the female part of a man's body."

"May I beg of you not to speak of it," urged De Courval, gravely.

"How may I promise for the lady?" laughed Schmidt as they moved through the fruit-trees. "Ah, here is the basket of roses for the Frau Von Courval."

A singular person, thought the vicomte, but surely a gentleman.

Madame de Courval, tired of looking for a home, had resolved to give no trouble to this kindly household and to accept their hours—the breakfast at seven, the noonday dinner, the supper at six. She was already dressed when she heard the step outside of her door, and looking up from her Bible, called "*Entrez*, my son. Ah, roses, roses! Did you gather them?"

"No; they are for you, with the compliments of our fellow-lodger, a German, I believe, Mr. Schmidt; another most strange person in this strange land. He speaks English well, but, *mon Dieu*, of the oddest. A well-bred man, I am sure; you will like him.''

''I do not know, and what matters it? I like very few people, as you know, René; but the place does appear to be clean and neat. That must suffice.''

He knew well enough that she liked few people. ''Are you ready, *maman?* Shall we go down?''

''Yes, I am ready. This seems to me a haven of rest, René—a haven of rest, after that cruel sea.''

''It so seems to me, *maman;* and these good Quakers. They *tutoyer* every one—every one. You must try to learn English. I shall give you lessons, and there is a note from Mr. Wynne, asking me to call at eleven. And one word more, *maman—*''

''Well, my son?''

''You bade me put aside the past. I shall do so; but you—can not you also do the same? It will be hard, for you made me make it harder.''

''I know—I know, but you are young—I old of heart. Life is before you, my son. It is behind me. I can not but think of my two lonely little ones in the graveyard and the quiet of our home life and, my God! of your father!'' To his surprise, she burst into tears. Any such outward display of emotion was in his experience of her more than merely unusual. ''Go down to breakfast, René. I shall try to live in your life. You will tell me everything—always. I shall follow you presently. We must not be late.''

''Yes,'' he said; but he did not tell her of his morning's adventure. Even had he himself been willing to speak of it, the German would not like it, and already Schmidt began to exercise over him that influence which was more or less to affect his life in the years yet to come. As he went down to the broad hall, he saw a floor thinly strewn with white sand, settles on both sides, a lantern hanging overhead, and the upper half of the front door open to let the morning air sweep through to the garden.

A glance to right and left showed on one side a bare, whitewashed front room, without pictures or mirrors, some colonial chairs with shells carved on feet and knees, and on a small table a china bowl of roses. The room to right he guessed at once to be used as a sitting-room by Schmidt.

The furniture was much as in the other room, but there were shining brass fire-dogs, silver candlesticks on the mantel, and over it a pair of foils, two silver-mounted pistols, and a rapier with a gold-inlaid handle. Under a window was a large secretary with many papers. There were books in abundance on the chairs and in a corner case. The claw-toed tables showed pipes, tobacco-jars, wire masks, and a pair of fencing-gloves. On one side of the hall a tall clock reminded him that he was some ten minutes late.

The little party was about to sit down at table when he entered. "This is Friend de Courval," said the widow.

"We have met in the garden," returned Schmidt, quietly.

"Indeed. Thou wilt sit by me, Friend de Courval, and presently thy mother on my right." As she spoke, Madame de Courval paused at the door while the hostess and her daughter bent in the silent grace of Friends. The new-comer took her place with a pleasant word of morning greeting in her pretty French; an old black woman brought in the breakfast. A tranquil courtesy prevailed.

"Will thy mother take this or that? Here are eggs my uncle sent from the country, and shad, which we have fresh from the river, a fish we esteem."

There was now for a somewhat short time little other talk. The girl of over sixteen shyly examined the new-comers. The young man approved the virginal curves of neck and figure, the rebellious profusion of dark chestnut-tinted hair, the eyes that could hardly have learned their busy attentiveness in the meeting-house. The gray dress and light gray silk kerchief seemed devised to set off the roses which came out in wandering isles of color on her cheeks. Madame's ignorance of English kept her silent, but she took note of the simple attire of her hostess, the exquisite neatness of the green apron, then common among Friends, and the high cap. The habit of the house was to speak only when there was need. There was no gossip even of the mildest.

"June was out all night," said Mrs. Swanwick. "That is our cat," she explained to De Courval.

"But she brought in a dead mouse," said the girl, "to excuse herself, I suppose." Schmidt smiled at the touch of humor, but during their first meal was more silent than usual.

"I did not tell thee, Margaret," said Mrs. Swanwick, "that William Westcott was here yesterday at sundown. I have no liking for him. I said thou wert out.''

"But I was only in the garden."

"I did say thou wert out, but not in the garden."

Schmidt smiled again as he set his teaspoon across his cup, the conventional sign that he wished no more tea.

Then the girl, with fresh animation, asked eagerly: "Oh, mother, I forgot; am I to have the book Ann Bingham thought delightful, and her father told thee I should read?"

"I am not so minded," replied the mother, and this seemed to end the matter. De Courval listened, amused, as again the girl asked cheerfully:

"Aunt Gainor will be here to take me with her to see some china, mother, at twelve. May I not go?"

"No, not to-day. There is the cider of last fall we must bottle, and I shall want thy help. The last time," she said, smiling, "thou didst fetch home a heathen god—green he was, and had goggle eyes. What would Friend Pennington say to that?"

"But I do not pray to it."

"My child!" said the mother, and then: "If thou didst pray to all Aunt Gainor's gods, thou wouldst be kept busy. I have my hands full with thee and Gainor Wynne's fal-lals and thy Uncle Langstroth's follies." She smiled kindly as she spoke, and again the girl quietly accepted the denial of her request, while De Courval listened with interest and amusement.

"I shall go with Miss Wynne," said Schmidt,

"and buy you a brigade of china gods. I will fill the house with them, Margaret." He laughed.

"Thou wilt do nothing of the kind," said Mrs. Swanwick.

"Well, Nanny would break them pretty soon. Brief would be the lives of those immortals. But I forgot; I have a book for thee, Pearl."

De Courval looked up. "Yes," he thought; "the Pearl, Marguerite. It does seem to suit."

"And what is it?" said the mother. "I am a little afraid of thee and thy books."

" 'The Vicar of Wakefield' it is called; not very new, but you will like it, Pearl."

"I might see it myself first."

"When Pearl and I think it fit for thee," said Schmidt, demurely. "I did see also in the shop Job Scott's 'The Opening of the Inward Eye, or Righteousness Revealed.' I would fetch thee that—for thyself."

The hostess laughed. "He is very naughty, Friend de Courval," she said, "but not as wicked as he seems." Very clearly Schmidt was a privileged inmate. Madame ate with good appetite, pleased by the attention shown her, and a little annoyed at being, as it were, socially isolated for want of English. As she rose she told her son that she had a long letter she must write to Cousin Rochefoucauld, and would he ask Mr. Wynne how it might be sent. Then Schmidt said to De Courval: "Come to my room. There we may smoke, or in the garden, not elsewhere. There is here a despotism; you will need to be careful."

"Do not believe him," said the Pearl. "Mother would let him smoke in meeting, if she were overseer."

"Margaret, Margaret, thou art saucy. That comes of being with the Willing girls and Gainor, who is grown old in sauciness—world's people!" and her eyebrows went up, so that whether she was quite in earnest or was the prey of some sudden jack-in-the-box of pure humor, De Courval did not know. It was all fresh, interesting, and somehow pleasant. Were all Quakers like these?

He followed Schmidt into his sitting-room, where his host closed the door. "Sit down," he said. "Not there. These chairs are handsome. I keep them to look at and for the occasional amendment of slouching manners. Five minutes will answer. But here are two of my own contrivance, democratic, vulgar, and comfortable. Ah, do you smoke? Yes, a pipe. I like that. I should have been disappointed if you were not a user of the pipe. I am going to talk, to put you in *pays de connaissance,* as you would say. And now for comments! My acquaintance of five years,—or five minutes, was it, that I was under water?—may justify the unloading of my baggage of gossip on a man whom I have benefited by the chance of doing a good deed, if so it be—or a kind one at least. You shall learn in a half hour what otherwise might require weeks."

De Courval, amused at the occasional quaintness of the English, which he was one day to have explained, blew rings of smoke and listened.

"I shall be long, but it will help you and save questions."

"Pray go on, sir. I shall be most thankful."

"*Imprimis,* there is Mrs. Swanwick, born in the Church of England, if any are born in church—Cyrilla Plumstead. She was brought up in luxury, which came to an end before they married her to a stiff Quaker man who departed this life with reasonable kindness, after much discipline of his wife in ways which sweeten many and sour some. She has held to it loyally—oh, more or less. That is the setting of our Pearl, a creature of divine naturalness, waiting until some Quaker Cupid twangs his bow. Then the kiss-defying bonnet will suffer. By the way, Mrs. Swanwick is a fair French scholar, but a bit shy with you as yet.

"Soon thou wilt see Josiah Langstroth, uncle of Mrs. Swanwick. Ah, there 's a man that mocks conjecture; for, being a Quaker by pride of ancestral damnation, he goes to meeting twice a year, swears a little to ease his soul, toasts George the Third of Sundays, and will surely tell you how, driven out of the country, he went to London and was presented to the king and triumphantly kept his hat on his head. He is rich and would provide for his niece, who will take help from no one. He does at times offer money, but is ever well pleased when she refuses. As for Hugh Wynne, I will go with you to see him, a Welsh squire to this day, like the best of them here. I shall leave you to make him out. He is a far-away cousin of Margaret's mother.

"It is a fine menagerie. Very soon you will hear

of Aunt Gainor Wynne,—every one calls her aunt;
I should not dare to do so,—a sturdy Federalist
lady, with a passion for old china, horses, and
matchmaking, the godmother of Mrs. Swanwick.
Take care; she will hate or love you at sight, and as
great a maker of mischief as ever perplexed good
sense; as tender an old woman at times as ever
lacked need of onions to fetch tears; a fine lady
when she chooses.

"There, I have done you a service and saved your
wits industry. You listen well. There is a savor of
grace in that. It is a virtue of the smoker. Question me if you like."

Nothing could better have pleased the young
man.

"I would know more of this town, sir," and he
told of his quest of a tavern. The German laughed.

"A good lesson—Federalists and ape democrats
—wild politics of a nation in its childhood. Three
great men,—Washington, Hamilton, James Wilson,
and perhaps John Adams; well—great merchants,
Willings, Bingham, and Girard; and besides these,
Quakers, many of them nobler for a creed unwork-
able in a naughty world, with offshoots of 'world's
people,' which saved some fortunes in the war; and,
ah, a sect that will die away,—Free Quakers, high-
minded gentlemen who made up for a century of
peace when they elected to draw the sword. I fear
I have been tedious."

"No, not at all; you are most kind, sir, and most
interesting. I am sure to like it all. I hope my
mother will be contented. We have never of late
years been used to luxuries."

"She can hardly fail to be satisfied; but it is a simple life. There are only two servants, Cicero, and Nanny, once a slave, now, as Mrs. Swanwick says, a servant friend—ah, and a stiff Episcopal. She has never ceased to wonder why her mistress ever became a Quaker. I am much of her way of thinking. Are you of a mind to walk and see a little of the city? Later we will call upon Mr. Wynne." As they rose, he added: "I did not speak of the wrecks of French nobles cast on these shores—only a few as yet. You will see them by and by. They are various—but in general perplexed by inheritance of helplessness. Once for all you are to understand that my room is always and equally yours. Of course you use the foils. Yes; well, we shall fence in the garden. And now come; let us go out."

"I forgot, sir. My mother bade me thank you for the roses. She has as yet no English, or would herself have thanked you."

"But I myself speak French—of a kind. It will serve to amuse madame; but never will you hear French at its best until Miss Wynne does talk it."

4

IV

AS they went northward on Front Street, with
the broad Delaware to the right, for as yet no
Water Street narrowed the river frontage, the German said: "I left out of my portrait gallery one
Schmidt, but you will come to know him in time.
He has a talent for intimacy. Come, now; you
have known him five years. What do you think of
him?"

More and more strange seemed this gentleman to
his young companion. He glanced aside at the tall,
strongly built man, with the merry blue eyes, and,
a little embarrassed and somewhat amused, replied
with habitual caution, "I hardly know as yet, but
I think I shall like him."

"I like the answer. You will like him, but we
may leave him and time to beget opinion. How dig-
nified these Georgian fronts are, and the stoops!
Once folks sat on them at evening, and gossiped of
the miseries of war. Now there are changed ways
and more luxury and a new day—less simpleness;
but not among the good people we have left. No.
They are of the best, and aristocrats, too, though
you may not suspect it. The habit of hospitality in
a new land remains. A lady with small means loses
no social place because, like our hostess, she receives

guests who pay. Here will come rich kinsfolk and friends, visitors on even terms—Whartons, Morrises, Cadwaladers, Logans,—the old, proud Welsh, grandsons of Welsh, with at times Quaker people and the men in office, for madame is clever and well liked. I tell her she has a Quaker salon, which is not my wit, but true."

"I had supposed Friends too rigid for this."

"Oh, there are Quakers and Quakers, and sometimes the overseers feel called upon to remonstrate; and then there is an unpleasantness, and our hostess is all of a sudden moved by the spirit to say things, and has her claws out. And my rose, my rose Pearl, can be prickly, too."

"She does not look like it, sir."

"No? When does a young woman look like what she is or may be? She is a good girl—as good as God makes them; her wits as yet a bit muzzled by the custom of Friends. A fair bud—prophetic of what the rose will be."

They wandered on to Arch Street and then westward. "Here," said Schmidt, as they turned into the open entrance of a graveyard—"here I come at evening sometimes. Read that. There are sermons in these stones, and history."

De Courval saw on a gray slab, "Benjamin Franklin and Deborah, his wife." He took off his hat, saying as he stood: "My father knew him. He came to Normandy once to see the model farms of our cousin, Rochefoucauld Liancourt."

"Indeed. I never knew the philosopher, but the duke—I knew the duke well,—in Paris,—oh, very well, long ago; a high-minded noble. We will come here again and talk of this great man, under the marble, quiet as never in life. You must not be late for Wynne. He will not like that."

Turning southward and walking quickly, they came in half an hour to the busy space in front of Wynne's warehouse. He met them at the door, where Schmidt, leaving them, said, "I leave you a man, Colonel Wynne."

Wynne said, smiling: "I am no longer a colonel, Vicomte, but a plain merchant. Have the kindness to follow me, Vicomte," and so passed on through a room where clerks were busy and into a small, neatly kept office.

"Sit down, Vicomte. We must have a long talk and come quickly to know one another. You speak English, I observe, and well, too. And, now, you have a letter of exchange on me for five thousand livres, or, rather, two hundred pounds. Better to leave it with me. I can give you interest at six per cent., and you may draw on me at need. Have you any present want?"

"No, sir; none—just yet none."

"I am told that you left France for England and have had, pardon me, much to lament."

"Yes, we have suffered like many others." He was indisposed to be frank where there was no need to say more.

"What do you purpose to do? A few thousand livres will not go far."

"I do not know. Anything which will help us to live."

"Anything? You may teach French like De Laisne, or fencing like Du Vallon, or dancing like the Marquis de Beau Castel. I offered him a clerk-ship."

"Offer me one," said De Courval. "I write a good hand. I speak and write English. I can learn, and I will."

Wynne took stock, as he would have said, of the rather serious face, of the eyes of gray which met his look, of a certain eagerness in the young man's prompt seizure of a novel opportunity.

"Can you serve under a plain man like my head clerk, run errands, obey without question—in a word, accept a master?"

"I have had two bitter ones, sir, poverty and misfortune."

"Can you come at eight thirty, sweep out the office, make the fires at need in winter, with an hour off, at noon, and work till six? Such is our way here."

The young man flushed. "Is that required?"

"I did it for a year, Vicomte, and used the sword for five years, and came back to prosper."

De Courval smiled. "I accept, sir; we have never been rich, and I ought to say that we are not of the greater noblesse. When our fortunes fell away, I worked with our peasants in the field. I have no false pride, and my sword is in a box in Mrs. Swanwick's attic. I fancy, sir, that I shall have no use for it here. Why gentlemen should prefer to teach French or dancing to good steady work I cannot understand."

"Nor I," said Wynne, beginning to like this grave and decisive young noble. "Think it over," he said.

"I have done so."

"Very good. You will receive thirty dollars a month—to be increased, I trust. When will you come?"

"To-morrow—at eight and a half, you said."

"Yes; but to-morrow a little earlier. The junior clerk you replace will tell you what you are to do, and for the rest Mr. Potts will give you your orders. A word more: you had better drop your title and be plain Mr. de Courval. When, as will chance, you go among our friends, it would be an affectation. Well, then, to-morrow; but,—and you will pardon me,—to-day we are two gentlemen, equals; to-morrow, here at least, you are a simple clerk among exact and industrious people, and I the master. Let us be clear as to this. That is all."

"I think I understand. And now may I ask how I may find the French minister? There is a letter my mother would send to her cousin, and I am at a loss, for I fear there are no mails I can trust."

"Jean de Ternant is the French minister, but he will hardly be likely to oblige a *ci-devant* vicomte. They talk of a new one. Give it to me; I will see that it goes by safe hands." With this he rose and added: "Mrs. Wynne will have the honor to call on the vicomtesse, and we shall be at her service."

"Thank you," said De Courval, a little overcome by his kindness. "My mother is in mourning, sir. She will, I fear, be unwilling to visit."

"Then my wife will come again. We may leave two good women to settle that; and now I must let you go." Then, seeing that De Courval lingered, he added, "Is there anything else?"

"Only a word of thanks, and may I ask why you are so good to us? I am—sadly unused to kindness. There was not much of it in England."

Wynne smiled. "I have heard a little about you —some things I liked—from my correspondents in Bristol and London; and, Vicomte, my mother was French. When you visit us at Merion you shall see her picture Stuart made for me from a miniature, and then you will understand why my heart goes out to all French people. But they are not easy to help, these unlucky nobles who will neither beg nor do a man's work. Oh, you will see them, and I, too, more and more, I fear. Good morning."

With this the young man walked thoughtfully away. Hugh Wynne watched him for a moment, and said to himself, "A good deal of a man, that; Schmidt is right." And then, having seen much of men in war and peace, "there must be another side to him, as there was to me. I doubt he is all meekness. I must say a word to Mary Swanwick," and he remembered certain comments his wife had made on Margaret's budding beauty. Then he went in.

The thoughts of the young man were far from women. He went along the road beside Dock Creek, and stood a moment on the bridge, amused at the busy throng of which he was now to become a part. On the west side of Second Street a noisy crowd at a shop door excited his curiosity.

"What is that?" he asked a passing mechanic. "I am a stranger here."

"Oh, that 's a vandoo of lottery shares. The odd numbers sell high, specially the threes. That 's what they 're after."

"Thank you," said De Courval, and then, as he drew nearer, exclaimed, *"Mon Dieu!"* The auctioneer was perched on a barrel. Just below him stood a young Frenchman eagerly bidding on the coveted number 33. Not until De Courval was beside him was he disillusioned. It was not Carteaux, nor was the man, on nearer view, very like him. When clear of the small crowd, De Courval moved away slowly, vexed with himself and disturbed by one of those abrupt self-revelations which prove to a man how near he may be to emotional insurrection.

"If it had been he," he murmured, "I should have strangled him, ah, there at once." He had been imprudent, lacking in intelligence. He felt, too, how slightly impressed he had been by his mother's desire that he should dismiss from his life the dark hour of Avignon. More than a little dissatisfied, he put it all resolutely aside and began to reconsider the mercantile career before him. He was about to give up the social creed and ways in which he had been educated. He had never earned a sou, and was now to become a part of the life of trade, a thing which at one time would have seemed to him impossible. Would his mother like it? No; but for that there was no help, and some of it he would keep to himself. Thirty dollars would pay

his own board, and he must draw on his small reserve until he made more. But there were clothes
to get and he knew not what besides; nor did he
altogether like it himself. He had served in the
army two years, and had then been called home,
where he was sorely needed. It would have been
strange if, with his training and traditions, he had
felt no repugnance at this prospect of a trader's life.
But it was this or nothing, and having made his
choice, he meant to abide by it. And thus, having
settled the matter, he went on his way, taking in
with observant eyes the wonders of this new country.

He made for his mother a neat little tale of how
he was to oblige Mr. Wynne by translating or writing French letters. Yes, the hours were long, but
he was sure he should like it, and Mrs. Swanwick
would, she had said, give him breakfast in time for
him to be at his work by half after eight o'clock;
and where was the letter which should be sent, and
Mrs. Wynne would call. The vicomtesse wished for
no company, and least of all for even the most respectable bourgeois society; but she supposed there
was no help for it, and the boarding-house was very
well, indeed, restful, and the people quiet. Would
she be expected to say thou to them? Her son
thought not, and after a rather silent noon dinner
went out for a pull on the river with Schmidt, and
bobbed for crabs to his satisfaction, while Schmidt
at intervals let fall his queer phrases as the crabs
let go the bait and slid off sideways.

"There is a man comes here to pester Mrs. Swan-

wick at times. He goes out of the doors sideways,
there, like that fellow in the water—Monsieur Crab,
I call him. He is meek and has claws which are
critical and pinch until madame boils over, and then
he gets red like a crab. That was when Pearl had
of Miss Gainor a gold locket and a red ribbon, and
wore it on a day when with Miss Gainor the girl
was by evil luck seen of our Quaker crab.

"But not all are like that. There is one, Israel
Morris, who looks like a man out of those pictures
by Vandyke you must have seen, and with the gen-
tleness of a saint. Were I as good as he, I should
like to die, for fear I could not keep it up. Ah
you got a nip. They can bite. It can not be entirely
true—I mean that man's goodness; but it is naturally performed. The wife is a fair test of humility.
I wonder how his virtue prospers at home."

De Courval listened, again in wonder where had
been learned this English, occasionally rich with odd
phrases; for usually Schmidt spoke a fluent English,
but always with some flavor of his own tongue.

The supper amused the young man, who was beginning to be curious and observant of these interesting and straightforward people. There were at
times long silences. The light give and take of the
better chat of the well-bred at home in France was
wanting. His mother could not talk, and there were
no subjects of common interest. He found it dull
at first, being himself just now in a gay humor.

After the meal he ventured to admire the buff-
and-gold china in a corner cupboard, and then two
great silver tankards on a sideboard. Mrs. Swan-

wick was pleased. "Yes," she said, "they are of
Queen Anne's day, and the arms they carry are of
the Plumsteads and Swanwicks."

He called his mother's attention to them. "But,"
she said, of course in French, "what have these people to do with arms?"

"Take care," he returned under his breath.
"Madame speaks French."

Mrs. Swanwick, who had a fair knowledge of the
tongue, quickly caught her meaning, but said with a
ready smile: "Ah, they have had adventures. When
my husband would not pay the war tax, as Friends
would not, the vendue master took away these tankards and sold them. But when the English came
in, Major André bought them. That was when he
stole Benjamin Franklin's picture, and so at last
Gainor Wynne, in London, years after, saw my arms
on them in a shop and bought them back, and now
they are Margaret's."

De Courval gaily related the tale to his mother
and then went away with her to her room, she exclaiming on the stair: "The woman has good manners. She understood me."

The woman and Pearl were meanwhile laughing
joyously over the sad lady's criticism. When once
in her bed-room, the vicomtesse said that on the
morrow she would rest in bed. Something, perhaps
the voyage and all this new life, had been too much
for her, and she had a little fever. A tisane, yes,
if only she had a tisane, but who would know how
to make one? No, he must tell no one that she was
not well.

He left her feeling that here was a new trouble and went down-stairs to join Schmidt. No doubt she was really tired, but what if it were something worse? One disaster after another had left him with the belief that he was marked out by fate for calamitous fortunes.

Schmidt cheered him with his constant hopefulness, and in the morning he must not fail Mr. Wynne, and at need Schmidt would get a doctor. Then he interested him with able talk about the stormy politics of the day, and for a time they smoked in silence. At last, observing his continued depression, Schmidt said: "Take this to bed with you—At night is despair, at morning hope—a good word to sleep on. Let the morrow take care of itself. Bury thy cares in the graveyard of sleep." Then he added with seriousness rare to him: "You have the lesson of the mid-years of life yet to learn—to be of all thought the despot. Never is man his own master till, like the centurion with his soldiers, he can say to joy come and to grief or anger or anxiety go, and be obeyed of these. You may think it singular that I, a three-days' acquaintance, talk thus to a stranger; but the debt is all one way so far, and my excuse is those five years under water, and, too, that this preacher in his time has suffered."

Unused till of late to sympathy, and surprised out of the reserve both of the habit of caste and of his own natural reticence, De Courval felt again the emotion of a man made, despite himself, to feel how the influence of honest kindness had ended his power to speak.

In the dim candle-light he looked at the speaker—tall, grave, the eagle nose, the large mouth, the heavy chin, a face of command, with now a little watching softness in the eyes.

He felt later the goodness and the wisdom of the German's advice. "I will try," he said; "but it does seem as if there were little but trouble in the world," and with this went away to bed.

Then Schmidt found Mrs. Swanwick busy over a book and said: "Madame de Courval is not well, I fear. Would you kindly see to her?"

"At once," she said, rising.

V

THE young man's anxiety about his mother kept him long awake, and his sleep was troubled, as at times later, by a dream of Carteaux facing him with a smile, and by that strange sense of physical impotence which sometimes haunts the dreamer who feels the need for action and cannot stir.

When at six in the morning De Courval went down-stairs, he met Mrs. Swanwick. She turned, and when in the hall said: "I have been with thy mother all night, and now Margaret is with her, but thou wilt do no harm to enter. She does not seem to me very ill, but we must have a doctor, and one who has her language. When after a little sleep she wakens, she wanders, and then is clear again." Seeing his look of anxiety, she added, "Be sure that we shall care for her."

He said no word of the pain he felt and scarce more than a word of his gratitude, but, going up-stairs again, knocked softly at a chamber door.

"Come in," he heard, and entered. A low voice whispered, "She is just awake," and the slight, gray figure of the girl went by him, the door gently closing behind her. In the dim light he sat down by his mother's bed, and taking a hot hand in his, heard her murmur: *"Mon fils*—my son. Angels—

angels! I was a stranger, and they took me in; naked and they clothed me, yes, yes, with kindness. What name did you say? Carteaux. Is he dead—Carteaux?"

The young man had a thrill of horror. "Mother," he said, "it is I, René."

"Ah," she exclaimed, starting up, "I was dreaming. These good people were with me all night. You must thank them and see that they are well paid. Do not forget—well paid—and a tisane. If I had but a tisane *de guimauve!*"

"Yes, yes," he said; "we shall see. Perhaps some lemonade."

"Yes, yes; go at once and order it." She was imperative; and her voice had lost its sweetness for a time. "I must not be made to wait."

"Very well, *maman.*" As he went out, the gray figure passed in, saying, "She is better this morning, and I am so grieved for thee."

"Thank you," he murmured, and went downstairs, seeing no one, and out to a seat in the garden, to think what he should do. Yes, there must be a doctor. And Carteaux—what a fool he had been to tell her his name! The name and the cropped hair of the Jacobin, the regular features, by no means vulgar, the blood-red eyes of greed for murder, he saw again as in that fatal hour. Whenever any new calamity had fallen upon him, the shrill murder-counseling voice was with him, heard at times like a note of discord even in later days of relief from anxiety, or in some gay moment of mirth. "He was wise," he murmured, remembering the

German's counsel, and resolutely put aside the disturbing thought. At last Nanny, the black maid, called him to breakfast. He was alone with Schmidt and Mrs. Swanwick. They discussed quietly what doctor they should call; not their friend, Dr. Redman, as neither he nor Dr. Rush spoke French. Schmidt said: "I have sent a note to Mr. Wynne not to expect you. Set your mind at ease."

There was need of the advice. De Courval felt the helplessness of a young man in the presence of a woman's illness. He sat still in his chair at breakfast, hardly hearing the German's efforts to reassure him.

It was near to eight. Nanny had gone up to relieve Margaret, who presently came in, saying, "Aunt Gainor is without, back from her morning ride."

There was a heavy footfall in the hall and a clear, resonant voice, "Mary Swanwick, where are you?"

In the doorway, kept open for the summer air to sweep through, the large figure of Gainor Wynne appeared in riding skirt and low beaver hat, a heavy whip in her hand. The years had dealt lightly with the woman, now far past middle life. There was a mass of hair time had powdered, the florid face, the high nose of her race, the tall, erect, massive build, giving to the observant a sense of masculine vigor. On rare occasions there was also a perplexing realization of infinite feminine tenderness, and, when she pleased, the ways and manners of an unmistakable gentlewoman.

As the two men rose, Mrs. Swanwick said quietly, "Aunt Gainor, Madame de Courval is ill."

"As much as to say, 'Do not roam through the house and shout.'"

"This is Friend de Courval," said Mrs. Swanwick.

"You must pardon me, Vicomte," said Miss Wynne. "You must pardon a rude old woman. I am Hugh Wynne's aunt. May I ask about your mother? Is she very ill? I meant to call on her shortly. I am heartily at your service."

"I fear she is very ill," he replied.

"Have you a doctor?"

"We were just now thinking whom we should have," said Mrs. Swanwick. "The vicomtesse speaks no English."

"Yes, yes," said Mistress Wynne; "who shall we have? Not Dr. Rush. He would bleed her, and his French—la, my cat can meow better French. Ah, I have it. I will fetch Chovet. We have not spoken for a month, because—but no matter, he will come."

There was nothing to do but to thank this resolute lady. "I will send for him at once, Aunt Gainor," said Mrs. Swanwick.

To De Courval's surprise, it was Margaret who answered. "He will come the quicker for Aunt Gainor, mother. Every one does as she wants." This was to De Courval.

"Except you, you demure little Quaker kitten. I must go," and the masterful woman in question was out of the house in a moment, followed by Schmidt and De Courval.

"A chair. I can't mount as I used to." Her black groom brought out a chair. In a moment she was on the back of the powerfully built stallion and

5

clattering up Front Street with perilous indifference
to an ill-paved road and any unwatchful foot-pas-
senger. She struck up Spruce Street and the un-
paved road then called Delaware Fifth Street and
so down Arch. It was mid-morning, and the street
full of vehicles and people a-foot. Suddenly, when
near her own house, she checked her horse as she
saw approaching a chaise with leather springs, the
top thrown back, and in front a sorry-looking white
horse. Within sat a man who would have served
for the English stage presentation of a Frenchman
—a spare figure, little, with very red cheeks under a
powdered wig; he was dressed in the height of the
most extravagant fashion of a day fond of color.
The conventional gold-headed cane of the physician
lay between his legs. At sight of Mistress Wynne
he applied the whip and called out to his horse in a
shrill voice, "*Allez.* Get on, Ça Ira!"

The spinster cried to him as they came near:
"Stop, stop, Doctor! I want you. Stop—do you
hear me?"

He had not forgotten a recent and somewhat fierce
political passage of arms, and turned to go by her.
With a quick movement she threw the big stallion
in front of Ça Ira, who reared, stopped short, and
cast the doctor sprawling over the dash-board. He
sat up in wrath. "*Sacré bleu!*" he cried, "I might
have been killed. *Quelle femme!* What a woman!
And my wig—" It was in the street dust.

"'Why did you not stop? Get the man's wig,
Tom." The groom, grinning, dismounted and stood
still, awaiting her orders, the dusty wig in his hand.

" With a quick movement she threw the big stallion in front of Ça Ira "

"My wig—give it to me."

"No, don't give it to him." The doctor looked ruefully from the black to the angry spinster.

"What means this, madame? My wig—"

"I want you to go at once to see a sick woman at Mrs. Swanwick's."

"I will not. I am sent for in haste. In an hour or two I will go, or this afternoon."

"I don't believe you. You must go now—now. Who is it is ill?" People paused, astonished and laughing.

"It is Citizen Jefferson. He is ill, very ill."

"I am glad of it. He must wait—this citizen."

"But he has a chill—*un diable* of a chill."

"If the devil himself had a chill,—Lord, but it would refresh him!—he would have to wait."

He tried to pass by. She seized the rein of his horse. Her blood was up, and at such times few men cared to face her.

"You will go," she cried, "and at once, or—there is a tale I heard about you last year in London from Dr. Abernethy. That highwayman—you know the story. Your wig I shall keep. It is freshly powdered. Lord, man, how bald you are!"

He grew pale around his rouge. "You would not, surely."

"Would I not? Come, now, I won't tell—oh, not every one. Be a good doctor. I have quarreled with Dr. Rush—and come and see me to-morrow. I have a horrid rheum. And as to Citizen Jefferson, he won't die, more 's the pity."

He knew from the first he must go, and by good

luck no one he knew was in sight to turn him into
ridicule for the pleasure of the great Federalist
dames.

"Give him his wig, Tom." The little doctor
sadly regarded the dusty wig. Then he readjusted
his head-gear and said he would go.

"Now, that 's a good doctor. Come," and she
rode off again after him, by no means inclined to set
him free to change his mind.

At Mrs. Swanwick's door, as he got out of his
chaise, she said: "This lady speaks only French.
She is the Vicomtesse de Courval. And now, mind
you, Doctor, no citizenesses or any such Jacobin
nonsense."

"*A votre service, madame,*" he said, and rapped
discreetly low, feeling just at present rather humble
and as meek as Ça Ira.

Mistress Wynne waited until the door closed
behind him, and then rode away refreshed. Turning to her black groom, she said, "If you tell, Tom,
I will kill you."

"Yes, missus."

"At all events, he won't bleed her," she reflected, "and he has more good sense than most of
them. That young fellow is a fine figure of a man.
I wonder what kind of clerk Hugh will make of him.
I must have him to dine."

"In the hall Dr. Chovet met Schmidt, who knew
him, as, in fact, he knew every one of any importance in the city.

"These are to me friends, Doctor," he said. "I
beg of you to come often," a request to the doctor's

liking, as it seemed to carry better assurance of pay than was the usual experience among his emigrant countrymen. He was at once a little more civil. He bowed repeatedly, was much honored, and after asking a few questions of De Courval, went upstairs with Mrs. Swanwick, reflecting upon how some day he could avenge himslf on Gainor Wynne.

De Courval, relieved by his presence and a little amused, said, smiling, "I hope he is a good doctor."

"Yes, he is competent. He manufactures his manners for the moment's need."

The doctor came down in half an hour, and, speaking French of the best, said: "Madame has had troubles, I fear, and the long voyage and no appetite for sea diet—bad, bad. It is only a too great strain on mind and body. There needs repose and shortly wine,—good Bordeaux claret,—and soon, in a week or two, to drive out and take the air. There is no cause for alarm, but it will be long, long."

Schmidt went with him to the door. De Courval sat down. Wine, drives, a doctor, and for how long? And perhaps additions to the simple diet of this modest household. Well, he must use some of the small means in Wynne's hands. And these women, with their cares, their brave self-denial of all help, how could he ever repay this unlooked-for kindness?

His mother soon grew better, and, having again seen Mr. Wynne, he felt that he might shortly take up the work which awaited him.

Meanwhile, the gentle nursing was effective, and went on without complaint and as a matter of course. Miss Wynne came at odd hours to inquire

or to fetch some luxury, and soon the vicomte must
call to see her.

The days went by, and there were strawberries
for madame from Mr. Langstroth and from Merion,
walks for De Courval, or a pull on the water with
Schmidt, and anxiously desired news from France.
At last, after a fortnight or more, well on into June,
the doctor insisted on claret, and De Courval asked
of Schmidt where it could be had. The German
laughed. "I might lie to you, and I should at need,
but I have already for the mother's use good Bordeaux in the cellar."

De Courval colored, and, hesitating, asked, "How
much am I in your debt?"

"Six months of the five years. It is I shall be
long in debt, I fear. It cannot be all on one side.
The life of a man! What credit hath it in the account of things? Suppose it had gone the other
way, would you contented bide?"

"Not I," laughed De Courval.

"Let us say, then, I have paid a score of thanks;
credit me with these—one should be prudent. Only
in the Bible it is a thank,—one. Be careful of the
coin. Let it rest there. So you go to work to-
morrow. It is well; for you have been anxious of
late, and for that exacting work is no bad remedy."

The next day De Courval found himself before
seven-thirty in the counting-house. "It is hard in
winter," said the clerk who was to instruct him.
"Got to make the fires then. Mr. Potts is particular. You must leave no dust, and here are brooms
in the closet." And so, perched cn a high stool,

the clerk, well amused, watched his successor, Louis René, Vicomte de Courval, sweep out the counting-house.

"By George!" said the critic, "you will wear out a broom a day. What a dust! Sweep it up in the dust-pan. Sprinkle it first with the watering-pot. Lord, man, don't deluge it! And now a little sand. Don't build a sea-beach. Throw out the dust on the ash-heap behind the house." It was done at last.

"Take your coat off next time. The clerks will be here soon, but we have a few minutes. Come out and I will show you the place. Oh, this is your desk, quills, paper, and sand, and 'ware old man Potts."

They went on to the broad landing between the warehouse and Dock Creek. "There are two brigs from Madeira in the creek, partly unloaded."

The great tuns of Madeira wine filled the air with vinous odors, and on one side, under a shed, were staves and salt fish from the North for return cargoes, and potatoes, flour, and onions in ropes for the French islands.

"The ship outside," said the clerk, "is from the Indies with tea and silks, and for ballast cheap blue Canton china."

The vessels and the thought of far-away seas pleased the young man. The big ship, it seemed, had been overhauled by a small British privateer.

"But there is no war?"

"No, but they claim to take our goods billed for any French port, and as many men as they choose to call English."

"And she beat them off?"

"Yes; Mr. Wynne gave the master a silver tank-ard, and a hundred dollars for the men."

De Courval was excited and pleased. It was no day of tame, peaceful commerce. Malayan pirates in the East, insolent English cruisers to be outsailed, the race home of rival ships for a market, made every voyage what men fitly called a venture. Commerce had its romance. Strange things and stranger stories came back from far Indian seas.

After this introduction, he thanked his instructor, and returning to the counting-house, was gravely welcomed and asked to put in French two long letters for Martinique and to translate and write out others. He went away for his noonday meal, and, returning, wrote and copied and resolutely rewrote, asking what this and that term of commerce meant, until his back ached when he went home at six. He laughed as he gave his mother a humorous account of it all, but not of the sweeping.

Then she declared the claret good, and what did it cost? Oh, not much. He had not the bill as yet.

VI

DESPITE the disgust he felt at the routine of daily domestic service, the life of the great merchant's business began more and more to interest De Courval. The clerks were mere machines, and of Mr. Wynne he saw little. He went in and laid letters on his desk, answered a question or two in regard to his mother, and went out with perhaps a message to a shipmaster fresh from the Indies and eager to pour out in a tongue well spiced with sea oaths his hatred of England and her ocean bullies.

The mother's recovery was slow, as Chovet had predicted, but at the end of June, on a Saturday, he told Mistress Wynne she might call on his patient, and said that in the afternoon the vicomtesse might sit out on the balcony upon which her room opened.

Madame was beginning to desire a little change of society and was somewhat curious as to this old spinster of whom René had given a kind, if rather startling, account. Her own life in England had been lonely and amid those who afforded her no congenial society, nor as yet was she in entirely easy and satisfactory relations with the people among whom she was now thrown. They were to her both new and singular.

The Quaker lady puzzled her inadequate experience—a *dame de pension,* a boarding-house keeper with perfect tact; with a certain simple sweetness, as if any common bit of service about the room and the sick woman's person were a pleasure. The quiet, gentle manners of the Quaker household, with now and then a flavor of some larger world, were all to Madame's taste. When, by and by, her hostess talked more and more freely in her imperfect French, it was unobtrusive and natural, and she found her own somewhat austere training beginning to yield and her unready heart to open to kindness so constant, and so beautiful with the evident joy of self-sacrifice.

During the great war the alliance with France had made the language of that country the fashion. French officers came and went, and among the Whig families of position French was even earlier, as in Mary Plumstead's case, a not very rare accomplishment. But of late she had had little opportunity to use her knowledge, and with no such courage as that of Gainor Wynne, had preferred the awkwardness of silence until her guest's illness obliged her to put aside her shy distrust in the interest of kindness. She soon found the tongue grow easier, and the vicomtesse began to try at short English sentences, and was pleased to amuse herself by correcting Margaret, who had early learned French from her mother, and with ready intelligence seized gladly on this fresh chance to improve her knowledge.

One day as Mrs. Swanwick sat beside her guest's couch, she said: "Thy son told me soon after thy coming that thou art not, like most of the French, of the Church of Rome." He, it seemed, desired to see a Friends' meeting, and his mother has expressed her own wish to do the same when well enough.

"No," said madame; "we are of the religion—Huguenots. There is no church of my people here, so my son tells me, and no French women among the emigrants."

"Yes, one or two. That is thy Bible, is it not?" pointing to the book lying open beside her. "I am reading French when times serve. But I have never seen a French Bible. May I look at it? I understand thy speech better every day, and Margaret still better; but I fear my French may be queer enough to thee."

"It is certainly better than my English," said the vicomtesse, adding, after a brief pause: "It is the French of a kind heart." The vicomtesse as she spoke was aware of a breach in her usual reserve of rather formal thankfulness.

"I thank thee for thy pretty way of saying a pleasant thing," returned Mrs. Swanwick. "I learned it—thy language—when a girl, and was foolishly shy of its use before I knew thee so well. Now I shall blunder on at ease, and Margaret hath the audacity of youth."

"A charming child," said madame, "so gay and so gentle and intelligent."

"Yes, a good girl. Too many care for her—ah,

the men! One would wish to keep our girls children, and she is fast ceasing to be a child.''

She turned to the Bible in her hand, open at a dry leaf of ivy. ''It has psalms, I see, here at the end.''

''Yes, Clement Marot's. He was burned at the stake for his faith.''

''Ah, cruel men! How strange! Here, I see, is a psalm for one about to die on the scaffold.''

''Yes—yes,'' said the vicomtesse.

''What strange stories it seems to tell! It was, I see, printed long ago.''

''Yes, two years before the massacre of St. Bartholomew.''

''And here is one for men about to go into battle for God and their faith.'' The hostess looked up. Her guest's face was stern, stirred as with some deep emotion, her eyes full of tears.

She had been thinking, as she lay still and listened to Mary Swanwick's comments, of death for a man's personal belief, for his faith, of death with honor. She was experiencing, of a sudden, that failure of self-control which is the sure result of bodily weakness; for, with the remembrance of her husband's murder, she recalled, amid natural feelings of sorrow, the shame with which she had heard of his failure at once to declare his rank when facing death. For a moment she lay still. ''I shall be better in a moment,'' she said.

''Ah, what have I done?'' cried Mrs. Swanwick, distressed, as she took the thin, white hand in hers. ''Forgive me.''

"You have done nothing—nothing. Some day I shall tell you; not now." She controlled herself with effectual effort, shocked at her own weakness, and surprised that it had betrayed her into emotion produced by the too vivid realization of a terrible past. She never did tell more of it, but the story came to the Quaker dame on a far-off day and from a less reserved personage.

At this moment Margaret entered. Few things escaped the watchful eyes that were blue to-day and gray to-morrow, like the waters of the broad river that flowed by her home. No sign betrayed her surprise at the evident tremor of the chin muscles, the quick movement of the handkerchief from the eyes, tear-laden, the mother's look of sympathy as she dropped the hand left passive in her grasp. Not in vain had been the girl's training in the ways of Friends. Elsewhere she was more given to set free her face to express what she felt, but at home and among those of the Society of Friends she yielded with the imitativeness of youth to the not unwholesome discipline of her elders. She quietly announced Aunt Gainor as waiting below stairs.

"Wilt thou see her?" said Mrs. Swanwick.

"Certainly; I have much to thank her for. And tell my son not to come up as yet," for, being Saturday, it was a half-holiday from noon, and having been out for a good walk to stretch his desk-cramped legs, he was singing in the garden bits of French songs and teasing June or watching her skilful hunt for grasshoppers. He caroled gaily as he lay in the shade:

"La fin du jour
Sauve les fleurs et rafraîchit les belles;
Je veux, en galant troubadour,
Célébrer, au nom de l'amour,
Chanter, au nom des fleurs nouvelles.
La fin du jour."

The message was given later, and as Mistress Gainor came in to his mother's room she was a striking figure, with the beaver hat tied under her chin and the long, dark-green pelisse cast open so as to reveal the rich silk of her gown. It was not unfit for her age and was in entire good taste, for as usual she was dressed for her rôle. Even her goddaughter was slightly surprised, well as she knew her. This was not the Gainor that Chovet knew, the woman who delighted to excite the too easily irritated Dr. Rush, or to shock Mrs. Adams, the Vice-President's wife, with well embroidered gossip about the Willing women and the high play at Landsdowne, where Mrs. Penn presided, and Shippens, Chews, and others came. This was another woman.

Margaret, curious, lingered behind Miss Wynne, and stood a moment, a hand on the door. Miss Wynne came forward, and saying in French which had amazed two generations, *"Bon jour, madame,"* swept the entirely graceful courtesy of a day when even the legs had fine manners, adding, as the vicomtesse would have risen, "No, I beg of you."

"The settle is on the balcony," said the hostess, "and Cicero will come up by and by and carry thee out. Not a step—not a step by thyself," she added, gently despotic.

As Miss Wynne passed by, the girl saw her courtesy, and, closing the door, said to herself, "I think I could do it," and fell to courtesying on the broad landing. "I should like to do that for Friend Nicholas Waln," and gaily laughing, she went out and down the garden to deliver her message to the young vicomte.

Neither man, woman nor the French tongue dismayed Mistress Wynne. *"C'était un long calembourg*, my son," the vicomtesse said later—"a long conundrum, a long charade of words to represent *le bon Dieu* knows what. Ah, a tonic, truly. I was amused as I am not often." In fact, she was rarely receptively humorous and never productively so. Now she spoke slowly, in order to be understood, comprehending the big woman and knowing her at once for a lady of her own world with no provincial drawbacks, a woman at her ease, and serenely unconscious of, or indifferent to, the quality of the astounding tongue in which she spoke.

She talked of London and of the French emigrant nobles in Philadelphia, of the Marquis de la Garde, who taught dancing; of the Comté du Vallon, who gave lessons in fencing; of De Malerive, who made ice-cream. Madame, interested, questioned her until they got upon unhappy France, when she shifted the talk and spoke of the kindness of Mr. Wynne.

"It will soon be too hot here," said Gainor, "and then I shall have you at the Hill—Chestnut Hill, and in a week I shall come for you to ride in my

landau,"—there were only four in the city,—"and
the vicomte shall drive with you next Saturday.
You may not know that my niece Mrs. Wynne was
of French Quakers from the Midi, and this is why
her son loves your people and has more praise for
your son than he himself is like to hear from my
nephew. For my part, when I hate, I let it out,
and when I love or like, I am frank," which was
true.

Just then came the old black servant man Cicero,
once a slave of James Logan the first, and so named
by the master, folks said, because of pride in his fine
translation of the "De Senectute" of Cicero, which
Franklin printed.

"Cicero will carry thee out," said Mrs. Swanwick.

"Will he, indeed?" said Gainor, seeing a shadow
of annoyance come over the grave face of the sick
woman as she said, "I can walk," and rose unsteadily. The pelisse was off, and before the amazed
vicomtesse could speak, she was in Gainor's strong
arms and laid gently down on a lounge in the outer
air.

"*Mon Dieu!*" was all she could say, "but you are
as a man for strength. Thank you."

The roses were below her. The cool air came over
them from the river, and the violet of the eastward
sky reflected the glow of the setting sun. A ship
with the tricolor moved up with the flood, a *bonnet
rouge* at the masthead, as was common.

"What flag is that?" asked the vicomtesse. "And
that red thing? I do not see well."

"I do not know," said Gainor, calmly fibbing; and seeing her goddaughter about to speak, she put a finger on her lips and thrust a hand ignorant of its strength in the ribs of the hostess as madame, looking down among the trees on the farther slope, said: "Who is that? How merry they are!"

"Adam and Eve—in the garden," replied Gainor.

"For shame!" murmured Mary Swanwick in English. "It is well she did not understand thee." Then she added to the vicomtesse: "It is Margaret, madame, and thy son."

Again gay laughter came up from the distance; the vicomtesse became thoughtful.

"I have left you lettuce and some fruit," said Miss Wynne, "and may I be pardoned for taking the place of Cicero?"

"Ah, madame, kindness in any form is easy to pardon." Then Gainor went away, while Mrs. Swanwick sat down, saying: "Now no more talk. Let me fan thee a little."

The next day being the first Sunday in July, Schmidt said after breakfast: "De Courval, you said last night that you would like to go to church. It shall be Christ Church, if you like—Episcopal they call it."

They set out early, and on Delaware Second Street saw the fine old church Dr. Kearsley planned, like the best of Christopher Wren's work, as De Courval at once knew.

"I shall go in. I may not stay," said Schmidt. "I do not like churches. They seem all too small for me. Men should pray to God out of doors. Well,

6

it has a certain stately becomingness. It will suit you; but the Druids knew best.''

They found seats near the chancel. Just before the service began, a black servant in livery entered by a side door. A large man, tall and erect, in full black velvet, followed. The servant opened a pew; the tall man sat down, and knelt in prayer; the servant went back to the door, and seated himself on the floor upon a cushion.

Schmidt whispered, ''That is George Washington.''

The young man, it is to be feared, paid small attention to the service or to good Bishop White's sermon. The grave, moveless, ruddy face held him with the interest of its history. The reverent attention of the great leader pleased him, with his Huguenot training. At the close the congregation remained standing until Washington had gone out.

''Come,'' said Schmidt, and crossing the church they waited at the south gate until the President passed. He raised his hand in soldierly salute, and bowing, took off his beaver as he met Mrs. Chew and the Chief-Justice.

The two men walked away, silent for a time. Then the German said: ''You have seen a great man, a great soldier,—says our Frederick, who ought to know,—a statesman, too, and baited now by Jefferson's creature Freneau. It must have pleased the Almighty to have decreed the making of a man like George Washington.''

That the God of Calvin should have pleasure in things made had never occurred to the young Huguenot, who was already getting lessons which in days to come would freely modify the effect of the stern tenets which through habit and education he accepted with small cost of thought. His mind, however, was of serious type, and inquiry was in the whole world's atmosphere of his time.

He said, "Herr Schmidt, can a man conceive of God as having enjoyment?"

"If you were God, the all-creative, the eternal power, the inconceivable master, would you not make for yourself pleasure, when you could make or mar all things? Does it shock you? Or has the thought of your church the clipped wings of an eagle that must ever stumble on the earth and yearn for the free flight of the heavens? Terrible shears are creeds."

De Courval was new to such comments. He felt hindered by all the child home-rule of habit, and the discipline of limiting beliefs held the more stringently for the hostile surroundings of neighbors and kinfolks of the Church of Rome.

The German was of no mind to perplex him. He had some clearly defined ideas as to what as a gentleman he could or could not do. As to much else he had no ruling conscience, but a certain kindliness which made him desire to like and be liked of men, and so now, with something akin to affection, he was learning to love the grave young noble to whom he owed a life endowed by nature with great power of varied enjoyment.

"We will talk of these things again," he said. "Once I was speaking of the making of men, and I said, 'If the father of Shakspere had married another woman, or his wife a year later, would "Hamlet" ever have been written?' "

De Courval laughed. "I do not know 'Hamlet.' "

The German looked around at him thoughtfully and said: "Is that indeed so? It is a sermon on the conduct of life. When once I spoke of this and how at birth we are fortuned, the king said to me, I think—" and he broke off his sentence. "You must not take me too seriously, De Courval. This is mere gossip of the imagination. I have lived too much in France with the philosophers, who are like Paul's men of Athens."

"I like it," said De Courval, pleased, puzzled, flattered, and immensely curious concerning the man at his side; but decent manners forbidding personal questions, he accepted the German's diversion of the talk and asked, "Who is that across the street?"

"A good soldier, General Wayne, and with him the Secretary of War, Knox. It is said he is one of the few whom Washington loves. He is a lonely man, the President, as are the kings of men, on thrones or elsewhere."

"To be loved of that man would be worth while," said his companion. He was to see him again in an hour of distress for himself and of trouble and grief for the harassed statesman.

When at home he told his mother he had seen Washington.

"What was he like?"

"I can not say—tall, straight, ruddy, a big nose."

She smiled at his description. "Your father,

René, once told me of a letter Marquis La Fayette had of him the day after he last parted with Washington. It was something like this: 'When our carriages separated, I said, I shall never see him again. My heart said Yes. My head said No; but these things happen. At least I have had my day.' That is not like a man, René. He must have strong affections."

"Men say not, mother."

VII

THE years which followed our long struggle for freedom were busy years for the mind of man. The philosophers in France were teaching men strange doctrines, and fashion, ever eager for change, reveled in the new political philosophy. The stir of unrest was in the air, among the people, in the talk of the salons.

The Bastille had long since fallen, and already in the provinces murder and pillage had begun. The terrible example set by Jourdan late in '91 was received in Paris with other than reprobation. He was to return to Avignon and, strange irony of fate, to be condemned as a moderate and to die by the guillotine amid the rejoicing of the children of his victims; but this was to be far away in '94.

The massacres of August, '92, when the king left the Swiss to their fate, all the lightning and thunder of the gathering storm of war without and frenzied murder within the tottering kingdom, had not as yet in this midsummer been heard of in America.

After four years as our minister in Paris, Mr. Jefferson had long ago come back to add the mischief of a notable intellect to the party which sincerely believed we were in danger of a monarchy, and was all for France and for Citizen Equality, who, as

Hamilton foresaw, might come to be the most cruel of tyrants.

The long battle of States' rights had begun in America. The Federalists, led by Hamilton, were for strong central rule; their opponents, the Republicans, later to be called Democrats, were gone mad in their Jacobin clubs of many cities, *bonnet rouge* at feasts, craze about titles, with Citizen for Mr., and eagerly expecting a new French minister.

Washington, a Federalist, smiled grimly at the notion of kingship, and the creature of no party, with his usual desire for peace, had made up, of both parties, a cabinet sure to disagree.

To hear the clamor of the Jacobin clubs, a stranger coming among us in '92 might have believed us ruined. Nevertheless, Hamilton had rescued our finance, assured a revenue not as yet quite sufficient, founded the bank, and assumed the State debts. The country was in peril only from disorders due to excess of prosperity, the podagra of the state. There was gambling in the new script, lotteries innumerable, and the very madness of speculation in all manner of enterprises—canals, toll-pike roads, purchases of whole counties.

Cool heads like Schmidt looked on and profited. The Quaker merchants, no wise perturbed by the rashness of speculation, accumulated irredeemable ground rents, and thriving, took far too little interest in the general party issues, but quietly created the great schools which are of our best to-day, endowed charities, and were to be heard of later as fearless Christian gentlemen in a time of death and despair, when men unafraid in battle shrank from the foe which struck and was never seen.

In the early August days, madame had driven now and then with Mistress Wynne, and at present was gone, not quite willingly, to stay a while at the Hill. Mrs. Wynne had called, and her husband, more than once, with a guarded word or two from his wife as to the manner of usefulness of his young clerk. "Mind you, Hugh, let it be secretary. Do not hurt the poor lady's pride." So counseled Darthea, kindly wise, and he obeyed, having come in time to accept his wife's wisdom in many matters social and other.

To the Hill farm came to call, on the vicomtesse, the Vicomte de Noailles, the prosperous partner of William Bingham; and, asked by the Wynnes, Mrs. Bingham, to be at a later day the acclaimed beauty of London; her kin, the Willings, with the gift of hereditary good looks; and the Shippens. The vicomtesse received them all with a certain surprise at their ceremonious good manners and their tranquil sense of unquestioned position. She would return no visits as yet, and her son was busy and, too, like herself, in mourning. In fact, she shrank from general contact with the prosperous, and dreaded for René this gay world of pretty young women. *Ciel!* What might not happen?

On their part, they were curious and kind. Emigrant ladies were rare; but, as to foreign titles, they were used to them in the war, and now they were common since a great influx of destitute French had set in, and not all who came were to their liking.

"There," said the German one evening, kindling
a great pipe, "enough of politics, De Courval; you
are of the insatiably curious. We are to dine to-
morrow at the fashionable hour of four with Mistress
Wynne and the maid, my Pearl. It is an occasion
of some worthiness. She has come to town for this
feast, one of her freaks. Did ever you see a great
actress?"

"I?" said De Courval. "No, or yes—once, in
France, Mademoiselle Mars. We of the religion do
not go to the theater. What actress do you speak
of?"

"Oh, women—all women; but to-morrow on the
stage will be Miss Gainor, become, by pretty courtesy
of possibilities declined, Mistress Gainor by bre-
vet—"

De Courval, delighted, cried: "But your little
Quaker lady—is she to have a rôle? She seems to
me very simple."

"Simple! Yes, here, or at meeting, I daresay.
Thou shouldest see her with Friend Waln. Her eyes
humbly adore his shoe-buckles—no, his shoe-ties—
when he exhorts her to the preservation of plainness
of attire, and how through deep wading, and a living
travail of soul, life shall be uplifted to good do-
minion. It is a godly man, no doubt, and a fine,
ripe English he talks; and Arthur Howell, too."

"I must hear them."

"You will hear noble use of the great English
speech. But best of all are the Free Quakers, like
Samuel Wetherill, an apostate, says Friend Pennington with malignant sweetness, but for me a sterling,

well-bred gentle, if ever God made one. Ah, then the
maid, all godliness and grace, will take his hat and
cane and, the head a bit aside, make eyes at him.
Ah, fie for shame! And how we purr and purr—
actresses, oh, all of them! There is the making of a
Quaker *Juliet* in that girl.''

''One would scarce think it. My mother is *éprise*
—oh, quite taken with Miss Margaret, and now, I
think, begins a little to understand this household,
so new and so wonderful to me and to her. But I
meant to ask you something. I have part paid the
queer doctor, and the bill, I suppose, is correct. It
is long—''

''And large, no doubt.''

''And what with a new gown my mother needs
and some clothes I must have—''

The German interrupted him. ''De Courval, may
I not help you, to whom I owe a debt which can
never be paid?''

''Oh, no, no. I shall soon have more wages.'' He
grew red as he spoke.

''But why is money such a wonder thing that only
some saleable article shall count against it? I lack
hospitality to entertain the thought.''

''Would you take it of me?''

''I? Yes. I took my life of you—a poor thing,
but mine own.''

''I think you had small choice in the matter,''
laughed René.

''*Der Teufel!* Very little. Let it be a loan, if you
will. Come, now. You make me unhappy. I lend
you five hundred *livres*—a hundred dollars we call it
here. You pay, when you can.''

De Courval hesitated. Was there not something ignoble in refusing a kindness thus offered? Schmidt laughed as he added: "Reverse it. Put it in this fashion: good master of my fate, let me drown. I would owe no coin of life to any. To end it, I put to-night in this left-hand drawer money. Use it freely. Leave a receipt each time, if you like."

"I am so little used to kindness," said De Courval, wavering.

"I know," returned Schmidt—"bittersweet to some men, but should not be to the more noble nature."

"No, no, not to me. I take it and gladly, but"— and once more he colored, as he said with a certain shyness—"would you mind calling me René? I—I should like it."

"And I, too," said the German, as he put a hand of familiar kindliness on the younger man's knee. "Now that is settled, and you have done me another favor. I have an errand at Germantown, and shall join you at Miss Wynne's at four to-morrow. Are there any ships come in? No? There will be, I fear, evil news from France, and storms, storms that will roll across the sea and beat, too, on these shores. It will stir here some foolish echoes, some feeble mockery of what over there cries murder." De Courval had had too much reason to believe him. "Ach, I am sleepy. Shall you go to see your mother on Sunday? There is my mare at your service."

Yes, he had meant to walk, but he would be glad of the horse.

When, on Saturday, Mrs. Swanwick knew that Schmidt had gone to the country, she said Margaret would walk with the vicomte, and show him the way. He felt a fresh surprise, a little embarrassment. Young women were not thus free in France; but as he was the only one thus amazed, he set out with the Pearl in some wonderment at what his mother would have said or thought.

They walked up Front Street, and at last along Fifth. She was now, as Schmidt had said, the other Margaret of whom De Courval had had brief knowledge at times. A frank, natural, gay good humor was in all her ways, a gentle desire to please, which was but the innocent coquetry of a young girl's heart. She stayed a moment as they crossed Walnut Street, and replying to a question, said: "Yes, that is the jail men called the Provostry in the war. My grandfather lay in it—oh, very long. We have his sword in the attic. I would hang it up down-stairs, but Friends would not approve, thou must know. And that is Independence Hall, but thou hast seen it."

"Yes. Are you proud of it?"

"Surely. My people shed our blood for what strong men did in that hall. My uncle and my grandfather came out of the jail to die, oh, both of them!"

"And of what party are you, Miss Margaret?"

"Of George Washington's," she cried. "But Friends must have no party, or their women, at least —not even tea-parties," and she laughed.

"I think I am of your party," said De Courval— "George Washington's."

The conventual shelter of the silk bonnet turned

toward him as she said: "Then we agree; but I am not sure that I like people to agree with me. It spoils talk, Mr. Schmidt says."

"Then I am all for Jefferson," he cried gaily, thinking in his grave way that this young girl was of a sudden older than her years.

"I am not sure that I like that either," she replied, and so chatting with easy freedom they came to Miss Wynne's door, opposite the Quakers' burial-ground, where their dead lay in unmarked graves. A negro servant in the brown livery of the Wynnes opened the door, and Aunt Gainor appeared in the hall in more than usual splendor.

"Good day, Vicomte," and to Margaret: "Take off your bonnet, child. How can any one, man or woman, kiss thee with that thing on thy head? It might be useful at need, but I do suppose you could take it off on such occasions."

"For shame, Aunt Gainor!" said the Pearl, flushing and glad of the bonnet she was in act to remove. Miss Wynne kissed her, whispering, "Good Lord! you are on the way to be a beauty!"

De Courval, who of course had called long since to thank his hostess, had so far dined in no one of the more luxuriously appointed homes of Philadelphia. Here were portraits; much, too much, china, of which he was no judge; and tables for work that Miss Wynne never did, or for cards at which she liked high play.

"Mr. Hamilton was to dine here, but was with me just now to be excused."

"He was with my mother an hour this morning,"

said Margaret, "about some small affairs we have in
New York. He is to be here again on Saturday sennight to tell mother all about it."

"I am sorry to miss him," said Gainor; "but if I
lose a guest I desired, I am to have one I do not
want. Mr. Josiah Langstroth has bidden himself to
dine with me."

"Uncle Josiah? I have not seen him for a
month."

"There is a joss in the corner like him, Vicomte,"
said Miss Wynne. "If you look at it, you will need
no presentation. I pray you to avoid the temptation
of a look." Of course both young persons regarded,
as she meant they should, the china god on his ebony
stand.

"A reincarnation of the bulldog," remarked
Gainor, well pleased with her phrase.

"If," said Margaret to the young man, "thou dost
take my aunt or Uncle Josiah seriously, it will be
what they never do one another. They fight, but
never quarrel. My mother thinks this is because
then they would stay apart and have no more the
luxury of fighting again, a thing they do love."

"Are you sure that is thy mother's wisdom, Margaret?" said Gainor. "It is not like her."

"If I said it was mine, thou wouldst box my ears."

"Did ever one hear the like?"

The young girl occasionally ventured, when with
aunt or uncle, upon these contributions of observation which now and then startle those who, seeing
little change from day to day, are surprised by the
sudden fruitage of developmental growth.

"I shall profit by Miss Swanwick's warning," said De Courval.

Miss Wynne, who kept both houses open, and now would not as usual, on account of the vicomtesse, fill her country house with guests, had come to town to dine Mr. Hamilton and to amuse herself with the young man. It cannot be said, despite her bluff kindness, that De Courval altogether or unreservedly liked her sudden changes of mood or the quick transitions which more or less embarrassed and at times puzzled him. Upon his inquiring for his mother, Miss Wynne replied:

"She is better, much better. You are to come to-morrow. You should come more often. It is absurd, most absurd, that you are so tied to the legs of a desk. I shall speak to my nephew."

"I beg of you, madame, to do no such thing. I am a clerk and the youngest." And then a little ashamed of his shame, he added: "I sweep out the office and lock up at evening. You would cause Mr. Wynne to think I had asked you." He spoke with decision.

"It is ridiculous. I shall explain, make it easy."

Then he said, "You will pardon me, who owe you so much, but I shall have to be beforehand and say I do not wish it."

"I retreat," said Miss Wynne. "I haul down my colors." He was quite sure that she never would.

"You are again kind, madame," he returned.

"I hear Mr. Schmidt and the joss," she said as she rose, while Margaret, unobserved, cast a thoughtful glance at the clerk. It was a new type to her. The gravity, the decisiveness, and the moral courage, although she may not have so labeled the qualities, appealed to her who had proudly borne the annoyances of restricted means among friends and kindred who lived in luxury. She had heard Schmidt say to her mother that this De Courval was a man on the way to the making of a larger manhood. Even young as she was, about to be seventeen in September, she had among the young Friends those she liked and some who were disposed to like her too well; but this was another kind of man.

When Schmidt entered, followed by Friend Langstroth, De Courval was struck by the truth of Gainor's reference to the joss. Short, very fat, a triple chin and pendant cheeks under small eyes, and a bald head—all were there.

"You are both late. My back of mutton will be overdone. The Vicomte de Courval—Mr. Langstroth."

"Glad to see thee; meant to come and see thee. I was to give thee this letter, Friend Schmidt. Mr. Wynne sent it. A messenger came up from Chester while I was with him at the counting-house. The *Saucy Sisters* was lying below for the flood."

Schmidt glanced at it, hesitated a moment, and put it in his pocket as they went in to dinner.

"Any news?" asked Langstroth. "Any news from France?"

"I do not know," said Schmidt. He had no mind to spoil the meal with what he knew must very likely be evil tidings. "It is from England," he added. Miss Gainor, understanding him, said: "We were to have had Mr. Hamilton. I think I told you."

"I saw him at the office of the Secretary of the Treasury," said Schmidt; "a less capable successor he has in his place. We talked much about the rage for lotteries, and he would stop them by a law."

"He should let things alone," said Langstroth. "A nice muddle he has made of it with his bank and his excise."

"And what do you know about it?" said Gainor, tartly.

"Fiddlesticks! I know that a man who cannot manage his own affairs had better leave larger things alone."

"He has," said Schmidt quietly, "as I see it, that rare double gift, a genius for government and finance."

"Humph!" growled Langstroth.

Schmidt was silent, and took the Wynne Madeira with honest appreciation, while the young man ate his dinner, amazed at the display of bad manners.

Then the girl beside him said in a half-whisper: "Fiddlesticks! Why do people say that? The violin is hard to play, I hear. Why do men say fiddlesticks?"

De Courval did not know, and Aunt Gainor asked, "What is that, Margaret?"

"I was saying that the violin must be hard to play."

"Ah, yes, yes," returned the hostess, puzzled, while Schmidt smiled, and the talk fell upon mild gossip and the last horse-race—and so on to more perilous ground.

7

"About lotteries," said Josiah, "I have bought thee a ticket, Margaret, number 1792—the lottery for the college of Princeton."

"A nice Quaker you are," said Miss Wynne. "I see they forbid lotteries in Massachusetts. The overseers of meeting will be after you."

"I should like to see them. A damn pretty business, indeed. Suppose thee were to win the big prize, child." He spoke the intolerable language then becoming common among Friends. "Thee could beat Gainor in gowns."

"I should not be let to wear them." Alas! she saw herself in brocades and lutestring underskirts. The young man ignorantly shared her distress.

"There is small chance of it, I fear," said Gainor. "A hundred lottery chances I have bought, and never a cent the richer." And so the talk went on, Langstroth abusing all parties, Schmidt calmly neutral, the young people taking small part, and regarding the lottery business as one of Josiah's annoying jokes—no one in the least believing him.

At last the cloth was off the well-waxed mahogany table, a fresh pair of decanters set before the hostess, and each guest in turn toasted.

Langstroth had been for a time comfortably unamiable. He had said abusive things of all parties in turn, and now Schmidt amused himself by adding more superlative abuse, while Gainor Wynne, enjoying the game, fed Langstroth with exasperating additions of agreement. The girl, knowing them all well, silently watched the German's face, his zest in annoying Josiah unexpressed by even the faintest smile—a perfect actor. De Courval, with less full understanding of the players, was at times puzzled, and heard in silence Schmidt siding with Josiah. "It was most agreeable, my dear," said Mistress Gainor next day to one of her favorites, Tacy Lennox. "Josiah should of right be a gentleman. He has invented the worst manners ever you saw, my dear Tacy. He was like a mad bull, eager for war, and behold—he is fed and petted. Ah, but he was furious and bedazed. Tacy, I would you had seen it."

It was at last quite too much of a trial for Josiah, who turned from Gainor to Schmidt, and then to De Courval, with wild opinions, to which every one in turn agreed, until at last, beginning to suspect that he was being played with, he selected a subject sure to make his hostess angry. A look of pugnacious greed for a bone of contest showed on his bulldog face as he turned to Mistress Wynne. "This Madeira is on its last legs, Gainor."

"All of us are," laughed Schmidt.

"It is hardly good enough for my toast."

"Indeed," said Gainor; "we shall know when we hear it."

Then Josiah knew that for her to agree with him would this time be impossible. He smiled. "When I am at home, Gainor, as thee knows, I drink to our lawful king." He rose to his feet. "Here 's to George the Third."

Gainor was equal to the occasion.

"Wait a little, Josiah. Take away Mr. Langstroth's glass, Cæsar. Go to the kitchen and fetch one of the glasses I use no more because the Hessian hogs used them for troughs when they were quartered on me in the war. Cæsar, a Hessian wine-glass for Mr. Langstroth.''

De Courval listened in astonishment, while Schmidt, laughing, cried, ''I will drink to George with pleasure.''

''I know,'' cried Margaret: ''to George Washington.''

Schmidt laughed. ''You are too sharp, Pearl. In a minute, but for your saucy tongue, I should have trapped our Tory friend. To George the greater,'' said Schmidt.

The Quaker turned down his glass. ''Not I, indeed.''

''I hope the poor man will never hear of it, Josiah,'' said Miss Wynne as she rose laughing, and presently Schmidt and the young people went away, followed shortly after by Langstroth.

For a while Margaret walked on in silence, De Courval and the German talking. At last she said: ''Thou shouldst know that my uncle is not as bad as he seems. He is really a kind and generous man, but he loves to contradict my aunt, and no one else can so easily make her angry.''

''Ah, Pearl, the Madeira was good,'' said Schmidt —''too good; or, rather, the several Madeiras. In the multitude of vinous counselers there is little wisdom, and the man's ways would tempt an angel to mischief.''

Mrs. Swanwick, being alone, had gone out to take supper with a friend, and as Margaret left them in the hall, Schmidt said to De Courval: ''Come in. I

have a great package from Gouverneur Morris, from
Paris. You may as well hear what news there is.
I saw your anxiety, but I was of no mind to have
that imitation Quaker discuss the agony of a great
nation.''

It took two months or more to hear from France,
and each week added to the gathering anxiety with
which De Courval awaited news. He was grateful
for the daily labor, with its steady exactions, which
forbade excessive thought of the home land, for no
sagacity of his friend or any forecast that man could
make three thousand miles away was competent to
predict the acts of the sinister historic drama on
which the curtain was rising far away in France.

As the German opened the envelop and set aside
letter after letter, he talked on in his disconnected
way. ''I could like some bad men more than Josiah
Langstroth. He has what he calls opinions, and will
say, 'Welladay,'—no, that is my bastard English,—
he will say 'Well, at all events, that is my opinion.'
What means 'all events,' Herr René? A kick would
change them. 'T is an event—a kick. And Mistress
Wynne is sometimes not easy to endure. She steps
heavily on tender toes, even when on errands of
goodness.'' The younger man scarce heard these
comments as letter after letter was put aside, until
at last he put down his pipe, and Schmidt said: ''I
was sorry to keep you, but now this last letter has it
all—all. There is no detail, my friend, but enough—
enough. He writes me all France is in a ferment.
This is from Mr. Morris, whom our mobocrats loathe
for an aristocrat. He writes: 'The King has vetoed

two bills, one about the priests and one of less moment. La Fayette is in disgrace, and wants the surgeon's courage to let blood. Worst of all, and I write in haste,' he says, 'a mob on June 20th broke into the Tuileries and there, in the Œil de Bœuf, a butcher mocked the King to his face as Monsieur Veto. The King laughed, it is said, and set their damned bonnet on his head, and drew his sword, and cried *"Vive la nation!"* The war goes ill or well as you please; ill for all, I fear. Dillon was murdered by his own regiment after a retreat.' "

"I knew him in the army," said De Courval. "I was young then. But the king—has he no courage? Are they all mad?"

"No. He has not the courage of action. He has the courage to endure, if that is to be so nominated. The other is needed just now. That is all—all."

"And too much."

"Yes. Come, let us go out and fence a bit in the garden, and sweat out too much Madeira. Come, there is still light enough."

VIII

THROUGH the quiet of a Sunday morning, De Courval rode slowly up Fifth Street, and into a land of farms and woodland, to spend a quiet day alone with his mother, Miss Wynne, not altogether to the young man's regret, having to remain in town over Monday. As he came to the scenes where Schmidt, in their walks of Sundays, had explained to him Washington's well-laid plan of the Germantown battle, he began at last to escape for a time the too sad reflection which haunted his hours of leisure in the renewed interest of a young soldier who had known only the army life, but never actual war. He bent low in the saddle, hat off to a group on the lawn at Cliveden, the once war-battered home of the Chews, and was soon after kissing his mother on the porch of the Hill farm.

There was disquieting news to tell of France, and he soon learned that despite the heat and mosquitos she preferred the tranquillity of the widow's home to the luxury of Miss Wynne's house. She was as usual calmly decided, and he did not urge her to stay longer. She would return to the city on Thursday. They talked of money matters, with reticence on his part in regard to Schmidt's kindness and good counsels, and concerning the satisfaction Mr. Wynne had expressed with regard to his secretary.

"It may be good training for thee, my son," she

said and then, after a pause, "I begin to comprehend these people," and, pleased with her progress, made little ventures in English to let him see how well she was learning to speak. An habitual respect made him refrain from critical corrections, but he looked up in open astonishment when she said rather abruptly: "The girl in her gray gowns is on the way to become one of the women about whom men go wild. Neither are you very ugly, my son. Have a care; but a word from me should suffice."

"Oh, mother," he exclaimed, "do not misunder-stand me!"

"My son, I know you are not as some of the light-minded cousins we knew in France; but a word of warning does no harm, even if it be not needed."

"I think you may be at ease, *maman*. You amaze me when you call her beautiful. A pleasant little maid she seems to me, and not always the same, and at times gay,—oh, when away from her mother,— and intelligent, too. But beautiful—oh, hardly. *Soyez tranquille, maman.*"

"I did not say she was beautiful. I said she was good-looking; or that at least was what I meant. Certainly she is unlike our too ignorant demoiselles; but contrast with the familiar may have its peril. It is quite another type from our young women at home, and attractive enough in its way—in its bour-geois way."

He smiled. "I am quite too busy to concern my-self with young women." In fact he had begun to find interest in a little study of this new type. "Yes, quite too busy."

"That is as well." But she was not at ease. On the whole, she thought it would be proper now for him to go to Mrs. Bingham's and to the President's receptions. Miss Wynne would see that he had the entrée. He was too occupied, he said once more, and his clothes were quite unfit. Neither was he inclined yet awhile. And so he rode away to town with several things to think about, and on Thursday the vicomtesse made clear to the well-pleased Mrs. Swanwick that she was glad of the quiet and the English lessons and the crisp talk of Schmidt, who spoke French, but not fluently, and concerning whom she was mildly jealous and, for her, curious. "Schmidt, my son? No; a name disguised. He is a gentleman to his finger-ends, but surely a strange one."

"It is enough, *maman*, that he is my friend. Often I, too, am curious; but—ah, well, I wonder why he likes me; but he does, and I am glad of it."

"You wonder. I do not," and she smiled.

"Ah, the vain *maman!*" he cried. It was very rare that she praised him, and she was by long habit given to no demonstrations of affection.

Two weeks ran on in the quiet routine of the Quaker home and the increasing work of the great shipping merchant. De Courval was more and more used by Wynne in matters other than copying letters in French. Sometimes, too, he was trusted with business affairs demanding judgment, and although Wynne spoke no word of praise, neither was there any word of censure, and he watched the clerk with interest and growing regard. Twice he sent him to New York, and once on an errand to Baltimore, where he successfully collected some long-standing debts. A new clerk had come, and De Courval, to his relief, was no longer expected to sweep out the counting-house.

By degrees Wynne fully realized that he had found a helper of unusual capacity, and more and more, as the great and varied business attracted De Courval, he was taken into Wynne's confidence, and saw the ships come and go, and longed to share the peril and see the wonders of the ocean. There were great tuns of wine from Madeira on the pier or in the cellars. Gentlemen came to taste it, men with historic names—General Wayne, Colonel Lear for the President, and Mr. Justice Yeates. De Courval was bade to knock out bungs and dip in tasting vials. Also Miss Wynne came to refill her cellar, but took small notice of him. He was out of favor for a season, and her nephew had laughed at her remonstrances.

"A thoroughbred put to the work of a farm-horse!"

"Nonsense, Aunt Gainor! Let him alone. You can not spoil him, as you did me. There is stuff in the fellow worth a dozen of my clerks. At six they are gone. If there is work to do, he stays till nine. What that man wants, he will get. What he sets himself to do, he does. Let him alone."

"A miserably paid clerk," she cried. "He deserves no better. I wash my hands of him."

"There is soap in the closet," he laughed.

She went away angry, and saw the young noble

talking with a ruddy gentleman whose taste in wine has made his name familiar at the dining-tables of the last hundred years. Major Butler was asking the vicomte to dine, and promising a perilous education in the vintages of Madeira.

When the major had gone, Mr. Wynne sent for his clerk. To be opposed was apt to stiffen his Welsh obstinacy. "Your wages are to be now, sir, two hundred and fifty livres,—fifty dollars a month,—and you are doing well, very well; but the clerks are not to know, except Mr. Potts." He owed this unusual advance to Miss Wynne, but probably the master was as little aware of what had caused it as was the irate spinster. De Courval thanked him quietly, knowing perfectly well that he had fairly earned what was so pleasantly given.

It was now the Saturday sennight mentioned by Margaret as the day when Mr. Hamilton was to come to settle certain small business matters with Mrs. Swanwick. Some wit, or jealous dame, as Schmidt had said, called Mrs. Swanwick's the Quaker salon; and, in fact, men of all types of opinion came hither. Friends there were, the less strict, and at times some, like Waln, to protest in their frank way against the too frequent company of world's people, and to go away disarmed by gentle firmness. Mrs. Swanwick's love of books and her keen interest in every new thing, and now the opening mind and good looks of Margaret, together with the thoughtful neutrality of Schmidt, captured men, young and old, who were apt to come especially on a Saturday afternoon, when there was leisure even for

busy statesmen. Hither came Aaron Burr—the wo-
man-hawk, Aunt Gainor called him, with his dark,
fateful face; Pickering, in after days of the War
Department; Wolcott, to be the scarce adequate successor of Hamilton; Logan, and gay cousins—not
often more than one or two at a time—with, rarely,
the Master of the Rolls and Robert Morris, and Mr.
Justice Chew—in fact, what was best in the social
life of the city.

Mr. Hamilton was shut up with Mrs. Swanwick
in the withdrawing-room, busy. It was now too late
to expect visitors—five o'clock of a summer afternoon. The vicomtesse avoided this interesting society, and at last René ceased to urge her to share
what he himself found so agreeable. Margaret sat
entranced in the "Castle of Otranto," hardly hearing the *click, click,* of the fencing-foils on the grass
plot not far away. Birds were in the air; a wood-
pecker was busy on a dead tree; bees, head down,
were accumulating honey for the hive at the foot of
the garden; and a breeze from the river was blowing through the hall and out at the hospitably open
front door—a peaceful scene, with still the ring
and clash of the foils and De Courval's merry
laughter.

"A hit, a palpable hit!" said a voice behind Margaret as she rose.

"Thou art dead for a ducat—dead, Friend de
Courval."

"Ah," said Schmidt, "a critic. Does it look easy,
Mr. de Forest?"

"I am a man of peace, how shouldst I know? but

"'Well played!' cried Schmidt—'the jest and the rapier'"

the game looks easy." He threw up his head and stretched out his hand. "Let me look at the thing."

"Then take off your coat and put on a mask. But I shall not hurt you; there is no need for the mask."

He was quietly amused, and if only Nicholas Waln would come; for now the Quaker gentleman had put aside hat and coat, and in plainest gray homespun faced him, a stalwart, soldierly figure.

"How does thee hold it, Friend Schmidt? Ah, so?"

In a moment the German knew that he was crossing blades with a master of the small sword. Margaret and De Courval looked on merrily exchanging gay glances.

"Dead," cried De Forest, as he struck fair over the German's heart, "and a damn good hit!"

"Well played!" cried Schmidt—"the jest and the rapier. Another bout—no!" To his surprise he saw the Quaker gentleman's face change as he hastily put on his coat.

"Thank thee," he said to De Courval as the young man handed him his hat, and without other words than "I bid thee good day. I shall not bide this afternoon," went into the hall and out of the farther door, passing with bowed head and without a word a gentleman who entered.

Schmidt showed little of the astonishment easily read on De Courval's face, who, however, said nothing, having been taught to be chary of comments on his elders; and now taking up his foil again, fell on guard.

"A man haunted by his past," said Schmidt, as was in fact explained at breakfast next day, when Mrs. Swanwick, being questioned, said: "Yes. He was a colonel in the war, and of reckless courage. Later he returned to Friends, and now and then has lapses in his language and his ways, and is filled with remorse."

"The call of the sword was too much for him," said Schmidt. "I can comprehend that. But he had a minute of the joy of battle."

"And then," said the Pearl, "he had a war with himself."

"The maid is beginning to think," said Schmidt to himself. But this was all on the next day.

As the tall man came out on the porch, Margaret said: "My mother is occupied. Friend Schmidt, thou knowest Friend Jefferson; and this is our new lodger," and she said boldly, "the Vicomte de Courval."

"Ah," exclaimed Jefferson, "we have met before. And madame is well, I trust?"

"Yes; but at this hour she rests. We owe you, sir, our thanks for the good chance of finding what has been to us most truly a home."

Margaret looked up pleased, she did not fully know why. And so he did really like them and their quiet home?

Presently Schmidt said to Jefferson: "There is sad news from France, Mr. Secretary."

"Good news, Citizen; altogether good. What if men die that a people may live? Men die in war. What is the difference? Titles will go, a king be

swept on to the dust-heap of history." A hot answer was on the lips of the young noble. He turned,
vexed at the loss of his chance as Alexander Hamilton and Mrs. Swanwick joined them. Jefferson
ceased to speak to Schmidt, and the two statesmen met with the formal courtesy of bitter hatred.
Jefferson could see no good in the brilliant finance
of the man who now talked with courteous ease to
one or another. The new-comer was slight of figure,
bright-eyed, with the deep line so rarely seen where
the nose meets the forehead, and above all graceful,
as few men are. The face was less mobile than that
of Jefferson, who resembled to a strange degree the
great actor of his name, a resemblance only to be explained by some common English ancestry in an un-
traceable past. He had been to a bad school in
France as minister, and perhaps had by this time
forgotten the day when he desired his agent in London to find for him a coat of arms.

Presently, after a talk with Mrs. Swanwick, Jefferson, ill-pleased to meet Hamilton, was of a mind to
go. Quite aware that he meant to leave a little
sting, he said: "I must be gone. Good-by"; and to
Hamilton: "You have heard, no doubt, the good
news from France—Citizen?"

"I have heard of needless murder and of a weak,
ill-served, kindly king insulted by a mob of ruffians."

Jefferson's thin face grew yet more somber; but
what reply the secretary might have made was put
aside by the cheerful coming of a man in plain, but
not Quaker clothes, a republican Jacobin of the mad-
dest, as was seen by his interchange of "Citizen"

with Jefferson, and the warm welcome he received. Thus reinforced, Jefferson lingered where Mrs. Swanwick and Margaret were busy with the hot chocolate, which Hamilton, from youthful habit, liked. At a word from their hostess, De Courval took a basket, and presently brought from the garden slope peaches such as any back yard among us grew in my childhood—yellow clingstones and open hearts. The widow ministered to the other statesman, who liked peaches and was not to be neglected even for her favorite Hamilton, now busily discussing with Schmidt the news sent by Gouverneur Morris.

The new-comer had paid no least attention to his hostess, but sat down at the table and fingered the jumbles, apees, and cake known as "lovers'-knots" of Nanny's make, until he discovered one to his fancy. Mrs. Swanwick gave no obvious sign of annoyance, but smilingly stirred the chocolate, while Margaret quietly removed the dish of cakes and gave the guest a slice of sweetened bread known as "Dutch loaf."

"There are fewer currants in the cake than there were last week," remarked the astronomer, for, as Schmidt said in an aside to De Courval and Hamilton, as they watched the great eat like lesser folk: "This is the famous astronomer, David Rittenhouse. He divides his thoughts between the heavens and his diet; and what else there is of him is Jacobin."

"I wish," said Hamilton, "that heaven equally engaged the rest of his party. May not I have my chocolate, Mrs. Swanwick?"

"Certainly; and might I be noticed a little?" said

Mrs. Swanwick to Rittenhouse. The absent-minded philosopher looked up and said:

"I forgot. Pardon me, Citess."

Hamilton laughed merrily. "Is that the last invention?"

"It sounds like the name of some wild little animal," said the Pearl.

"Neat, that, Margaret," said Hamilton; "and might I, too, have a peach? Mr. Jefferson has emptied the basket."

Margaret rose, and with De Courval went down the garden, a fair presentment of the sexes, seen and approved by Hamilton, while Jefferson said gaily:

"The transit of Venus, Rittenhouse," for it was that observation which had given this star-gazer fame and recognition abroad.

"My compliments, sir," said Schmidt. "I regret not to have said it."

Jefferson bowed. He was at his best, for neither manners nor wit were wanting in his social hour. The astronomer, without comment, went on eating sweet bread. They drank chocolate and chatted idly of the new luxury—ice-cream, which Monsieur de Malerive made for a living, and sold on the mall we now call Independence Square. They talked, too, of the sad influx of people from San Domingo; the widow, attentive, intellectually sympathetic, a pleasant portrait of what the silver-clad Pearl would be in days to come; she, the girl, leaning against a pillar of the porch, a gray figure silently watchful, curious, behind her for background the velvets of the rival statesmen, the long broidered

8

waistcoats, the ribbon-tied queues, and the two strongly contrasted faces. Perhaps only Schmidt recognized the grace and power of the group on the porch.

The warm August evening was near its close, and a dark storm, which hung threateningly over the Jersey shore, broke up the party. Warned by rolling thunder, the three men went away in peaceful talk.

"The hate they have buried in their bellies," said Schmidt; "but, René, they are of the peerage, say what they may. Equality! *Der gute Himmel!* All men equal—and why not all women, too! He left that out. Equal before the law, perhaps—not his slaves; before God, no—nor man. Does he think Hamilton his equal? He does not love the gentleman entirely. But these two are, as fate, inevitable withal, rulers of men. I have seen the labeled creatures of other lands—kings, ministers. These men you saw here are the growth of a virgin soil—*Ach!* 'There were giants in those days,' men will say." Mrs. Swanwick listened quietly, considering what was said, not always as quick as Margaret to understand the German. He spoke further of the never-pleased Virginian, and then the widow, who had kindness for all and respect for what she called experienced opinion, avoiding to be herself the critic and hiding behind a quotation, said, " 'There be many that say, Who will shew us any good?' "

"Fine Bible wisdom," said Schmidt.

By and by when she had gone away with·Margaret about household matters, Schmidt said to De Courval: "That is one of the beautiful flowers of the for-

mal garden of Fox and Penn. The creed suits the
temperament—a garden rose; but my Pearl—*Ach!*
a wild rose, creed and creature not matched; nor
ever will be.''

''I have had a delightful afternoon,'' said René,
unable or indisposed to follow the German's lead.
''Supper will be late. You promised me the new
book.''

''Yes; Smith's 'Wealth of Nations,' not easy reading, but worth while.''

Thereafter the busy days ran on into weeks, and
in October of this tragic 1792 came the appalling
news of the murdered Swiss, self-sacrificed for no
country and no large principle beyond the pledge of
an oath to a foreign king. More horrible was the massacre of the priests in the garden of the Carmelites.

To René's relief, these unlooked-for riots of murder seemed to affect his mother less than he had
feared might be the case. ''My husband's death
was, my son, a prophecy of what was to come.'' To
her it was all personal. For him it was far more,
and the German alone understood the double anguish
of a man in whom contended a puzzled horror at
deaths without apparent reason, of murders of women like the Princesse de Lamballe,—an orgy of obscene insult,—and a wild anger at the march of the
Duke of Brunswick upon Paris. It was his country,
after all, and he left his mother feeling disappointed
that she did not share his hostile feeling in regard to
the *émigrés* in the German army.

The wonderful autumn colors of October and November came and passed, a new wonder to the young

man; his mother, to all seeming contented, spending her evenings with him over English lessons, or French books out of Logan's excellent library, or busy with never-finished embroidery. On Sundays they went to Gloria Dei, the modest little church of the Swedes. There to-day, amid the roar of trade and shipyards, in the churchyard the birds sing over the grave of their historian, Wilson, and worn epitaphs relate the love and griefs of a people whose blood is claimed with pride by the historic families of Pennsylvania.

During these months, Aunt Gainor was long absent in Boston on a visit, a little to the relief of the vicomtesse. Schmidt, too, was away in New York, to the regret of René, who had come more and more to feel wholesomely his influence and increasing attachment. The money help had set him at ease, and he could now laugh when, on counting the coin in the drawer, he found it undiminished. He had remonstrated in vain. The German smiled. "A year more, and I shall be out of debt." Had René not heard of the widow's cruse? "I must be honest. 'T is my time. The grateful bee in my bonnet does but improve the shining hour of opportunity. What was there to do but laugh?" And René at last laughed.

December came with snow and gray skies, and the great business De Courval had grown to feel his own felt the gathering storm caused by the decree of freedom to white and black in the French islands. The great shipmasters, Clark, Willing, Girard, the free-thinking merchant, and Wynne, were all looking as bleak as the weather, and prudently ceased to make their usual sea-ventures before the ice formed, while at the coffee-houses the war between England and France, more and more near, threatened new perils to the commerce of the sea.

On January 27, 1793, being Saturday, while De Courval, Wolcott, and Gilbert Stuart, the artist, sat chatting with Hamilton in the dining-room and drinking the widow's chocolate, the painter was begging leave to make a picture of Margaret, and asking them to come and see the portrait of Mrs. Jackson, one of the three charming sisters of Mr. Bingham.

"No, there must be no portrait. It is against the way of Friends," said the mother. "I should hear of it from Friend Waln and others, too."

What more there was, René did not learn. The painter was urgent. Stuart did paint her long afterward, in glorious splendor of brocade, beautiful with powder and nature's rouge. But now came Nanny, the black maid, and waited while Margaret shyly won a little talk with Hamilton, who loved the girl. "I have been thinking," she said, "of Friend Jefferson. Why, sir, do they have any titles at all, even Citizen? I think a number would be still more simple." She was furnishing an elder with another of the unlooked-for bits of humor which attest the florescence of a mind gathering sense of the comic as the years run on and the fairy godmother, Nature, has her way.

"Good heaven, child! if Mr. Jefferson had his will with your numeration, I should be zero, and he the angel of arithmetic alone knows what."

"What is it, Nanny?" said the mother.

"Massa Wynne want to see Massa Courval—right away in the front room."

De Courval, wondering what had happened, and why he was wanted in haste, found Wynne in Schmidt's sitting-room. "Close the door," said the master, "and sit down. I have much to say to you, and little time. There is great disturbance in San Domingo. I have debts due me there, and, by ill chance, a cargo probably to be there soon—the *George Washington*, as you may remember. You made out the bill of lading in French."

"I recall it, sir."

"The debts may go for hopeless. The cargo is lost if landed. Port au Prince and Cap Français are in terror, the planters flying to the towns, the plantations in ruins. The decree of freedom for the black has roused the devil among the slaves, and the low-class whites are ruling the towns." He paused to think, and then added: "I send out to-morrow with the flood my fastest ship, the schooner *Marie*, without cargo, mind you. Will you go, nominally as supercargo? You are more thoughtful than your years would imply. You are twenty-seven, I think you said. What you are worth in danger—and there will be much—I do not know. There may be questions involving grave decisions, involving courageous action, not merely what every gentleman has—mere personal fearlessness. I am plain, I trust."

De Courval was silent.

"If you get there first, I save a large loss. Once ashore, the cargo will be seized, and not a cent paid for it. It is to take or leave, Mr. de Courval; I shall not blame you if you say no. But if you do say no, I must go. The loss may be serious.''

Here was a chance to repay much kindness, and the threat of danger stirred the young man's blood. "How long should I be absent?"

"I do not know. The ship may have gone to Martinique, also. There were goods for both islands.''

"There is but one question, sir—my mother. She has no one else. And may I talk to Mr. Schmidt?"

"To no one better, if he were here. He is not, and I cannot wait. I shall call for your answer at nine to-night. The tide serves at 6 A.M. I ought to say that your perfect English and as perfect French enable you to pass for being of one nation or the other. Best to be an American. And De Courval? No; that is too plainly French.''

"I am Louis René. Why not Mr. Lewis, sir, at need?''

"Good! Excellent! I shall write my instructions with care. They will be full; but much must be left to you and the master.''

"Captain Biddle, I suppose.''

"Yes. A resolute old sea-dog, but who will obey because I order it. Good night. At nine—I must know at nine.''

De Courval lost no time. His mother was alone, as usual avoiding the Saturday visitors.

"Oh,'' he said to himself as he stood outside of her door, "you must let me go.''

He paused before he knocked. Gratitude, interest, awakened eagerness for perilous adventure, called him to this voyage. He had then, as on later occasions one source of indecision—the mother. If she said no, he must stay; but would she? He knocked gently, and in a moment was standing at her side.

She set aside her embroidery-frame. "What is wrong?" she said. "I do not want to hear any more evil news—or at least, no details. Who else is dead of those we cared for?"

"No one, mother. Mr. Wynne wishes me to sail for him at dawn to-morrow for San Domingo. I may be in time to save him much money."

"Well," she said coldly, "what else?" Her face, always grave, became stern. "And so, to save a trader's money, I am to be left alone."

"Mother, it seems hard for you to understand these people; and there is another side to it. I have been treated with kindness for which there seems to me small reason. Twice my wages have been raised, and this offer is a compliment, as well as a chance to oblige a man I like."

"Wages!" she cried. "Do not imagine me deceived by these good-natured bourgeois, nor by your desire to spare me. Secretary, indeed! Do they fancy me a fool? You are a clerk."

"I am," he said; "but that is not now of importance. He has said that he must go or I must go."

"Then let him go. You must not disobey me, René."

"Mother," he said, "these people have, God knows why, found us a home, and covered us with obligations never possible to be repaid. Here at last comes a chance—and you know our old French saying."

"Yes, yes, I know. But any clerk could go. It is —oh, my son!—that I should miss you day and night."

"Any clerk could not go, *maman*. It asks this thing—a man not afraid. No timid clerk can go. Do not you see, *maman?*"

"He will think you afraid if you stay?"

"Oh, mother, do understand this man better! He is a gentleman—of—of as good a race as ours, a soldier of distinction in the war. He will not think me afraid; but others may."

"Is there danger, my son?"

"Yes. To be honest, very great danger. The blacks are free. The lower whites rule the seaports. It is to be more terrible than the riot of murder at home."

He had remained standing while he talked. For half a minute the dark figure and unchanging face bent over the embroidery-frame without a word of reply. Then rising, she set a hand on each of his shoulders and said, "You must go, René." Centuries of the training and creed of a race of warlike men could not have failed to defeat love-born anxiety, and the dread of loss, in a woman through whom had passed into the making of a man certain ancestral qualities. "You must go," she repeated.

"Thank you, mother. I was afraid—"

"Of what?" she cried. "That I should be afraid for a man of my blood to risk life where duty calls him?"

"No, mother; I was afraid that you might not see it all as I do."

"If, René, this were but a peaceful errand of months away, I should have said no. The debts, all —all might have stood. I should have been ashamed, but obstinate, my son. We will not discuss it. You must go. And is it for long?" The clear, sweet voice broke a little. "Is it for very long?"

"I do not know."

"Ah, well. I do not want to see you in the morning. When you are ready to-night, you will say good-by."

"Yes, mother. And now I must pack my bag." And he left her.

That was strange, he thought. What would have made some women say no decided her to say go. He smiled proudly. "It was like her," he murmured.

When at eight that night he came to say good-by, she kissed him and said only, "Write to me when you can." At nine Hugh Wynne had the answer he confidently expected.

At dusk of day, the old black Cicero tramped after De Courval through the snow, as full of thought he went on, his camlet cloak about him, and under it the sword he had left in the Quaker's attic. He had told Mrs. Swanwick and left a letter for Schmidt, taking, after some hesitation, fifty dollars out of the drawer.

At daybreak, on the slip, Mr. Wynne waited with the captain. "Here," said the merchant, "are your instructions. Use your good sense. You have it. Have no fear of assuming responsibility. Captain Biddle, in case of doubt, trust Mr. Lewis to decide any question involving money."

"Oh, that is his name—Lewis."

"Yes; Mr. Lewis will show you my instructions."
Then taking De Courval aside, "You said no word
of pay."

"No, sir."

"Very good. Some men would have bargained. I
shall see that your salary while absent, eighty dollars
a month, is put in Mary Swanwick's hands for your
mother."

"Thank you. That leaves me at ease."

"Ah, here is some of my own Maryland tobacco
and a pipe the Germans call meerschaum; and one
word more: you have infinitely obliged me and my
wife. God bless you! Good-by! *Bon voyage!* Your
boat is ready, and Captain Biddle is impatient to be
gone."

In a few minutes the *Marie*, wing-and-wing, was
flying down the Delaware with the first of the ebb,
the skim of ice crackling at her bow and a fair wind
after her. They were like enough to carry the ebb-
tide with them to the capes or even to outsail it.

De Courval stood on the quarter-deck, in the clear,
sharp wintry air, while the sun rose over Jersey and
deepened the prevalent reds which had so struck his
mother when in May, nine months before, they first
saw the city. Now he recalled his sad memories of
France, their unhappy poverty in England until
their old notary in Paris contrived to send them the
few thousand livres with which they had come to
Pennsylvania with the hopes which so often deceived
the emigrant, and then God had found for them
friends. He saw as he thought of them, the German,
who held to him some relation of affectionate near-

ness which was more than friendship and seemed like such as comes, though rarely, when the ties of blood are drawn closer by respect, service, and love. He had ceased to think of the mystery which puzzled many and of which Hamilton and Mr. Justice Wilson were believed to know more than any others. Being of the religion, he had said to Schmidt in a quiet, natural way that their coming together was providential, and the German had said: "Why not? It was provided." Then he saw Gainor Wynne, so sturdy and full of insistent kindness; the strong, decisive nephew; the Quaker homes; all these amazing people; and, somehow with a distinctness no other figure had, the Pearl in the sunlight of an August evening.

The name Margaret fits well—ah—yes. To sing to her the old French verse—there in the garden above the river—well, that would be pleasant—and to hear how it would sound he must try it, being in a happy mood.

The captain turned to listen, for first he whistled the air and then sang:

LE BLASON DE LA MARGUERITE

> En Avril où naquit amour,
> J'entrai dans son jardin un jour,
> Où la beauté d'une fleurette
> Me plut sur celles que j'y vis.
> Ce ne fut pas la pâquerette,
> L'oeillet, la rose, ni le lys:
> Ce fut la belle Marguerite,
> Qu'au cœur j'aurai toujours écrite.

He laughed. That would hardly do—"*au coeur écrite*"; but then, it is only a song.

"Well sung," said the captain, not ignorant of French. "Do you sing that to the lady who is written in your heart?"

"Always," laughed De Courval—"always."

IX

IT is well for us to follow the fortunes of some of those who were in De Courval's mind as the *Marie* lost sight of the steeple of Christ Church.

Mrs. Swanwick, born in the creed and customs of the Church of England, was by many ties of kindred allied to the Masters, Willings, Morrises, and to that good Whig rector, the Rev. Richard Peters. She had conformed with some doubts to the creed of John Swanwick, her dead husband, but was of no mind to separate her daughter altogether from the gay cousins whose ways her simpler tastes in no wise always approved.

It was also black Nanny's opinion that the girl should see the gayer world, and she expressed herself on this matter to her mistress with the freedom of an old servant. She could neither read nor even tell the time, and never left the house or garden, except for church or the funeral of some relative. Just now, a week after the vicomte had gone, she was busy in the kitchen when Mrs. Swanwick came in.

"Were there many at thy cousin's burial?" asked the mistress.

"Yes, there was; but this goin' out don't agree with me. I ain't young enough to enjoy it." Then she said abruptly: "Miss Margaret she 's pinin' like. She ain't no Quaker—no more than me."

Mrs. Swanwick smiled, and Nanny went on peeling potatoes.

"I don't go with Friends—I 'm church people, and I likes the real quality."

"Yes, I know, Nanny." She had heard all this many times.

"I heard the Governor askin' you—"

"Yes, yes. I think she may go, Nanny."

"She 'll go, and some time she 'll stay," said Nanny.

"Indeed? Well—I shall see," said the mistress.

"Potatoes ain't what they used to be, and neither is folks."

Now and then, with more doubt as Margaret grew and matured, her mother permitted her to stay for a day at Belmont, or at Cliveden with the Chews, but more readily with Darthea Wynne. Just now an occasional visitor, Mr. John Penn, the Proprietary, had come with his wife to ask the girl to dine at Landsdowne. It would be a quiet party. She could come with Mr. Schmidt, who, like Nanny, seeing the girl of late somewhat less gay than usual and indisposed to the young Quaker kinsfolk, with whom she had little in common, urged the mother to consent. She yielded reluctantly. "Ann," said the gentleman in the ruby-colored coat, "would take care of her." This Ann, the daughter of the Chief Justice Allen, was a friend of Mary Swanwick's youth. There was advice given, and some warnings, which the pleased girl, it is to be feared, thought little of as, wrapped in furs, Schmidt drove her in his sleigh over the float bridge at the middle ferry, and at last along the Monument Road from the Lancaster Pike to the front of the Italian villa John Penn built where now in the park stands the Horticultural Hall.

The sky was clear, the sun brilliant. There were far-away glimpses of the river, and on the terrace to meet them, at three o'clock, a group of gay young cousins, who came out with Mrs. Byrd of Westover, the hostess, Ann Penn, very splendid in gown and powder, with Mr. Peters, their neighbor, of late made a judge, and the Governor in purple velvet short-clothes and gold buckles. He put out in welcome a lace-ruffled hand, of which he was said to be proud. A hood, and over it a calash for shelter from cold, had replaced the girl's Quaker bonnet, and now it was cast back, and the frost-red cheeks were kissed, and the profuse compliments of the day paid to the really charming face of Margaret, whom nature had set off with color and whom stern decrees of usage had clad for contrast in relieving gray silks.

There was whispering among those madcap cousins as they hurried her away to Ann Greenleaf's room, a niece of Mrs. Penn, "to set thy hair in order for dinner, thou darling Quaker." She was used to their ways, and went merry with the rest up the great stairway whence William Penn, in the serene beauty of his youth, looked down at the noisy party, now bent upon a prank altogether in the fashion of their day.

As Margaret entered the room, she saw Miss Ann Greenleaf being tossed up in stays by a black maid.

"Why, dear, is the room so dark?" asked Margaret; for the curtains were drawn, and there were candles on the mantel and in sconces.

"The better to see how we shall look—in the evening," replied Miss Willing.

Gowns, silken hose, high, red-heeled shoes, and powder-puffs lay about on bed and chairs.

"We have a little secret," cried Miss Willing, "and we will never tell, dear."

"Never!" cried they.

"We want to dress thee just for to see how thou wouldst look in the gown of decent Christians."

"I could never think of it."

"Come, girls," cried Miss Willing, "let us dress her just once."

"Oh, but just for a half-hour," they said, and gathered around her, laughing, urgent.

Nice Christians these! She would not. Mother would not like it, and—ah, me, she was not unwilling to see herself once in the long cheval-glass. She had had naughty dreams of brocade and powder. Despite her resistance, they had off the prim Quaker dress, and blushing, half-angry, half-pleased, she was in slim attire, saying: "Thou really must not. My stockings, oh, not my stockings! Oh, Molly Greenleaf, how can I? It is dreadful—please not." But the silk stockings were on, and the garters, with compliments my modest pen declines to preserve. There was enough of the maiden neck in view above the undervest, and very splendid length of brocade gown, with lace of the best, and a petticoat, pearl-tinted, "Because, dear, we are all Quakers," they cried. "And do keep still, or the powder will be all

9

over thee. What color, girls! Can it be real? I must kiss thee to see if it be rouge.''

"For shame!" cried Margaret, between tears and laughter.

"Now a fan—and patches, Molly Greenleaf! No. The old women wear them; but gloves, crumpled down at the elbow. So!" She had given up at last.

It was only for a frolic half-hour. "Go now and see thyself.'' Two of the merriest seized lighted candles, for the room was made dark by the drawn curtains, and stood on each side of the long cheval-glass, a pretty picture, with Margaret before the mirror, shy and blushing. "Great heavens! you are a wonder! Isn't she, oh, isn't she, the sweetest thing!"

The Quaker maiden looked down at the rich brocade and then looked up, and knew that she was beautiful. She stood still, amazed at the revelation, and the gods who give us uncalled-for thoughts set in her mind for a moment the figure of the young vicomte. She colored, and cried, laughing, as she turned away from the glass: "You have had your way with me, and now—undress me, girls, please. I should scarce know how.''

"Oh, the sweet, innocent thing!" cried they. "But wait a little. Now thy hair—so—and so, and a bit more powder. La, but you are dangerous! Where are thy Quaker gown and stockings? Where can they be! Molly Greenleaf, what have you done with them? And, oh, Cinderella, the slippers fit to a charm." No one knew where had gone the gown, the shoes, the shawl, the rest of the simple garb.

"The fairy godmother has done it," cried Miss Cadwalader. "What shall we do?" cried Betty Morris. The gong, a new fashion, rang for dinner. The girl was angry.

"This passes the limit of a jest," she cried. "Go down? I? No. I will die first." They implored, laughing; but she refused, saying, "I sit here till I have my gown," and would speak no more.

At this minute came Mrs. Penn. "What is all this noise, young women? Good Lord! Margaret Swanwick! So this is what these minxes have been at all the morning?"

"I have been tricked," said Margaret, "and—and I will never forgive them—never."

"But come down to dinner, my dear. You will have your revenge when the men see you. There, the Governor dislikes to wait. He has sent up to say dinner is ready."

"I want my gown," said the Pearl, "and I will not go down." Only anger kept her from tears.

"But the Governor must see you. Come, no one will know, and, bless me! but you are a beauty!"

"Is n't she?" they cried in chorus. A glance at the mirror and a triumphant sense of victorious capacities to charm swept over the hesitating girl. Life of late had been as gray as her garb.

"Come, dear. You really must. You are making too much, quite too much, of a bit of innocent fun. If you wait to dress, I shall have to explain it all, and the Governor will say you lack courage; and must I say I left you in tears? And the mutton, my dear child—think of the mutton!"

"I am not in tears, and I hate you all, every one of you; but I will go."

Her head was up, as fan in hand she went down in front of the cousins, now mildly penitent, Mrs. Penn at her side. "Did they think to show off an awkward Quaker cousin, these thoughtless kittens? Give them a lesson, my dear."

"I mean to," said Margaret, her eyes flashing.

The men were about the fire in the great drawing-room, one little girl just slipping out, the future wife of Henry Baring. The party was large—young Mr. Rawle and General Wayne and the Peters from Belmont near by.

The men turned to bow as Mrs. Penn stepped aside, and left to view a startling vision of innocence and youth and loveliness. The girl swept a curtsey, the practice when dreams of the world were teasing her had not been in vain. Then she rose and moved into the room. For a moment there was silence. Except Schmidt, no one knew her. The Governor, bowing, cried, "By George! Margaret, you beat them all! What fairies have metamorphosed you?"

"We, we," cried the chorus. The men paid her compliments after the downright fashion of their set. She was gay, quick to reply, amazingly at ease. Schmidt watched her, comprehending as no one else did the sudden revelation to the young woman of the power and charm of her beauty and the primal joy of unused weapons. To the younger men she was a little reserved and quiet, to the elder men all grace and sweetness, to the trickster cousins, disconcertingly cool.

"Where on earth did she learn it all?" said Mrs. Byrd, as she went out to dinner with Mr. Penn.

"Heaven knows. But it was a saucy trick and she will pay for it, I fear, at home."

"Will she tell?" said Morris, the master of the rolls, as he followed behind them with Mrs. Wayne.

"Yes," said Mrs. Byrd, "she will tell; but whether or not, the town will ring with it, in a day or two. A pity, too, for the child is brought up in the straightest way of Friends. None of Madame Logan's fine gowns and half-way naughtiness for her."

At dinner Margaret quietly amused Mr. Morris with Schmidt's terror of June, the cat, and with Mr. Jefferson's bout with Hamilton, and the tale of the sad lapse of De Forest, which greatly pleased General Wayne, her right-hand neighbor. When they left the men to their Madeira, she insisted on changing her dress. A not duly penitent bevy of maids assisted, and by and by it was a demure Quaker moth who replaced the gay butterfly and in the drawing-room helped Madame Penn to make tea. They paid her fair compliments, and she smiled, saying: "I, dear Mrs. Penn—was I here? Thou must be mistaken. That was Grandmama Plumstead thou didst have here. Oh, a hundred years ago."

"Ask her to come again," said Mrs. Penn.

"And to stay," said Mrs. Wayne; "a charming creature."

"The maid is clever," said Mrs. Masters.

Meanwhile the wine went round on the coasters over the mahogany table in the dining-room, and men talked of France, and grew hot with wine and more politics than pleased their host, who had no definite opinions, or, if any, a sincere doubt as to the quality of a too aged Madeira.

He gave a toast: "The ladies and our Quaker Venus." They drank it standing.

"This wine needs fining," said his reverence, the rector of Christ Church. They discussed it seriously.

Mr. Rawle cried, "A toast: George Washington and the Federal party."

"No politics, gentlemen," said Penn; "but I will drink the first half of it—His Excellency."

MR. LANGSTROTH on this day rode to town, and there learned that Margaret was at Landsdowne, and also a surprising piece of news with which he did not regale Mary Swanwick.

Full of what he had heard, Mr. Langstroth, being now on horseback and on his way to Gray Pines, his home, was suddenly minded to see his great-niece. Therefore he rode up the avenue at Landsdowne, and hitching his horse, learned that the men were still over their wine. "I will go in," he said, well pleased.

"Ah," said Penn, rising, "you are just in time for the punch." He hated the man and all his positive ways, but, the more for that, was courteous, if rather formal. "A glass for Mr. Langstroth. Your health, sir; your very good health."

"It is not good," said the new-comer.

"But the wine I trust is," said the Governor.

"It might supply goodness," Langstroth replied, "if it were not a bit pricked." It was a tender subject, and his host, feeling grossly wronged, was silent.

"Any fresh news?" said the attorney-general.

"Yes, sir; yes. The Princeton College lottery was drawn this morning, and guess who drew a prize?"

"Not I"—"Nor I," they cried. "Who was it? Not you?"

"I! No such luck."

"Who, then?"

"Well, I bought ten chances in the fall, and one for my great-niece, Margaret Swanwick. Her mother did not like it. Friends are all for putting an end to lotteries."

"And she won?"

"She did. I chose for luck the number of her age and the last two figures of the year—1792. That took it."

"How much? How much?" they shouted, the wine and rum punch having done their work. "How much?"

"Eight thousand, nine hundred, and thirty-four dollars, as I 'm a sinner."

"The girl may have gay gowns now," cried one.

"Let us go out, and tell her," said the Governor, as men still called him; and upon this, having had wine and rum more than was well, they went laughing into the drawing-room.

"Oh, news! news!" cried one and another.

Mrs. Penn looked annoyed. "What is it?" she asked.

"Ho, ho! Fine news!" said Langstroth. "Mar-

garet has the great prize in the Princeton lottery—
eight thousand and more. It was drawn this morning."

"What luck!" cried the ladies. "And you are not
jesting?"

"No. It is true. I bought it for her," roared Langstroth, triumphant. "Think of that, Margaret—eight
thousand and—"

"For me—mine!" said the girl, rising as she
spoke. "Don't speak to me, Cousin Penn. I have
had too much to-day. I am troubled. I must go."
No, she did not want to discuss it. She must go
home. "May I not go, Friend Schmidt? If this is a
joke, uncle, it is not to my taste. I must go."

"Certainly. The sleigh is at the door."

Langstroth was angry. He had had no thanks,
not a word. There was some embarrassment, but
the women must need felicitate the unwilling winner.
She made short answers.

"The puss has her claws out," murmured Mrs.
Byrd, as she heard in reply to her congratulations:
"I think it is a misfortune—a—a—what will my
mother say? I must go." She was a child again.
Mrs. Penn, understanding the girl, went out with
her, saying kind things, and helping her to put on
her over-wrap.

"Damn the fool!" said her uncle, who had followed her into the hall, and to whom she would not
speak.

The gentlemen were silent, not knowing how to
sympathize with a misfortune so peculiar. Schmidt,
tranquil and undisturbed, made the usual formal

adieus and followed her out of the room. He tucked
in the furs with kindly care, and through the early
evening dusk they drove away across the snow, the
girl silent, the man respectful of her mood.

X

IT was after dark when Schmidt left Margaret at her home. As he was about to drive away to the stable, he said, "Those are wild girls, but, my dear child, you were so very pretty, I for one almost forgave them."

"Oh, was I?" she cried, shyly pleased and a little comforted. "But the lottery prize; I shall hear about that, and so will my mother, too. I never gave it a thought when uncle spoke of it long ago."

"It is a small matter, Pearl. We will talk about it later. Now go in and quit thinking of it. It is shrewd weather, and nipping."

Margaret knew very well that she had good cause to be uneasy. Friends had been of late much exercised over the evil of lotteries, and half of Langstroth's satisfaction in this form of gambling was due to his love of opposition and his desire to annoy the society of which he still called himself a member. Although, to his anger, he had long ago been disowned, he still went to meeting once or twice a year. He had had no such sacrificial conscience in the war as made Clement Biddle and Wetherill "apostates," as Friends called them. He was by birthright a member of the society, and stood for King George, and would pay no war tax. But when the vendue-master took his old plate and chairs, he went privately and bought them back; and so, having thus paid for the joy of apparent opposition, drank to the king in private, and made himself merry over the men who sturdily accepting loss for conscience's sake, sat at meals on their kitchen chairs, silently unresistant, but, if human, a little sorrowful concerning the silver which came over with Penn and was their only material reminder of the Welsh homes their fathers had left that they might worship God in their own simple way.

The one person Langstroth loved was his great-niece, of whose attachment to the German he was jealous with that keen jealousy known to those who are capable of but one single love. He had meant to annoy her mother; and, with no least idea that he would win a prize for her child, was now vexed at Margaret's want of gratitude, and well pleased with the fuss there would be when the news got out and Friends came to hear of it.

When Pearl threw herself into the mother's arms and broke into tears, sobbing out the double story, for a moment Mrs. Swanwick was silent.

"My dear," she said at last, "why didst thou let them dress thee?"

"I—I could not help it, and—and—I liked it, mother. Thou didst like it once," she added, with a look of piteous appeal. "Don't scold me, mother. Thou must have liked it once."

"I, dear? Yes, I liked it. But—scold thee? Do I ever scold thee? 'T is but a small matter. It will be the talk of a week, and Gainor Wynne will laugh, and soon it will be forgotten. The lottery is more serious.''

"But I did not do it.''

"No.''

"They will blame thee, mother, I know—when it was all my uncle's doing. Let them talk to him.''

The widow smiled. "Nothing would please him better; but—they have long since given up Josiah for a lost sheep—''

"Black, mother?'' She was a trifle relieved at the thought of an interview between Friend Howell, the gentlest of the gentle, and Josiah.

"Brown, not black,'' said the mother, smiling. "It will someway get settled, my child. Now go early to bed and leave it to thy elders. I shall talk of it to Friend Schmidt.''

"Yes, mother.'' Her confidence in the German gentleman, now for five years their guest, was boundless.

"And say thy prayers with a quiet heart. Thou hast done no wrong. Good night, my child. Ask if Friend de Courval wants anything. Since her son went away, she has been troubled, as who would not be. Another's real cause for distress should make us feel how small a matter is this of ours.'' She kissed her again, and the girl went slowly up-stairs, murmuring: "He went away and never so much as said good-by to me. I do not think it was civil.''

Meanwhile the mother sat still, with only the click, click of the knitting-needles, which somehow seemed always to assist her to think. She had steadily refused help in money from Uncle Josiah, and now, being as angry as was within the possibilities of a temper radiant with the sunshine of good humor, she rejoiced that she owed Josiah nothing.

"He shall have a piece of my mind," she said aloud, and indeed a large slice would have been a sweetening addition to his crabbed sourness. "Ah, me!" she added, "I must not think of the money; but how easy it would make things!" Not even Schmidt had been permitted to pay more than a reasonable board. No, she would not repine; and now madame, reluctantly accepting her son's increased wages, had insisted that his room be kept vacant and paid for, and was not to be gainsaid about the needed fur-lined roquelaure she bought for her hostess and the extra pay for small luxuries.

"May God forgive me that I have been unthankful for His goodness," said Mary Swanwick, and so saying she rose and putting aside her thoughts with her knitting, sat down to read a little in the book she had taken from the library, to Friend Poulson's dismay. "Thou wilt not like it, Mary Swanwick." In a minute of mischief young Mr. Willing had told her of a book he had lately read—a French book, amusing and witty. He had left her wishing he could see her when she read it, but self-advised to stay away for a time.

She sat down with anticipative satisfaction. "What hard French!" she thought. "I must ask help of madame," as she often called her, Friend Courval being, as she saw plainly, too familiar to her guest. As she read, smiling at the immortal wit and humor of a day long passed, suddenly she shut the

book with a quick movement, and set it aside.
"What manner of man was this Rabelais? Friend
Poulson should have been more plain with me; and
as for Master Willing, I shall write to him, too, a
bit of my mind." But she never did, and only said
aloud: "If I give away any more pieces of my mind,
I shall have none left," and turned, as her diary records, to the "Pilgrim's Progress," of which she
remarked, "an old book by one John Bunyan, much
read by Friends and generally approved, ridiculed
by many, but not by me. It seems to me good, pious
wit, and not obscene like the other. I fear I sin
sometimes in being too curious about books." Thus
having put on paper her reflections, she went to
bed, having in mind a vague and naughty desire to
have seen Margaret in the foolish garb of worldly
folk.

Margaret, ashamed, would go nowhere for a week,
and did more than the needed housework, to Nanny's
disgust, whose remembrances were of days of luxury
and small need for "quality folks" to dust rooms.
The work over, when tired of her labor, Margaret sat
out in the winter sunshine in the fur-lined roquelaure, madame's extravagant gift, and, enraptured,
read "The Mysteries of Udolpho," or closing the
book, sailed with the *Marie,* and wondered what San
Domingo was like.

Meanwhile the town, very gay just now with dinners Mr. John Adams thought so excessive, and with
sleigh-riding parties to Belmont and Cliveden, rang
with wild statements of the dressing scene and the
lottery. Very comic it was to the young bucks, and,

"Pray, Mrs. Byrd, did the garters fit?" "Fie, for shame!" "And no stays, we hear," wives told their husbands, and once in the London Coffee-house, in front of which, long ago, Congo slaves were sold and where now men discussed things social, commercial, and political, Schmidt had called a man to stern account and exacted an apology. The gay girls told their Quaker cousins, and at last Friends were of a mind to talk to Mary Swanwick, especially of the lottery.

Before graver measures were taken, it was advisable that one should undertake to learn the truth, for it was felt not to be desirable to discipline by formal measures so blameless a member where clearly there had been much exaggeration of statement.

Ten days after the dinner at Landsdowne, John Pemberton was met in the hall of the Swanwick house by Mr. Schmidt, both women being out. The German at once guessed the errand of this most kindly of Quaker gentles, and said, "Mr. Pemberton, you are come, I suppose, to speak for Friends of the gossip about these, my own friends. Pray be seated. They are out."

"But my errand is not to thee, who art not of the Society of Friends."

"I am of the society of these friends. I know why you are come. Talk to me."

"I am advised in spirit that it may be as well to do so. Thou art a just man. I shall speak."

On this he sat down. It was a singular figure the German saw. The broad, white beaver hat, which the Quaker gentleman kept on his head, was turned up in front and at the back over abundant gray hair. A great eagle nose overhanging a sharp chin, brought near to it by the toothless jaws of age, gave to the side face a queer look of rapacity, contradicted by the refinement and serene kindliness of the full face now turned upon the German.

"Friend Schmidt," he said, "our young friend, we are told, has been unwise and exhibited herself among those of the world in unseemly attire. There are those of us who, like Friend Logan, are setting a bad example in their attire to the young. I may not better state how we feel than in the words of William Penn: 'Choose thy clothes by thine own eye, not by another's; the more simple and plain they are the better; neither unshapely nor fantastical, and for use and decency, not for pride.' I think my memory serves me."

"I shall not argue with you, sir, but being in part an eye-witness, I shall relate what did occur," and he told very simply of the rude jest, and of the girl's embarrassment as he had heard it from the mother.

"I see," said Pemberton. "Too much has been made of it. She will hear no more of it from Friends, and it may be a lesson. Wilt thou greet her with affectionate remembrance from an old man and repeat what I have said?"

"I will do so."

"But there is a matter more serious. We are told that she bought a lottery-ticket, and has won a great prize. This we hear from Josiah Langstroth."

"Did he say this—that she bought a ticket?"

"We are so advised."

"Then he lied. He bought it in her name, without asking her."

"Art thou sure? Thy language is strong."

"Yes, I am sure."

"And what will Mary Swanwick do with this money won in evil ways?"

"I do not know."

"It is well that she should be counseled."

"Do you not think, sir, as a man of sense and a gentleman and more, that it may be well to leave a high-minded woman to dispose of this matter? If she goes wrong, will it not then be time to interfere? There is not a ha'-penny of greed in her. Let her alone."

The Quaker sat still a moment, his lean figure bent over his staff. "Thou art right," he said, looking up. "The matter shall rest, unless worse come of it."

"Why not see Mr. Langstroth about it?" said the German, mischievously inclined. "He is of Friends, I presume."

"He is not," said Pemberton. "He talked in the war of going forth from us with Wetherill, but he hath not the courage of a house-fly. His doings are without conscience, and now he is set in his ways. He hath been temperately dealt with long ago and in vain. An obstinate man; when he sets his foot down thou hast to dig it up to move him. I shall not open the matter with Josiah Langstroth. I have been led to speak harshly. Farewell."

When Mrs. Swanwick heard of this and had talked of it to Margaret, the Pearl said, "We will not take the money, and uncle cannot; and it may go." Her

10

decisiveness both pleased and astonished the mother. It was a maturing woman who thus anticipated Schmidt's advice and her own, and here for a little while the matter lay at rest.

Not all Friends, however, were either aware of what Pemberton had learned or were fully satisfied, so that one day Daniel Offley, blacksmith, a noisy preacher in meetings and sometimes advised of elders to sit down, resolved to set at rest alike his conscience and his curiosity. Therefore, on a February afternoon, being the 22d, and already honored as the birthday of Washington, he found Margaret alone, as luck would have it. To this unusual house, as I have said, came not only statesmen, philosophers, and the rich. Hither, too, came the poor for help, the lesser Quakers, women and men, for counsel or a little sober gossip. All were welcome, and Offley was not unfamiliar with the ways of the house.

He found Margaret alone, and sitting down, began at once and harshly to question her in a loud voice concerning the story of her worldly vanity, and asked why she could thus have erred.

The girl had had too much of it. Her conscience was clear, and Pemberton, whom she loved and respected, had been satisfied, as Schmidt had told them. She grew red, and rising, said: "I have listened to thee; but now I say to thee, Daniel Offley, that it is none of thy business. Go home and shoe thy horses."

He was not thus to be put down. "This is only to add bad temper to thy other faults. As a Friend and for many of the Society, I would know what thee has done with thee devil wages of the lottery."

"'Thou canst not shoe my conscience'"

She looked at him a moment. The big, red, coarse face struck her as comical. Her too often repressed sense of humor helped her, and crying, "Thou canst not shoe my conscience, Daniel Offley," she fled away up-stairs, her laughter ringing through the house, a little hysterical, perhaps, and first cousin to tears. The amazed preacher, left to his meditations, was shocked into taking off his beaver and saying strong words out of a far away and naughty past.

She was angry beyond the common, for Schmidt had said it was all of it unwise and meddlesome, nor was the mother better pleased than he when she came to hear of Offley's visit. "I am but half a Friend," she confessed to Schmidt, not liking altogether even the gentler inquiries of John Pemberton.

When on the next Sunday Madame de Courval was about to set out for the Swedes' church, Mrs. Swanwick said, "It is time to go to meeting, my child."

"I am not going, mother."

"But thou didst not go last First Day."

"No. I cannot, mother. May I go with madame?"

"Why not?" said Schmidt, looking up from his book. And so the Pearl went to Gloria Dei.

"They have lost a good Quaker by their impertinence," said Schmidt to himself. "She will never again go to meeting." And, despite much gentle urging and much persuasive kindness, this came at last to be her custom, although she still wore unchanged her simple Quaker garb. Madame at least was pleased, but also at times thoughtful of the future when the young vicomte would walk between them down Swanson Street to church.

There was, of course, as yet no news of the *Marie,* and many bets on the result of the bold venture were made in the coffee-houses, for now, in March of the year '93, the story of the king's death and of war between France and England began further to embitter party strife and alarm the owners of ships. If the vicomtesse was anxious, she said no word of what she felt. Outside of the quiet home where she sat over her embroidery there was an increase of political excitement, with much abuse, and in the gazettes wild articles over classic signatures. With Jacobin France for exemplars, the half-crazed Republicans wore tricolor cockades, and the *bonnet rouge* passed from head to head at noisy feasts when "Ça Ira" and the "Marseillaise" were sung. Many persons were for war with England, but the wiser of both parties were for the declaration of neutrality, proclaimed of late amid the fury of extreme party sentiment. The new French minister eagerly looked for by the republicans was soon to come and to add to the embarrassment of the Government whatever of mischief insolent folly could devise.

Meanwhile the hearts of two women were on the sea, and the ship-owners were increasingly worried; for now goods for French ports would be seized on the ocean and sailors claimed as English at the will of any British captain.

Amid all this rancor of party and increase of anxiety as to whether America was to be at war or peace, the small incident of a girl's change of church was soon forgotten. It was not a rare occurrence, and only remarkable because, as Schmidt said to Gainor

Wynne somewhat later. it proved what a convincing preacher is anger.

Mistress Wynne had come home from Boston after a week's travel, and being tired, went to bed and decided to have a doctor, with Chovet for choice, because Rush had little gossip. She was amply fed with it, including the talk about the change of dress and the lottery. So good was the effect that, on the doctor's departure, she threw his pills out of the window, and putting on pattens, took her cane and went away through the slush to see Margaret. On the way many things passed through her mind, but most of all she remembered the spiritual struggles of her own young days, when she, too, had broken with Friends.

And now when she met Margaret in the hall, it was not the girl who wept most, as Gainor cried to Schmidt to go and not mock at two women in tears no man could understand.

"Ah," cried Schmidt, obediently disappearing, "he who shall explicate the tears of women shall be crowned by the seraphs." Thus he saw Gainor in her tender mood, such as made her to be forgiven much else of men and of angels. She comforted the girl, and over the sad story of the stays and garters she laughed—not then, but in very luxury of unfettered mirth on her homeward way.

He who got the largest satisfaction out of poor Margaret's troubles was Josiah Langstroth, as he reflected how for the first time in his life he had made Mary Swanwick angry, had stirred up Friends, and at last had left the Presbyterian ministers of the trustees of Princeton College in a hopeless quandary.

If the owner of the prize in their lottery would not take it, to whom did it belong? And so at last it was left in Miss Swanwick's name in the new bank Hamilton had founded, to await a use of which as yet no man dreamed.

XI

WHEN De Courval lost sight of the red city, and while the unusual warmth of the winter weather was favoring their escape from the ice adrift on the bay, the young man reflected that above all things it was wise to be on good terms with his captain.

Accordingly, he said: "It is fit, sir, that you should advise me as to Mr. Wynne's instructions. Have the kindness to read them. I have not done so."

Much gratified, the captain took the paper. "Hum!" he exclaimed, "to reach Port au Prince in time to prevent unloading of the *George Washington*. To get her out and send her home with her cargo." He paused. "We may be in time to overhaul and stop her; but if she has arrived, to carry her out from under the guns of the fort is quite another matter. 'To avoid the British cruisers.' Well, yes, we are only in ballast,"—he looked up with pride at the raking masts and well-trimmed sails,— "the ship does not float can catch the *Marie*. 'Free to do as seems best if we are stopped by privateers.' Ah, he knows well enough what I should do."

"He seems to have provided for that," said De Courval, glancing at the carronades and the long Tom astern such as many a peaceful ship prudently carried.

The captain grinned. "That is like Hugh Wynne. But these island fools rely on us for diet. They will be starving, and if the *George Washington* reach the island before we do, they will lose no time, and, I guess, pay in worthless bills on France, or not at all. However, we shall see." This ended the conversation.

They had the usual varied luck of the sea; but the master carried sail, to the alarm of his mates, and seeing none of the dreaded cruisers, overtook a French merchant ship and learned with certainty of the outbreak of war between France and Great Britain, a fresh embarrassment, as they well knew.

At sundown on February the 15th, the lookout on the crosstrees saw the mountains of San Domingo back of the city of Port au Prince, and running in under shelter of one of the many islands which protect the bay, the captain and the supercargo took counsel as to what they should do.

"If," said De Courval, "I could get ashore as a French sailor at night, and learn something of how things stand, we might be helped."

The captain feared risks neither for himself nor for another, and at last said: "I can run you in at dark, land you on a spit of sand below the town, and wait for you."

Thus it was that in sailor garb, a tricolor cockade in his hat, De Courval left the boat at eight at night and began with caution to approach the town. The brilliant moon of a clear tropic night gave sufficient light, and following the shore, he soon came upon the warehouses and docks, where he hoped to learn what ships were in the harbor. Soon, however, he was halted by sentries, and being refused permission to pass, turned away from the water-front. Passing among rude cabins and seeing almost no one, he came out at last on a wide, well-built avenue and into a scene of sorrowful misery. Although the new commissioners of the republic had put down the insurrection of the slaves with appalling slaughter, their broken bands were still busy with the torch and the sword, so that the cities were filled with refugees of the plantation class—men and women who were quite helpless and knew not where to turn for shelter or for the bread of the day.

De Courval had been quite unprepared for the wretchedness he now saw. Indistinct in the moon-made shadows, or better seen where the light lay, were huddled groups of women and children, with here and there near by a man made helpless by years of the ownership of man. Children were crying, while women tried in vain to comfort them. Others were silent or wildly bewailing their fate. To all seeming, indifferent to the oft-repeated appeals of misery, went by officials, army officers, smoking cigarettes, drunken sailors, and such women as a seaport educates to baseness. Half of the town had been for months in ashes. The congestion of the remainder was more and more felt as refugees from ruined plantations came hither, hungry and footsore, to seek food where was little and charity where was none.

Unable to do more than pity, the young vicomte went his way with care along a street strangely crowded with all manner of people, himself on the lookout for a café where he might find seamen. Presently he found what he sought, and easily fell into sea-talk with a group of sailors. He learned only that the town was without the usual supplies of food from the States; that the troops lived on fish, bananas, and yams, and that General Esbarbé had ruthlessly put down the negro insurrection. Only one ship had come in of late. The outbreak of war between England and France had, in fact, for a time put an end to our valuable trade with the islands. Learning nothing of value, he paid his score and stood a moment in the doorway, the drunken revel of idle sailors behind him and before him the helpless wretchedness of men and women to whom want had been hitherto unknown. He must seek elsewhere for what he wished to learn. As he hesitated, two men in white linen went by with a woman. They were laughing and talking loudly, apparently indifferent to the pitiable groups on door-steps or on the sidewalks.

"Let us go to the Cocoanut," said the woman. One of the men said "Yes." They went on, singing a light drinking song. No one seemed to care for any one else: officials, sailors, soldiers, destitute planters seemed all to be in a state of detachment, all kindly human ties of man to man broken. In fact, for a year the island had been so gorged with tragedy that it no longer caused remark.

De Courval followed the men and women, presuming that they were going to a café. If he learned nothing there, he would go back to the ship.

Pushing carelessly by a group of refugees on the

247K.

outside of the "Cocoanut," the party went in, and one, an official, as he seemed to be, sat down at a table with the woman. De Courval, following, took the nearest table, while the other companion of the woman went to the counter to give an order. The woman sat still, humming a coarse Creole love-song, and the vicomte looked about him. The room was dimly lighted, and quite half of it was occupied by the same kind of unhappy people who lay about on the streets, and may have paid for leave to sit in the café. The unrestrained, noisy grief of these well-dressed women amazed the young man, used to the courage and self-control of the women of his own class. The few tables near by were occupied by small parties of officers, in no way interested in the wretchedness about them. A servant came to De Courval. What would he have? Fried fish there was, and baked yams, but no other dish. He asked for wine, paid for it, and began to be of a sudden curious about the party almost within touch. The woman was a handsome quadroon. Pinned in her high masses of black hair were a dozen of the large fireflies of the tropics, a common ornament of a certain class of women. From moment to moment their flashing lanterns strangely illuminated her hair and face. As he watched her in wonder, the man who had gone to the counter came back and sat down, facing the crowd.

"Those *sacrés enfants*," he said, "they should be turned out; one can hardly hear a word for the bawling. I shall be glad to leave—"

"When do you go, Commissioner?" said the woman.

"In a day or two. I am to return to France as soon as possible and make our report."

De Courval was startled by the voice, and stared at the speaker. The face was no longer clean-shaven, and now wore the mustache, a recent Jacobin fashion. The high-arched eyebrows of the man of the Midi, the sharp voice, decided him. It was Carteaux. For a moment René had the slight vertigo of a man to whose intense passion is forbidden the relief of physical action. The scene at Avignon was before him, and instantly, too, the sense of need to be careful of himself, and to think solely of his errand. He swallowed his wine in haste, and sat still, losing no word of the talk, as the other man said:

"They will unload the American ship to-morrow, I suppose."

"Yes," said Carteaux; "and pay in good republican *assignats* and promises. Then I shall sail on her to Philadelphia, and go thence to France. Our work here is over."

De Courval had heard enough. If the ship went to the States, there he would find his enemy. To let him go, thus unpunished, when so near, was obviously all that he could do. He rose and went out. In a few minutes he had left the town behind him and was running along the beach, relieved by rapid action. He hailed the boat, lying in wait off the shore, and had, as he stood, the thought that with his father's murderer within reach, duty had denied him the privilege of retributive justice. It was like the dreams with which at times he was troubled—when he saw Carteaux smiling and was himself unable to move. Looking back, as the boat ran on to the beach, he saw a red glow far away, and over it the pall of smoke where hundreds of plantations were burning, with everywhere, as he had heard, ruin, massacre, and ruthless executions of the revolted slaves set free. Such of the upper class as could leave had departed, and long since Blanchelande, ex-governor, had been sent to France, to be remembered only as the first victim of the guillotine.

The captain, uneasy, hurried De Courval into the boat, for he had been gone two hours. There was a light, but increasing wind off shore to help them and before them a mile's pull. As they rowed to the ship, the captain heard De Courval's news. "We must make sure it is our ship," said the captain. "I could row in and see. I should know that old tub a hundred yards away—yes, sir, even in the night."

"The town, Captain, is in confusion—full of planters, men, women, and children lying about the streets. There is pretty surely a guard on board that ship. Why not beat in closer without lights, and then, with all the men you can spare, find the ship, and if it is ours, take her out?"

"If we can. A good idea. It might be done."

"It is the only way. It must be done. Give me the mate and ten men."

"What! Give you my men, and sit down and wait for you? No, sir. I shall go with you." He was of a breed which has served the country well on sea and land, and whose burial-places are battle-fields and oceans.

It was soon decided to wait to attack until the

town was asleep. In the interval De Courval, in case of accident, wrote to his mother and to Schmidt, but with no word of Carteaux. Then for a while he sat still, reflecting with very mingled feelings that success in carrying the ship would again cut him off from all chance of meeting Carteaux. It did seem to him a malignant fate; but at last dismissing it, he buckled on his sword, took up his pistols, and went on deck.

At midnight the three boats set out with muffled oars, and after a hard pull against an off-shore wind, through the warm tropic night, they approached the town.

The captain whistled softly, and the boats came together.

"Speak low," he said to De Courval. "It is the *George Washington* and no mistake. They are wide-awake, by ill luck, and singing."

"Yes, I hear them."

"But they are not on deck. There are lights in the cabin." The "Ça Ira" rang out in bits across the water. The young noble heard it with the anguish it always awakened; for unfailingly it gave back to memory the man he longed to meet, and the blood-dabbled mob which came out of the hall at Avignon shouting this Jacobin song.

The captain said: "We will board her on this side, all together. She is low in the water. Pull in with your boat and secure the watch forward and I will shut the after hatches and companionway. Look out for the forecastle. If her own men are on board, they will be there."

De Courval's heart alone told him of the excitement he felt; but he was cool, tranquil, and of the temperament which rises to fullest competence in an hour of danger. A minute later he was on deck, and moving forward in the silence of the night, came upon the watch. "Hush!" he said; "no noise. Two to each man. They are asleep. There—choke hard and gag. Here, cut up this rope; a good gag." In a moment three scared sailors awoke from dreams of their Breton homes, and were trussed with sailor skill.

"Now, then," he said in French, "a pistol ball for the man who moves. Stay by them, you Jones, and come, the rest of you. Rouse the crew in the forecastle, mate. Call to them. If the answer is in French, let no man up. Don't shoot, if you can help it."

He turned quickly, and, followed by four men, ran aft, hearing wild cries and oaths. A man looking out of a port-hole had seen two boats and the glint of muskets. As the captain swung over the rail, half a dozen men ran up on deck shouting an alarm. The captain struck with the butt of his pistol. A man fell. De Courval grappled with a burly sailor, and falling, rose as the mate hit the guard on the head with a marline-spike. Then an officer fired, and a sailor went down wounded. It was savage enough, but brief, for the American crew and captain released, were now running aft from the forecastle, and the French were tumbled into the companionway and the hatches battened down in haste, but no man killed.

"Get up sail!" cried the captain. "An ax to the

cable; she is moored to a buoy. Tumble into the
boats, some of you! Get a rope out ahead, and pull
her bow round. Now, then, put out the lights, and
hurry, too!'' As he gave his orders, and men were
away up the rigging, shot after shot from the cabin
windows drew, as was meant, the attention of the
town. Lights were seen moving on the pier, the
sound of oars was heard. There was the red flare of
signals on shore; cries and oaths came from below
and from the shore not far away.

It was too late. The heavy ship, as the cable
parted, swung round. The wind being off the land,
sail after sail filled, and picking up his boats in haste,
the captain stood by the helm, the ship slowly gathering way, while cannon-shots from the batteries fell
harmless in her wake.

''Darn the old sea-barrel!'' the captain cried.
Two boats were after them. ''Down! All of you,
down!'' A dozen musket-balls rattled over them.
''Give them a dose, boys!''

''No, no!'' cried De Courval. ''Shoot over them!
Over! Ah, good! Well done!'' For at the reply
the boats ceased rowing, and, save for a few spent
bullets, the affair was ended. The brig, moving more
quickly, soon left their pursuers, and guided by
lights on the *Marie,* they presently joined her.

''Now, then,'' said the captain, ''get out a boat!''
When one by one the disgusted guard came on deck
and in the darkness were put in the boat, their officer
asked in French who had been their captors.

De Courval, on hearing this, replied, ''His Ma-
jesty's schooner *St. George,* privateer of Bristol.''

"But, *mon dieu*," cried the bewildered man, "this ship is American. It is piracy."

"No, monsieur; she was carrying provisions to a French port." The persistent claim of England, known as the "provision order," was well in force, and was to make trouble enough before it was abandoned.

The officer, furious, said: "You speak too well our tongue. Ah, if I had you on shore!"

De Courval laughed. "Adieu, Citizen." The boat put off for the port, and the two ships made all sail.

By and by the captain called to De Courval to come to the cabin. "Well, Mr. Lewis,—if that is to be your name,—we are only at the beginning of our troubles. These seas will swarm with ships of war and English privateers, and we must stay by this old tub. If she is caught, they will go over the manifest and take all they want out of her, and men, too, damn 'em."

"I see," said De Courval. "Is there anything to do but take our chance on the sea?"

"I shall run north and get away from the islands out of their cruising grounds."

"What if we run over to Martinique? How long would it take?"

"Three days and a half as we sail, or as that old cask does. But what for?"

"I heard that things are not so bad there. We might sell the old tub's cargo."

"Sell it? They would take it."

"Perhaps. But we might lie off the port if there

11

is no blockade and—well, negotiate. Once rid of the cargo, she would sail better."

"Yes; but Mr. Wynne has said nothing of this. It is only to risk what we have won. I won't risk it."

"I am sorry," said De Courval, "but now I mean to try it. Kindly run your eye over these instructions. This is a matter of business only."

The captain reddened angrily as he said, "And I am to obey a boy like you?"

"Yes, sir."

The master knew Hugh Wynne well, and after a pause said grimly: "Very good. It is out of the frying-pan into the fire." He hated it, but there was the order, and obedience to those over him and from those under him was part of his sailor creed.

In four days, about dawn, delayed by the slower ship, they were off the port of St. Pierre. The harbor was empty, and there was no blockade as yet.

"And now," said the captain, "what to do? You are the master, it seems. Run in, I suppose?"

"No, wait a little, Captain. If, when I say what I want done, it seems to you unreasonable, I shall give it up. Get a bit nearer; beat about; hoist our own flag. They will want to understand, and will send a boat out. Then we shall see."

"I can do that, but every hour is full of risk." Still he obeyed, beginning to comprehend his supercargo and to like the audacity of the game.

Near to six o'clock the bait was taken. A boat put out and drew near with caution. The captain began to enjoy it. "A nibble," he said.

"Give me a boat," said De Courval. "They will

not come nearer. There are but five men. I must risk it. Let the men go armed.'' In ten minutes he was beside the Frenchmen, and seeing a young man in uniform at the tiller, he said in French: ''I am from that brig. She is loaded with provisions for this port or San Domingo, late from the States.''

''Very well. You are welcome. Run in. The vicomte will take all, and pay well. *Foi d'honneur,* monsieur; it is all as I say. You are French?''

''Yes; an *émigré.*''

''We like not that, but I will go on board and talk it over.''

When on the *Marie* they went to the cabin with the captains of the two American ships. ''And now let us talk,'' said De Courval. ''Who commands here for the republic?''

''Citizen Rochambeau; a good Jacobin, too.''

De Courval was startled. ''A cousin of my mother —the vicomte—a Jacobin!''

''Is monsieur for our side?'' asked the officer.

''No; I am for the king.''

''King, monsieur! The king was guillotined on January 21.''

''*Mon Dieu!*''

''May I ask your name, monsieur?''

''I am the Vicomte de Courval, at your service.''

''By St. Denis! I know; you are of Normandy, of the religion, like ourselves. I am the Comte de Lourmel.''

''And with the Jacobins?''

''Yes. I have an eminent affection for my head. When I can, my brother and I will get away.''

"Then we may talk plainly as two gentlemen."

"Assuredly."

"I do not trust that vicomte of yours—a far-away cousin of my mother, I regret to say."

"Nor would I trust him. He wished the town illuminated on account of the king's death."

"It seems incredible. Poor Louis! But now, to our business. Any hour may bring a British cruiser. This cargo is worth in peace twenty thousand dollars. Now it is worth thirty-two thousand,—salt beef, potatoes, pork, onions, salt fish, and some forty casks of Madeira. Ordinarily we should take home coffee and sugar, but now it is to be paid for in louis d'or or in gold joes, here—here on board, monsieur."

"But the cargo?"

"The sea is quiet. When the money is on deck, we will run in nearer, and you must lighter the cargo out. I will give you one day, and only one. There is no other way. We are well armed, as you see, and will stand no Jacobin tricks. Tell the vicomte Sans Culottes I am his cousin, De Courval. Stay, I shall write a note. It is to take on my terms, and at once, or to refuse."

"He will take it. Money is plenty; but one cannot eat louis d'ors. How long do you give us?"

"Two hours to go and return; and, monsieur, I am trusting you."

"We will play no tricks." And so presently the boat pushed off and was away at speed.

"And now what is all that damned parley-vouing? It was too fast for me," said the captain; but on hearing, he said it would work. He would hover round the *George Washington* with cannon loaded and men armed. Within the time set the officer came back with another boat. "I have the money," he said. "The vicomte swore well and long, and would much desire your company on shore." De Courval laughed. "I grieve to disappoint him."

"The lighters are on the way," said De Lourmel— "a dozen; and upon my honor, there will be no attempt at capture."

The ship ran in nearer while the gold was counted, and then with all possible haste the cargo, partly a deck-load, was lightered away, the wind being scarcely more than a breeze. By seven at night the vessel was cleared, for half of the *Marie's* men had helped. A small barrel of wine was put in the count's boat, and a glad cheer rang out as all sail was set.

Then at last the captain came over to where De Courval, leaning against the rail, allowed himself the first pipe of the busiest day of his life; for no man of the crew had worked harder.

"I want to say you were right, young man, and I shall be glad to say so at home. I came darn near to not doing it."

"Why, without you, sir," said De Courval, "I should have been helpless. The cutting out was yours, and this time we divide honors and hold our tongues."

"Not I," said the master; nor did he, being as honest as any of his race of sea-dogs.

The lumbering old brig did fairly well. After three stormy weeks, in mid-March off the Jersey coast they came in sight of a corvette flying the tricolor. The captain said things not to be put on record, and signaled his clumsy consort far astern to put to sea. "An Englishman all over," said the captain. Then he sailed straight for the corvette with the flag he loved flying. There was a smart gale from the east, and a heavy sea running. Of a sudden, as if alarmed, the Stars and Stripes came down, a tricolor went up, and the *Marie* turned tail for the Jersey coast. De Courval watched the game with interest. The captain enjoyed it, as men who gamble on sea chances enjoy their risks, and said, laughing, "I wonder does that man know the coast? He 's a morsel reckless."

The corvette went about and followed. "Halloa! He 's going to talk!" A cannon flash was followed by a ball, which struck the rail.

"Not bad," said the captain, and turning, saw De Courval on the deck. "Are you hit, man?" he cried.

"Not badly." But the blood was running freely down his stocking as he staggered to his feet.

"Get him below!"

"No, no!" cried De Courval. The mate ripped open his breeches. "A bad splinter wound, sir, and an ugly bruise." In spite of his protests, they carried him to the cabin and did some rude sea surgery. Another sharp fragment had cut open his cheek, but what Dr. Rush would have called "diachylon plaster" sufficed for this, and in great pain he lay and listened, still for a time losing blood very freely. The corvette veered and let go a broadside while the captain looked up at the rigging anxiously. "Too much

sea on," he said. "I will lay his damn ribs on Abse-
com Beach, if he holds on."

Apparently the corvette knew better, and ma-
nœuvered in hope to catch a too wary foe, now flying
along the shallow coast in perilous waters. At nightfall the corvette gave up a dangerous chase, got
about, and was off to sea. At morning the English
war-ship caught the brig, being clever enough to lie
off the capes. The captain of the *George Washington*
wisely lacked knowledge of her consort the schooner,
and the Englishman took out of his ship five men, de-
claring them Britons, although they spoke sound,
nasal Cape Cod American.

XII

AN express-rider from Chester had ridden through the night to carry to Mr. Wynne at Merion the news of his ships' return and a brief note from the captain to say that all had gone well.

Though weaker than he was willing to believe, De Courval was able with some help to get on deck and was welcomed by Wynne, who saw with sudden anxiety the young man's pallor; for although neither wound was serious, he had lost blood enough to satisfy even the great Dr. Rush, and limped uneasily as he went to the rail to meet the ship-owner.

"Are you hurt?" asked Wynne.

"Not badly. We had a little bout with a British corvette. Captain Biddle will tell you, sir. St. Denis! but it was fun while it lasted; and the cutting out, too."

"I envy you," said Wynne, with swift remembrance of the market-place in Germantown, the glow of battle in his gray Welsh eyes.

De Courval's face lighted up at the thought of it. "But now," he said—"now I must see my mother—oh, at once."

"The tide is at full flood. A boat shall drop you at the foot of the garden. Can you walk up from the shore, or shall I send you a chaise?"

"I can walk, sir." He was too eager to consider

his weakness, and strong hands helping him into and out of the boat, in a few minutes, for the distance was small, he was set ashore at the foot of the garden, now bare and leafless. He dismissed the men with thanks, and declared he required no further help. With much-needed care he limped up the slope, too aware of pain and of an increase of weakness that surprised him, but nevertheless with a sense of exhilaration at the thought of coming home —yes, home—after having done what he well knew would please his mother. No other thought was in his mind.

Of a sudden he heard voices, and, looking up, saw Mrs. Swanwick and Margaret. Gay, excited, and happy, he stumbled forward as they came, the girl crying out: "The vicomte, mother!"

"Ah, but it is good to see you!" he said as he took the widow's hand and kissed it, and then the girl's, who flushed hot as he rose unsteadily. Seeing her confusion, he said: "Pardon me. It is our way at home, and I am so, so very glad to get back to you all!"

"But—thou art lame!" cried the widow, troubled.

"And his face—he is hurt, mother!"

"Yes, yes; but it is of no moment. We had a one-sided battle at sea." Then he reeled, recovering himself with effort. "My mother is well?"

"Yes. Lean on me. Put a hand on my arm," said Mrs. Swanwick. "Ah, but the mother will be glad!" And thus, the Pearl walking behind, they went into the house. "Tell madame he is here, Margaret." The young woman went by them and up-stairs to the vicomtesse's bedroom, breathless as she entered in haste.

The vicomtesse said sharply: "Always knock, child."

"I forgot. He is come. He is here. I—we are so glad for thee."

"My son?" She rose.

"Yes, yes." Margaret fled away. It was not for other eyes; she knew that. The vicomtesse met him on the landing, caught him in her arms, kissed him, held him off at arm's-length, and cried. "Are you ill, René?"

"No, no; a little hurt, not badly. I have lost blood," and then, tottering, added faintly, "a wound, a wound," and sank to the floor. She called loudly in alarm, and Schmidt, coming in haste from his room and lifting him, carried him to his bed-chamber. He had overestimated his strength and his power of endurance.

Mother and hostess took possession of him. Nanny hurried with the warming-pan for the bed; and reviving, he laughed as they came and went, acknowledged the welcome comfort of lavender-scented sheets and drank eagerly the milk-punch they brought.

Within an hour Schmidt had the little French surgeon at his bedside, and soon René's face and torn thigh were fitly dressed. There was to be quiet, and only madame or Mrs. Swanwick, and a little laudanum and no starvation. They guarded him well, and, as he said, "fiercely," and, yes, in a week he might see people. "Not Mistress Wynne," said the doctor; "a tornado, that woman: but Mr. Schmidt and Mr. Wynne." He was impatient enough as he lay abed and ate greedily wonderful dishes from Darthea Wynne; and there, from the only greenhouse in the town, were flowers, with Mrs. Robert Morris's compliments, and books, the latest, from Mistress Gainor, "for the hero, please," for by now the town was astir with Captain Biddle's story. The German wrote for him notes of thanks, but as yet would not talk. He could wait to hear of his voyage.

He was on a settle one morning alone with Schmidt. There came a discreet knock at the door. "Come in," called Schmidt, and Margaret entered, saying: "These are the first. I gathered them myself at Uncle Josiah's," from which it may be understood that Josiah had made his peace.

"I found them on the Wissahickon. Smell of them," she said as she set her bowl of fragrant trailing-arbutus before him, coloring a little, and adding: "Mother said I must not stay. We are glad thou art better."

"Oh, thank you, thank you," said the young man. The air of spring, the youth of the year, was in the room. As the door closed behind Margaret, Schmidt asked: "René, did you ever see the Quaker lady?— the flower, I mean."

"Yes, once. And now again. How she grows!"

"Yes, she does grow," said Schmidt. "I have noticed that at her age young women grow." While he spoke, Mr. Wynne came in, a grave, reserved, sturdy man, in whom some of the unemotional serenity of his Quaker ancestry became more notable as he went on into middle life.

Schmidt excused himself, and Wynne sat down, saying: "You seem quite yourself, Vicomte. I have heard the whole story from Captain Biddle. You have made one more friend, and a good one. You will be amused to learn that the French party is overjoyed because of your having victualed the starving Jacobins. The Federals are as well pleased, and all the ship-owners at the baffling of the corvette. No, don't speak; let me finish. The merchants at the coffee-house have voted both of you tankards, and five hundred dollars for the crew, and what the women will say or do the Lord knows. You will have need to keep your head cool among them all."

"Ah, Mr. Wynne, if my head was not turned by what you said to me when we parted, it is safe enough."

"My opinion has been fully justified; but now for business. Both ships are in. You have made an unlooked-for gain for me. Your share—oh, I shall take care of the captain, too—your share will be two thousand dollars. It is now in the bank with what is left of your deposit with me. I can take you again as my clerk or Stephen Girard will send you as supercargo to China. For the present I have said my say."

"I thank you, sir. It is too much, far too much. I shall go back to my work with you."

"And I shall be glad to have you. But I fear it may not be for life—as I should wish."

"No, Mr. Wynne. Some day this confusion in

France must end, and then or before, though no Jacobin, I would be in the army.''

"I thought as much," said Wynne. "Come back now to me, and in the fall or sooner something better may turn up; but for a month or two take a holiday. Your wages will go on. Now, do not protest. You need the rest, and you have earned it.'' With this he added: "And come out to Merion. My wife wants to thank you; and madame must come, too. Have you heard that we are to have a new French minister in April?''

"Indeed? I suppose he will have a great welcome from the Republicans.''

"Very likely," said Wynne.

It was more from loss of blood that René had suffered than from the gravity of the wound. His recovery was rapid, and he was soon released from the tyranny which woman loves to establish about the sickness-fettered man. The vicomtesse had some vague regret when he asserted his independence, for again he had been a child, and her care of him a novel interest in a life of stringent beliefs, some prejudices, and very few positive sources of pleasure. The son at this time came to know her limitations better and to recognize with clearer vision how narrow must always have been a life of small occupations behind which lay, as yet unassailed, the pride of race and the more personal creed of the obligations of a caste which no one, except Mistress Wynne, ventured to describe to Schmidt as needing social spectacles. "A provincial lady," she said; "a lady, but of the provinces.'' The German smiled, which was often his only comment upon her shrewd insight and unguarded talk.

The vicomtesse settled down again to her life of books, church, and refusals to go anywhere except to Darthea at Merion, where she relaxed and grew tender among the children. She would have her son go among gayer people, and being free for a time he went as bidden, and was made much of at the town houses of the gay set. But as he would not play loo for money, and grew weary at last of the rôle of Othello and of relating, much against his will, his adventures to a variety of attentive Desdemonas who asked questions about his life in France, of which he had no mind to speak, he soon returned to the more wholesome company of Schmidt and the tranquil society of the widow's house.

Schmidt, with increasing attachment and growing intimacy of relation, began again the daily bouts with the foils, the long pulls on the river, and the talks at night when the house was quiet in sleep.

The grave young Huguenot was rather tired of being made to pass as a hero, and sternly refused the dinners of the Jacobin clubs, declining to claim for himself the credit of relieving the Jacobin vicomte, his kinsman.

The more certain news of war between France and Great Britain had long since reached Philadelphia, and when, one afternoon in April, Mr. Alexander Hamilton, just come from a visit to New York, appeared at the widow's, he said to Schmidt that Citizen Genêt, the French minister, had reached Charleston in the *Ambuscade*, a frigate. He had brought commissions for privateers, and had already sent out two, the *Citizen Genêt* and the *Sans Culottes*, to wage war on English commerce. The Secretary of State, Jefferson, had protested against the French consul's condemning prizes, but the republican Jacobins, gone mad with joy, took sides against their leader, and mocked at the President's proclamation of neutrality. Such was his news. Mr. Hamilton was depressed and had lost his usual gaiety. It was all bad, very bad. The man's heart ached for the difficulties of his friend, the harassed President.

Meanwhile imitative folly set the Jacobin fashions of long pantaloons and high boots for good republicans. The young men took to growing mustachios. Tricolor cockades appeared in the streets, while the red cap on barbers' poles and over tavern signs served, with news of the massacres in France, to keep in De Courval's mind the thought of his father's fate. In the meantime, amid feasts and clamorous acclaim, Genêt came slowly north with his staff of secretaries.

Schmidt saw at this time how depressed his young friend had become and felt that in part at least it was due to want of steady occupation. Trying to distract him one evening, he said: "Let us go to the fencing school of the Comte du Vallon. I have long meant to ask you. It is late, but the *émigrés* go thither on a Friday. It will amuse you, and you want something I cannot teach. Your defense is slow, your attack too unguarded."

"But," said De Courval, "I cannot afford lessons at a dollar. It is very well for Morris and Lloyd."

Schmidt laughed. "I let the comte have the rooms free. The house is mine. Yes, I know, you avoid the *émigrés;* but why? Oh, yes, I know you have been busy, and they are not all to your taste, nor to mine; but you will meet our bookseller De Méry and De Noailles, whom you know, and you will like Du Vallon."

It was nine o'clock when, hearing foils ringing and laughter, they went up-stairs in an old warehouse on the north side of Dunker's Court, and entered presently a large room amid a dozen of what were plainly French gentlemen, who were fencing in pairs and as merry as if no heads of friends and kindred were day by day falling on the guillotine. Schmidt knew them all and had helped many. They welcomed him warmly.

"*Bonjour, monsieur.* We amuse ourselves well, and forget a little," said Du Vallon. "Ah, the Vicomte de Courval! Enchanted to see you here. Allow me to present Monsieur de Malerive. He is making a fortune with the ice-cream, but he condescends to give us a lesson now and then. Gentlemen, the Vicomte de Courval." The foils were lowered and men bowed. Scarce any knew him, but several came forward and said pleasant things, while, as they left to return to their fencing, Schmidt made his brief comments. "That is the Chevalier Pontgibaud, René,—the slight man,—a good soldier in the American war. The Vicomte de Noailles is a partner of Bingham."

"Indeed!" said René. "He is in trade, as I am— a Noailles!"

"Yes; may you be as lucky. He has made a fortune, they say."

"Take a turn with the marquis," said Du Vallon. The marquis taught fencing. De Courval replied, "With pleasure," and the clatter of foils began again, while Du Vallon and Schmidt fell apart into quiet talk.

"The young man is a clerk and I hear has won credit and money. *Bon chien, bonne chasse.* Do you know his story? Ah, my sad Avignon! La Rochefoucauld told me they killed his father; but of course you know all about it."

"No, I have heard but little," said Schmidt. "I know only that his father was murdered. Des Aguilliers told me that; but as De Courval has not, does not, speak of it, I presume him to have his reasons. Pray let us leave it here."

"As you please, *mon ami.*" But Du Vallon thought the German strangely lacking in curiosity.

The time passed pleasantly. De Courval did better with Tiernay, who taught French to the young women and was in the shabby splendor of clothes which, like their owner, had seen better days.

They went away late. Yes, he was to have lessons from Du Vallon, who had courteously criticized his defense as weak. But the remedy had answered the German's purpose. Here was something to learn which as yet the young man did badly. The lessons went on, and Schmidt at times carried him away into the country with fowling-pieces, and they came home loaded with wood pigeons; and once, to De Courval's joy, from the Welsh hills with a bear on

12

the back of their chaise and rattles for Pearl from what De Courval called the *serpent à sonnettes*—"a nice Jacobin snake, *Mademoiselle*." And so the quiet life went on in the Quaker house with books, walks, and the round of simple duties, while the young man regained his former vigor.

The spring came in with flowers and blossoms in the garden, and, on the 21st of May, Citizen Genêt was to arrive in this year of '93. The French frigate *Ambuscade,* lying in the river and hearing from Chester in due season, was to warn the republicans with her guns of the coming of the minister.

"Come," said Schmidt, as the casements shook with the signal of three cannon. "Pearl said she would like to see it, and the farce will be good. We are going to be amused; and why not?"

"Will Friend de Courval go with us?" asked Margaret. Walks with the young woman were somehow of late not so easily had. Her mother had constantly for her some interfering duties. He was glad to go.

At the signal-guns, thousands of patriots gathered in front of the State House, and in what then was called the Mall, to the south of it. Schmidt and the young people paused on the skirts of the noisy crowd, where were many full of liquor and singing the "Marseillaise" with drunken variations of the tune. "A sight to please the devil of laughter," said Schmidt. "There are saints for the virtues, why not devils for men's follies? The mischief mill for the grinding out of French Jacobins from Yankee grain will not run long. Let us go on around the Mall and get before these foolish folk. Ah, to insult this perfect day of May with drunkenness! Is there not enough of gladness in the upspring of things that men must crave the flattery of drink?'' He was in one of those moods when he was not always, as he said, understandable, and when his English took on queer ways.

Pausing before the gray jail at the corner of Delaware, Sixth Street, and Walnut, they saw the poor debtors within thrust out between the bars of the windows long rods with bags at the end to solicit alms. Schmidt emptied his pockets of shillings, and they went on, the girl in horror at the blasphemies of those who got no coin. Said Schmidt: ''Our friend Wynne lay there in the war for months. Ask Madam Darthea for the tale, De Courval. 'T is pretty, and worth the ear of attention. When I rule the world there will be no prisons. I knew them once too well.''

So rare were these glimpses of a life they knew not of that both young people, surprised, turned to look at him.

''Wert thou in jail, sir?'' said the Pearl.

''Did I say so? Life is a jail, my good Margaret; we are all prisoners.'' The girl understood, and asked no more. Crossing the Potter's Field, now Washington Square, they leaped over the brook that ran through it from the northwest.

''Here below us lie the dead prisoners of your war, Pearl. The jail was safe, but now they are free. God rest their souls! There 's room for more.'' Scarcely was there room in that summer of '93. Passing the Bettering House on Spruce Street

Road, and so on and out to the Schuylkill, they
crossed the floating bridge, and from the deep cutting
where Gray's Lane descended to the river, climbed
the slope, and sat down and waited.

Very soon across the river thousands of men
gathered and a few women. The bridge was lined
with people and some collected on the bank and in
the lane below them, on the west side of the stream.

Hauterive, the French consul at New York, and
Mr. Duponceau and Alexander Dallas of the Democratic Club, stood near the water on the west end
of the bridge, waiting to welcome Genêt. "I like it
very well," said Schmidt; "but the play will not run
long."

"Oh, they are coming!" cried Margaret. This
was interesting. She was curious, excited and
with her bonnet off, as De Courval saw, bright-eyed,
eager, and with isles of color mysteriously passing
over her face, like rose clouds at evening.

A group of horsemen appeared on the top of the
hill above them, one in front. "Genêt, I suppose,"
said De Courval. A good-looking man, florid, smiling, the tricolor on the hat in his hand, he bowed to
right and left, and honored with a special salute
mademoiselle, near-by on the bank. He had the
triumphant air of a very self-conscious conqueror.
Cheers greeted him. *Vive la république!* D——
George Washington! Hurrah for Citizen Genêt!"
with waving of French flags. He stopped below
them in the lane. A boy in the long pantaloons of
protest, with the red cap of the republic on his head,
was lifted up to present a bouquet of three colors

made of paper flowers. Citizen Genêt gave him the fraternal kiss of liberty, and again the crowd cheered. "Are these people crazy?" asked the Quaker maiden, used to Friends' control of emotion.

"Mad? Yes, a little." Genêt had paused at the bridge. Mr. Dallas was making him welcome to the capital. David Rittenhouse stood by, silent in adoration, his attention divided between Genêt and a big bun, for he had missed his dinner.

"It is all real," said the German. "The bun doth equally well convince. Oh, David, didst thou but dream how comic thou art!" Meanwhile De Courval by turns considered the fair face and the crowd, too tragically reminded to be, like Schmidt, altogether amused.

But surely here indeed was comedy, and for many of this careless multitude a sad ending of politics in the near summer months.

The crowd at the water's-edge closed around Genêt, while the group of four or five men on horseback who followed him came to a halt on the roadway just below where were seated Schmidt and his companions. The riders looked around them, laughing. Then one spoke to a young secretary, and the man thus addressed, turning, took off his hat and bowed low to the Quaker maid.

"*Mon Dieu!*" cried De Courval, springing up as the attachés moved on. "*C'est Carteaux!* It is he!"

Schmidt heard him; the girl to the left of Schmidt less plainly. "What is it?" she cried to De Courval. His face as she saw it was of a sudden white, the eyes wide open, staring, the jaw set, the hands half-open, the figure as of a wild creature about to leap on its prey. "Take care!" said Schmidt. "Take care! Keep quiet!" He laid a strong hand on De Courval's shoulder. "Come away! People are looking at you."

"Yes, yes." He straightened, wiping the sweat from his forehead.

"Art thou ill?" asked Margaret.

"No, no. I am glad—glad as never before. Let us go. It will keep. It will keep." She looked at him with wonder. They climbed the bank and went up the hill across the Woodlands, Andrew Hamilton's estate, and homeward by the middle ferry at High Street, no one speaking.

The girl, troubled and apprehensive, walked on, getting now and then from the bonnet's seclusion a quick side glance at a face a little flushed and wearing a look of unwonted satisfaction. Schmidt was as silent as his companions. Comedy again, he thought, and as ever behind it the shadow tragedy. "If I were that man, I should be afraid—a secretary of this accursed envoy. I must know more. Ah, here is the other man behind the every-day De Courval."

De Courval went in and up-stairs to his room and at the five-o'clock supper showed no sign of the storm which had swept over him. After the meal he followed his mother, and as usual read aloud to her a chapter of the French Bible. Then at dusk he pulled out on the river, and, finding refreshment in a cold plunge, rowed to shore, returning in full control of the power to consider with Schmidt, as now he knew he must do, a situation not so simple as it seemed when he set eyes on his enemy.

"I have been waiting for you, René. I guess enough to know this for a very grave matter. You will want to tell me."

"I have often wanted to talk to you, but, as you may or may not know, it was also too painful to discuss until the need came; but now it has come."

"You will talk to me, René, or not, as seems the better to you."

"I shall speak, and frankly; but, sir, wait a little."

Without replying further, the German took up a book and read. The young man let fall his head on his hands, his elbows on a table. He had tried to forget, but now again with closed eyes and, with that doubtful gift of visual recall already mentioned he saw the great, dimly lighted hall at Avignon, the blood-stained murderers, the face of his father, his vain appeal. The tears rained through his fingers. He seemed to hear again: "Yvonne! Yvonne!" and at last to see, with definiteness sharpened by the morning's scene, the sudden look of ferocity in a young man's face—a man not much older than himself. He had thought to hear from it a plea for mercy. Ah, and to-day he had seen it gay with laughter. One day it would not laugh. He wiped away tears as he rose. The German gentleman caught him to his broad breast. "What is it, my son? Ah, I would that you were my son! Let us have it out—all of it. I, too, have had my share of sorrow. Let me hear, and tell it quietly. Then we can talk."

Thus it came about that with a sense of relief René told his story of failing fortunes, of their château in ruins, and of how, on his return from Avignon, he had found his mother in a friendly farm refuge. He told, too, with entire self-command of the tragedy in the papal city, his vain pursuit of Carteaux, their flight to England, and how on the voyage his mother had wrung from him the whole account of his father's death.

"Does she know his name?" asked Schmidt.

"Carteaux? Yes. I should not have told it, but I did. She would have me tell it."

"And that is all." For a little while the German, lighting his pipe, walked up and down the room without a word. Then at last, sitting down, he said: "René, what do you mean to do?"

"Kill him."

"Yes, of course," said Schmidt, coolly; "but—let us think a little. Do you mean to shoot him as one would a mad dog?"

"Certainly; and why not?"

"You ask 'Why not?' Suppose you succeed? Of course you would have to fly, leave your mother alone; or, to be honest with you, if you were arrested, the death of this dog would be, as men would look at it, the murder of an official of the French legation. You know the intensity of party feeling here. You would be as sure to die by the gallows as any common criminal; and—there again is the mother to make a man hesitate."

"That is all true; but what can I do, sir? Must I sit down and wait?"

"For the present, yes. Opinion will change. Time is the magician of opportunities. The man will be here long. Wait. Go back to your work. Say nothing. There are, of course, the ordinary ways—a quarrel, a duel—"

"Yes, yes; anything—something—"

"Anything—something, yes; but what thing? You must not act rashly. Leave it to me to think over; and promise me to do nothing rash—to do nothing in fact just yet."

De Courval saw only too clearly that his friend was wiser than he. After a moment of silence he said: "I give you my word, sir. And how can I thank you?"

"By not thanking me, not a rare form of thanks. Now go to bed."

When alone, Schmidt said to himself: "Some day he will lose his head, and then the tiger will leap. It was clear from what I saw, and who could sit quiet and give it up? Not I. A duel? If this man I have learned to love had Du Vallon's wrist of steel or mine, it would be easy to know what to do. Ah, if one could know that rascal's fence—or if I—no; the boy would never forgive me; and to cheat a man out of a just vengeance were as bad as to cheat him of a woman's love." As for killing a man with whom he had no personal quarrel, the German, unreproached by conscience, considered the matter entirely in his relation to De Courval. And here, as he sat in thought, even a duel troubled him, and it was sure to come; for soon or late, in the limited society of the city, these two men would meet. He was deeply disturbed. An accident to De Courval was possible; well, perhaps his death. He foresaw even this as possible, since duels in that time were not the serio-comic encounters of the French duel of to-day.

As Schmidt sat in self-counsel as to what was advisable he felt with curious joy that his affection for the young noble was disturbing his judgment of what as a gentleman he would have advised. The situation was, as he saw, of terrible significance. A large experience of men and events failed to assist him to see his way.

No less bewildered and even more deeply troubled, De Courval lay awake, and, as the hours went by, thought and thought the thing over from every point of view. Had he met Carteaux that morning alone, away from men, he knew that he would have throttled the slighter man with his strong young hands, glad of the joy of brute contact and of personal infliction of the death penalty with no more merciful weapon than his own strength. He thrilled at the idea; but Schmidt, coldly reasonable, had brought him down to the level of common-sense appreciation of unregarded difficulties. His mother! He knew her now far better than ever. His mother would say, "Go, my son." She would send him out to take his chances with this man, as for centuries the women of her race had sent their men to battle. He was more tender for her than she would be for herself. His indecision, the product of a larger duty to her lonely, helpless life, increased by what Schmidt had urged, left him without a helpful thought, while ever and ever in the darkness he felt, as his friend had felt, that in some moment of opportune chance he should lose for her and himself all thought of consequences.

Perhaps of those who saw the episode of sudden passionate anger in Gray's Lane none was more puzzled and none more curious than Margaret Swanwick. Anything as abrupt and violent as De Courval's irritation was rare in her life of tranquil experiences, and nothing she had seen of him prepared her for this outbreak. Of late, it is to be confessed, De Courval had been a frequent guest of her thoughts, and what concerned him began greatly to concern her. Something forbade her to ask of Schmidt an explanation of what she had seen. Usually she was more frank with him than with any one else, and why now, she thought, should she not question him? But then, as if relieved by the decision, she concluded that it was not her business, and put aside the curiosity, but not completely the anxiety which lay behind it.

If she told her mother and asked of her what De Courval's behavior might have meant, she was sure that her eagerness would be reproved by a phrase which Mrs. Swanwick used on fitting occasions—"Thou shalt not covet thy neighbor's secrets." Many things were to happen before the girl would come to understand why, in the quiet of a May morning, a rather reserved gentleman had of a sudden looked like a wild animal.

XIII

A CHEERING crowd escorted Genêt to Oeller's Hotel. A few days later Washington received the minister, De Ternant's successor, with a coldly formal speech, and the envoy came away in wrath; for had he not seen in the parlor of the President, medallions of decapitated Citizen Capet and his family? His insolent demands for money owing to France, but not yet due, and for a new and more liberal compact, are matters of history. There were wild claims for the right of French consuls to condemn prizes without intermediation of our courts, and yet more and more absurd requests and specious arguments, to which Jefferson replied with decision, but with more tenderness than pleased the Federalists.

When the privateer *Citizen Genêt* anchored off Market Street wharf, two enlisted Americans on board were arrested, and the cabinet, being of one opinion, the President ordered the privateer to leave. Genêt appealed to the Secretary of State for delay and against this inconceivable wrong to a sister republic, and as the cabinet remained firm, and the democrats raged, the town was for days on the verge of riot and bloodshed.

On the 27th of May, while on an errand for Mr. Wynne, about four in the afternoon, De Courval

saw the crowd going into Oeller's Hotel for a great
dinner in honor of Genêt. On the steps stood a man
waving the tricolor. It was Carteaux. *"Mon
Dieu!"* murmured De Courval, "shall I get used to
it?" His errand took him past the house of the
Vice-President, John Adams. Servants and friends
were carrying in muskets. A noisy mob hooted and
drifted away to Oeller's. There had been threats
of destroying the house, and Adams meant to be
ready. The young man went on deep in thought.
In front of the Senate House he bowed to Edmund
Randolph, an occasional visitor at the Quaker salon
and now Attorney-General at the age of thirty-
eight.

Returning, De Courval met Stephen Girard, who
stopped him. Short, sallow, a little bald, and still
slight of build, he was watching with a look of
amusement the noisy mob in front of the hotel.
"Ah, bonjour, monsieur. And you would not go as
my supercargo. It is open for the asking." He
spoke French of course. "These yonder are children, but they are not as serious as they think themselves. Come this afternoon to my farm on the
neck and eat of my strawberries. There will be
the French consul-general and the secretary Carteaux. No politics, mind you. My heart is with the
revolutionary government at home, but my politics
in America are here," and he struck his breeches'
pocket. "I am not for war, *monsieur.*"

De Courval excused himself, and went away murmuring: "Again, again! It must end. I must make
it end. Ah, mother, mother!"

Schmidt, troubled by the young man's gloom and loss of spirits, did all he could, but characteristically made no effort to reopen a subject on which he had as yet reached no other decision than the counsel of delay.

The mother questioned her son. It was nothing. He was not quite well, and the heat of July was great. The German was yet more disturbed when one evening after the fencing lesson Du Vallon said: "I had here to-day two of the staff of that *sacré* Citizen Genêt. There is already talk of his recall for insolence to the President. *Le bon Dieu* be praised!"

"Why, Marquis, do you permit these cattle to come here?"

"One must live, Monsieur Schmidt."

"Perhaps."

"One of them is a pleasure to fence with—a Monsieur Carteaux, a meager Jacobin. I could not touch him."

"I should like to, with the buttons off the foils," said Schmidt.

"I also. That does make a difference."

Schmidt went away thoughtful. The next afternoon, feeling the moist heat, the vicomtesse went to Darthea at Merion. The two men fenced as usual, while mother and daughter sat in shadow on the porch, and a faint, cool air came up from the river.

"*Ach, du lieber Himmel!* but it is hot!" cried the German, casting down his foil. "You are doing better. Let us go and cool off in the river. Come."

They went down the garden, picking the ripe

plums as they went. "What is wrong with you, René? You promised me."

"It is the heat. Miss Margaret looks ill. No one could endure it, and in the counting-house it is dreadful, and with no work to distract me."

"The Pearl goes again to Gray Court to-morrow," said the German.

"Indeed."

"Yes. I shall miss her, but it is as well. And, you, René—it is not the heat. Why do you put me off with such excuses?"

"Well, no. It is of course that villain," and he told of Girard and the invitation.

"René, a day will come when you will meet that man, and then the thing will somehow end. You cannot go on suffering as you are doing."

"I know; but a devil of indecision pursues me."

"An angel, perhaps."

"Oh, yes. Pity me. My mother stands like a wall I may not pass between me and him. It is horrible to think that she—she is protecting my father's murderer. If I told her, by Heaven! she would bid me go and kill him. You do not know her. She would do it; but, then, who knows what might chance? If I die, she is alone, friendless. I fear to risk it. *Mon Dieu*, sir, I am afraid!"

"And yet some day you will have to put an end to all this doubt. Comfort yourself with this: Fate, which plays with us will take you in hand. Let it go just now."

"I will try to. I will. If I were as these good Quakers—ah, me, I should sit down,"—and he smiled,—"and thee and thou Providence, and be quiet in the armor of meek unresistance."

"They do kill flies," said the German.

"Ah, I wish then they would attend to the mosquitos," cried De Courval, laughing.

"As to non-resistance, friend, it hath its limitations. Did I tell thee of Daniel Offley? My Pearl told me," and he related the defeat of the blacksmith.

"Insolent," said René.

"No; the man believed that he had a mission. I should like to have his conscience for a week or two, to see how it feels; and, as for non-resistance, canst thou keep a secret?"

"I? Why not? What is it?" He was curious. As they talked, standing beside the river, René watched the flat stones he threw ricochet on the water.

"Once on a time, as they say in Madame Swanwick's book of sixty-five tales, by Nancy Skyrin, a man, one Schmidt, came into the dining-room and sat down quietly to read at an open window for the sake of the breeze from the river. It might have been on Second Day. It chanced to be the same time a Quaker man who hath of late come often sat without on the step of the porch, a proper lad, and young, very neat in gray. Near by sat a maid. Up from the river came the little god who is of all religions and did tempt the young man. The man within lost interest in his book."

Then René gave up the game of skip-stone, and, turning, said, "*Mon Dieu,* you did not listen?"

"Did he not? He had listened to the talk in the

book, and wherefore not to them? It amused him more. For a little the maid did not seem greatly displeased.''

''She did not seem displeased?''

''No. And then—and then that Friend who was perverted into a lover would *brusquer* matters, as you say, and did make a venture, being tempted by the little devil called Cupid. The man who listened did not see it, but it does seem probable she was kissed, because thereupon was heard a resounding smack, and feeling that here had been a flagrant departure from non-resistance, the man within, having been satisfactorily indiscreet, fell to reading again and the Quaker went away doubly wounded. Dost thou like my story, Friend de Courval?''

''No, I do not.'' He was flushing, angry.

''I told you I had no conscience.''

''Upon my word, I believe you. Why did you not kick him?''

''I leave you the privilege.''

''Come. I hate your story,''—and laughing, despite his wrath,—''your conscience needs a bath.''

''Perhaps.'' And they went down to the boat, the German still laughing.

''What amuses you?''

''Nothing. Nothing amuses one as much as nothing. I should have been a diplomatist at the court of Love.'' And to himself: ''Is it well for these children? Here is another tangle, and if—if anything should go amiss here are three sad hearts. D—— the Jacobin cur! I ought to kill him. That would settle things.''

13

For many days De Courval saw nothing of his enemy. Schmidt, who owned many houses and mortgages and good irredeemable ground rents, was busy.

Despite the fear of foreign war and the rage of parties, the city was prosperous and the increase of chariots, coaches, and chaises so great as to cause remark. House rents rose, the rich of the gay set drank, danced, gambled, and ran horses on the road we still call Race Street. Wages were high. All the wide land felt confidence, and speculation went on, for the poor in lotteries, for the rich in impossible canals never to see water.

On August 6 of this fatal year '93, Uncle Josiah came to fetch the Pearl away for a visit, and, glad as usual to be the bearer of bad news, told Schmidt that a malignant fever had killed a child of Dr. Hodge and three more. It had come from the *Sans Culottes,* privateer, or because of damaged coffee fetched from he knew not where.

The day after, Dr. Redman, President of the College of Physicians, was of opinion that this was the old disease of 1762—the yellow plague. Schmidt listened in alarm. Before the end of August three hundred were dead, almost every new case being fatal. On August 20, Schmidt was gone for a day. On his return at evening he said: "I have rented a house on the hill above the Falls of Schuylkill. We move out to-morrow. I know this plague. *El vomito* they call it in the West Indies."

Mrs. Swanwick protested.

"No," he said; "I must have my way. You have cared for me in sickness and health these five years.

Now it is my turn. This disease will pass along the water-front. You are not safe an hour." She gave way to his wishes as usual, and next day they were pleasantly housed in the country.

Business ceased as if by agreement, and the richer families, if not already in the country, began to flee. The doom of a vast desertion and of multiplying deaths fell on the gay and prosperous city. By September 10 every country farm was crowded with fugitives, and tents received thousands along the Schuylkill and beyond it. Sooner or later some twenty-three thousand escaped, and whole families camped in the open air and in all weather. More would have gone from the city, but the shops were shut, money ceased to circulate, and even the middle class lacked means to flee. Moreover, there was no refuge open, since all the towns near by refused to receive even those who could afford to leave. Hence many stayed who would gladly have gone.

Madame de Courval was at Merion, and Margaret had now rejoined her mother, brought over by her uncle. He had ventured into the city and seen Matthew Clarkson, the mayor, on business. He would talk no business. "Terrible time," said Josiah— "terrible! Not a man will do business." Did he feel for these dying and the dead? Schmidt doubted it, and questioned him quietly. The doctors were not agreed, and Rush bled every one. He, Josiah, was not going back. Half a dozen notes he held had been protested; a terrible calamity, but fine for debtors; a neat excuse.

Mr. Wynne had closed his counting-house, and

was absent on the Ohio, and De Courval was left to brood; for now the French legation had gone to the country, the cabinet fled to Germantown, and the President long before to Mount Vernon for his summer rest.

The day after Josiah's visit, Schmidt left a letter on Mrs. Swanwick's table, and rode away to town without other farewell.

"Look at that, my friend," said the widow to René, and burst into tears. He read and re-read the letter:

DEAR MADAM: The city has no nurses, and help is needed, and money. I have a note from Girard. He has what Wetherill once described as the courage of the penny, not the cowardice of the dollar. I go to help him, for how long I know not, and to do what I can. My love to my friend René. I shall open your house. I have taken the key. I shall write when I can. I leave in my desk money. Use it. I owe what no money can ever repay.

I am, as always, your obedient, humble servant,

J. S.

There was consternation in the home and at Merion, where he was a favorite, and at the Hill, which Gainor had filled with guests; but day after day went by without news. No one would carry letters. Few would even open those from the city. The flying men and women told frightful stories. And now it was September. Two weeks had gone by without a word from Schmidt. The "National Gazette" was at an end, and the slanderer Freneau gone. Only one newspaper still appeared, and the flight went on: all fled who could.

At length De Courval could bear it no longer. He had no horse, and set off afoot to see his mother at Merion, saying nothing of his intention to Mrs. Swanwick. He learned that Wynne was still on the Ohio; ignorant of the extent of the calamity at home.

"Mother," he said, "again I must go into danger. Mr. Schmidt has gone to the city to care for the sick. For two weeks we have been without news of him. I can bear it no longer. I must go and see what has become of him."

"Well, and why, my son, should you risk your life for a man of whom you know nothing? When before you said it was a call of duty I bade you go. Now I will not."

"Mother, for a time we lived on that man's generous bounty."

"What!" she cried.

"Yes. It was made possible for me because I had the good fortune to save him from drowning. I did not tell you."

"No, of course not."

He told briefly the story of his rescue of the German.

"If he is well, I must know it. He is more than merely my friend. If he is ill, I must care for him. If he is dead—oh, dear mother, I must go!"

"I forbid it absolutely. If you go, it is against my will."

He saw that she meant it. It was vain to protest. He rose.

"I have no time to lose, mother. Pray for me."

"That I do always, but I shall not forgive you; no—yes, kiss me. I did not mean that; but think of my life, of yours, what it owes me. You will not go, my son."

"Yes, I am going. I should be base, a coward, ungrateful, if I did not go. Good-by, mother. Let them know at Mrs. Swanwick's."

He was gone. She sat still a little while, and then rising, she looked out and saw him go down the garden path, a knapsack on his back.

"His father would never have left me. Ah, but he is my son—all of him. He was right to go, and I was weak, but, my God, life is very hard!" For a moment she looked after his retreating figure, and then, fearless, quiet, and self-contained, took up again the never-finished embroidery.

XIV

IN the summer of 1793, the city of Penn numbered forty-five thousand souls, and lay in the form of an irregularly bounded triangle, the apex being about seven squares, as we say, west of the Delaware. From this it spread eastward, widening until the base, thinly builded with shops, homes, and warehouses, extended along the Delaware River a distance of about two miles from Callowhill Street to Cedar. It was on the parts nearest to the river that the death-cloud lay.

De Courval had walked from the Falls of Schuylkill late in the morning, and, after having been ferried across the Schuylkill, passed by forest and farm roads over a familiar, rolling country, and arrived at Merion, in the Welsh barony, where he parted from his mother. To this distance he was now to add the seven miles which would bring him to the city.

He soon reached the Lancaster road, and after securing a bowl of bread and milk, for which he paid the exorbitant price of two shillings at a farm-house, he lay down in the woods and, lighting his meerschaum pipe, rested during the early afternoon, glad of shelter from the moist heat of the September day.

He had much to think about. His mother he dismissed, smiling. If, after what he had said, he had not obeyed the call of duty and gratitude, he knew full well that she would have been surprised, despite her protests and the terror with which his errand filled her. He, too, felt it, for it is the form which peril takes rather than equality of risk which makes disease appal many a man for whom war has the charm which awakens the lust of contest, and not such alarm as the presence of the unseen foe which gives no quarter. He dismissed his fears with a silent appeal for strength and support.

He thought then of his enemy. Where was he? This pestilence, the inexplicable act of an all-powerful God, had for a time been set as a barrier between him and his foe. If either he or Carteaux died of it, there was an end of all the indecisions that affection had put in his way. He had a moral shock at the idea that he was unwilling to believe it well that the will of God should lose him the fierce joy of a personal vengeance. How remote seemed such a feeling from the religious calm of the Quaker home! And then a rosy face, a slight, gray-clad figure, came before him with the clearness of visual perception which was one of his mental peculiarities. The sense of difference of rank which his mother had never lost, and would never lose, he had long since put aside. Margaret's refinement, her young beauty, her gay sweetness, her variety of charm, he recalled as he lay; nor against these was there for him any available guard of common sense, that foe of imprudent love, to sum up the other side with the arithmetic of worldly wisdom. He rose, disturbed a little at the consciousness of a power beginning to get beyond his control, and went on his way down the long, dusty road, refreshed by the fair angel company of Love and Longing.

Very soon he was recalled from his dreams. As he came within a mile of the city, he saw tents as for an army, camp-fires, people cooking, men, women, and children lying about by the roadside and in the orchards or the woods. Two hungry-looking mechanics begged help of him. He gave them each a shilling and went on. The nearer shore of the quiet Schuylkill was lined with tents. Over the middle-ferry floating bridge came endlessly all manner of vehicles packed with scared people, the continuous drift from town of all who could afford to fly, a pitiful sight in the closing day. Beyond the river were more tents and half-starved families.

At dusk, as he went eastward on Market Street, there were fewer people, and beyond Sixth Street almost none. The taverns were closed. Commerce was at an end. Turning south, he crossed the bridge over Dock Creek at Second Street and was soon in a part of the city where death and horror had left only those whom disease, want of means, or some stringent need, forbade to leave their homes. Twenty-four thousand then or later fled the town. A gallant few who could have gone, stayed from a sense of duty.

Exposure at night was said to be fatal, so that all who could were shut up indoors, or came out in fear only to feed with pitch and fence palings the fires kindled in the streets which were supposed to give protection, but were forbidden later. A canopy of rank tar-smoke hung over the town and a dull, ruddy glow from these many fires. Grass grew in the roadway of the once busy street, and strange silence reigned where men were used to move amid the noises of trade. As he walked on deep in thought, a woman ran out of a house, crying: ''They are dead! All are dead!'' She stopped him. ''Is my baby dead, too?''

''I—I do not know,'' he said, looking at the wasted, yellow face of the child in her arms. She left it on the pavement, and ran away screaming. He had never in his life touched the dead; but now, though with repugnance, he picked up the little body and laid it on a door-step. Was it really dead? he asked himself. He stood a minute looking at the corpse; then he touched it. It was unnaturally hot, as are the dead of this fever. Not seeing well in the dusk, and feeling a strange responsibility, he laid a hand on the child's heart. It was still. He moved away swiftly through the gathering gloom of deserted streets. On Front Street, near Lombard, a man, seeing him approach, ran from him across the way. A little farther, the sense of solitude and loneliness grew complete as the night closed dark about him. He had been long on his way.

A half-naked man ran out of an alley and, standing before him, cried: ''The plague is come upon us because they have numbered the people. Death! death! you will die for this sin.'' The young man, thus halted, stood appalled and then turned to look after the wild prophet of disaster, who ran up Lombard Street, his sinister cries lost as he disappeared in the gloom. René recalled that somewhere in the Bible he had read of how a plague had come on the Israelites for having numbered the people. Long afterward he learned that a census of Philadelphia had been taken in 1792. He stood still a moment in the gloom, amid the silence of the deserted city and then of a sudden moved rapidly onward.

He had reached the far edge of the town, his mind upon Schmidt, when he saw to his surprise by the glow of a dying fire a familiar form. "Mr. Girard!" he cried, in pleased surprise; for in the country little was as yet known of the disregard of death with which this man and many more were quietly nursing the sick and keeping order in a town where, except the comparatively immune negroes, few aided, and where the empty homes were being plundered. The quick thought passed through René's mind that he had heard this man called an atheist by Daniel Offley.

He said to Girard: "Ah, Monsieur, have you seen Monsieur Schmidt?"

"Not for three days. He has been busy as the best. There is one man who knows not fear. Where is he, Vicomte?"

"We do not know. We have heard nothing since he left us two weeks ago. But he meant to live in Mrs. Swanwick's house."

"Let us go and see," said Girard; and with the man who already counted his wealth in millions René hurried on. At the house they entered easily, for the door was open, and went up-stairs.

In Schmidt's room, guided by his delirious cries,

they found him. Girard struck a light from his steel
and flint, and presently they had candles lighted,
and saw the yellow face, and the horrors of the
vomito, in the disordered room.

"*Mon Dieu!* but this is sad!" said Girard. "Ah,
the brave gentleman! You will stay? I shall send
you milk and food at once. Give him water freely,
and the milk. Bathe him. Are you afraid?"

"I—yes; but I came for this, and I am here to
stay."

"I shall send you a doctor; but they are of little
use."

"Is there any precaution to take?"

"Yes. Live simply. Smoke your pipe—I believe
in that. You can get cooler water by hanging out in
the air demijohns and bottles wrapped in wet linen
—a West-Indian way, and the well water is cold. I
shall come back to-morrow." And so advising, he
left him.

De Courval set the room in order, and lighted his
pipe, after obeying Girard's suggestions. At intervals he sponged the hot body of the man who was
retching in agony of pain, babbling and crying
out about courts and princes and a woman—ever of
a woman dead and of some prison life. De Courval
heard his delirious revelations with wonder and a
pained sense of learning the secrets of a friend.

In an hour came Dr. Rush, with his quiet manner
and thin, intellectual face. Like most of those of his
profession, the death of some of whom in this battle
with disease a tablet in the College of Physicians
records to-day, he failed of no duty to rich or poor.

But for those who disputed his views of practice he had only the most virulent abuse. A firm friend, an unpardoning hater, and in some ways far ahead of his time, was the man who now sat down as he said: "I must bleed him at once. Calomel and blood-letting are the only safety, sir. I bled Dr. Griffith seventy-five ounces to-day. He will get well." The doctor bled everybody, and over and over.

His voice seemed to rouse Schmidt. He cried out: "Take away that horse leech. He will kill me." He fought them both and tore the bandage from his arm. The doctor at last gave up, unused to resistance. "Give him the calomel powders."

"Out with your drugs!" cried the sick man, striking at him in fury, and then falling back in delirium again, yellow and flushed. The doctor left in disgust, with his neat wrist ruffles torn. On the stair he said: "He will die, but I shall call to-morrow. He will be dead, I fear."

"Is he gone?" gasped Schmidt, when, returning, René sat down by his bedside.

"Yes, sir; but he will come again."

"I do not want him. I want air—air." As he spoke, he rose on his elbow and looked about him. "I knew you would come. I should never have sent for you. *Mein Gott!*" he cried hoarsely, looking at the room and the bedclothes. "Horrible!" His natural refinement was shocked at what he saw. "*Ach!* to die like a wallowing pig is a torture of disgust! An insult, this disease and torment." Then wandering again: "I pray you, sir, to hold me excused."

The distracted young man never forgot that night.
The German at dawn, crying, "Air, air!" got up,
and despite all De Courval could do staggered out
to the upper porch and lay uncovered on a mattress
upon which De Courval dragged him. The milk and
food came, and at six o'clock Stephen Girard.

"I have been up all night," he said; "but here is
a black to help you."

To De Courval's delight, it was old Cicero, who,
lured by high wages given to the negro, whom even
the pest passed by, had left the widow's service.

"Now," said Girard, "here is help. Pay him well.
Our friend will die, I fear; and, sir, you are a brave
man, but do not sit here all day."

De Courval, in despair at his verdict, thanked
him. But the friend was not to die. Cicero proved
faithful, and cooked and nursed and René, as
the hours of misery went on, began to hope. The
fever lessened in a day or two, but Schmidt still lay
on the porch, speechless, yellow and wasted, swear-
ing furiously at any effort to get him back to bed.
As the days ran on he grew quiet and rejoiced to feel
the cool breeze from the river and had a smile
for René and a brief word of cheer for Girard, who
came hither daily, heroically uncomplaining, spending his strength lavishly and his money with less indifference. Schmidt, back again in the world of human interests, listened to his talk with René, himself
for the most part silent.

Twice a day, when thus in a measure relieved, as
the flood served, De Courval rowed out on the river,
and came back refreshed by his swim. He sent com-

forting notes by Cicero to his mother and to Mrs.
Swanwick, and a message of remembrance to Margaret, and was careful to add that he had "fumed"
the letters with sulphur, that things were better
with Schmidt, and he himself was well. Cicero
came back with glad replies and fruit and milk and
lettuce and fresh eggs and what not, while day after
day three women prayed at morning and night for
those whom in their different ways they loved.

One afternoon Dr. Rush came again and said it
was amazing, but it would have been still better if
he had been let to bleed him, telling how he had bled
Dr. Mease six times in five days, and now he was
safe. But here he considered that he would be no
further needed. Schmidt had listened civilly to the
doctor with the mild, tired, blue eyes and delicate
features; feeling, with the inflowing tide of vigor,
a return of his normal satisfaction in the study of
man, he began, to De Courval's joy, to amuse himself.

"Do you bleed the Quakers, too?" he asked.

"Why not?" said the doctor, puzzled.

"Have they as much blood as other people? You
look to be worn out. Pray do not go. Sit down.
Cicero shall give you some chocolate."

The doctor liked few things better than a chance
to talk. He sat down again as desired, saying:
"Yes, I am tired; but though I had only three hours'
sleep last night, I am still, through the divine Goodness, in perfect health. Yesterday was a triumph
for mercury, jalap, and bleeding. They saved at
least a hundred lives."

"Are the doctors all of your way of thinking?"

"No, sir. I have to combat prejudice and falsehood. Sir, they are murderers."

"Sad, very sad!" remarked Schmidt.

"I have one satisfaction. I grieve for the blindness of men, but I nourish a belief that my labor is acceptable to Heaven. Malice and slander are my portion on earth; but my opponents will have their reward hereafter."

"Most comforting!" murmured Schmidt. "But what a satisfaction to be sure you are right!"

"Yes, to know, sir, that I am right and these my enemies wrong, does console me; and, too, to feel that I am humbly following in the footsteps of my Master. But I must go. The chocolate is good. My thanks. If you relapse, let me know, and the lancet will save you. Good-by."

When René returned, having attended the doctor to the door, Schmidt was smiling.

"Ah, my son," he said, "only in the Old Testament will you find a man like that—malice and piety, with a belief in himself no man, no reason, can disturb."

"Yes, I heard him with wonder."

"He has done me good, but now I am tired. He has gone—he said so—to visit Miss Gainor, at the Hill. I should like to hear her talk to him."

An attack of gout had not improved that lady's temper, and she cruelly mocked at the great doctor's complaints of his colleagues. When she heard of De Courval, and how at last he would not agree to have Schmidt held for the doctor to bleed him she said he was a fine fellow; and to the doctor's statement that he was a fool, she retorted: "You have changed your religion twice, I do hear. When you are born again, try to be born a fool."

The doctor, enraged, would have gone at once, but the gout was in solid possession, and the threat to send for Dr. Chovet held him. He laughed, outwardly at least, and did not go. The next day he, too, was in the grip of the fever, and was bled to his satisfaction, recovering later to resume his gallant work.

And now that, after another week, Schmidt, a ghastly frame of a man, began to eat, but still would not talk, De Courval, who had never left him except for his swim or to walk in the garden, leaving Cicero in charge, went out into the streets to find a shop and that rare article, tobacco.

It was now well on into this fatal September. The deaths were three hundred a week. The sick no man counted, but probably half of those attacked died. At night in his vigils, De Courval heard negroes, with push-carts or dragging chaises, cry: "Bring out your dead! Bring out your dead!" The bodies were let down from upper windows by ropes or left outside of the doorways until the death-cart came and took them away.

It was about noon when René left the house. As he neared the center of the city, there were more people in the streets than he expected to see; but all wore a look of anxiety and avoided one another, walking in the middle of the roadway. No one shook hands with friend or kinsman. Many smoked;

14

most of them wore collars of tarred rope, or chewed garlic, or held to their faces vials of "vinegar of the four thieves" once popular in the plague. He twice saw men, stricken as they walked, creep away like animals, beseeching help from those who fled in dismay. Every hour had its sickening tragedy.

As he stood on Second Street looking at a man chalking the doors of infected houses, a lightly clad young woman ran forth screaming. He stopped her. "What is it? Can I help you?" A great impulse of desire to aid came over him, a feeling of pitiful self-appeal to the manhood of his courage.

"Let me go! My husband has it. I won't stay! I am too young to die."

A deadly fear fell upon the young Huguenot. "I, too, am young, and may die," he murmured; but he went in and up-stairs. He saw an old man, yellow and convulsed; but being powerless to help him, he went out to find some one.

On the bridge over Dock Creek he met Daniel Offley. He did not esteem him greatly, but he said, "I want to know how I can help a man I have just left."

The two men who disliked each other had then and there their lesson. "I will go with thee." They found the old man dead. As they came out, Offley said, "Come with me, if thee is minded to aid thy fellows," and they went on, talking of the agony of the doomed city.

Hearses and push-carts went by in rows, heavy with naked corpses in the tainted air. Very few well-dressed people were seen. Fashion and wealth had gone, panic-stricken, and good grass crops could have been cut in the desolate streets near the Delaware.

Now and then came some scared man, walking in the roadway, for few, as I said, used the sidewalk, would turn, shocked at hearing the Quaker's loud voice; for, as was noticed, persons who met, spoke softly and low, as if feeling the nearness of the unseen dead in the houses. While De Courval waited, Offley went into several alleys on their way, and came out more quiet.

"I have business here," said Offley, as he led the way over the south side of the Potter's Field we now call Washington Square. He paused to pay two black men who were digging wide pits for the fast-coming dead cast down from the death-carts. A Catholic priest and a Lutheran clergyman were busy, wearily saying brief prayers over the dead.

Offley looked on, for a minutè silent. "The priest is of Rome," he said, "one Keating—a good man; the other a Lutheran."

"Strange fellowship!" thought De Courval.

They left them to this endless task, and went on, Daniel talking in his oppressively loud voice of the number of the deaths. The imminence of peril affected the spirits of most men, but not Offley. De Courval, failing to answer a question, he said: "What troubles thee, young man? Is thee afeared?"

"A man should be—and at first I was; but now I am thinking of the Papist and Lutheran—working together. That gives one to think, as we say in French."

"I see not why," said Offley. "But we must hasten, or the health committee will be gone."

In a few minutes they were at the State House. Daniel led him through the hall and up-stairs. In the council-room of Penn was seated a group of notable men.

"Here," said Offley in his great voice, "is a young man of a will to help us."

Girard rose. "This, gentlemen, is my countryman, the Vicomte de Courval."

Matthew Clarkson, the mayor, made him welcome.

"Sit down," he said. "We shall presently be free to direct you."

De Courval took the offered seat and looked with interest at the men before him.

There were Carey, the future historian of the plague; Samuel Wetherill, the Free Quaker; Henry de Forrest, whom he had met; Thomas Savory; Thomas Wistar; Thomas Scattergood; Jonathan Seargeant; and others. Most of them, being Friends, sat wearing their white beaver hats. Tranquil and fearless, they were quietly disposing of a task from which some of the overseers of the poor had fled. Six of those present were very soon to join the four thousand who died before November. When the meeting was over Girard said to De Courval: "Peter Helm and I are to take charge of the hospital on Bush Hill. Are you willing to help us? It is perilous; I ought to tell you that."

"Yes, I will go," said René; "I have now time, and I want to be of some use."

"We thank you," said Matthew Clarkson. "Help is sorely needed."

"Come with me," said Girard. "My chaise is here. Help is scarce. Too many who should be of us have fled." As they went out, he added: "I owe this city much, as some day it will know. You are going to a scene of ungoverned riot, of drunken negro nurses; but it is to be changed, and soon, too."

James Hamilton's former country seat on Bush Hill was crowded with the dying and the dead; but there were two devoted doctors, and soon there was better order and discipline.

De Courval went daily across the doomed city to his loathsome task, walking thither after his breakfast. He helped to feed and nurse the sick, aided in keeping the beds decent, and in handling the many who died, until at nightfall, faint and despairing, he wandered back to his home. Only once Schmidt asked a question, and hearing his sad story, was silent, except to say: "I thought as much. God guard you, my son!"

One day, returning, he saw at evening on Front Street a man seated on a door-step. He stopped, and the man looked up. It was the blacksmith Offley.

"I am stricken," he said. "Will thee help me?"

"Surely I will." De Courval assisted him into the house and to bed. He had sent his family away. "I have shod my last horse, I fear. Fetch me Dr. Hutchinson."

"He died to-day."

"Then another—Dr. Hodge; but my wife must

not know. She would come. Ask Friend Pennington to visit me. I did not approve of thee, young man. I ask thee pardon; I was mistaken. Go, and be quick.''

"I shall find some one." He did not tell him that both Pennington and the physician were dead.

De Courval was able to secure the needed help, but the next afternoon when he returned, the blacksmith was in a hearse at the door. De Courval walked away thoughtful. Even those he knew avoided him, and he observed, what many noticed, that every one looked sallow and their eyes yellow. A strange thing it seemed.

And so, with letters well guarded, that none he loved might guess his work, September passed, and the German was at last able to be in the garden, but strangely feeble, still silent, and now asking for books. A great longing was on the young man to see those he loved; but October, which saw two thousand perish, came and went, and it was well on into the cooler November before the pest-house was closed and De Courval set free, happy in a vast and helpful experience, but utterly worn out and finding his last week's walks to the hospital far too great an exertion. What his body had lost for a time, his character had gained in an exercised charity for the sick, for the poor, and for the opinions of men on whom he had previously looked with small respect.

A better and wiser man on the 20th of November drove out with Schmidt to the home of the Wynnes at Merion, where Schmidt left him to the tender care of two women, who took despotic possession.

"At last!" cried the mother, and with tears most rare to her she held the worn and wasted figure in her arms. *"Mon Dieu!"* she cried, as for the first time she heard of what he had done. For only to her was confession of heroic conduct possible. "And I—I would have kept you from God's service. I am proud of you as never before." All the long afternoon they talked, and Mr. Wynne, just come back, and Darthea would have him to stay for a few days.

At bedtime, as they sat alone, Hugh said to his wife, "I was sure of that young man."

"Is he not a little like you?" asked Darthea.

"Nonsense!" he cried. "Do you think every good man like me? I grieve that I was absent."

"And I do not."

XV

THE weeks before Mrs. Swanwick's household returned to the city were for De Courval of the
happiest. He was gathering again his former
strength in the matchless weather of our late autumnal days. To take advantage of the re-awakened
commerce and to return to work was, as Wynne
urged, unwise for a month or more. The American
politics of that stormy time were to the young noble
of small moment, and the Terror, proclaimed in
France in September on Barras's motion, followed
by the queen's death, made all hope of change in
his own land for the present out of the question.

With the passing of the plague, Genêt and his staff
had come back; but for René to think of what he
eagerly desired was only to be reminded of his own
physical feebleness.

Meanwhile Genêt's insolent demands went on, and
the insulted cabinet was soon about to ask for his
recall, when, as Schmidt hoped, Carteaux would also
leave the country. The enthusiasm for the French
republic was at first in no wise lessened by Genêt's
conduct, although his threat to appeal to the country against Washington called out at last a storm
of indignation which no one of the minister's viola-
tions of law and of the courtesies of life had yet oc-
casioned. At first it was held to be an invention of

"black-hearted Anglican aristocrats," but when it came out in print, Genêt was at once alarmed at the mischief he had made. He had seriously injured his Republican allies,—in fact, nearly ruined the party, said Madison,—for at no time in our history was Washington more venerated. The Democratic leaders begged men not to blame the newly founded republic, "so gloriously cemented with the blood of aristocrats," for the language of its insane envoy. The Federalists would have been entirely pleased, save that neither England nor France was dealing wisely with our commerce, now ruined by the exactions of privateers and ships of war. Both parties wailed over this intolerable union of insult and injury; but always the President stood for peace, and, contemplating a treaty with England, was well aware how hopeless would be a contest on sea or land with the countries which, recklessly indifferent to international law, were ever tempting us to active measures of resentment. For De Courval the situation had, as it seemed, no personal interest. There has been some need, however, to remind my readers of events which were not without influence upon the fortunes of those with whom this story is concerned.

Schmidt was earnestly desirous that they should still remain in the country, and this for many reasons. De Courval and he would be the better for the cool autumn weather, and both were quickly gathering strength. Madame de Courval had rejoined them. The city was in mourning. Whole families had been swept away. There were houses which no one owned, unclaimed estates, and men missing of whose deaths there was no record, while every day or two the little family of refugees heard of those dead among the middle class or of poor acquaintances of whose fates they had hitherto learned nothing. Neither Schmidt nor René would talk of the horrors they had seen, and the subject was by tacit agreement altogether avoided.

Meanwhile they rode, walked, and fished in the Schuylkill. Schmidt went now and then to town on business, and soon, the fear of the plague quite at an end, party strife was resumed, and the game of politics began anew, while the city forgot the heroic few who had served it so well, and whom to-day history also has forgotten and no stone commemorates.

One afternoon Schmidt said to De Courval: "Come, let us have a longer walk!"

Margaret, eager to join them, would not ask it, and saw them go down the garden path toward the river. "Bring me some goldenrod, please," she called.

"Yes, with pleasure," cried De Courval at the gate, as he turned to look back, "if there be any left."

"Then asters," she called.

"A fair picture," said Schmidt, "the mother and daughter, the bud and the rose. You know the bluets folks hereabouts call the Quaker ladies,—oh, I spoke of this before,—pretty, but it sufficeth not. Some sweet vanity did contrive those Quaker garments."

It was in fact a fair picture. The girl stood, a

gray figure in soft Eastern stuffs brought home by our ships. One arm was about the mother's waist, and with the other she caught back the hair a playful breeze blew forward to caress the changeful roses of her cheek.

"I must get me a net, mother, such as the President wore one First Day at Christ Church."

"Thou must have been piously attending to thy prayers," returned Mrs. Swanwick, smiling.

"Oh, but how could I help seeing?"

"It is to keep the powder off his velvet coat, my dear. When thou art powdered again, we must have a net."

"Oh, mother!" It was still a sore subject.

"I should like to have seen thee, child."

"Oh, the naughty mother! I shall tell of thee. Ah, here is a pin in sight. Let me hide it, mother."

The woman seen from the gate near-by was some forty-five years old, her hair a trifle gray under the high cap, the face just now merry, the gown of fine, gray linen cut to have shown the neck but for the soft, silken shawl crossed on the bosom and secured behind by a tie at the waist. A pin held it in place where it crossed, and other pins on the shoulders. The gown had elbow sleeves, and she wore long, openwork thread glove mitts; for she was expecting Mistress Wynne and Josiah and was pleased in her own way to be at her best.

Schmidt, lingering, said: "It is the pins. They must needs be hid in the folds not to be seen. Ah, vanity has many disguises. It is only to be neat, thou seest, René, and not seem to be solicitous concerning appearances.'' Few things escaped the German.

They walked away, and as they went saw Mistress Gainor Wynne go by in her landau with Langstroth. ''That is queer to be seen—the damsel in her seventies and uncle bulldog Josiah. He had a permanent ground rent on her hill estate as lasting as time, a matter of some ten pounds. They have enjoyed to fight over it for years. But just now there is peace. Oh, she told me I was to hold my tongue. She drove to Gray Court, and what she did to the man I know not; but the rent is redeemed, and they are bent on mischief, the pair of them. As I was not to speak of it, I did not; but if you tell never shall I be forgiven.'' He threw his long bulk on the grass and laughed great laughter.

''But what is it?'' said René.

''*Guter Himmel,* man! the innocent pair are gone to persuade the Pearl and the sweet mother shell— she that made it—to take that lottery prize. I would I could see them.''

''But she will never, never do it,'' said René.

''No; for she has already done it.''

''What, truly? *Vraiment!*''

''Yes. Is there not a god of laughter to whom I may pray? I have used up my stock of it. When Cicero came in one day, he fetched a letter to Stephen Girard from my Pearl. She had won her mother to consent, and Girard arranged it all, and, lo! the great prize of money is gone long ago to help the poor and the sick. Now the ministers of Princeton College may pray in peace. Laugh, young man!''

But he did not. "And she thought to do that?''

"Yes; but as yet none know. They will soon, I fear.''

"But she took it, after all. What will Friends say?''

"She was read out of meeting long ago, disowned, and I do advise them to be careful how they talk to Madame of the girl. There is a not mild maternal tigress caged somewhere inside of the gentlewoman. 'Ware claws, if you are wise, Friend Waln!'' De Courval laughed, and they went on their way again, for a long time silent.

At Flat Rock, above the swiftly flowing Schuylkill, they sat down, and Schmidt, saying, "At last the pipe tastes good,'' began to talk in the strain of joyous excitement which for him the beautiful in nature always evoked, when for a time his language became singular. "Ah, René, it is worth while to cross the ocean to see King Autumn die thus gloriously. How peaceful is the time! They call this pause when regret doth make the great Reaper linger pitiful—they call it the Indian summer.''

"And we, the summer of St. Martin.''

"And we, in my homeland, have no name for it, or, rather, *Spätsommer;* but it is not as here. See how the loitering leaves, red and gold, rock in mid-air. A serene expectancy is in the lingering hours. It is as still as a dream of prayer that awaiteth answer. Listen, René, how the breeze is stirring the spruces, and hark, it is—ah, yes—the Angelus of evening.''

His contemplative ways were familiar, and just now suited the young man's mood. "A pretty carpet," he said, "and what a gay fleet of colors on the water!"

"Yes, yes. There is no sorrow for me in the autumn here, but after comes the winter." His mood of a sudden changed. "Let us talk of another world, René—the world of men. I want to ask of you a question; nay, many questions." His tone changed as he spoke. "I may embarrass you."

De Courval knew by this time that on one subject this might very well be the case. He said, however, "I do not know of anything, sir, which you may not freely ask me."

He was more at ease when Schmidt said, "We are in the strange position of being two men one of whom twice owes his life to the other."

"Ah, but you forget to consider what unending kindness I too owe—I, a stranger in a strange land; nor what your example, your society, have been to me."

"Thank you, René; I could gather more of good from you than you from me."

"Oh, sir!"

"Yes, yes; but all that I have said is but to lead up to the wide obligation to be frank with me."

"I shall be."

"When I was ill I babbled. I was sometimes half-conscious, and was as one man helplessly watching another on the rack telling about him things he had no mind to hear spoken."

"You wandered much, sir."

"Then did I speak of a woman?"

"Yes; and of courts and battles."

"Did I speak of—did I use my own name, my title? Of course you know that I am not Herr Schmidt."

"Yes; many have said that."

"You heard my name, my title?"

"Yes; I heard them."

For a minute there was silence. Then Schmidt said: "There are reasons why it must be a secret— perhaps for years or always. I am Graf von Ehrenstein; but I am more than that—much more and few even in Germany know me by that name. And I did say so?"

"Yes, sir."

"It must die in your memory, my son, as the priests say of what is heard in confession."

This statement, which made clear a good deal of what De Courval had heard in the German's delirium, was less singular to him than it would have seemed to-day. More than one mysterious titled person of importance came to the city under an assumed name, and went away leaving no one the wiser.

"It is well," continued Schmidt, "that you, who are become so dear to me, should know my story. I shall make it brief.

"Soon after my marriage, a man of such position as sometimes permits men to insult with impunity spoke of my wife so as to cause me to demand an apology. He fell back on his higher rank, and in my anger I struck him on the parade-ground at

Potsdam while he was reviewing his regiment. A lesser man than I would have lost his life for what I did. I was sent to the fortress of Spandau, where for two years I had the freedom of the fortress, but was rarely allowed to hear from my wife or to write. Books I did have, as I desired, and there I learned my queer English from my only English books, Shakespeare and the Bible.''

"Ah, now I understand," said De Courval; "but it is not Shakespeare you talk. Thanks to you, I know him."

"No, not quite; who could? After two years my father's interest obtained my freedom at the cost of my exile. My wife had died in giving birth to a still-born child. My father, an old man, provided me with small means, which I now do not need, nor longer accept, since he gave grudgingly, because I had done that which for him was almost unpardonable. I went to England and France, and then came hither to breathe a freer air, and, as you know, have prospered, and am, for America, rich. You cannot know the disgust in regard to arbitrary injustice with which I left my own land. I felt that to use a title in this country would be valueless, and subject me to comment and to inquiry I wished to avoid. You have earned the right to know my story, as I know yours. Mr. Alexander Hamilton and my business adviser, Mr. Justice Wilson, alone know my name and title, and, I may add, Mr. Gouverneur Morris. I shall say to the two former that you share this knowledge. They alone know why it is reasonable and, indeed, may have been prudent that, until

my return home, I remain unknown. It is needless
to go farther into the matter with you. This simple
life is to my taste, but I may some day have to go
back to my own land—I devoutly trust never. We
shall not again open a too painful subject.''

De Courval said, ''I have much to thank you for,
but for nothing as for this confidence.''

''Yet a word, René. For some men—some young
men—to know what now you know of me, would
disturb the intimacy of their relation. I would
have it continue simple. So let it be, my son. Come,
let us go. How still the woods are! There is here a
quiet that hath the quality of a gentle confessor who
hears and will never tell. Listen to that owl!''

As they drew near to the house the German said:
''*Ach,* I forgot. In December I suppose we must go
to the city. You are not as yet fit for steady work;
but if I can arrange it with Wynne, why not let me
use you? I have more to do here and in New York
than I like. Now, do not be foolish about it. There
are rents to gather in, journeys to make. Let
me give you five hundred *livres* a month. You will
have time to ride, read, and see the country. I
shall talk to Hugh Wynne about the matter.'' Thus,
after some discussion and some protest, it was arranged, the young man feeling himself in such relation to the older friend as made this adjustment
altogether agreeable and a glad release from a return
to the routine of the counting-house.

Too often the thought of Carteaux haunted him,
while he wondered how many in France were thus
attended. When in after years he saw go by men

15

who had been the lesser agents in the massacres, or those who had brought the innocent to the guillotine, he wondered at the impunity with which all save Marat had escaped the personal vengeance of those who mourned, and, mourning, did nothing. Even during the Terror, when death seemed for so many a thing to face smiling, the man who daily sent to the guillotine in Paris or the provinces uncounted thousands, walked the streets unguarded, and no one, vengeful, struck. In fact, the Terror seemed to paralyze even the will of the most reckless. Not so felt the young noble. He hungered for the hour of relief, let it bring what it might.

The simple and wholesome life of the Quaker household had done much to satisfy the vicomtesse, whose life had never of late years been one of great luxury, and as she slowly learned English, she came to recognize the qualities of refinement and self-sacrifice which, with unusual intelligence, made Mrs. Swanwick acceptably interesting. It became her custom at last to be more down-stairs, and to sit with her embroidery and talk while the knitting-needles clicked and the ball of wool hanging by its silver hoop from the Quaker lady's waist grew smaller. Sometimes they read aloud, French or English, or, with her rare smile, the vicomtesse would insist on sharing some small household duty. The serene atmosphere of the household, and what Schmidt called the gray religion of Friends, suited the Huguenot lady. As concerned her son, she was less at ease, and again, with some anxiety, she had spoken to him of his too evident pleasure in the society of

Margaret, feeling strongly that two such young and attractive people might fall easily into relations which could end only in disappointment for one or both. The girl's mother was no less disturbed, and Schmidt, as observant, but in no wise troubled, looked on and, seeing, smiled, somewhat dreading for René the inevitable result of a return to town and an encounter with his enemy.

Genêt had at last been recalled, in December, but, as Du Vallon told Schmidt, Carteaux was to hold his place as chargé d'affaires to Fauchet, the new minister, expected to arrive in February, 1794.

On the day following the revelations made by Schmidt, and just after breakfast, Margaret went out into the wood near by to gather autumn leaves. Seeing her disappear among the trees, De Courval presently followed her. Far in the woods he came upon her seated at the foot of a great tulip-tree. The basket at her side was full of club moss and gaily tinted toadstools. The red and yellow leaves of maple and oak, falling on her hair and her gray gown, made, as it seemed to him, a pleasant picture.

De Courval threw himself at her feet on the ground covered with autumn's lavished colors.

"We have nothing like this in France. How wonderful it is!"

"Yes," she said; "it is finer than ever I saw it." Then, not looking up, she added, after a pause, the hands he watched still busy: "Why didst thou not bring me any goldenrod last evening? I asked thee."

"I saw none."

"Ah, but there is still plenty, or at least there are asters. I think thou must have been gathering *pensées*, as thy mother calls them; pansies, we say."

"Yes, thoughts, thoughts," he returned with sudden gravity—"*pensées*."

"They must have been of my cousin Shippen or of Fanny Cadwalader, only she is always laughing." This young woman, who still lives in all her beauty on Stuart's canvas, was to end her life in England.

"Oh, neither, neither," he said gaily, "not I. Guess better."

"Then a quiet Quaker girl like—ah—like, perhaps, Deborah Wharton."

He shook his head.

"No? Thou art hard to please," she said. "Well, I shall give them up—thy *pensées*. They must have been freaked with jet; for how serious thou art!"

"What is that—freaked with jet?"

She laughed merrily. "Oh, what ignorance! That is Milton, Monsieur—'Lycidas.'" She was gently proud of superior learning.

"Ah, I must ask Mr. Schmidt of it. I have much to learn."

"I would," and her hands went on with their industry of selecting the more brilliantly colored leaves. "I have given thee something to think of. Tell me, now, what were the thoughts of jet in thy *pensées*—the dark thoughts."

"I cannot tell thee. Some day thou wilt know, and that may be too soon, too soon"; for he thought: "If I kill that man, what will they think of revenge, of the guilt of blood, these gentle Quaker people?"

Aloud he said: "You cannot think these thoughts of mine, and I am glad you cannot."

He was startled as she returned quickly, without looking up from her work: "How dost thou know what I think? It is something that will happen," and, the white hands moving with needless quickness among the gaily tinted leaves, she added: "I do not like change, or new things, or mysteries. Does Madame, thy mother, think to leave us? My mother would miss her."

"And you? Would not you a little?"

"Yes, of course; and so would friend Schmidt. There, my basket will hold no more. How pretty they are! But thou hast not answered me."

"We are not thinking of any such change."

"Well, so far that is good news. But I am still curious. Mr. Schmidt did once say the autumn has no answers. I think thou art like it." She rose as she spoke.

"Ah, but the spring may make reply in its time— in its time. Let me carry thy basket, Miss Margaret." She gave it to him with the woman's liking to be needlessly helped.

"I am very gay with red and gold," she cried, and shook the leaves from her hair and gown. "It is worse than the brocade and the sea-green petticoat my wicked cousins put on me." She could laugh at it now.

"But what would Friends say to the way the fine milliner, Nature, has decked thee, Mademoiselle? They would forgive thee, I think. Mr. Schmidt says the red and gold lie thick on the unnamed graves at Fourth and Mulberry streets, and no Quaker doth protest with a broom.''

''He speaks in a strange way sometimes. I often wonder where he learned it.''

''Why dost thou not ask him?''

''I should not dare. He might not like it.''

''But thou art, it seems, more free to question some other people.''

''Oh, but that is different; and, Monsieur,'' she said demurely, ''thou must not say thou and thee to me. Thy mother says it is not proper.''

He laughed. ''If I am thou for thee, were it not courteous to speak to thee in thy own tongue?''

She colored, remembering the lesson and her own shrewd guess at the lady's meaning, and how, as she was led to infer, to *tutoyer*, to say thou, inferred a certain degree of intimacy. ''It is not fitting here except among Friends.''

''And why not? In France we do it.''

''Yes, sometimes, I have so heard.'' But to explain further was far from her intention. ''It sounds foolish here, in people who are not of Friends. I said so—''

''But are we not friends?''

''I said Friends with a big F, Monsieur.''

''I make my apologies,''—he laughed with a formal bow,—''but one easily catches habits of talk.''

''Indeed, I am in earnest, and thou must mend thy habits. Friend Marguerite Swanwick desires to be excused of the Vicomte de Courval,'' and, smiling, she swept the courtesy of reply to his bow as the autumn leaves fell from the gathered skirts.

"As long as thou art thou, it will be hard to obey," he said, and she making no reply, they wandered homeward through level shafts of sunlight, while fluttering overhead on wings of red and gold, the cupids of the forest enjoyed the sport, and the young man murmured: "Thou and thee," dreaming of a walk with her in his own Normandy among the woodlands his boyhood knew.

"Thou art very silent," she said at last.

"No, I am talking; but not to you—of you, perhaps."

"Indeed," and she ceased to express further desire to be enlightened, and fell to asking questions about irregular French verbs.

Just before they reached the house, Margaret said: "I have often meant to ask thee to tell me what thou didst do in the city. Friend Schmidt said to mother that Stephen Girard could not say too much of thee. Tell me about it, please."

"No," he returned abruptly. "It is a thing to forget, not to talk about."

"How secretive thou art!" she said, pouting, "and thou wilt never, never speak of France." In an instant she knew she had been indiscreet as he returned:

"Nor ever shall. Certainly not now."

"Not—not even to me?"

"No." His mind was away in darker scenes.

Piqued and yet sorry, she returned, "Thou art as abrupt as Daniel Offley."

"Mademoiselle!"

"What have I said?"

"Daniel Offley is dead. I carried him into his own house to die, a brave man when few were brave."

"I have had my lesson," she said. There were tears in her eyes, a little break in her voice.

"And I, Pearl; and God was good to me."

"And to me," she sobbed; "I beg thy pardon— but I want to say—I must say that thou too wert brave, oh, as brave as any—for I know—I have heard."

"Oh, Pearl, you must not say that! I did as others did." She had heard him call her Pearl un- reproved, or had she not? He would set a guard on his tongue. "It is chilly. Let us go in," for they had stood at the gate as they talked.

It was their last walk, for soon the stripped trees and the ground were white with an early snowfall and the autumn days had gone, and on the first of December reluctantly they moved to the city.

XVI

LEAST of all did De Courval like the change to the busy life of the city. A growing love, which he knew would arouse every prejudice his mother held dear, occupied his mind when he was not busy with Schmidt's affairs or still indecisively on the outlook for his enemy. Genêt, dismissed, had gone to New York to live, where later he married De Witt Clinton's sister, being by no means willing to risk his head in France. His secretary, as De Courval soon heard, was traveling until the new minister arrived. Thus for the time left more at ease, De Courval fenced, rode, and talked with Schmidt.

December of this calamitous year went by and the rage of parties increased. Neither French nor English spared our commerce. The latter took the French islands, and over a hundred and thirty of our ships were seized as carriers of provisions and ruthlessly plundered, their crews impressed and many vessels left to rot, uncared for, at the wharves of San Domingo and Martinique. A nation without a navy, we were helpless. There was indeed enough wrong done by our old ally and by the mother-country to supply both parties in America with good reasons for war.

The whole land was in an uproar and despite the news of the Terror in France, the Jacobin clubs multiplied in many cities North and South, and broke out in the wildest acts of folly. In Charleston they pulled down the statue of the great statesman Pitt. The Democratic Club of that city asked to be affiliated with the Jacobin Club in Paris, while the city council voted to use no longer the absurd titles "Your Honour" and "Esquire."

Philadelphia was not behindhand in folly, but it took no official form. The astronomer Rittenhouse, head of the Republican Club, appeared one day at the widow's and showed Schmidt a copy of a letter addressed to the Vestry of Christ Church. He was full of it, and when, later, Mr. Jefferson appeared, to get the chocolate and the talk he dearly liked, Rittenhouse would have had him sign the appeal.

"This, Citizen," said the astronomer, "will interest and please you."

The Secretary read, with smiling comments: " 'To the Vestry of Christ Church: It is the wish of the respectable citizens that you cause to be removed the image of George the Second from the gable of Christ Church.' Why not?" said the Secretary, as he continued to read aloud: " 'These marks of infamy cause the church to be disliked.' " .

"Why not remove the church, too?" said Schmidt.

" 'T is of as little use," said Jefferson, and this Mrs. Swanwick did not like. She knew of his disbelief in all that she held dear.

"Thou wilt soon get no chocolate here," she said; for she feared no one and at times was outspoken.

"Madame, I shall go to meeting next First Day with the citizen Friends. My chocolate, please." He read on, aloud: " 'It has a tendency to keep the young and virtuous away.' That is you and I, Rittenhouse—'the young and virtuous.' '' But he did not sign, and returned this amazing document, remarking that his name was hardly needed.

"They have refused," said the astronomer, "actually refused, and it is to be removed by outraged citizens to-day, I hear. A little more chocolate, Citess, and a bun—please."

"Citess, indeed! When thou art hungry enough to speak the King's English," said Mrs. Swanwick, "thou shalt have thy chocolate; and if thy grammar be very good, there will be also a slice of sally-lunn."

The philosopher repented, and was fed, while Schmidt remarked on the immortality a cake may confer; but who Sally was, no one knew.

"You will be pleased to hear, Rittenhouse, that Dr. Priestly is come to the city," said the Secretary. "He is at the Harp and Crown on Third Street."

"I knew him in England," said Schmidt; "I will call on him to-day. A great chemist, René, and the finder of a new gas called oxygen."

When the star-gazer had gone away the Secretary, after some talk about the West Indian outrages, said: "I shall miss your chocolate, Madame, and my visits. You have heard, no doubt, of the cabinet changes."

"Some rumors, only," said Schmidt.

"I have resigned, and go back to my home and my farming. Mr. Hamilton will also fall out this January, and General Knox, no very great loss. Colonel Pickering takes his place."

"And who succeeds Hamilton, sir?"

"Oh, his satellite, Wolcott. The ex-Secretary means to pull the wires of his puppets. He loves power, as I do not. But the chocolate, alas!"

"And who, may I ask," said Mrs. Swanwick, "is to follow thee, Friend Jefferson?"

"Edmund Randolph, I believe. Bradford will have his place of Attorney-General. And now you have all my gossip, Madame, and I leave next week. I owe you many thanks for the pleasant hours in your home. Good-by, Mr. Schmidt; and Vicomte, may I ask to be remembered to your mother? I shall hope to be here now and then."

"We shall miss thee, Friend Jefferson," said the widow.

"I would not lessen thy regrets," he said. "Ah, one lingers." He kissed the hand he held, his bright hazel eyes aglow. "Good-by, Miss Margaret." And bowing low, he left them.

Schmidt looked after him, smiling.

"Now thou art of a mind to say naughty things of my friend," said Mrs. Swanwick. "I know thy ways."

"I was, but I meant only to criticize his politics. An intelligent old fox with golden eyes. He is of no mind to accept any share of the trouble this English treaty will make, and this excise tax."

René, who was beginning to understand the difficulties in a cabinet where there was seldom any unanimity of opinion, said: "There will be more peace for the President."

"And less helpful heads," said Schmidt. "Hamilton is a great loss, and Jefferson in some respects.

They go not well in double harness. Come, René, let us go and see the philosopher. I knew him well. Great men are rare sights. A Jacobin philosopher! But there are no politics in gases.''

The chemist was not at home, and hearing shouts and unusual noise on Second Street, they went through Church Alley to see what might be the cause. A few hundred men and boys of the lower class were gathered in front of Christ Church, watched by a smaller number of better-dressed persons, who hissed and shouted, but made no attempt to interfere when, apparently unmolested, a man, let down from the roof of the gable, tore off the leaden medallion of the second George [1] amid the cheering and mad party cries of the mob.

Schmidt said: "Now they can say their prayers in peace, these Jacobin Christians."

In one man's mind there was presently small thought of peace. When the crowd began to scatter, well pleased, Schmidt saw beside him De la Forêt, consul-general of France, and with him Carteaux. He threw his great bulk and broad shoulders between De Courval and the Frenchmen, saying: "Let us go. Come, René."

As he spoke, Carteaux, now again in the service, said: "We do it better in France, Citizen Consul. The Committee of Safety and Père Couthon would have shortened the preacher by a head. Oh, they are leaving. Have you seen the caricature of the aristocrat Washington on the guillotine? It has made the President swear, I am told."

[1] The leaden bas-relief has since been replaced.

As he spoke, De Courval's attention was caught by the French accents and something in the voice, and he turned to see the stranger who spoke thus insolently.

"Not here, René. No! no!" said Schmidt. He saw De Courval's face grow white as he had seen it once before.

"Let us go," said De la Forêt.

"A feeble mob of children," returned Carteaux.

As he spoke, De Courval struck him a single savage blow full in the face.

"A fight! a fight!" cried the crowd. "Give them room! A ring! a ring!"

There was no fight in the slighter man, who lay stunned and bleeding, while René struggled in Schmidt's strong arms, wild with rage.

"You have done enough," said the German; "come!" René, silent, himself again, stared at the fallen man.

"What is the meaning of this outrage?" said De la Forêt. "Your name, sir?"

"I am the Vicomte de Courval," said René, perfectly cool. "You will find me at Madame Swanwick's on Front Street."

Carteaux was sitting upon the sidewalk, still dazed and bleeding. The crowd looked on. "He hits hard," said one.

"Come, René," said the German, and they walked away, René still silent.

"I supposed it would come soon or late," said Schmidt. "We shall hear from them to-morrow."

"René struggled in Schmidt's arms, wild with rage"

"*Mon Dieu,* but I am glad. It is a weight off my mind. I shall kill him."

Schmidt was hardly as sure. Neither man spoke again until they reached home.

"Come to my room, René," said the German after supper. "I want to settle that ground-rent business."

As they sat down, he was struck with the young man's look of elation. "Oh, my pipe first. Where is it? Ah, here it is. What do you mean to do?"

"Do? I do not mean to let him think it was only the sudden anger of a French gentleman at a Jacobin's vile speech. He must know why I struck."

"That seems reasonable."

"But I shall not involve in my quarrel a man of your rank. I shall ask Du Vallon."

"Shall you, indeed! There is wanted here a friend and an older head. What rank had I when you saw me through my deadly duel with El Vomito? Now, no more of that." De Courval yielded.

"I shall write to him and explain my action. He may put it as he pleases to others."

"I see no better way. Write now, and let me see your letter."

René sat at the table and wrote while Schmidt smoked, a troubled and thoughtful man. "He is no match for .that fellow with the sword; and yet"— and he moved uneasily—"it will be, on the whole, better than the pistol." Any thought of adjustment or of escape from final resort to the duel he did not consider. It would have been out of the question for himself and, as he saw it, for any man of his beliefs and training.

"Here it is, sir," said René. The German gentleman laid down his long pipe and read:

SIR: I am desirous that you should not consider my action as the result of what you said in my hearing to M. de la Forêt. I am the Vicomte de Courval. In the massacre at Avignon on the twelfth of September, 1791, when my father was about to be released by Jourdan, your voice alone called for his condemnation. I saw him die, butchered before my eyes. This is why I struck you.

LOUIS RENÉ DE COURVAL.

"That will do," said Schmidt. "He shall have it to-night. You will have a week to spend with Du Vallon. No prudent man would meet you in the condition in which you left him."

"I suppose not. I can wait. I have waited long. I regret the delay chiefly because in this city everything is known and talked about, and before we can end the matter it will be heard of here."

"Very probably; but no one will speak of it before your mother, and you may be sure that these good people will ask no questions, and only wonder and not realize what must come out of it."

"Perhaps, perhaps." He was not so sure and wished to end it at once.

It had been in his power to have made the social life of the better republicans impossible for his father's murderer; but this might have driven Carteaux away and was not what he desired. The constant thought of his mother had kept him as undecided as Hamlet, but now a sudden burst of anger had opened the way to what he longed for. He was glad.

When, that night, Jean Carteaux sat up in bed and read by dim candlelight De Courval's letter, he, too, saw again the great hall at Avignon and recalled the blood madness. His Jacobin alliances had closed to him in Philadelphia the houses of the English party and the Federalists, and in the society he frequented, at the official dinners of the cabinet officers, he had never seen De Courval, nor, indeed, heard of him, or, if at all casually, without his title and as one of the many *émigrés* nobles with whom he had no social acquaintance. It was the resurrection of a ghost of revenge. He had helped to send to the guillotine others as innocent as Jean de Courval, and then, at last, not without fear of his own fate, had welcomed the appointment of commissioner to San Domingo and, on his return to France, had secured the place of secretary to Genêt's legation. The mockery of French sentiment in the clubs of the American cities, the cockades, and red bonnets, amused him. It recoiled from personal violence, and saying wild things, did nothing of serious moment. The good sense and the trust of the great mass of the people throughout the country in one man promised little of value to France, as Carteaux saw full well when the recall of Genêt was demanded. He felt the chill of failure in this cooler air, but was of no mind to return to his own country. He was intelligent, and, having some means, meant that his handsome face should secure for him an American

16

wife, and with her a comfortable dowry; for who knew of his obscure life in Paris? And now here was that affair at Avignon and the ruin of his plans. He would at least close one mouth and deny what it might have uttered. There was no other way, and for the rest —well, a French *émigré* had heard him speak rashly and had been brutal. The Jacobin clubs would believe and stand by him. De la Forêt must arrange the affair, and so far this insolent *ci-devant* could have said nothing else of moment.

De la Forêt called early the next day, and was referred to Schmidt as René left the room. No pacific settlement was discussed or even mentioned. The consul, well pleased, accepted the sword as the weapon, and this being Sunday, on Thursday at 7 A.M. there would be light enough, and they would cross on the ice to New Jersey; for this year one could sleigh from the city to the capes, and from New York to Cape Cod—or so it was said.

Meanwhile the Jacobin clubs rang with the insult to a French secretary, and soon it was the talk in the well-pleased coffee-houses and at the tables of the great merchants. René said nothing, refusing to gratify those who questioned him.

"A pity," said Mrs. Chew to Penn, the Governor, as men still called him. "And why was it? The young man is so serious and so quiet and, as I hear, religious. I have seen him often at Christ Church with his mother, or at Gloria Dei."

"One can get a good deal of religion into a blow," remarked Hamilton, "or history lies. The man in-

sulted him, I am told, and the vicomte struck him.''
Even Hamilton knew no more than this.

''Still, there are milder ways of calling a man to account,'' said young Thomas Cadwalader, while Hamilton smiled, remembering that savage duel in which John Cadwalader, the father, had punished the slanderer, General Conway.

''Will there be a fight?'' said Mrs. Byrd.

''Probably,'' said Penn, and opinion among the Federals was all for the vicomte. Meanwhile no one spoke of the matter at the widow's quiet house, where just now the severe winter made social visits rare.

As for De Courval he fenced daily with Du Vallon, who was taken into their confidence and shared Schmidt's increasing anxiety.

XVII

O N Thursday, at the dawn of a gloomy winter
morning, the two sleighs crossed over a mile of
ice to the Jersey shore. Large flakes of snow were
falling as Schmidt drove, the little doctor, Chovet,
beside him, De Courval silent on the back seat. Nothing could keep Chovet quiet very long. "I was in the
duel of Laurens, the President of the Congress. Oh,
it was to be on Christmas Day and near to Seven
Street. Mr. Penn—oh, not the fat governor but the
senator from Georgia—he slipped in the mud on
the way, and Laurens he help him with a hand, and
they make up all at once and no further go, and I
am disappoint.'' It was an endless chatter. "And
there was the Conway duel, too. Ah, that was good
business!''

Schmidt, out of patience, said at last, "If you talk
any more, I will throw you out of the sleigh.''

"Oh, *le diable!* and who then will heal these which
go to stick one the other? Ha! I ask of you that?''

"The danger will be so much the less,'' said
Schmidt. Chovet was silenced.

On the shore they met De la Forêt and Carteaux,
and presently found in the woods an open space
with little snow. The two men stripped to the shirt,
and were handed the dueling-swords, Schmidt whispering: "Be cool; no temper here. Wait to attack.''

"And now," said the consul, as the seconds fell back, "on guard, Messieurs!"

Instantly the two blades rang sharp notes of meeting steel as they crossed and clashed in the cold morning air. "He is lost!" murmured Schmidt. The slighter man attacked furiously, shifting his ground, at first imprudently sure of his foe. A prick in the chest warned him. Then there was a mad interchange of quick thrusts and more or less competent defense, when De Courval, staggering, let fall his rapier and dropped, while Carteaux, panting, stood still.

Schmidt knelt down. It was a deep chest wound and bled but little outwardly. De Courval, coughing up foamy blood, gasped, "It is over for a time— over." Chovet saw no more to do than to get his man home, and so strangely does associative memory play her tricks that Schmidt, as he rose in dismay, recalled the words of the dying *Mercutio*. Then, with apparent ease, he lifted René, and, carrying him to the sleigh, wrapped him in furs, and drove swiftly over the ice to the foot of the garden. "Fasten the horse, Doctor," he said, "and follow me." René smiled as the German carried him. "The second time of home-coming wounded. How strange! Don't be troubled, sir. I do not mean to die. Tell my mother yourself."

"If you die," murmured Schmidt, "he shall follow you. Do not speak, René."

He met Margaret on the porch. "What is it?" she cried, as he went by her with his burden. "What is the matter?"

"A duel. He is wounded. Call your mother."
Not waiting to say more, he went carefully up-
stairs, and with Chovet's help René was soon in his
bed. It was quietly done, Mrs. Swanwick, distressed,
but simply obeying directions, asked no questions
and Margaret, below-stairs, outwardly calm, her
Quaker training serving her well, was bidding
Nanny to cease crying and to get what was needed.

Once in bed, René said only, "My mother—tell
her, at once." She had heard at last the quick haste
of unwonted stir and met Schmidt at her chamber
door.

"May I come in?" he asked.

"Certainly, Monsieur. Something has happened
to René. Is he dead?"

"No; but, he is hurt—wounded."

"Then tell me the worst at once. I am not of
those to whom you must break ill news gently. Sit
down." He obeyed her.

"René has had a duel. He is badly wounded in
the lung. You cannot see him now. The doctor in-
sists on quiet."

"And who will stop me?" she said.

"I, Madame," and he stood between her and the
door. "Just now you can only do him harm. I beg
of you to wait—oh, patiently—for days, perhaps.
If he is worse, you shall know it at once."

For a moment she hesitated. "I will do as you
say. Who was the man?"

"Carteaux, Madame."

"Carteaux here! *Mon Dieu!* Does he live?"

"Yes. He was not hurt."

"And men say there is a God! Christ help me; what is it I have said? How came he here, this man?"

He told her the whole story, she listening with moveless, pale, ascetic face. Then she rose: "I am sorry I did not know of this beforehand. I should have prayed for my son that he might kill him. I thank you, Monsieur. I believe you love my René."

"As if he were my son, Madame."

Days went by, darkened with despair or brightened with faint hope. Alas! who has not known them? The days grew to weeks. There were no longer guests, only anxious inquirers and a pale, drooping young woman and two mothers variously troubled.

But if here there were watching friendship and love and service and a man to die to-day or tomorrow to live, in the darkened room were spirits twain ever whispering love or hate. Outside of the house where De Courval lay, the Jacobin clubs rejoiced and feasted Carteaux, who burned De Courval's note and held his tongue, while Fauchet complained of the insult to his secretary, and Mr. Randolph neither would nor could do anything.

The February of 1794 passed, and March and April, while Glentworth, Washington's physician, came, and afterward Dr. Rush, to Chovet's disgust. Meanwhile the young man lay in bed wasting away with grim doubts of phthisis in the doctors' minds until in May there was a gain, and, as once before, he was allowed a settle, and soon was in the air on the upper porch, and could see visitors.

Schmidt, more gaunt than ever, kissed the hand of the vicomtesse in his German fashion, as for the first time through all the long vigils they had shared with Mary Swanwick she thanked him for positive assurance of recovery.

"He is safe, you tell me. May the God who has spared my son remember you and bless you through all your days and in all your ways!"

He bent low. "I have my reward, Madame."

Some intuitive recognition of what was in his mind was perhaps naturally in the thought of both. She said, "Will it end here?"

Seeing before him a face which he could not read, he replied, "It is to be desired that it end here, or that some good fortune put the sea between these two."

"And can you, his friend, say that? Not if he is the son I bore. I trust not," and, turning away, she left him; while he looked after her and murmured: "There is more mother in me than in her," and going out to where René lay, he said gaily: "Out of prison at last, my boy. A grim jail is sickness."

"Ah, to hear the birds who are so free," said René. "Are they ever ill, I wonder?"

"Mr. Hamilton is below, René—just come from New York. He has been here twice."

"Then I shall hear of the world. You have starved me of news." There was little good to tell him. The duke, their cousin, had fled from France, and could write to madame only of the Terror and of deaths and ruin.

The Secretary came up fresh with the gaiety of a world in which he was still battling fiercely with the Republican party, glad of the absence of his rival, Jefferson, who saw no good in anything he did or said.

"You are very kind," said De Courval, "to spare me a little of your time, sir." Indeed he felt it. Hamilton sat down, smiling at the eagerness with which René questioned him.

"There is much to tell, Vicomte. The outrages on our commerce by the English have become unendurable, and how we are to escape war I do not see. An embargo has been proclaimed by the President; it is for thirty days, and will be extended to thirty more. We have many English ships in our ports. No one of them can leave."

"That ought to bring them to their senses," said René.

"It may," returned Hamilton.

"And what, sir, of the treaty with England?"

Hamilton smiled. "I was to have been sent, but there was too much opposition, and now, as I think, wisely, Chief-Justice Jay is to go to London."

"Ah, Mr. Hamilton, if there were but war with England,—and there is cause enough,—some of us poor exiles might find pleasant occupation."

The Secretary became grave. "I would do much, yield much, to escape war, Vicomte. No man of feeling who has ever seen war desires to see it again. If the memory of nations were as retentive as the memory of a man, there would be an end of wars."

"And yet, sir," said René, "I hardly see how you—how this people—endure what you so quietly accept."

"Yes, yes. No man more than Washington feels the additions of insult to injury. If to-day you could give him a dozen frigates, our answer to England would not be a request for a treaty which will merely secure peace, and give us that with contempt, and little more. (What it personally costs that proud gentleman, our President, to preserve his neutral attitude few men know.")

René was pleased and flattered by the thoughtful gravity of the statesman's talk.

"I see, sir," he said. "There will be no war."

"No; I think not. I sincerely hope not. But now I must go. My compliments to your mother; and I am glad to see you so well."

As he went out, he met Schmidt in the hall. "Ah, why did you not prevent this duel?" he said.

"No man could, sir. It is, I fear, a business to end only when one of them dies. It dates far back of the blow. Some day we will talk of it, but I do not like the outlook."

"Indeed." He went into the street thoughtful. In principle opposed to duels, he was to die in the prime of life a victim to the pistol of Burr.

The pleasant May weather and the open air brought back to De Courval health and the joys of life. The girl in the garden heard once more his bits of French song, and when June came with roses he was able to lie on the lower porch, swinging at ease in a hammock sent by Captain Biddle, and it seemed

as if the world were all kindness. As he lay, Schmidt
read to him, and he missed only Margaret, ordered
out to the country in the care of Aunt Gainor, while,
as he grew better, he had the strange joy of senses
freshened and keener than in health, as if he were
reborn to a new heritage of tastes and odors, the
priceless gift of wholesome convalescence.

He asked no questions concerning Carteaux or
what men said of the duel; but as Schmidt, musing,
saw him at times gentle, pleased, merry, or again
serious, he thought how all men have in them a brute
ancestor ready with a club. "Just now the devil is
asleep." He alone, and the mother, fore-looking,
knew; and so the time ran on, and every one wanted
him. The women came with flowers and strawberries, and made much of him, the gray mother not
ill-pleased.

In June he was up, allowed to walk out or to
lie in the boat while Schmidt caught white perch
or crabs and talked of the many lands he had seen.
Then at last, to René's joy, he might ride.

"Here," said Schmidt, "is a note from Mistress
Gainor. We are asked to dine and stay the night.
No, not you. You are not yet fit for dinners and gay
women. These doctors are cruel. There will be,
she writes, Mr. Jefferson, here for a week; Mr. Lang-
stroth, and a woman or two; and Wolcott of the
Treasury, 'if Hamilton will let him come,' she says."
For perhaps wisely the new official followed the ex-
Secretary's counsels, to the saving of much needless
thinking. "A queer party that!" said Schmidt.
"What new mischief are she and the ex-Quaker

Josiah devising?'' He would be there at three, he wrote, the groom having waited a reply.

"Have you any message for Miss Margaret, René?" he asked next day.

"Tell her that all that is left of me remembers her mother's kindness." And, laughing, he added: "That there is more of me every day."

"And is that all?"

"Yes; that is all. Is there any news?"

"None of moment. Oh, yes, I meant to tell you. The heathen imagine a vain thing—a fine republican mob collected in front of the Harp and Crown yesterday. There was a picture set up over the door in the war—a picture of the Queen of France. A painter was made to paint a ring of blood around the neck and daub the clothes with red. If there is a fool devil, he must grin at that."

"*Canaille!*" said René. "Poor queen! We of the religion did not love her; but to insult the dead! Ah, a week in Paris now, and these cowards would fly in fear."

"Yes; it is a feeble sham." And so he left René to his book and rode away with change of garments in his saddle-bags.

XVIII

MISS GAINOR being busy at her toilette, Schmidt was received at the Hill Farm by the black page, in red plush for contrast, and shown up to his room. He usually wore clothes of simple character and left the changing fashions to others. But this time he dressed as he did rarely, and came down with powdered hair, in maroon-colored velvet with enameled buttons, ruffles at the wrists, and the full lace neck-gear still known as a Steenkirk.

Miss Gainor envied him the gold buckles of the broidered garters and shoes, and made her best courtesy to the stately figure which bent low before her.

"They are late," she said. "Go and speak to Margaret in the garden." He found her alone under a great tulip-tree.

"*Ach!*" he cried, "you are looking better. You were pale." She rose with a glad welcome as he saw and wondered. "How fine we are, Pearl!"

"Are we not? But Aunt Gainor would have it. I must courtesy, I suppose."

The dress was a compromise. There were still the gray silks, the underskirt, open wider than common in front, a pale sea-green petticoat, and, alas! even powder—very becoming it seemed to the German gentleman. I am helpless to describe the prettiness of it. Aunt Gainor had an artist's eye, though she herself delighted in too gorgeous attire.

He gave Margaret the home news and his message from René, and no; she was not yet to come to town. It was too hot, and not very healthy this summer.

"Why did not the vicomte write?" she said with some hesitation. "That would have been nicer."

"*Ach, guter Himmel!* Young men do not write to young women."

"But among Friends we are more simple."

"*Ach,* Friends—and in this gown! Shall we be of two worlds? That might have its convenience."

"Thou art naughty, sir," she said, and they went in.

There was Colonel Lennox and his wife, whom Schmidt had not met, and Josiah. "You know Mrs. Byrd, Mr. Schmidt? Mrs. Eager Howard, may I present to you Mr. Schmidt?" This was the Miss Chew who won the heart of the victor of the Cowpens battle; and last came Jefferson, tall, meager, red-cheeked, and wearing no powder, a lean figure in black velvet, on a visit to the city.

"There were only two good noses," said Gainor next day to a woman with the nose of a pug dog—"mine and that man Schmidt's—Schmidt, with a nose like a hawk and a jaw most predacious."

For mischief she must call Mr. Jefferson "Excellency," for had he not been governor of his State?

He bowed, laughing. "Madame, I have no liking for titles. Not even those which you confer."

"Oh, but when you die, sir," cried Mrs. Howard,

"and you want to read your title clear to mansions in the skies?"

"I shall want none of them; and there are no mansions in the skies."

"And no skies, sir, I suppose," laughed Mrs. Byrd. "Poor Watts!"

"In your sense none," he returned. "How is De Courval?"

"Oh, better; much better."

"He seems to get himself talked about," said Mrs. Howard. "A fine young fellow, too."

"You should set your cap for him, Tacy," said Gainor to the blond beauty, Mrs. Lennox.

"It was set long ago for my Colonel," she cried.

"I am much honored," said her husband, bowing.

"She was Dr. Franklin's last love-affair," cried Gainor. "How is that, Tacy Lennox?"

"Fie, Madam! He was dying in those days, and, yes, I loved him. There are none like him nowadays."

"I never thought much of his nose," said Gainor, amid gay laughter; and they went to dinner, the Pearl quietly attentive, liking it well, and still better when Colonel Howard turned to chat with her and found her merry and shyly curious concerning the great war she was too young to remember well, and in regard to the men who fought and won. Josiah, next to Mrs. Lennox, contributed contradictions, and Pickering was silent, liking better the company of men.

At dusk, having had their Madeira, they rode away, leaving only Margaret and Schmidt. The

evening talk was quiet, and the girl, reluctant, was
sent to bed early.

"I have a pipe for you," said Gainor. "Come out
under the trees. How warm it is!"

"You had a queer party," said Schmidt, who
knew her well, and judged better than many her
true character.

"Yes; was it not? But the women were to your
liking, I am sure."

"Certainly; but why Josiah, and what mischief
are you two after?"

"I? Mischief, sir?"

"Yes; you do not like him. You never have him
here to dine if you can help it."

"No; but now I am trying to keep him out of
mischief, and to-day he invited himself to dine."

"Well!" said Schmidt, blowing great rings of
smoke.

"General Washington was here yesterday. His
horse cast a shoe, and he must needs pay me a
visit. Oh, he was honest about it. He looked
tired and aged. I shall grow old; but aged, sir,
never. He is deaf, too. I hope he may not live to
lose his mind. I thought of Johnson's lines about
Marlborough."

"I do not know them. What are they?"

"From Marlb'rough's eyes the streams of dotage flow,
  And Swift expires, a driv'ler and a show."

"Yes," said Schmidt thoughtfully—"yes; that is
the ending I most should fear."

"He is clear-headed enough to-day; but the men

around him think too much of their own interests, and he of his country alone.''

''It may be better with this new cabinet.''

''No; there will be less head.''

''And more heart, I hope,'' said Schmidt.

''I could cry when I think of that man's life.''

''Yes, it is sad enough; but suppose,'' said Schmidt, ''we return to Josiah.''

''Well, if you must have it, Josiah has one honest affection outside of a love-affair with Josiah—Margaret, of course.''

''Yes; and what more?''

''He thinks she should be married, and proposes to arrange the matter.''

The idea of Uncle Josiah as a matchmaker filled the German with comic delight. He broke into Gargantuan laughter. ''I should like to hear his plan of campaign.''

''Oh, dear Aunt Gainor,'' cried a voice from an upper window, ''what is the joke? Tell me, or I shall come down and find out.''

''Go to bed, minx!'' shouted Miss Gainor. ''Mr. Schmidt is going to be married, and I am to be bridesmaid. To bed with you!''

''Fie, for shame, Aunt! He will tell me to-morrow.'' The white figure disappeared from the window.

''Oh, Josiah is set on it—really set on it, and you know his possibilities of combining folly with obstinacy.''

''Yes, I know. And who is the happy man?''

''The Vicomte de Courval, please.''

17

Schmidt whistled low. "I beg your pardon, Mistress Gainor. Cannot you stop him? The fool! What does he propose to do?"

"I do not know. He has an odd admiration for De Courval, and that is strange, for he never contradicts him."

"The admiration of a coward for a brave man— I have known that more than once. He will do Heaven knows what, and end in making mischief enough."

"I have scared him a little. He talked, the idiot, about his will, and what he would or would not do. As if that would help, or as if the dear child cares or would care. I said I had money to spare at need. He will say nothing for a while. I do not mean to be interfered with. I told him so."

"Did you, indeed?"

"I did."

"Mistress Gainor, you had better keep your own hands off and let things alone. Josiah would be like an elephant in a rose garden."

"And I like—"

"A good, kindly woman about to make a sad mistake. You do not know the mother's deep-seated prejudices, nor yet of what trouble lies like a shadow on René's life. I should not dare to interfere."

"What is it?" she said, at once curious and anxious.

"Mistress Gainor, you are to be trusted, else you would go your way. Is not that so?"

"Yes; but I am reasonable and Margaret is dear to me. I like the vicomte and, as for his mother, she thinks me a kind, rough old woman; and for her nonsense about rank and blood, stuff! The girl's blood is as good as hers.''

"No doubt; but let it alone. And now I think you ought to hear his story and I mean to tell it.'' And sitting in the darkness, he told her of Avignon and Carteaux and the real meaning of the duel and how the matter would go on again some day, but how soon fate alone could determine. She listened, appalled at the tragic story which had come thus fatefully from a far-away land into the life of a quiet Quaker family.

"It is terrible and sad,'' she said. "And he has spoken to no one but you of this tragedy? It must be known to many.''

"The death, yes. Carteaux's share in it, no. He was an unknown young *avocat* at the time.''

"How reticent young De Courval must be! It is singular at his age.''

"He had no reason to talk of it; he is a man older than his years. He had in fact his own good reason for desiring not to drive this villain out of his reach. He is a very resolute person. If he loves this dear child, he will marry her, if a dozen mothers stand in the way.''

"There will be two. I see now why Mary Swanwick is always sending Margaret to me or to Darthea Wynne. I think the maid cares for him.''

"Ah, my dear Miss Gainor, if I could keep them apart for a year, I should like it. God knows where the end will be. Suppose this fellow were to kill him! That they will meet again is sadly sure, if I know De Courval.''

"You are right," she returned. "But if, Mr. Schmidt, this shadow did not lie across his path, would it please you? Would you who have done so much for him—would you wish it?"

"With all my heart. But let it rest here, and let time and fate have their way."

"I will," she said, rising. "It is cool. I must go in. It is a sad tangle, and those two mothers! I am sometimes glad that I never married and have no child. Good night. I fear that I shall dream of it."

"I shall have another pipe before I follow you. We are three old cupids," he added, laughing. "We had better go out of business."

"There is a good bit of cupidity about one of us, sir."

"A not uncommon quality," laughed Schmidt.

Pleased with her jest, she went away, saying, "Tom will take care of you."

To the well-concealed satisfaction of the vicomtesse, it was settled that Margaret's health required her to remain all summer at the Hill; but when June was over, De Courval was able to ride, and why not to Chestnut Hill? And although Gainor never left them alone, it was impossible to refuse permission for him to ride with them.

They explored the country far and wide with Aunt Gainor on her great stallion, a rash rider despite her years. Together they saw White Marsh and the historic lines of Valley Forge, and heard of Hugh Wynne's ride, and, by good luck, met General Wayne one day and were told the story of that dismal winter when snow was both foe and friend. Aunt Gainor rode in a riding-mask, and the Quaker bonnet was worn no longer, wherefore, the code of lovers' signals being ingeniously good, there needed no cupids old or young. The spring of love had come and the summer would follow in nature's course. Yet always René felt that until his dark debt was paid he could not speak.

Therefore, sometimes he refrained from turning his horse toward the Hill and went to see his mother, now again, to her pleasure, with Darthea, or else he rode with Schmidt through that bit of Holland on the Neck and saw sails over the dikes and the flour windmills turning in the breeze. Schmidt, too, kept him busy, and he visited Baltimore and New York, and fished or shot.

"You are well enough now. Let us fence again," said Schmidt, and once more he was made welcome by the *émigrés* late in the evening when no others came.

He would rarely touch the foils, but "*Mon Dieu,* Schmidt," said de Malerive, "he has with the pistol skill."

Du Vallon admitted it. But: "*Mon ami*, it is no weapon for gentlemen. The Jacobins like it. There is no tierce or quarte against a bullet."

"Do they practise with the pistol here?"

"No. Carteaux, thy lucky friend, ah, very good, —of the best with the foil,—but no shot." René smiled, and Schmidt understood.

"Can you hit that, René?" he said, taking from his pocket the ace of clubs, for playing-cards were often used as visiting-cards, the backs being white, and other material not always to be had.

René hit the edge of the ace with a ball, and then the center. The gay crowd applauded, and Du Vallon pleased to make a little jest in English, wished it were a Jacobin club, and, again merry, they liked the jest.

XIX

THE only man known to me who remembered Schmidt is said to have heard Alexander Hamilton remark that all the German lacked of being great was interest in the noble game of politics. It was true of Schmidt. The war of parties merely amused him, with their honest dread of a monarchy, their terror of a bonded debt, their disgust at the abominable imposition of a tax on freemen, and, above all, an excise tax on whisky. Jefferson, with keen intellect, was trying to keep the name Republican for the would-be Democrats, and while in office had rebuked Genêt and kept Fauchet in order, so that, save for the smaller side of him and the blinding mind fog of personal and party prejudice, he would have been still more valuable in the distracted cabinet he had left.

Schmidt looked on it all with tranquillity, and while he heard of the horrors of the Terror with regret for individual suffering, regarded that strange drama much as an historian looks back on the records of the past.

Seeing this and the man's interest in the people near to him, in flowers, nature, and books, his attitude of mind in regard to the vast world changes seemed singular to the more intense character of De Courval. It had for him, however, its value in the midst of the turmoil of a new nation and the temptations an immense prosperity offered to a people who were not as yet acclimated to the air of freedom.

In fact Schmidt's indifference, or rather the neutrality of a mind not readily biased, seemed to set him apart, and to enable him to see with sagacity the meaning and the probable results of what appeared to some in America like the beginning of a fatal evolution of ruin.

Their companionship had now the qualities of one of those rare and useful friendships between middle age and youth, seen now and then between a father and son, with similar tastes. They were much together, and by the use of business errands and social engagements the elder man did his share in so occupying De Courval as to limit his chances of seeing Margaret Swanwick; nor was she entirely or surely displeased. Her instincts as a woman made her aware of what might happen at any time. She knew, too, what would then be the attitude of the repellent Huguenot lady. Her pride of caste was recognized by Margaret with the distinctness of an equal but different pride, and with some resentment at an aloofness which, while it permitted the expression of gratitude, seemed to draw between Mrs. Swanwick and herself a line of impassable formality of intercourse.

One of the lesser accidents of social life was about to bring for De Courval unlooked-for changes and materially to affect his fortunes. He had seemed to Schmidt of late less troubled, a fact due to a decision which left him more at ease.

The summer of 1794 was over, and the city gay and amusing. He had seen Carteaux more than once, and seeing him, he had been but little disturbed. On an evening in September, Schmidt and he went as usual to the fencing-school. There were some new faces. Du Vallon said, "Here, Schmidt, is an old friend of mine, and Vicomte, let me present Monsieur Brillat-Savarin."

The new-comer greeted De Courval and his face expressed surprise as he bowed to the German. "I beg pardon," he said—"Monsieur Schmidt?"

"Yes, at your service."

He seemed puzzled. "It seems to me that we have met before—in Berne, I think."

"Berne. Berne," said Schmidt, coldly. "I was never in Berne."

"Ah, I beg pardon. I must be mistaken."

"Are you here for a long stay?"

"Only for a few days. I am wandering in a land of lost opportunities."

"Of what?" asked Schmidt.

"Oh, of the cook. Think of it, these angelic reed-birds, the divine terrapin, the duck they call canvas, the archangelic wild turkey, unappreciated, crudely cooked; the Madeira—ah, *mon dieu!* I would talk of them, and, behold, the men talk politics! I have eaten of that dish at home, and it gave me the colic of disgust."

"But the women?" said a young *émigré*.

"Ah, angels, angels. But can they make an ome-let? The divine Miss Morris would sing to me when I would speak seriously of my search for truffles.

Oh, she would sing the 'Yankee Dudda'[1] and I must hear the 'Lament of Major André.' Who was he?"

De Courval explained.

"It is the truffle I lament. Ah, to marry the truffle to the wild turkey."

The little group laughed. "Old gourmand," cried Du Vallon, "you are still the same."

"Gourmet," corrected Savarin. "Congratulate me. I have found here a cook—Marino, a master, French of course, from San Domingo. You will dine with me at four to-morrow; and you, Monsieur Schmidt, certainly you resemble—"

"Yes," broke in the German. "A likeness often remarked, not very flattering."

"Ah, pardon me. But my dinner—Du Vallon, you will come, and the vicomte, and you and you, and there will be Messieurs Bingham and Rawle and Mr. Meredith, and one Jacobin,—Monsieur Girard, —as I hear a lover of good diet—ah, he gave me the crab which is soft, the citizen crab. Monsieur Girard —I bless him. I have seen women, statesmen, kings, but the crab, ah! the crab 'which is soft.' "

All of them accepted, the *émigrés* gladly, being, alas! none too well fed.

"And now, adieu. I must go and meditate on my dinner."

The next day at four they met at Marino's, the new restaurant in Front Street then becoming fashionable.

"I have taken the liberty," said Bingham, "to send half a dozen of Madeira, 1745, and two de-

[1] He so writes it in his "Physiologie du goût."

canters of grape juice, what we call the white. The rest—well, of our best, all of it."

They sat down expectant. "The turkey I have not," said Savarin; "but the soup—ah, you will see —soup *a la reine*. Will Citizen Girard decline?"

The dinner went on with talk and laughter. Savarin talking broken English, or more volubly French.

"You are to have the crabs which are soft, Monsieur Girard, *en papillotte*, more becoming crabs than women, and at the close reed-birds. Had there been these in France, and the crab which is soft, and the terrapin, there would have been no Revolution. And the Madeira—perfect, perfect, a revelation. Your health, Mr. Bingham."

Bingham bowed over his glass, and regretted that canvasback ducks and terrapin were not yet in season. The *émigrés* used well this rare chance, and with talk of the wine and jest and story (anything but politics), the dinner went on gaily. Meanwhile Girard, beside De Courval, spoke of their sad experiences in the fever, and of what was going on in the murder-scourged West Indian Islands, and of the ruin of our commerce. Marino in his white cap and long apron stood behind the host, quietly appreciative of the praise given to his dinner.

Presently Savarin turned to him. "Who," he asked, "dressed this salad. It is a marvel, and quite new to me."

"I asked Monsieur de Beauvois to do me the honor."

"Indeed! Many thanks, De Beauvois," said the

host to a gentleman at the farther end of the table. "Your salad is past praise. Your health. You must teach me this dressing."

"A secret," laughed the guest, as he bowed over his glass, "and valuable."

"That is droll," said De Courval to Bingham.

"No; he comes to my house and to Willing's to dress salad for our dinners. Ten francs he gets, and lives on it, and saves money."

"Indeed! I am sorry for him," said René.

Then Mr. Bingham, being next to Girard, said to him: "At the State Department yesterday, Mr. Secretary Randolph asked me, knowing I was to see you to-day, if you knew of any French gentleman who could act as translating clerk. Of course he must know English."

"Why not my neighbor De Courval?" said the merchant. "But he is hardly of Mr. Randolph's politics."

"And what are they?" laughed Mr. Bingham. "Federal, I suppose; but as for De Courval, he is of no party. Besides, ever since Freneau left on account of the fever, the Secretaries are shy of any more clerks who will keep them in hot water with the President. For a poet he was a master of rancorous abuse."

"And who," said Girard, "have excelled the poets in malignancy? Having your permission, I will ask our young friend." And turning to René, he related what had passed between him and Mr. Bingham.

Somewhat surprised, René said: "I might like it, but I must consult Mr. Schmidt. I am far from having political opinions, or, if any, they are with the Federals. But that would be for the Secretary to decide upon. An exile, Mr. Girard, should have no political opinions unless he means to become a citizen, as I do not.''

''That seems reasonable,'' said Bingham, the senator for Pennsylvania, overhearing him. ''Your health, De Courval, I commend to you the white grape juice. And if the place please you, let it be a receipt in full for my early contribution of mud.'' And laughing, he told Girard the story.

''Indeed, sir, it was a very personal introduction,'' returned René.

''I should like well to have that young man myself,'' said Girard in an aside to Bingham. ''This is a poor bit of advancement you offer—all honor and little cash. I like the honor that attends to a draft.''

The senator laughed. ''Oh, Schmidt has, I believe, adopted De Courval or something like it. He will take the post for its interest. Do you know,'' he added, ''who this man Schmidt may be?''

''I—no; but all Europe is sending us mysterious people. By and by the kings and queens will come. But Schmidt is a man to trust, that I do know.''

''A good character,'' cried Schmidt. coming behind them. ''My thanks.''

''By George! It was lucky we did not abuse you,'' said Bingham.

''Oh, Madeira is a gentle critic, and a good dinner does fatten amiability. Come, René, we shall get on even terms of praise with them as we walk home.''

The party broke up, joyous at having dined well.

As they went homeward, Schmidt said: "Our host, René, is not a mere gourmet. He is a philosophic student of diet, living in general simply, and, I may add, a gentleman of courage and good sense, as he showed in France."

"It seems difficult, sir, to judge men. He seemed to me foolish."

"Yes; and one is apt to think not well of a man who talks much of what he eats. He recognized me, but at once accepted my obvious desire not to be known. He will be sure to keep my secret."

When having reached home, and it was not yet twilight—they sat down with their pipes, René laid before his friend this matter of the secretaryship.

Schmidt said: "My work is small just now, and the hours of the State Department would release you at three. You would be at the center of affairs, and learn much, and would find the Secretary pleasant. But, remember, the work may bring you into relations with Carteaux."

"I have thought of that; but my mother will like this work for me. The business she disliked."

"Then take it, if it is offered, as I am sure it will be." "He is very quiet about Carteaux," thought Schmidt. "Something will happen soon. I did say from the first that I would not desire to be inside of that Jacobin's skin."

The day after, a brief note called De Courval to the Department of State.

The modest building which then housed the Secretary and his affairs was a small dwelling-house on High Street, No. 379, as the old numbers ran.

No mark distinguished it as the vital center of a nation's foreign business. René had to ask a passer-by for the direction.

For a brief moment De Courval stood on the outer step before the open door. A black servant was asleep on a chair within the sanded entry.

The simplicity and poverty of a young nation, just of late having set up housekeeping, were plainly to be read in the office of the Department of State. Two or three persons went in or came out. ·

Beside the step an old black woman was selling peanuts. René's thoughts wandered for a moment from his Norman home to a clerk's place in the service of a new country.

"How very strange!"—he had said so to Schmidt, and now recalled his laughing reply: "We think we play the game of life, René, but the banker Fate always wins. His dice are loaded, his cards are marked." The German liked to puzzle him. "And yet," reflected De Courval, "I can go in or go home." He said to himself: "Surely I am free,— and, after all, how little it means for me! I am to translate letters." He roused the snoring negro, and asked, "Where can I find Mr. Randolph?" As the drowsy slave was assembling his wits, a notably pleasant voice behind René said: "I am Mr. Randolph, at your service. Have I not the pleasure to see the Vicomte de Courval?"

"Yes, I am he."

"Come into my office." René followed him, and they sat down to talk in the simply furnished front room.

The Secretary, then in young middle age, was a largely built man and portly, dark-eyed, with refined features and quick to express a certain conciliatory courtesy in his relations with others. He used gesture more freely than is common with men of our race, and both in voice and manner there was something which René felt to be engaging and attractive.

He liked him, and still more after a long talk in which the duties of the place were explained and his own indisposition to speak of his past life recognized with tactful courtesy.

Randolph said at last, "The office is yours if it please you to accept."

"I do so, sir, most gladly."

"Very good. I ought to say that Mr. Freneau had but two hundred and fifty dollars a year. It is all we can afford."

As René was still the helper of Schmidt, and well paid, he said it was enough. He added: "I am not of any party, sir. I have already said so, but I wish in regard to this to be definite."

"That is of no moment, or, in fact, a good thing. Your duties here pledge you to no party. I want a man of honor, and one with whom state secrets will be safe. Well, then, you take it? We seem to be agreed."

"Yes; and I am much honored by the offer."

"Then come here at ten to-morrow. There is much to do for a time."

Madame was pleased. This at least was not commerce. But now there was little leisure, and no time

for visits to the Hill, at which the two conspiring
cupids, out of business and anxious, smiled, doubtful
as to what cards Fate would hold in this game: and
thus time ran on.

The work was easy and interesting. The Secretary, courteous and well-pleased, in that simpler
day, came in person to the little room assigned to
De Courval and brought documents and letters
which opened a wide world to a curious young man,
who would stay at need until midnight, and who
soon welcomed duties far beyond mere French let-
ter-writing.

By and by there were visits with papers to Mr.
Wolcott at the Treasury Department, No. 119 Chestnut Street, and at last to Fauchet at Oeller's Hotel.

He was received with formal civility by Le Blanc,
a secretary, and presently Carteaux, entering,
bowed. De Courval did not return the salute, and,
finishing his business without haste, went out.

He felt the strain of self-control the situation had
demanded, but, as he wiped the sweat from his forehead, knew with satisfaction that the stern trials of
the years had won for him the priceless power to be
or to seem to be what he was not.

"The *ci-devant* has had his little lesson," said Le
Blanc. "It will be long before he insults another
good Jacobin."

Carteaux, more intelligent, read otherwise the set
jaw and grave face of the Huguenot gentleman. He
would be on his guard.

The news of the death of Robespierre, in July,
1794, had unsettled Fauchet, and his subordinate,

18

sharing his uneasiness, meant to return to France if
the minister were recalled and the Terror at an end,
or to find a home in New York, and perhaps, like
Genêt, a wife. For the time he dismissed De Courval from his mind, although not altogether self-as-
sured concerning the future.

XX

"AND now about this matter of dress," said Miss Gainor.

"Thou art very good, Godmother, to come and consult me," said Mrs. Swanwick. "I have given it some thought, and I do not see the wisdom of going half-way. The good preacher White has been talking to Margaret, and I see no reason why, if I changed, she also should not be free to do as seems best to her."

"You are very moderate, Mary, as you always are."

"I try to be; but I wish that it were altogether a matter of conscience with Margaret. It is not. Friends were concerned in regard to that sad duel and considered me unwise to keep in my house one guilty of the wickedness of desiring to shed another's blood, Margaret happened to be with me when Friend Howell opened the subject, and thou knowest how gentle he is."

"Yes. I know. What happened, Mary?"

"He said that Friends were advised that to keep in my house a young man guilty of bloodshed was, as it did appear to them, undesirable. Then, to my surprise, Margaret said: 'But he was not guilty of bloodshed.' Friend Howell was rather amazed, as thou canst imagine; but before he could say a word more, Miss Impudence jumped up, very red in the face, and said: 'Why not talk to him instead of troubling mother? I wish he had shed more blood than his own.' ''

"Ah, the dear minx! I should like to have been there," said Gainor.

"He was very near to anger—as near as is possible for Arthur Howell; but out goes my young woman in a fine rage about what was none of her business."

"And what did you say?"

"What could I say except to excuse her, because the young man was our friend, and at last that I was very sorry not to do as they would have had me to do, but would hear no more. He was ill-pleased, I do assure thee."

"Were you very sorry, Mary Swanwick?"

"I was not, although I could not approve the young man nor my child's impertinence."

"Well, my dear, I should have said worse things. I may have my way in the matter of dress, I suppose?"

"Yes," said the widow, resigned. "An Episcopalian in Friends' dress seems to me to lack propriety; but as to thy desire to buy her fine garments, there are trunks in my garret full of the world's things I gave up long ago."

"Were you sorry?"

"A little, Aunt Gainor. Wilt thou see them?"

"Oh, yes, Margaret," she called, "come in."

She entered with De Courval, at home by good luck. "And may I come, too?" he asked.

"Why not?" said Mistress Gainor, and they went up-stairs, where Nanny, delighted, opened the trunks and took out one by one the garments of a gayer world, long laid away unused. The maid in her red bandana head-gear was delighted, having, like her race, great pleasure in bright colors.

The widow, standing apart, looked on, with memories which kept her silent, as the faint smell of lavender, which seems to me always to have an ancient fragrance, hung about the garments of her youth.

Margaret watched her mother with quick sense of this being for her something like the turning back to a record of a girlhood like her own. De Courval had eyes for the Pearl alone. Gainor Wynne, undisturbed by sentimental reflections, enjoyed the little business.

"Goodness, my dear, what brocade!" cried Miss Wynne. "How fine you were, Mary! And a white satin, with lace and silver gimp."

"It was my mother's wedding-gown," said the widow.

"And for day wear this lutestring will fit you to a hair, Margaret; but the sleeves must be loose. And lace—what is it?" She held up a filmy fabric.

"I think I could tell." And there, a little curious, having heard her son's voice, was the vicomtesse, interested, and for her mildly excited, to René's surprise.

Miss Gainor greeted her in French I dare not venture upon, and this common interest in clothes seemed somehow to have the effect of suddenly bringing all these women into an intimacy of the minute, while the one man stood by, with the unending wonder of the ignorant male, now, as it were, behind the scenes. He fell back and the women left him unnoticed.

"What is it, Madame?" asked Margaret.

"Oh, French point, child, and very beautiful."

"And this other must be—"

"It is new to me," cried Miss Wynne.

"Permit me," said the vicomtesse. "Venetian point, I think—quite priceless, Margaret, a wonder." She threw the fairy tissue about Pearl's head, smiling as she considered the effect.

"Is this my mother?" thought her son, with increase of wonder. He had seen her only with restricted means, and knew little of the more luxurious days and tastes of her youth.

"Does you remember this, missus?" said Nanny.

"A doll," cried Gainor, "and in Quaker dress! It will do for your children, Margaret."

"No, it is not a child's doll," said Mrs. Swanwick. "Friends in London sent it to Marie Wynne, Hugh's mother, for a pattern of the last Quaker fashions in London—a way they had. I had quite forgotten it."

"And very pretty, quite charming," said the vicomtesse.

"And stays, my dear, and a modesty fence," cried Miss Wynne, holding them up. "You will have to fatten, Pearl."

Upon this the young man considered it as well to retire. He went down-stairs unmissed, thinking of the agreeable intimacy of stays with the fair figure he left bending over the trunk, a mass of black lace in her hand.

"She threw the fairy tissue about Pearl's head, smiling as
she considered the effect"

"Spanish, my dear," said Madame, with animation; "quite a wonder. Oh, rare, very rare. Not quite fit for a young woman—a head veil."

"Are they all mine, Mother?" cried Margaret.

"Yes, my child."

"Then, Madame," she said, with rising color and engaging frankness, "may I not have the honor to offer thee the lace?"

"Why not?" said Gainor, pleased at the pretty way of the girl.

"Oh, quite impossible, child," said the vicomtesse. "It is quite too valuable."

"Please!" said Pearl. "It would so become thee."

"I really cannot."

"Thy roquelaure," laughed Mrs. Swanwick, "was —well—I did remonstrate. Why may not we too have the pleasure of extravagance?"

"I am conquered," said Madame, a trace of color in her wan cheeks as Mrs. Swanwick set the lace veil on her head, saying: "We are obliged, Madame. And where is the vicomte? He should see thee."

"Gone," said Miss Gainor; "and just as well, too," for now Nanny was holding up a variety of lavender-scented delicacies of raiment, fine linens, and openwork silk stockings.

René, still laughing, met Schmidt in the hall.

"You were merry up-stairs."

"Indeed we were." And he gaily described his mother's unwonted mood; but of the sacred future of the stays he said no word.

"And so our gray moth has become a butterfly. I

think Mother Eve would not have abided long without a milliner. I should like to have been of the party up-stairs."

"You would have been much enlightened," said Miss Wynne on the stair. "I shall send for the boxes, Mary." And with this she went away with Margaret, as the doctor had declared was still needful.

"Why are you. smiling, Aunt?" said Margaret.

"Oh, nothing." Then to herself she said: "I think that if René de Courval had heard her talk to Arthur Howell, he would have been greatly enlightened. Her mother must have understood; or else she is more of a fool than I take her to be."

"And thou wilt not tell me?" asked the Pearl.

"Never," said Gainor, laughing—"never."

Meanwhile there was trouble in the western counties of Pennsylvania over the excise tax on whisky, and more work than French translations for an able and interested young clerk, whom his mother spoke of as a secretary to the minister.

"It is the first strain upon the new Constitution," said Schmidt; "but there is a man with bones to his back, this President." And by November the militia had put down the riots, and the first grave trial of the central government was well over; so that the President was free at last to turn to the question of the treaty with England, already signed in London.

Then once more the clamor of party strife broke out. Had not Jay kissed the hand of the queen? "He had prostrated at the feet of royalty the sovereignty of the people."

Fauchet was busy fostering opposition long before the treaty came back for decision by the Senate.
The foreign office was busy, and Randolph ill
pleased with the supposed terms of the coming document.

To deal with the causes of opposition to the treaty
in and out of the cabinet far into 1795 concerns this
story but indirectly. No one was altogether satisfied,
and least of all Fauchet, who at every opportunity
was sending despatches home by any French war-
ship seeking refuge in our ports.

A little before noon, on the 29th of November, of
this year, 1794, a date De Courval was never to forget, he was taking the time for his watch from the
clock on the western wall of the State House. As he
stood, he saw Dr. Chovet stop his chaise.

"Bonjour, citizen,'' cried the doctor. ''Your too
intimate friend, Monsieur Carteaux, is off for
France. He will trouble you no more.'' As usual,
the doctor, safe in his chaise, was as impertinent as
he dared to be.

Too disturbed to notice anything but this startling
information in regard to his enemy, De Courval
said: ''Who told you that? It cannot be true. He
was at the State Department yesterday, and we were
to meet this afternoon over the affair of a British
ship captured by a French privateer.''

''Oh, I met him on Fifth Street on horseback just
now—a little while ago.''

''Well, what then?''

'' 'I am for New York,' he said. I asked: 'How
can I send letters to France?' He said: 'I cannot

wait for them. I am in a hurry. I must catch that corvette, the *Jean Bart,* in New York.' Then I cried after him: 'Are you for France?' And he: 'Do you not wish you, too, were going? Adieu. Wish me *bon voyage.*' "

"Was he really going? We would have heard of it."

"*Le diable,* I think so; but he nas a mocking tongue. I think he goes. My congratulations that you are rid of him. Adieu!"

"Insolent!" muttered De Courval. Was it only insolence, or was it true that his enemy was about to escape him? The thought that he could not leave it in doubt put an instant end to his indecisions.

"I shall not risk it," he said, and there was no time to be lost. His mother, Margaret, the possible remonstrance from Schmidt, each in turn had the thought of a moment and then were dismissed in turn as he hurried homeward. Again he saw Avignon and Carteaux' dark face, and heard the echoing memory of his father's death-cry, "Yvonne! Yvonne!" He must tell Schmidt if he were in; if not, so much the better, and he would go alone. He gave no thought to the unwisdom of such a course. His whole mind was on one purpose, and the need to give it swift and definite fulfilment.

He was not sorry that Schmidt was not at home. He sat down and wrote to him that Carteaux was on his way to embark for France and that he meant to overtake him. Would Schmidt explain to his mother his absence on business? Then he took Schmidt's pistols from their place over the mantel, loaded and

primed them, and put half a dozen bullets and a
small powder-horn in his pocket. To carry the pistols, he took Schmidt's saddle-holsters. What next?
He wrote a note to the Secretary that he was called
out of town on business, but would return next day,
and would Schmidt send it as directed. He felt sure
that he would return. As he stood at the door of
Schmidt's room, Mrs. Swanwick said from the foot
of the stairs: "The dinner is ready."

"Then it must wait for me until to-morrow. I
have to ride on a business matter to Bristol."

"Thou hadst better bide for thy meal."

"No, I cannot." As Mrs. Swanwick passed into
the dining-room, Margaret came from the withdrawing-room, and stood in the doorway opposite to him, a
china bowl of the late autumnal flowers in her hands.
Seeing him cloaked and booted to ride, she said:

"Wilt thou not stay to dine? I heard thee tell
mother thou wouldst not."

"No; I have a matter on hand which requires
haste."

She had learned to read his face.

"It must be a pleasant errand," she said. "I
wish thee success." Thinking as he stood how some
ancestor going to war would have asked for a glove,
a tress of hair, to carry on his helmet, he said: "Give
me a flower for luck."

"No; they are faded."

"Ah, I shall think your wish a rose—a rose that
will not fade."

She colored a little and went by him, saying nothing, lest she might say too much.

"Good-by!" he added, and went out the hall door, and made haste to reach the stables of the Bull and Bear, where Schmidt kept the horses De Courval was free to use. He was about to do a rash and, as men would see it, a foolish thing. He laughed as he mounted. He knew that now he had no more power to stop or hesitate than the stone which has left the sling.

He had made the journey to New York more than once, and as he rode north up the rode to Bristol in a heavy downfall of rain he reflected that Carteaux would cross the Delaware by the ferry at that town, or farther on at Trenton.

If the doctor had been correct as to the time; Carteaux had started at least an hour and a half before him.

It was still raining heavily as he rode out of the city, and as the gray storm-clouds would shorten the daylight, he pushed on at speed, sure of overtaking his enemy and intently on guard. He stayed a moment beside the road to note the distance, as read on a mile-stone, and knew he had come seven miles. That would answer. He smiled as he saw on the stone the three balls of the Penn arms, popularly known as the three apple dumplings. A moment later his horse picked up a pebble. It took him some minutes to get it out, the animal being restless. Glancing at his watch, he rode on again, annoyed at even so small a loss of time.

When, being about three miles from Bristol town, and looking ahead over a straight line of road, he suddenly pulled up and turned into the shelter of a wood. Some two hundred yards away were two or three houses. A man stood at the roadside. It was Carteaux. René heard the clink of a hammer on the anvil.

To be sure of his man, he fastened his horse and moved nearer with care, keeping within the edge of the wood. Yes, it was Carteaux. The doctor had not lied. If the secretary were going to France, or only on some errand to New York, was now to De Courval of small moment. His horse must have cast a shoe. As Carteaux rode away from the forge. De Courval mounted, and rode on more rapidly.

Within two miles of Bristol, as he remembered, the road turned at a sharp angle toward the river. A half mile away was an inn where the coaches for New York changed horses. It was now five o'clock, and nearing the dusk of a November day. The rain was over, the sky darkening, the air chilly, the leaves were fluttering slowly down, and a wild gale was roaring in the great forest which bounded the road. He thought of the gentler angelus of another evening, and, strange as it may seem, bowed his head, and like many a Huguenot noble of his mother's race, prayed God that his enemy should be delivered into his hands. Then he stopped his horse and for the first time recognized that it had been raining heavily and that it were well to renew the priming of his pistols. He attended to this with care, and then rode quickly around the turn of the road, and came upon Carteaux walking his horse.

"Stop, Monsieur!" he called, and in an instant he was beside him.

Carteaux turned at the call, and, puzzled for a moment, said: "What is it?"—and then at once knew the man at his side.

He was himself unarmed, and for a moment alarmed as he saw De Courval's hand on the pistol in his holster. He called out, "Do you mean to murder me?"

"Not I. You will dismount, and will take one of my pistols—either; they are loaded. You will walk to that stump, turn, and yourself give the word, an advantage, as you may perceive."

"And if I refuse?"

"In that case I shall kill you with no more mercy than you showed my father. You have your choice. Decide, and that quickly."

Having dismounted as he spoke, he stood with a grip on Carteaux' bridle, a pistol in hand, and looking up at the face of his enemy. Carteaux hesitated a moment, with a glance up and down the lonely highway.

"Monsieur," said De Courval, "I am not here to wait on your decision. I purpose to give you the chance I should give a gentleman; but take care—at the least sign of treachery I shall kill you."

Carteaux looked down at the stern face of the Huguenot and knew that he had no choice.

"I accept," he said, and dismounted. De Courval struck the horses lightly, and having seen them turn out of the road, faced Carteaux, a pistol in each hand.

"I have just now renewed the primings," he said. As he spoke, he held out the weapons. For an instant the Jacobin hesitated, and then said quickly:

"I take the right-hand pistol."

"When you are at the stump, look at the priming," said De Courval, intently on guard. "Now, Monsieur, walk to the stump beside the road. It is about twelve paces. You see it?"

"Yes, I see it."

"Very good. At the stump, cock your pistol, turn, and give the word, 'Fire!' Reserve your shot or fire at the word—an advantage, as you perceive."

The Jacobin turned and moved away, followed by the eye of a man distrustfully on the watch.

René stood still, not yet cocking his weapon. Carteaux walked away. When he had gone not over half the distance René heard the click of a cocked pistol and at the instant Carteaux, turning, fired.

René threw himself to right and felt a sharp twinge of pain where the ball grazed the skin of his left shoulder. "Dog of a Jacobin!" he cried, and as Carteaux extended his pistol hand in instinctive protest, De Courval fired. The man's pistol fell, and with a cry of pain he reeled, and, as the smoke blew away, was seen to pitch forward on his face.

At the moment of the shot, and while René stood still, quickly reloading, he heard behind him a wild gallop, and, turning, saw Schmidt breathless at his side, and in an instant out of the saddle. "*Lieber Himmel!*" cried the German, "have you killed him?"

"I do not know; but if he is not dead. I shall kill him; not even you can stop me."

"*Ach!* but I will, if I have to hold you." As he spoke he set himself between René and the prostrate man. "I will not let you commit murder. Give me that pistol."

For a moment René stared at his friend. Then a quick remembrance of all this man had been to him, all he had done for him, rose in his mind.

"Have your way, sir!" he cried, throwing down his weapon; "but I will never forgive you, never!"

"*Ach!* that is better," said Schmidt. "To-morrow you will forgive and thank me. Let us look at the rascal."

Together they moved forward, and while De Courval stood by in silence, Schmidt, kneeling beside Carteaux, turned over his insensible body.

"He is not dead," he said, looking up at René.

"I am sorry. Your coming disturbed my aim. I am sorry he is alive."

"And I am not; but not much, *der Teufel!* The ball has torn his arm, and is in the shoulder. If he does live, he is for life a maimed man. This is vengeance worse than death." As he spoke, he ripped open Carteaux' sleeve. "*Saprement!* how the beast bleeds! He will fence no more." The man lay silent and senseless as the German drew from Carteaux' pocket a handkerchief and tied it around his arm. "There is no big vessel hurt. *Ach, der, Teufel!* What errand was he about?" A packet of paper had fallen out with the removal of the handkerchief. "It is addressed to him. We must know. I shall open it."

"Oh, surely not!" said René.

Schmidt laughed. "You would murder a man, but respect his letters."

"Yes, I should."

"My conscience is at ease. This is war." As he spoke, he tore open the envelop. Then he whistled low. "Here is a devil of a business, René!"

"What is it, sir?"

"A despatch from Fauchet to the minister of Foreign Affairs in Paris. Here is trouble, indeed. You waylay and half-kill the secretary of an envoy—you, a clerk of the State Department—"

"*Mon Dieu!* Must he always bring me disaster?" cried René. He saw with utter dismay the far-reaching consequences of his rash act.

"It is to the care of the captain of the *Jean Bart*, New York Harbor. The Jacobin party will have a fine cry. The State Department will have sent a man to rob a bearer of despatches. Who will know or believe it was a private quarrel?"

"How could I know his errand?"

"That will not save you. Your debt is paid with interest, but at bitter cost. And what now to do?" He stood in the road, silent for a moment, deep in thought. "If he dies, it must all be told."

"I should tell it myself. I do not care."

"But I very much care. If he lives, he will say you set upon him, an unarmed man, and stole his despatches."

"Then leave them."

"That were as bad. I saw his treachery; but who will believe me? I must stay by him, and see what I can do."

Meanwhile the man lay speechless. René looked down at him and then at Schmidt. He, too, was

19

thinking. In a moment he said: "This at least is
clear. I am bound in honor to go on this hound's
errand, and to see that these papers reach the *Jean
Bart.*"

"You are right," said Schmidt; "entirely right.
But you must not be seen here. Find your way
through the woods, and when it is dark—in an hour
it will be night—ride through Bristol to Trenton,
cross the river there at the ferry. No one will be
out of doors in Trenton or Bristol on a night like
this. Listen to the wind! Now go. When you are
in New York, see Mr. Nicholas Gouverneur in Beaver
Street. At need, tell him the whole story; but not
if you can help it. Here is money, but not enough.
He will provide what you require. Come back
through the Jerseys, and cross at Camden. I shall
secure help here, go to town, get a doctor, and return. I must talk to this man if he lives, else he will
lie about you."

"You will excuse me to the Secretary?"

"Yes; yes, of course. Now go. These people at
the inn must not see you."

He watched him ride away into the wood. "It is
a sorry business," he said as he knelt down to give
the fallen man brandy from the flask he found in his
saddle-bag.

Within an hour Carteaux, still insensible, was at
Bisanet's Inn, a neighboring doctor found, and that
good Samaritan Schmidt, after a fine tale of highwaymen, was in the saddle and away to town, leaving Carteaux delirious.

He went at once to the house of Chovet and found

him at home. It was essential to have some one who could talk French.

"At your service," said the doctor.

"Why the devil did you send De Courval after Carteaux this morning?"

"I never meant to."

"But you did. You have made no end of mischief. Now listen. I need you because you speak French. Can you hold your tongue, if to hold it means money? Oh, a good deal. If you breathe a word of what you hear or see, I will half-kill you."

"Oh, Monsieur, I am the soul of honor."

"Indeed. Why, then, does it trouble you? Owing to your damned mischief-making, De Courval has shot Carteaux. You are to go to the inn, Bisanet's, near Bristol, to-night, and as often afterward as is needed. I shall pay, and generously, if he does not—but, remember, no one is to know. A highwayman shot him. Do you understand? I found him on the road, wounded."

"Yes; but it is late."

"You go at once."

"I go, Monsieur."

Then Schmidt went home, and ingeniously accounted to Madame, and in a note to Randolph, for René's absence in New York.

As he sat alone that night he again carefully considered the matter. Yes, if Carteaux died not having spoken, the story would have to be told. The despatch would never be heard of, or if its singular fortune in going on its way were ever known and discussed, that was far in the future, and Schmidt had a strong belief in many things happening or not happening.

And if, too, despite his presumed power to close Carteaux' lips, the injured man should sooner or later charge René with his wound and the theft of the despatch, Schmidt, too, would have a story to tell.

Finally—and this troubled his decisions—suppose that at once he frankly told Fauchet and the Secretary of State what had happened. Would he be believed by Fauchet in the face of what Carteaux would say, or would René be believed or that he had honorably gone on his enemy's errand? The *Jean Bart* would have sailed. Months must pass before the news of the reception of the despatch could in the ordinary state of things be heard of, and now the sea swarmed with British cruisers, and the French frigates were sadly unsafe. To-morrow he must see Carteaux, and at once let Fauchet learn the condition of his secretary. He returned to his trust in the many things that may happen, and, lighting a pipe, fell upon his favorite Montaigne.

He might have been less at ease could he have dreamed what mischief that despatch was about to make or what more remote trouble it was to create for the harassed President and his cabinet.

XXI

AT noon next day a tired rider left his horse at an inn in Perth Amboy and boarded the sloop which was to take him to New York, if tide and wind served. Both at this time were less good to him than usual, and he drifted the rest of the afternoon and all night on the bay.

At length, set ashore on the Battery, he was presently with a merchant, in those days of leisurely ventures altogether a large personage, merchant and ship-master, capable, accurate, enterprising, something of the great gentleman, quick to perceive a slight and at need to avenge it, a lost type to-day— a Dutch cross on Huguenot French. Mr. Nicholas Gouverneur was glad to see once more the Vicomte de Courval. His own people, too, had suffered in other days for their religion, and if René's ancestors had paid in the far past unpleasant penalties for the respectable crime of treason to the king, had not one of Mr. Gouverneur's ancestors had a similar distinction, having been hanged for high treason? "Ah, of course he told you the story, René," said Schmidt when he heard of this interview.

Mr. Gouverneur, having offered the inevitable hospitality of his sideboard, was in no hurry.

René, although in hot haste to be done with his

strange errand, knew better than to disturb the formalities of welcome. He must inquire after Mrs. Gouverneur, and must answer for his mother. At last his host said: "You do small justice to my rum, Vicomte. It is as unused to neglect as any young woman. But, pardon me, you look tired, and as if you had made a hard journey. I see that you are anxious and too polite to interrupt a garrulous man. What can I do for you or our friend Schmidt?"

"I have this packet of papers which should go at once to the corvette *Jean Bart*. One François-Guillaume Need is the Captain."

"And I have been delaying you. Pray pardon me. Despatches, I suppose, for my cousin Gouverneur Morris." René did not contradict him. "We will see to it at once, at once. The *Jean Bart* sails to-night, I hear. She has waited, we knew not why."

"For these despatches, sir. Can I not be set aboard of her at once?"

"Surely," said Gouverneur; "come with me."

As they walked toward the water Mr. Gouverneur said: "You have, I think you told me, a despatch for the captain of the corvette. Let me urgently advise you not to board that vessel. My boat shall take you to the ship,—deliver your despatch,—but let nothing tempt you to set foot on her deck. We are not on very good terms with France; you are still a French citizen. Several of the corvette's officers have been in Philadelphia. If you are recognized as a French noble, you will never see America again. You know what fate awaits an émigré in Paris; not even your position in the Department of State would save you."

De Courval returned: "You are no doubt right, sir. I had already thought of the risk—"

"There need be none if you are prudent."

"But I ought to receive a receipt for the papers I deliver."

"That is hardly needed—unusual, I should say; Mr. Randolph will scarcely expect that."

De Courval was not inclined to set the merchant right in regard to the character of the despatches, for it might then be necessary to tell the whole story. He made no direct reply, but said merely: "I am most grateful—I shall have the honor to take your advice. Ah, here is the boat."

"It is my own barge," said Gouverneur. "Be careful. Yonder is the corvette, a short pull. I shall wait for you here.

In a few minutes De Courval was beside the gangway of the corvette. He called to a sailor on the deck that he wished to see an officer. Presently a young lieutenant came down the steps. De Courval said in French, as he handed the officer the packet of papers:

"This is a despatch, Citizen, from Citizen Minister Fauchet, addressed to the care of your captain. Have the kindness to give it to him and ask for a receipt."

The lieutenant went on deck and very soon returned.

"The receipt, please," said De Courval.

"Captain Need desires me to say that, although it

is unusual to give a receipt for such papers, he will do so if you will come to the cabin. He wishes to ask questions about the British cruisers, and may desire to send a letter to Citizen Minister Fauchet.''

"I cannot wait. I am in haste to return," said De Courval.

"*Le diable*, Citizen! He will be furious. We sail at once—at once; you will not be delayed."

René thought otherwise.

"Very well; I can but give your reply. It seems to me strange. You will hear of it some day, Citizen.''

As soon as the officer disappeared, René said to his boatman: "Quick! Get away—get me ashore as soon as you can!''

Pursuit from a man-of-war boat was possible, if one lay ready on the farther side of the corvette. He had, however, only a ten minutes' row before he stood beside Mr. Gouverneur on the Battery slip.

"I am a little relieved," said the older man. "Did you get the acknowledgment of receipt you wanted?''

"No, sir. It was conditioned upon my going aboard to the captain's cabin.''

"Ah, well, I do not suppose that Mr. Randolph will care.''

"Probably not.'' René had desired some evidence of his singular mission, but the immense importance of it as proof of his good faith was not at the time fully apprehended. The despatch had gone on its way, and he had done honorably his enemy's errand.

"And now," said the merchant, "let us go to my

house and see Mrs. Gouverneur, and above all have dinner.''

René had thought that flight might be needed if he carried out his fatal purpose, and he had therefore put in his saddle-bags enough garments to replace the muddy dress of a hard ride. He had said that he must leave at dawn, and having laid aside the cares of the last days, he gave himself up joyously to the charm of the refined hospitality of his hosts.

As they turned away, the corvette was setting her sails and the cries of the sailors and the creak of the windlass showed the anchor was being raised. Before they had reached Gouverneur's house she was under way, with papers destined to make trouble for many.

As René lay at rest that night within the curtained bed, no man on Manhattan Island could have been more agreeably at ease with his world. The worry of indecision was over. He felt with honest conviction that his prayer for the downfall of his enemy had been answered, and in this cooler hour he knew with gratitude that his brute will to kill had been wisely denied its desire. It had seemed to him at the time that to act on his instinct was only to do swift justice on a criminal; but he had been given a day to reflect and acknowledged the saner wisdom of the morrow.

Further thought should have left him less well pleased at what the future might hold for him. But the despatch had gone, his errand was done. An image of Margaret in the splendor of brocade and lace haunted the dreamy interval between the waking state and the wholesome sleep of tired youth. Moreover, the good merchant's Madeira had its power of somnolent charm, and, thus soothed, De Courval passed into a world of visionless slumber.

He rode back through the Jerseys to avoid Bristol and the scene of his encounter, and, finding at Camden a flat barge returning to Philadelphia, was able, as the river was open and free of ice, to get his horse aboard and thus to return with some renewal of anxiety to Mrs. Swanwick's house. No one was at home; but Nanny told him that Mr. Schmidt, who had been absent, had returned two days before, but was out. Miss Margaret was at the Hill, and June, the cat, off for two days on love-affairs or predatory business.

He went up-stairs to see his mother. Should he tell her? On the whole, it was better not to speak until he had seen Schmidt. He amused her with an account of having been sent to New York on business and then spoke of the Gouverneur family and their Huguenot descent. He went away satisfied that he had left her at ease, which was not quite the case. "Something has happened," she said to herself. "By and by he will tell me. Is it the girl? I trust not. Or that man? Hardly."

The supper passed in quiet, with light talk of familiar things, the vicomtesse, always a taciturn woman, saying but little.

As De Courval sat down, her black dress, the silvery quiet of Mrs. Swanwick's garb, her notably gentle voice, the simple room without colors, the sanded floor, the spotless cleanliness of the table furniture, of a sudden struck him as he thought of the violence and anger of the scene on the Bristol road. What would this gentle Friend say, and the Pearl? What, indeed!

"Supper was just over when, to René's relief, Schmidt appeared. He nodded coolly to René and said, laughing: "Ah, Frau Swanwick, I have not had a chance to growl; but when I go again to the country, I shall take Nanny. I survive; but the diet!" He gave an amusing account of it. "Pork— it is because of the unanimous pig. Pies—ach!— cabbage, a sour woman and sour bread, chicken rigged with hemp and with bosoms which need not stays." Even the vicomtesse smiled. "I have dined at Mr. Morris's, to my relief. Come, René, let us smoke."

When once at ease in his room, he exclaimed: "*Potstausend,* René, I am out of debt. The years I used to count to be paid are settled. Two days' watching that delirious swine and bottling up the gossiping little demon Chovet! A pipe, a pipe, and then I shall tell you."

"Indeed, I have waited long."

"Chovet told Fauchet at my request of this regrettable affair. He is uneasy, and he well may be, concerning all there is left of his secretary."

"Then he is alive," said René; "and will he live?"

"Alive? Yes, very much alive, raving at times like a madman haunted by hell fiends. I had to stay. After a day he was clear of head, but as weak as a man can be with the two maladies of a ball in a palsied shoulder and a doctor looking for it. Yes, he will live; and alive or dead will make mischief.''

''Did he talk to you?''

''Yes. He has no memory of my coming at the time he was shot. I think he did not see me at all.''

''Well, what else?''

''I told him the whole story, and what I had seen him do. I was plain, too, and said that I had found his despatch, and you, being a gentleman, must needs see that it went. He saw, I suspect, what other motive you had—if he believed me at all.''

''But did he believe you? Does he?''

''No, he does not. I said, 'You are scamp enough to swear that we set on you to steal your papers, a fine tale for our Jacobin mobocrats.' A fellow can't lie with his whole face. I saw his eyes narrow, but I told him to try it if he dared, and out comes my tale of his treachery. We made a compact at last, and he will swear he was set upon and robbed. I left him to invent his story. But it is plainly his interest to keep faith, and not accuse you.''

''He will not keep faith. Sometime he will lie about me. The despatch has gone by the *Jean Bart,* but that part of our defense is far to reach.''

''Well, Chovet is gold dumb, and as for the Jacobin, no man can tell. If he be wise, he will stick to his tale of highwaymen. Of course I asked Chovet to let the minister learn of this sad accident, but he did not arrive until after I had the fellow well scared.''

''Is that all?''

''No. The man is in torment. Damn! if I were

in pain like that, I should kill myself. Except that
fever, I never had anything worse than a stomach-
ache in all my life. The man is on the rack, and
Chovet declares that he will never use the arm again,
and will have some daily reminder of you so long as
he lives. Now, René, a man on the rack may come
to say things of the gentleman who turned on the
torture.''

''Then some day he will lie, and I, *mon Dieu,* will
be ruined. Who will believe me? The State Department will get the credit of it, and I shall be
thrown over—sacrificed to the wolves of party slander.''

''Not if I am here.''

''If you are here?''

''Yes. At any time I may have to go home.''

''Then let us tell the whole story.''

''Yes, if we must; but wait. Why go in search of
trouble? For a time, perhaps always, he will be
silent. Did you get a receipt for the despatch?''

''No. The captain would not give one unless I
went to his cabin and that I dared not do.''

''I, as the older man, should have pointed out to
you the need of using every possible means to get
an acknowledgment from the captain; but you were
right. Had you gone on board the ship, you would
never have left her. Well, then there is more need
to play a silent, waiting game until we know, as we
shall, of the papers having reached their destination. In fact, there is nothing else to do. There will
be a nice fuss over the papers, and then it will all be
forgotten.''

"Yes, unless he speaks."

"If he does, there are other cards in my hand. Meanwhile, being a good Samaritan, I have again seen Carteaux. He will, I think, be silent for a while. Be at ease, my son; and now I must go to bed. I am tired."

This was one of many talks; none of them left René at ease. How could he as yet involve a woman he loved in his still uncertain fate? He was by no means sure that she loved him; that she might come to do so he felt to be merely possible, for the modesty of love made him undervalue himself and see her as far beyond his desserts. His mother's prejudices troubled him less. Love consults no peerage and he had long ago ceased to think as his mother did of a title which had no legal existence.

It was natural enough that an event as grave as this encounter with Carteaux should leave on a young man's mind a deep impression; nor had his talk with Schmidt, the night before, enabled him, as next day he walked to the State Department, to feel entirely satisfied. The news of the highway robbery had been for two days the city gossip, and already the gazettes were considering it in a leisurely fashion; but as no journals reached the widow's house unless brought thither by Schmidt, the amenities of the press in regard to the assault and the administration were as yet unseen by De Courval. On the steps of the Department of State he met the Marquis de Noailles, who greeted him cheerfully, asking if he had read what Mr. Bache and the "Aurora" said of the attack on Carteaux.

René felt the cold chill of too conscious knowledge as he replied: "Not yet, Marquis. I am but yesterday come from New York."

"Well, it should interest Mr. Randolph. It does appear to Mr. Bache that no one except the English party and the Federals could profit by the theft. How they could be the better by the gossip of this *sacré* Jacobin actor in the rôle of a minister the *bon Dieu* alone knows."

René laughed. "You are descriptive, Marquis."

"Who would not be? But, my dear De Courval, you must regret that you were not the remarkable highwayman who stole Fauchet's eloquence and left a gold watch and seals; but here comes Mr. Randolph. He may explain it; at all events, if he confides to you the name of that robber, send the man to me. I will pay five dollars apiece for Jacobin scalps. *Adieu.* My regrets that you are not the man."

Mr. Randolph was cool as they went in together, and made it plain that absence without leave on the part of a clerk was an embarrassment to the public service of the State Department, in which were only three or four clerks. De Courval could only say that imperative private business had taken him out of town. It would not occur again. Upon this Mr. Randolph began to discuss the amazing assault and robbery with which town gossip was so busy. Mr. Fauchet had been insolent, and, asking aid in discovering the thief, had plainly implied that more than he and his government would suffer if the despatch were not soon restored to the minister. Mr. Randolph had been much amused, a little angry and also puzzled. "It had proved," he said, "a fine weapon in the hands of the Democrats." The young man was glad to shift the talk, but wherever he went for a few days, people, knowing of his duel, were sure to talk to him of this mysterious business. Later the "Aurora" and Mr. Bache, who had taken up the rôle in which Mr. Freneau had acted with skill and ill temper, made wild use of the story and of the value of the stolen papers to a criminal cabinet. Over their classic signatures Cato and Aristides challenged Democratic Socrates or Cicero to say how General Washington would be the better for knowledge of the rant of the strolling player Fauchet. Very soon, however, people ceased to talk of it. It was an unsolved mystery. But for one man torment of body and distress of mind kept ever present the will and wish to be without risk revenged. He was already, as he knew, *persona non grata,* and to have Schmidt's story told and believed was for the secretary to be sent home in disgrace. He waited, seeing no way as yet to acquit himself of this growing debt.

January of 1795 came in with the cabinet changes already long expected. Carteaux was still very ill in bed, with doctors searching for the bullet. As yet he told only of being robbed of his despatches and that he had lost neither watch nor purse, which was conclusive. Whereupon Fauchet talked and insulted Randolph, and the Democratic clubs raved with dark hints and insinuations, while the despatch went on its way, not to be heard of for months to come. René, who was for a time uneasy and disliked the secrecy thrown about an action of which he was far from ashamed, began at last to feel relieved, and thus the midwinter was over and the days began noticeably to lengthen.

XXII

"LET us skate to-night. I have tried the ice," said Schmidt, one afternoon in February. "Pearl learned, as you know, long ago." She was in town for a week, the conspirators feeling assured of René's resolution to wait on this, as on another matter, while he was busy with his double work. Her mother had grown rebellious over her long absence, and determined that she should remain in town, as there seemed to be no longer cause for fear and the girl was in perfect health. Aunt Gainor, also, was eager for town and piquet and well pleased with the excuse to return, having remained at the Hill long after her usual time.

"The moon is a fair, full matron," said Schmidt. "The ice is perfect. Look out for air-holes, René," he added, as he buckled on his skates. "Not ready yet?" René was kneeling and fastening the Pearl's skates. It took long.

"Oh, hurry!" she cried. "I cannot wait." She was joyous, excited, and he somehow awkward.

Then they were away over the shining, moon-lighted ice of the broad Delaware with that exhilaration which is caused by swift movement, the easy product of perfect physical capacity. For a time they skated quietly side by side, Schmidt, as usual,

enjoying an exercise in which, says Graydon in his
memoirs, the gentlemen of Philadelphia were un-
rivaled. Nearer the city front, on the great ice plain,
were many bonfires, about which phantom figures
flitted now an instant black in profile, and then lost
in the unillumined spaces, while far away, opposite
to the town, hundreds of skaters carrying lanterns
were seen or lost to view in the quick turns of the
moving figures. "Like great fireflies," said Schmidt.
A few dim lights in houses and frost-caught ships
and faint, moonlit outlines alone revealed the place
of the city. The cries and laughter were soon lost
to the three skaters, and a vast solitude received
them as they passed down the river.

"Ah, the gray moonlight and the gray ice!" said
Schmidt, "a Quaker night, Pearl."

"And the moon a great pearl," she cried.

"How one feels the night!" said the German. "It
is as on the Sahara. Only in the loneliness of great
spaces am I able to feel eternity; for space is time."
He had his quick bits of talk to himself. Both young
people, more vaguely aware of some sense of awe in
the dim unpeopled plain, were under the charm of
immense physical joy in the magic of easily won
motion.

"Surely there is nothing like it," said René,
happy and breathless, having only of late learned to
skate, whereas Pearl had long since been well taught
by the German friend.

"No," said Schmidt; "there is nothing like it,
except the quick sweep of a canoe down a rapid.
A false turn of the paddle, and there is death. Oh,

but there is joy in the added peril! The blood of the Angles finds the marge of danger sweet.''

''Not for me,'' said Pearl; ''but we are safe here.''

''I have not found your Delaware a constant friend. How is that, René?''

''What dost thou mean?'' said Pearl. ''Thou art fond of teasing my curiosity, and I am curious, too. Tell me, please. Oh, but thou must!''

''Ask the vicomte,'' cried Schmidt. ''He will tell you.''

''Oh, will he, indeed?'' said René, laughing. ''Ah, I am quite out of breath.''

''Then rest a little.'' As they halted, a swift skater, seeking the loneliness of the river below the town, approaching, spoke to Margaret, and then said: ''Ah, Mr. Schmidt, what luck to find you! You were to give me a lesson. Why not now?''

''Come, then,'' returned Schmidt. ''I brought you hither, René, because it is safer away from clumsy learners, and where we are the ice is safe. I was over it yesterday, but do not go far. I shall be back in a few minutes. If Margaret is tired, move up the river. I shall find you.''

''Please not to be long,'' said Margaret.

''Make him tell you when your wicked Delaware was not my friend, and another was. Make him tell.''

As he spoke, he was away behind young Mr. Morris, singing in his lusty bass snatches of German song and thinking of the ripe mischief of the trap he had baited with a nice little Cupid. ''I want it to come soon,'' he said, ''before I go. She will be

curious and venture in, and it will be as good as
the apple with knowledge of good and—no, there
is evil in neither.''

She was uneasy, she scarce knew why. Still at
rest on the ice, .she turned to De Courval. ''Thou
wilt tell me?'' she said.

''I had rather not.''

''But if I ask thee?''

''Why should I not?'' he thought. It was against
his habit to speak of himself, but she would perhaps
like him the better for the story.

''Then, Miss Margaret, not because he asked and
is willing, but because you ask, I shall tell you.''

''Oh, I knew thou wouldst. He thought thou
wouldst not and I should be left puzzled. Sometimes he is just like a boy for mischief.''

''Oh, it was nothing. The first day I was here I
saved him from drowning. A boat struck his head
while we were swimming, and I had the luck to be
near. There, that is all.'' He was a trifle ashamed
to tell of it.

She put out her hand as they stood. ''Thank thee.
Twice I thank thee, for a dear life saved and because thou didst tell, not liking to tell me. I could
see that. Thank thee.''

''Ah, Pearl,'' he exclaimed, and what more he
would have said I do not know, nor had he a chance,
for she cried: ''I shall thank thee always, Friend de
Courval. We are losing time.'' The peril that
gives a keener joy to sport was for a time far too
near, but in other form than in bodily risk. ''Come,
canst thou catch me?'' She was off and away, now

near, now far, circling about him with easy grace,
merrily laughing as he sped after her in vain. Then
of a sudden she cried out and came to a standstill.

"A strap broke, and I have turned my ankle. Oh,
I cannot move a step! What shall I do?"

"Sit down on the ice."

As she sat, he undid her skates and then his own
and tied them to his belt. "Can you walk?" he
said.

"I will try. Ah!" She was in pain. "Call Mr.
Schmidt," she said. "Call him at once."

"I do not see him. We were to meet him opposite
the Swedes' church."

"Then go and find him."

"What, leave you? Not I. Let me carry you."

"Oh, no, no; thou must not." But in a moment
he had the slight figure in his arms.

"Let me down! I will never, never forgive thee!"
But he only said in a voice of resolute command,
"Keep still, Pearl, or I shall fall." She was silent.
Did she like it, the strong arms about her, the head
on his shoulder, the heart throbbing as never before?
He spoke no more, but moved carefully on.

They had not gone a hundred yards when he
heard Schmidt calling. At once he set her down,
saying, "Am I forgiven?"

"No—yes," she said faintly.

"Pearl, dear Pearl, I love you. I meant not to
speak, oh, for a time, but it has been too much for
me. Say just a word." But she was silent as
Schmidt stopped beside them and René in a few
words explained.

"Was it here?" asked Schmidt.

"No; a little while ago."

"But how did you come so far, my poor child?"

"Oh, I managed," she said.

"Indeed. I shall carry you."

"If thou wilt, please. I am in much pain."

He took off his skates, and with easy strength walked away over the ice, the girl in his arms, so that before long she was at home and in her mother's care, to be at rest for some days.

"Come in, René," said Schmidt, as later they settled themselves for the usual smoke and chat. The German said presently: "It was not a very bad sprain. Did you carry her, René?"

"I—"

"Yes. Do you think, man, that I cannot see?"

"Yes, I carried her. What else could I do?"

"Humph! What else? Nothing. Was she heavy, Herr de Courval?"

"Please not to tease me, sir. You must know that, God willing, I shall marry her."

"Will you, indeed? And your mother, René, will she like it?"

"No; but soon or late she will have to like it. For her I am still a child, but now I shall go my way."

"And Pearl?"

"I mean to know, to hear. I can wait no longer. Would it please you, sir?"

"Mightily, my son; and when it comes to the mother, I must say a word or two."

"She will not like that. She likes no one to come between us."

"Well, we shall see. I should be more easy if only that Jacobin hound were dead, or past barking. He is in a bad way, I hear. I could have wished that you had been of a mind to have waited a little longer before you spoke to her."

René smiled. "Why did you leave us alone to-night? It is you, sir, who are responsible."

"*Potstausend! Donnerwetter!* You saucy boy! Go to bed and repent. There are only two languages in which a man can find good, fat, mouth-filling oaths, and the English oaths are too naughty for a good Quaker house."

"You seem to have found one, sir. It sounds like thunder. We can do it pretty well in French."

"Child's talk, prattle. Go to bed. What will the mother say? Oh, not yours. Madame Swanwick has her own share of pride. Can't you wait a while?"

"No. I must know."

"Well, Mr. Obstinate Man, we shall see." The wisdom of waiting he saw, and yet he had deliberately been false to the advice he had more than once given. René left him, and Schmidt turned, as he loved to do, to the counselor Montaigne, just now his busy-minded comrade, and, lighting upon the chapter on reading, saw what pleased him.

"That is good advice, in life and for books. To have a 'skipping wit.' We must skip a little time. I was foolish. How many threads there are in this tangle men call life!" And with this he read over the letters just come that morning from Germany. Then he considered Carteaux again.

"If that fellow is tormented into taking his revenge, and I should be away, as I may be, there will be the deuce to pay.

"Perhaps I might have given René wiser advice; but with no proof concerning the fate of the despatch, there was no course which was entirely satisfactory. Best to let the sleeping dog lie. But why did I leave them on the ice? *Sapristi!* I am as bad as Mistress Gainor. But she is not caught yet, Master René."

XXIII

IN a few days Margaret was able to be afoot, although still lame; but René had no chance to see her. She was not to be caught alone, and would go on a long-promised visit to Merion. Thus February passed, and March, and April came, when personal and political matters abruptly broke up for a time their peaceful household.

Margaret had been long at home again, but still with a woman's wit she avoided her lover. Aunt Gainor, ever busy, came and went, always with a dozen things to do.

Her attentions to Madame de Courval lessened when that lady no longer needed her kindness and, as soon happened, ceased to be interesting. She would not gamble, and the two women had little in common. Miss Gainor's regard for René was more lasting. He was well-built and handsome, and all her life she had had a fancy for good looks in men. He had, too, the virile qualities she liked and a certain steadiness of purpose which took small account of obstacles and reminded her of her nephew Hugh Wynne. Above all, he had been successful, and she despised people who failed and too often regarded success as a proof of the right to succeed, even when the means employed were less creditable than those by which René had made his way. Moreover, had he not told her once that her French was wonderful? Miss Gainor changed her favorites often, but René kept in her good graces and was blamed only because he did not give her as much of his time as she desired; for after she heard his history from Schmidt, he won a place in her esteem which few men had ever held. She had set her heart at last on his winning Margaret, and the lifelong game of gambling with other folks' fortunes and an honest idolatry for the heroic, inclined her to forgive a lack of attention due in a measure to his increasing occupations.

To keep her eager hands off this promising bit of match-making had been rather a trial, but Schmidt was one of the few people of whom she had any fear, and she had promised not to meddle. At present she had begun to think that the two human pawns in the game she loved were becoming indifferent, and to let things alone was something to which she had never been inclined. Had she become aware of the German's mild treachery that night on the ice, she would in all likelihood have been angry at first and then pleased or annoyed not to have had a hand in the matter.

Mistress Wynne, even in the great war, rarely allowed her violent politics to interfere with piquet, and now Mr. Dallas had asked leave to bring Fauchet, the new French minister, to call upon her. He was gay, amusing, talked no politics, played piquet nearly as well as she, and was enchanted, as he assured her, to hear French spoken without accent.

If to De la Forêt, the consul-general, he made merry concerning his travels in China, as he called her drawing-room, saying it was perilously over-populous with strange gods, she did not hear it, nor would she have cared so long as she won the money of the French republic.

One evening in early April, after a long series of games, he said: "I wish I could have brought here my secretary Carteaux. He did play to perfection, but now, poor devil, the wound he received has palsied his right arm, and he will never hold cards again—or, what he thinks worse, a foil. It was a strange attack."

"Does he suffer? I have heard about him."

"Horribly. He is soon going home to see if our surgeons can find the bullet; but he is plainly failing."

"Oh, he is going home?"

"Yes; very soon."

"How did it all happen? It has been much talked about, but one never knows what to believe."

"I sent him to New York with despatches for our foreign office, but the *Jean Bart* must have sailed without them; for he was waylaid, shot, and robbed of the papers, but lost no valuables."

"Then it was not highwaymen?"

"No; I can only conjecture who were concerned. It was plainly a robbery in the interest of the Federalists. I do not think Mr. Randolph could have these despatches, or if he has, they will never be heard of." Upon this he smiled.

"Then they are lost?"

"Yes. At least to our foreign office. I think Mr. Wolcott of the Treasury would have liked to see them."

"But why? Why Mr. Wolcott?" She showed her curiosity quite too plainly.

"Ah, that is politics, and Madame forbids them."

"Yes—usually; but this affair of Monsieur Carteaux cannot be political. It seems to me an incredible explanation."

"Certainly a most unfortunate business," said the minister.

He had said too much and was on his guard. He had, however, set the spinster to thinking, and remembering what Schmidt had told her of De Courval, her reflections were fertile. "Shall we have another game?"

A month before the day on which they played, the *Jean Bart,* since November of 1794 at sea, after seizing an English merchantman was overhauled in the channel by the British frigate *Cerberus* and compelled to surrender. The captain threw overboard his lead-weighted signal-book and the packet of Fauchet's despatches. A sailor of the merchant ship, seeing it float, jumped overboard from a boat and rescued it. Upon discovering its value, Captain Drew of the *Cerberus* forwarded the despatches to Lord Grenville in London, who in turn sent them as valuable weapons to Mr. Hammond, the English minister in Philadelphia. There was that in them which might discredit one earnest enemy of the English treaty, but months went by before the papers reached America.

Miss Gainor, suspecting her favorite's share in this much-talked-of affair, made haste to tell Schmidt of the intention of Carteaux to sail, to the relief of the German gentleman, who frankly confided to her the whole story. He spoke also once more of De Courval and urged her for every reason to leave the young people to settle their own affairs. Meanwhile Josiah was in bed with well-earned gout.

On the afternoon of the 14th of April, René came home from the State office and said to Schmidt: "I have had paid me a great compliment, but whether I entirely like it or not, I do not know. As usual, I turn to you for advice."

"Well, what is it?"

"The President wants some one he can trust to go to the western counties of this State and report on the continued disturbance about the excise tax. I thought the thing was at an end. Mr. Hamilton, who seems to have the ear of the President, advised him that as a thoroughly neutral man I could be trusted. Mr. Randolph thinks it a needless errand."

"No. It is by no means needless. I have lands near Pittsburg, as you know, and I hear of much disaffection. The old fox, Jefferson, at Monticello talks about the excise tax as 'infernal,' and what with the new treaty and Congress and other things the Democrats are making trouble enough for a weak cabinet and a strong President. I advise you to accept. You can serve me, too. Take it. You are fretting here for more reasons than one. I hear that Carteaux is out of bed, a crippled wreck, and Fauchet says is soon to go to France. In August the minister himself will leave and one Adet take his place. I think you may go with an easy mind. We are to be rid of the whole pestilent lot.''

''Then I shall accept and go as soon as I receive my instructions. But I do dread to leave town. I shall go, but am at ease only since you will be here.''

''But I shall not be, René. I have hesitated to tell you. I am called home to Germany, and shall sail from New York for England on to-day a week. I shall return, I think; but I am not sure, nor if then I can remain. It is an imperative call. I am, it seems, pardoned, and my father is urgent, and my elder brother is dead. If you have learned to know me, you will feel for me the pain with which I leave this simpler life for one which has never held for me any charm. Since Carteaux is soon to sail, and I hear it is certain, I feel less troubled. I hope to be here again in August or later. You may, I think, count on my return.''

''Have you told Mrs. Swanwick, sir?''

''Yes, and the Pearl. Ah, my son, the one thing in life I have craved is affection; and now—''

''No one will miss you as I shall—no one—'' He could say no more.

''You will of course have charge of my affairs, and Mr. Wilson has my power of attorney, and there is Hamilton at need. Ah, but I have had a scene with these most dear people!''

The time passed quickly for De Courval. He himself was to be gone at least two months. There was a week to go, as he must, on horseback, and as much to return. There were wide spaces of country to cover and much business to settle for Schmidt. His stay was uncertain and not without risks.

Over three weeks went by before he could be spared from the thinly officered department. Schmidt had long since gone, and René sat alone in the library at night and missed the large mind and a temperament gayer than his own. His mother had asked no questions concerning Carteaux, and as long as there was doubt in regard to his course, he had been unwilling to mention him; but now he felt that he should speak freely and set his mother's mind at rest before he went away.

Neither, despite what he was sure would be the stern opposition he would have to encounter from his mother, could he go without a word to Margaret —a word that would settle his fate and hers. The Carteaux business was at an end. He felt free to act. Fortune for once favored him. Since he had spoken to his mother of his journey and the lessened household knew of it, Pearl had even more sedulously avoided the pleasant talks in the garden and the rides, now rare, with Aunt Gainor and himself. The mother, more and more uneasy, had spoken to her daughter very decidedly, and Madame grew less familiarly kind to the girl; while she herself, with a mind as yet in doubt, had also her share of pride and believed that the young vicomte had ceased to care for her, else would he not have created an opportunity to say what long ago that night on the ice seemed to make a matter of honor? She was puzzled by his silence, a little vexed and not quite sure of herself.

He put off to the last moment his talk with his mother and watched in vain for a chance to speak to Margaret. His instructions were ready, his last visits made. He had had an unforgettable half-hour with the President and a talk with Hamilton, now on a visit from New York. The ex-secretary asked him why he did not cast in his lot frankly with the new land, as he himself had done. He would have to give notice in court and renounce his allegiance to his sovereign, so ran the new law.

"I have no sovereign," he replied, "and worthless as it now seems, I will not renounce my title, as your law requires."

"Nor would I," said Hamilton. "You will go home some day. The chaos in France will find a master. The people are weary of change and will accept any permanent rule."

"Yes, I hope to return. Such is my intention," and they fell into talk of Schmidt.

De Courval's last day in the city had come. Schmidt had left him the free use of his horses, and he would try one lately bought to see how it would answer for his long journey.

About eleven of a sunny June morning he mounted and rode westward up Chestnut Street. At Fifth and Chestnut streets, Congress having just adjourned, the members were coming out of the brick building which still stands at the corner. He knew many, and bowed to Gallatin and Fisher Ames. Mr. Madison stopped him to say a word about the distasteful English treaty. Then at a walk he rode on toward the Schuylkill, deep in thought.

21

Beyond Seventh there was as yet open country, with few houses. It was two years since, a stranger, he had fallen among friends in the Red City, made for himself a sufficient income and an honorable name and won the esteem of men. Schmidt, Margaret, the Wynnes; his encounters with Carteaux, the yellow plague, passed through his mind. God had indeed dealt kindly with the exiles. As he came near to the river and rode into the thinned forest known as the Governor's Woods, he saw Nanny seated at the roadside.

"What are you doing here, Nanny?" he asked.

"The missus sent me with Miss Margaret to carry a basket of stuff to help some no-account colored people lives up that road. I has to wait."

"Ah!" he exclaimed, and, dismounting, tied his horse. "At last," he said, and went away up the wood road. Far in the open forest he saw her coming, her Quaker bonnet swinging on her arm.

"Oh, Miss Margaret!" he cried. "I am glad to have found you. You know I am going away to-morrow for two months at least. It is a hard journey, not without some risk, and I cannot go without a word with you. Why have you avoided me as you have done?"

"Have I?" she replied.

"Yes; and you know it."

"I thought—I thought—oh, let me go home!"

"No; not till you hear me. Can you let me leave in this way without a word? I do not mean that it shall be. Sit down here on this log and listen to me." He caught her hand.

"Please, I must go."

"No; not yet. Sit down here. I shall not keep you long—a woman who wants none of me. But I have much to say—explanations, ah, much to say." She sat down.

"I will hear thee, but—"

"Oh, you will hear me? Yes, because you must? Go, if you will. It will be my answer."

"I think the time and the place ill chosen,"— she spoke with simple dignity,—"but I will hear thee."

"I have had no chance but this. You must pardon me." She looked down and listened. "It is a simple matter. I have loved you long. No other love has ever troubled my life. Save my mother, I have no one. What might have been the loves for brothers and sisters are all yours, a love beyond all other loves, the love of a lonely man. Whether or not you permit me to be something more, I shall still owe you a debt the years can never make me forget—the remembrance of what my life beside you in your home has given me."

The intent face, the hands clasped in her lap, might have shown him how deeply she was moved; for now at last that she had heard him she knew surely that she loved him. The long discipline of Friends in controlling at least the outward expression of emotion came to her aid as often before. She felt how easy it would have been to give him the answer he longed for; but there were others to think about, and from her childhood she had been taught the lesson of consideration for her elders. She set herself to reply to him with stern repression of feeling not very readily governed.

"How can I answer thee? What would thy mother say?" He knew then what her answer might have been. She, too, had her pride, and he liked her the more for that.

"Thou art a French noble. I am a plain Quaker girl without means. There would be reason in the opposition thy mother would make."

"A French noble!" he laughed. "A banished exile, landless and poor—a pretty match I am. But, Pearl, the future is mine. I have succeeded here, where my countrymen starve. I have won honor, respect, and trust. I would add love."

"I know, I know; but—"

"It is vain to put me off with talk of others. I think you do care for me. My mother will summon all her prejudices and in the end will yield. It is very simple, Pearl. I ask only a word. If you say yes, whatever may then come, we will meet with courage and respect. Do you love me, Pearl?"

She said faintly, "Yes."

He sat silent a moment, and then said, "I thank God!" and, lifting her hand, kissed it.

"Oh, René," she cried, "what have I done!" and she burst into tears. "I did not mean to."

"Is it so hard, dear Pearl? I have made you cry."

"No, it is not hard; but it is that I am ashamed to think that I loved thee long—long before thou didst care for me. Love thee, René! Thou dost not dream how—how I love thee."

Her reticence, her trained reserve, were lost in this

"'I know, I know, but—'"

passion of long-restrained love. Ah, here was Schmidt's Quaker Juliet!

He drew her to him and kissed her wet cheek. "You will never, never regret," he said. "All else is of no moment. We love each other. That is all now. I have so far never failed in anything, and I shall not now."

He had waited long, he said, and for good reasons. Some day, but not now in an hour of joy, he would tell her the story of his life, a sad one, and of why he had been what men call brutal to Carteaux and why their friend Schmidt, who knew of his love, had urged him to wait. She must trust him yet a little while longer.

"And have I not trusted thee?"

"Yes, Pearl."

"We knew, mother and I, knowing thee as we did, that there must be more cause for that dreadful duel than we could see."

"More? Yes, dear, and more beyond it; but it is all over now. The man I would have killed is going to France."

"Oh, René—killed!"

"Yes, and gladly. The man goes back to France and my skies are clear for love to grow."

He would kill! A strange sense of surprise arose in her mind, and the thought of how little even now she knew of the man she loved and trusted. "I can wait, René," she said, "and oh, I am so glad; but mother—I have never had a secret from her, never."

"Tell her," he said; "but then let it rest between us until I come back."

"That would be best, and now I must go."

"Yes, but a moment, Pearl. Long ago, the day after we landed, a sad and friendless man, I walked out to the river and washed away my cares in the blessed waters. On my return, I sat on this very log, and talked to some woodmen, and asked the name of a modest flower. They said, 'We call it the Quaker lady.' And to think that just here I should find again, my Quaker lady."

"But I am not a Quaker lady. I am a naughty 'Separatist,' as Friends call it. Come, I must go, René. I shall say good-by to thee to-night. Thou wilt be off early, I do suppose. And oh, it will be a weary time while thou art away!"

"I shall be gone by six in the morning."

"And I sound asleep," she returned, smiling. He left her at the roadside with Nanny, and, mounting, rode away.

XXIV

THE widow allowed no one to care for Schmidt's library except her daughter or herself. It contained little of value except books, but even those Indian arrow-heads he found on Tinicum Island and the strange bones from near Valley Forge were dusted with care and regarded with the more curiosity because, even to the German, they spoke no language the world as yet could read.

As she turned from her task and Margaret entered, she saw in her face the signal of something to be told. It needed not the words, "Oh, mother," as she closed the door behind her—"oh, mother, I am afraid I have done a wrong thing; but I met René de Courval,—I mean, he met me,—and—and he asked me to marry him—and I will; no one shall stop me." There was a note of anticipative defiance in the young voice as she spoke.

"Sit down, dear child."

The girl sunk on a cushion at her feet, her head in the mother's lap. "I could not help it," she murmured, sobbing.

"I saw this would come to thee, long ago," said the mother. "I had hoped thou wouldst be so guided as not to let thy heart get the better of thy head."

"It is my head has got me into this—this sweet

trouble. Thou knowest that I have had others, and some who had thy favor; but, mother, here for two years I have lived day by day in the house with René, and have seen him so living as to win esteem and honor, a tender son to his mother, and so respectful to thee, who, for her, art only the keeper of a boarding-house. Thou knowest what Friend Schmidt says of him. I heard him tell Friend Hamilton. He said —he said he was a gallant gentleman, and he wished he were his son. You see, mother, it was first respect and then—love. Oh, mother, that duel! I knew as I saw him carried in that I loved him.'' She spoke rapidly, with little breaks in her voice, and now was silent.

"It is bad, very bad, my child. I see no end of trouble—oh, it is bad, bad, for thee and for him!''

"It is good, good, mother, for me and for him. He has waited long. There has been something, I do not know what, kept him from speaking sooner. It is over now.''

"I do not see what there could have been, unless it were his mother. It may well be that. Does she know?''

"When he comes back he will tell her.''

"I do not like it, and I dislike needless mysteries. From a worldly point of view,—and I at least, who have drunk deep of poverty, must somewhat think for thee. Here are two people without competent means—''

"But I love him.''

"And his mother?''

"But I love him.'' She had no other logic. "Oh,

I wish Mr. Schmidt were here! René says he will like it.''

"That, at least, is a good thing." Both were silent a little while. Mrs. Swanwick had been long used to defer to the German's opinions, but looking far past love's limited horizon, the widow thought of the certain anger of the mother, of the trap she in her pride would think set for her son by designing people, her prejudices intensified by the mere fact of the poverty which left her nothing but exaggerated estimates of her son and what he was entitled to demand of the woman he should some day marry. And too, René had often spoken of a return to France. She said at last: "We will leave the matter now, and speak of it to no one; but I should say to thee, my dear, that apart from what for thy sake I should consider, and the one sad thing of his willingness to avenge a hasty word by possibly killing a fellow-man,—how terrible!—apart from these things, there is no one I had been more willing to give thee to than René de Courval."

"Thank thee, mother." The evil hour when the vicomtesse must hear was at least remote, and something akin to anger rose in the widow's mind as she thought of it.

René came in to supper. Mrs. Swanwick was as usual quiet, asking questions in regard to Margaret's errand of charity, but of a mind to win time for reflection, and unwilling as yet to open the subject with René.

When, late in the evening, he came out of the study where he had been busy with the instructions left by

Schmidt, he was annoyed to learn that Margaret had gone up-stairs. There was still before him the task of speaking to his mother of what he was sure was often in her mind, Carteaux. She had learned from the gossip of guests that a Frenchman had been set upon near Bristol and had been robbed and wounded. Incurious and self-centered, the affairs of the outer world had for her but little real interest. Now she must have her mind set at ease, for René well knew that she had not expected him to rest contented or to be satisfied with the result of his unfortunate duel. Her puritan creed was powerless here as against her social training, and her sense of what so hideous a wrong as her husband's murder should exact from his son.

"I have something to tell you, *maman*," he said; "and before I go, it is well that I should tell you."

"Well, what is it?" she said coldly, and then, as before, uneasily anxious.

"On the twenty-ninth of November I learned that Carteaux had started for New York an hour before I heard of it, on his way to France. I had waited long —undecided, fearing that again some evil chance might leave you alone in a strange land."

"You did wrong, René. There are duties which ought to permit of no such indecision. You should not have considered me for a moment. Go on."

"How could I help it, thinking of you, mother? I followed, and overtook this man near Bristol. I meant no chance with the sword this time. He was unarmed. I gave him the choice of my pistols, bade him pace the distance, and give the word. He walked away some six feet, half the distance, and, turning suddenly, fired, grazing my shoulder. I shot him—ah, a terrible wound in arm and shoulder. Schmidt had found a note I left for him, and, missing his pistols, inquired at the French legation, and came up in time to see it all and to prevent me from killing the man."

"Pre—vent you! How did he dare!"

"Yes, mother; and it was well. Schmidt found, when binding up his wound, that he was carrying despatches from the Republican Minister Fauchet to go by the corvette *Jean Bart,* waiting in New York Harbor.

"What difference did that make?"

"Why, mother, I am in the State Department. To have killed a member of the French legation, or stopped his journey, would have been ruin to me and a weapon in the hands of these mock Jacobins."

"But you did stop him."

"Yes; but I delivered the despatch myself to the corvette."

"Yes, you were right; but what next? He must have spoken."

"No. The threat from Schmidt that he would tell the whole story of Avignon and his treachery to me has made him lie and say he had been set upon by unknown persons and robbed of his papers. He has wisely held his tongue. He is crippled for life and has suffered horribly. Now he goes to France a broken, miserable man, punished as death's release could not punish."

"I do not know that. I have faith in the vengeance of God. You should have killed him. You did not. And so I suppose there is an end of it for a time. Is that all, René?''

"Yes, that is all. The loss of the despatch remains a mystery, and the Democrats are foolish enough to believe we have it in the foreign office. No one of them but Carteaux knows and he dare not speak. The despatch will never come back here, or if it does, Carteaux will have gone. People have ceased to talk about it, and now, mother, I am going away with an easy mind. Do not worry over this matter. Good night.''

"Worry?" she cried. "Ah, I would have killed the Jacobin dog!''

"I mean to," he said, and left her.

At dawn he was up and had his breakfast and there was Pearl in the hall and her hands on his two shoulders. "Kiss me," she said. "God bless and guard thee, René!''

XXV

WHILE Schmidt was far on his homeward way, De Courval rode through the German settlements of Pennsylvania and into the thinly settled Scotch-Irish clearings beyond the Alleghenies, a long and tedious journey, with much need to spare his horse.

His letters to government officers in the village of Pittsburg greatly aided him in his more remote rides. He settled some of Schmidt's land business, and rode with a young soldier's interest over Braddock's fatal field, thinking of the great career of the youthful colonel who was one of the few who kept either his head or his scalp on that day of disaster.

He found time also to prepare for his superiors a reassuring report, and on July 18 set out on his return. He had heard nothing from his mother or from any one else. The mails were irregular and slow,—perhaps one a week,—and very often a flood or an overturned coach accounted for letters never heard of again. There would be much to hear at home.

On July Fourth of 1795, while the bells were ringing in memory of the nation's birthday, Fauchet sat in his office at Oeller's Hotel. He had been recalled and was for various reasons greatly troubled. The ıeaction in France against the Jacobins had set in, and they, in turn were suffering from the violence of the returning royalists and the outbreaks of the Catholic peasantry in the south. Marat's bust had been thrown into the gutter and the Jacobin clubs closed. The minister had been able to do nothing of value to stop the Jay treaty. The despatch on which he had relied to give such information as might enable his superiors to direct him and assure them of his efforts to stop the treaty had disappeared eight months ago, as he believed by a bold robbery in the interest of the English party, possibly favored by the cabinet, which, as he had to confess, was less likely. He was angry as he thought of it and uneasy as concerned his future in distracted France. He had questioned Carteaux again and again but had never been quite satisfied. The theft of the despatch had for a time served his purpose, but had been of no practical value. The treaty with England would go to the senate and he return home, a discredited diplomatic failure. Meanwhile, in the trying heat of summer, as during all the long winter months, Carteaux lay for the most part abed, in such misery as might have moved to pity even the man whose bullet had punished him so savagely. At last he was able to sit up for a time every day and to arrange with the captain of a French frigate, then in port, for his return to France.

Late in June he had dismissed Chovet with only a promise to pay what was in fact hard-earned money. Dr. Glentworth, Washington's surgeon, had replaced him, and talked of an amputation, upon which, cursing doctors in general, Carteaux swore that he would prefer to die.

Chovet, who dosed his sick folk with gossip when other means failed, left with this ungrateful patient one piece of news which excited Carteaux's interest. Schmidt, he was told, had gone to Europe, and then, inaccurate as usual, Chovet declared that it was like enough he would never return, a fact which acquired interest for the doctor himself as soon as it became improbable that Carteaux would pay his bill. When a few days later Carteaux learned from De la Forêt that his enemy De Courval was to be absent for several weeks, and perhaps beyond the time set for his own departure, he began with vengeful hope to reconsider a situation which had so far seemed without resource.

Resolved at last to make for De Courval all the mischief possible before his own departure, with such thought as his sad state allowed he had slowly matured in his mind a statement which seemed to him satisfactorily malignant. Accordingly on this Fourth of July he sent his black servant to ask the minister to come to his chamber.

Fauchet, somewhat curious, sat down by the bedside and parting the chintz curtains, said, "I trust you are better."

The voice which came from the shadowed space within was weak and hoarse. "I am not better—I never shall be, and I have little hope of reaching home alive."

"I hoped it not as bad as that."

"And still it is as I say. I do not want to die

without confessing to you the truth about that affair in which I was shot and my despatch stolen.''

Men who had lived through the years of the French Revolution were not readily astonished, but at this statement the Minister sat up and exclaimed: "*Mon Dieu!* What is this?''

"I am in damnable pain; I must be brief. I was waylaid near Bristol by Schmidt and De Courval, and when I would not stop, was shot by De Courval. They stole the despatch, and made me swear on threat of death that I had been attacked by men I did not know.''

Fauchet was silent for a while, and then said: "That is a singular story—and that you kept the promise, still more singular.''

"I did keep it. I had good reason to keep it.'' He realized, as he told the tale, how improbable it sounded, how entirely Fauchet disbelieved him. If he had not been dulled by opiates and racked past power of critical thought, he was far too able a man to have put forth so childish a tale. He knew at once that he was not believed.

"You do not believe me, Citizen.''

"I do not. Why did you not tell me the truth at first?''

"It was not the threat to kill me which stopped me. I was of the tribunal at Avignon which condemned the *ci-devant* vicomte, the young man's father. To have had it known here would have been a serious thing to our party and for me ruin. I was ill, feeble, in their hands, and I promised Schmidt that I would put it all on some unknown person.''

Fauchet listened. He entirely distrusted him. "Is that all? Do you expect any reasonable man to believe such a story?"

"Yes, I do. If I had told you at the time, you would have used my statement at once and I should have suffered. Now that both these cursed villains are gone, I can speak."

"Indeed," said Fauchet, very desirous of a look at the face secure from observation within the curtained bed, "but why do you speak now? It is late. Why speak at all?"

"For revenge, Monsieur. I am in hell."

Fauchet hesitated. "That is a good reason; but there is more in this matter than you are willing to tell."

"That is my business. I have told you enough to satisfy my purpose and yours."

"Rather late for mine. But let us understand each other. This man, then, this De Courval, had a double motive—to avenge his father's death and to serve his masters, the Federalists. That is your opinion?"

"Yes, his desire for revenge made him an easy tool. I cannot talk any more. What shall you do about it?"

"I must think. I do not know. You are either a great fool or a coward or both. I only half trust you."

"Ah, were I well, Monsieur, no man should talk to me as you are doing."

"Luckily for me you are not well; but will you swear to this, to a written statement?"

22

"I will." Whether it was to be a truthful statement or not concerned the minister but little if he could make use of it. Upon this, the consul-general and a secretary, Le Blanc, being called in, to their amazement Carteaux dictated a plain statement and signed it with his left hand, the two officials acting as witnesses.

The minister read it aloud:

Oeller's Hotel, July 4, 1795.

I, George Carteaux, being *in extremis*, declare that on the 29th of November, about 5 P.M., near Bristol, I was set upon and shot and a despatch taken from me by one Schmidt and a Frenchman by name De Courval. No valuables were taken. By whom they were set on or paid I do not know.

George Carteaux.

Witnesses:

  Louis Le Blanc,
  Jean de la Forêt.

The two members of the legation silently followed the minister out of the room.

"That is a belated story," said De la Forêt. "Do you credit it?"

'It is not all, you may be sure; a rather lean tale," replied Le Blanc, whose career in the police of Paris had taught him to distrust men. "He lied both times, but this time it is a serviceable lie."

"A little late, as you say," remarked Fauchet. "Once it might have helped us."

"Ah, if," said the consul-general, "he could tell who has your despatch!"

"Not Mr. Randolph," said Le Blanc.

"No," returned Fauchet; "or if he has, it will never be seen by any one else."

"Why?" asked Le Blanc.

The minister, smiling, shook his head. "If ever it turns up in other hands, you will know why, and Mr. Randolph, too."

The minister later in the day assured Carteaux that he would make such use of the deposition as would force the administration to rid itself of a guilty clerk. He was in no haste to fulfil his pledge. Two or three months earlier, when the general opposition to the English treaty promised to delay or prevent it, this damaging paper would have had some value. Apart, however, from any small practical utility the confession might still possess, it promised Fauchet another form of satisfaction. Being a man of great vanity, he felt injured and insulted by the coolness of his diplomatic reception and by the complete absence of pleasant social recognition in the homes of the great Federalist merchants. He would give Carteaux's statement to the Secretary of State and demand that De Courval be dismissed and punished. He felt that he could thus annoy and embarrass the administration; but still, distrusting Carteaux, he waited. His delay was ended by the gossip which began to be rumored about in regard to the attack on Carteaux, and concerning the mysterious loss of Despatch No. 10.

Chovet had been abruptly dismissed, unpaid, and the German having gone away in some haste with no thought of his promise to pay, none knew when he would return. The little doctor was furious. His

habit of imprudent gossip had been controlled by
Schmidt's threats and still more surely by his
pledge of payment. By and by, in his exasperation,
he let drop hints, and soon the matter grew. He had
been cheated by Carteaux, and if people only knew
the truth of that story, and so on, while he won self-
importance from holding what he half believed to be
a state secret.

At last, increasingly uneasy about his fee, it occurred to him to ask Miss Wynne if it were certain
that Schmidt would not return. If not—ah, there
was the young man who must pay, or the whole story
should be told.

That Miss Gainor kept him waiting for half an
hour he felt as a slight and regarded it as an addition to the many wrongs he had suffered at the hands
of a woman who had learned from time and experience no lessons in prudence.

Increasingly vexed at her delay, when she came in
he was walking about with reckless disregard of the
priceless china with which she delighted to crowd
her drawing-room. As she entered he looked at his
watch, but Mistress Gainor was to-day in high good
humor, having won at piquet of Mrs. Bingham the
night before enough to make her feel comfortably
pleased with Gainor Wynne.

"Bonjour, Monsieur," she said in her fluent an-
glicized French. "I beg pardon for keeping you
waiting; I was dressing." Chovet had rarely been
able to sacrifice his liking to annoy to the practical
interests of the moment, and now, disbelieving her,
he said, "If you will speak English, I may be able to

understand you." This was a little worse than usual.

"Sir," she said, with dignity, "your manners are bad. Never do I permit such things to be said to me. I might say something such as you have said to me in regard to your English and there would be an end of our conversation," upon which she laughed outright. "What makes you so cross, Doctor, and to what do I owe the honor of a visit?"

Then he broke out. "I have been cheated by Mr. Carteaux. He has not paid me a cent. He has got another doctor."

"Wise man, Mr. Carteaux; but what on earth have I to do with that Jacobin?"

In his anger the doctor had quite lost sight for the moment of the object of his visit, which was to know if Schmidt had gone never to return, as was freely reported. Now he remembered.

"I desire to know if Mr. Schmidt will come back. He promised to pay if Carteaux did not. Oh, it is a fine story—of him and De Courval. A despatch has been stolen—every one knows that. I am not to be trifled with, Madame. I can tell a nice tale."

"Can you, indeed? I advise you to be careful what you say. Mr. Schmidt will return and then you will get some unusual interest on your money. Have you no sense of honor that you must talk as you have done?"

"I do never talk," he said, becoming uneasy.

Miss Gainor rose, having heard all she wished to hear. "Lord! man, talk! You do nothing else. You have been chattering about this matter to Mrs.

Byrd. If I were you, I should be a bit afraid. How much money is owing you?"

"Three hundred dollars, and—I have lost patients, too. I have—"

"Sit down," she said. "Don't behave like a child." She went to her desk, wrote a check and gave it to him. "May I trouble you for a receipt?" He gave it, surprised and pleased. "And now do hold your tongue if you can, or if Mr. Schmidt does not beat you when he comes home, I will. You have no more decency than you have hair."

This set him off again. "Ah you think it is only money, money. You, a woman, can say things. I am insult," he cried. "I will have revenge of Schmidt, if he do come. I will have blood."

"Blood, I would," she said. "Get your lancet ready." She broke into laughter at the idea of a contest with the German. "I will hear no more. These are my friends." When in one of her fits of wrath, now rare, she was not choice of her words. Both were now standing. "A flea and a bear, you and Schmidt! Lord, but he will be scared—poor man!"

He too was in a fine rage, such as he never allowed himself with men. "Oh, I am paid, am I? That will not be all of it." He rose on tiptoe, gesticulating wildly, and threw his hands out, shaking them. There was a sudden clatter of broken china.

"Great heavens!" cried Gainor. "Two of my gods gone, and my blue mandarin!"

For a moment he stood appalled amid the wreck of precious porcelain, looking now at Miss Wynne and now at the broken deities.

The owner of the gods towered over the little doctor. Wrath and an overwhelming sense of the comic contended for expression. "Two gods, man! Where now do you expect to go when you die—"

"Nowhere," he said.

"I agree with you. Neither place would have you. You are not good enough for one and not bad enough for the other." She began to enjoy the situation. "I have half a mind to take away that check. It would not pay, but still—"

"I regret—I apologize." He began to fear lest this terrible old woman might have a whole mind in regard to the check.

"Oh," she laughed, "keep it. But I swear to you by all my other gods that if you lie any more about my friends, I shall tell the story Dr. Abernethy told me. In your greed and distrust of men whose simple word is as sure as their bond, you threaten to tell a tale. Well, I will exchange stories with you. I shall improve mine, too."

"Ah," he cried, "you do promise, and keep no word. You have told already Schmidt of me."

"I did—and one other; but now the whole town shall hear. You were ingenious, but the poor highwayman was too well hanged."

Chovet grew pale. "Oh, Madame, you would not. I should be ruined."

"Then be careful and—go away. I sometimes lose my temper, but never my memory. Remember."

He looked up at the big woman as she stood flushed with anger, and exclaiming under his breath, "*Quelle diablesse!*" went out scared and uneasy.

Looking from the window, she saw him walk away. His hands hung limp at his sides, his head was dropped on his breast; not even Ça Ira looked more dejected.

"Good heavens! the man ought to have a bearing-rein. I much fear the mischief is done. The little brute! He is both mean and treacherous."

She turned to look down at the wreckage of her household Lares and rang the bell.

Cæsar appeared. "Sweep up my gods, and take them away. Good heavens! I ought to have flattered the man. I promised the blue mandarin to Darthea Wynne because he always nodded yes to her when she wanted advice to her liking. Well, well, I am a blundering old idiot." She had indeed made mischief, and repentance, as usual with her, came late. She had, however, only added to the mischief. Chovet had already said enough, and the loss of the despatch and the attack on Carteaux by a clerk of the Department of State aroused anew the Democrats and fed the gossip of the card-tables, while René rode on his homeward way with a mind at ease. Nothing had so disturbed the social life of the city for many a day. Before long the matter came to the ear of the Secretary of State, who saw at once its bearing upon his department and the weapon it would be in the hands of party. It was, however, he said to Mr. Bingham, too wild a story for ready credence, and De Courval would soon be at home.

A day later, Fauchet presented to the amazed and angry Secretary of State Carteaux's formal state-

ment, but made no explanation of its delay except
the illness of his attaché. The man was near to
death. He himself believed his statement, the words
of a man about to die. Randolph stood still in
thought. "Your charge, sir," he said, and he spoke
French well, "is that my clerk, the Vicomte de Courval, has stolen your despatch and perhaps fatally
wounded the gentleman commissioned to deliver it."

"You state it correctly. I am not surprised."

The tone was so insolent that Randolph said
sharply: "You are not surprised? Am I to presume
that you consider me a party to the matter?"

"I have not said so, but subordinates are sometimes too zealous and—"

"And what, sir?"

"It is idle to suppose that the theft had no motive.
There was some motive, but what it was perhaps the
English party may be able to explain. My despatch
is lost. Your secretary took it with the help of one
Schmidt. The loss is irreparable and of great moment. I insist, sir, that the one man who has not
fled be dealt with by you, and by the law."

"I shall wait, sir, until I hear the vicomte's story.
He is a gentleman of irreproachable character, a
man of honor who has served us here most faithfully.
I shall wait to hear from him. Your secretary seems
to have lied at first and waited long to tell this amazing story."

The minister did not explain, but said sharply:

"It will be well if that despatch can be found. It
was meant only for the Ministry of Foreign Affairs."

"I do not understand you."

Fauchet laughed. "I trust that you may never have occasion to understand me better." He was angry, and lost both his prudence and what little manners he ever possessed. "It is desirable, or at least it is to be hoped that the thief destroyed it."

"The gentleman you condemn, sir, is not yet on trial, and this has gone far enough and too far. I shall lay the matter in due time before the President." Upon which he bowed out the Republican envoy.

Greatly annoyed, Mr. Randolph put the matter before the members of the cabinet, who agreed that in justice they must wait for De Courval's return.

Meanwhile Chovet's gossip had done its work, and there were a dozen versions which amused many, made others angry, and fed the strife of parties; for now Fauchet spoke of it everywhere with the utmost freedom.

"It is incredible," said Governor Penn; and the women, too, were all on the side of De Courval, while Mr. Wynne, in great anxiety, thought fit to call at Mrs. Swanwick's for news of the vicomte.

He saw in a moment that the widow had heard some of the stories so freely talked about. She had found to her relief some one to whom she could speak. "What is all this," she asked, "I hear about Friend de Courval? My Uncle Josiah has been to tell me and I could make nothing of it?"

"I know, Mary, only the wildest tales. But when De Courval returns, I desire to see him at once."

"His mother heard from him to-day and we look for him possibly to-morrow. Gainor Wynne has been here, in a fine rage. The young man has very warm friends, Hugh. I cannot believe a word of it.''

"Nor I, what I hear. But let him see me at once." The widow was distressed. "Something there must have been. Alas, my poor Margaret!''

Her life had been for many years a constant struggle with poverty, made harder by remembrance of early days of ease and luxury. She bore it all with high-hearted courage and the pride which for some inexplicable reason will accept any gift except money. It became an easier life when Schmidt took of her his two rooms and became by degrees their friend, while the fact that the daughter, inheriting her beauty, was like herself of Friends, did in a measure keep their lives simple and free from the need for many luxuries she saw in the homes of their cousins. Mrs. Swanwick thought, too, of these strangers whom she had nursed, of the vicomtesse, at times a little trying with her sense of what was due to her; of her son, kindly, grave, thoughtful of others, religious,—that was singular,—and twice, as it was said, engaged in bloody quarrels. How could one understand that?

She knew what her bountiful nature had given these exiles. Now she was again to be a reproach among Friends and to feel that these people had brought into her quiet home for her child only misfortune and sorrow. If Schmidt were but here! Margaret was at home, busy and joyful, knowing nothing of what lay before her or of this sinister story of attempted murder and robbery. Resolutely setting it all aside, Mrs. Swanwick went out to provide for the wants of the day.

A half hour later De Courval crossed the city, riding along High Street. A pleasant comrade—Joy—went with him as he turned down Front Street, past widely separated houses and gardens gay with flowers. Once they had been country homes, but now the city was slowly crowding in on them with need for docks. He left his horse at the stable and walked swiftly homeward.

Mrs. Swanwick's house was still remote enough to be secure from the greed of commerce. The dusty, gray road before him, dry with the intense heat of August, ran southward. No one was in sight. There was something mysteriously depressing in the long highway without sign of life, a reminder of that terrible summer when day by day he had come out of the house and seen no one.

As he drew near Mrs. Swanwick's door, he met Captain Biddle. "Oh, by George!" said the sailor, "so you are come at last, and none too soon. I have been here thrice."

"What is the matter, Captain? Is any one ill?"

"No; but there is a lot of lies about you. There is neither decency nor charity ashore. Have you been at the State Department or seen any one?"

"No. I am this moment come back. But, for God's sake, Captain, tell me what it is."

"A fellow named Carteaux has charged you with half killing him and stealing his despatches. That is all I know."

"Is that all? *Diable!* I am sorry I did not

wholly kill him. I knew this would come out soon or late. Of course he is lying; but I did shoot him.''

''There is a malignant article in the 'Aurora' to-day—there, I marked it.''

René looked it over as he stood. ''So I am the thief, I am the agent of the cabinet or the Federal party, and *mon Dieu*, Schmidt—''

''It is serious,'' said the captain. ''A horsewhip is the weapon needed here, but I am at your service in every way.''

''Thank you; but first of all, I must see Mr. Randolph; and, oh, worst of all, Schmidt is absent!'' He felt that he could not meet Margaret until he had put an end to this slander. He foresaw also that to meet with success would, in Schmidt's absence, be difficult. Thanking his sailor friend, he made haste to see his official superior.

''Ah,'' said Randolph, ''I am both glad and sorry to see you. Sit down. Have you heard of the charges against you made by Mr. Fauchet for his secretary, Carteaux?''

''Nothing very clear, sir; but enough to bring me here instantly to have the thing explained to me.''

''Pray read this statement.''

De Courval read Carteaux's deposition and, flushing with sudden anger he threw the paper on the table. ''So it seems I deliberately waylaid and shot the secretary of an envoy in order to steal his despatches.''

''That is the charge, made by a man who I am assured is dying. You can have no objection to my asking you a few questions.''

"None. I shall like it."

"Did you shoot this man?"

"I did. He was of the mock court which murdered my father at Avignon. Any French gentleman here can tell you—Du Vallon for one, and De Noailles. Of the direct personal part this man took in causing my father's death I have not talked. Twice he has had the equal chance I would have given a gentleman. Yes, I meant to kill him."

"But, Vicomte—"

"Pardon me." And he told briefly the story of Carteaux's treacherous shot and of why for a while it seemed well to Schmidt to silence the man.

"It was unwise. A strange and sad affair," said the secretary, "but, Monsieur, it is only this recent matter which concerns me, and the fact, the unfortunate fact, that your enemy was a bearer of despatches. Who can substantiate your statement as against that of a man said to be dying? Who can I call upon?"

"No one. Mr. Schmidt saw it. He is in Europe. The man lies. It is his word or mine. He says here nothing of its being only a personal quarrel; and why did he wait? Ah, clearly until Schmidt, who saw it all, had gone to Europe and I was absent."

"Why he waited I cannot say. The rest concerns me greatly. Did you destroy his despatches?"

"*Mon Dieu!* I? No. Mr. Schmidt, in cutting open his clothes to get at his wound, found those papers, and then seeing what I had done, and how the department might be credited with it, or at least the English party, I myself carried the despatch to its address, the captain of the *Jean Bart*."

"Did you get a receipt?"

"I asked for it. It was refused. The captain was angry at what he said had been dangerous delay, and refused unless I would come on board and talk to him. I of course declined to do so. I would certainly have been carried to France."

"She has sailed, the *Jean Bart?*"

"Yes, sir."

"Then what proof have you as against the deposition of a man *in extremis?*"

"None but my word, that I gave to an officer of the corvette a package of papers."

"The minister was insolent enough to hint that this was a robbery in the interest of my service and a plot of the Federalist English sympathizers. In fact, he implied even more. I am asked to dismiss you as proof that we at least are in no way a party to the matter."

"One moment, Mr. Secretary—would that be proof?"

"No, sir. Pardon me. This affair has been twice before the cabinet, where, to be frank, some difference of opinion existed. The President—but no matter. You admit the fact of the assault and, well, the taking of the paper. You do not deny either. You have no evidence in favor of your explanation, —none."

"Pardon me; I have said De Noailles could assure you that I had cause for a personal quarrel."

"Admit the personal motive, it does not help you. The Republicans are using this scandal freely, and we have quite enough complications, as you know.

If these people urge it, the law may be appealed to. To conclude, this is not a cabinet matter, and it was so decided. It affects the honor of my own department.''

''Sir, the honor!'' De Courval rose as he spoke. ''You have said what I could permit no one but my official superior to say.''

''I regret to have been so unpleasant, but having duly considered the matter, I must reluctantly ask you not to return to the office until you can clear yourself by other evidence than your own. I deeply regret it.''

''You are plain enough, sir, and I most unfortunate. It does seem to me that my life here might at least give my word value as against that of this lying Jacobin.''

The Secretary made no reply. Randolph, although a kindly man and courteous, had nothing more to say to the young clerk. He was but one of many *émigré* nobles cast on our shores, and his relations with the Secretary had been simply official, although, as the latter would have admitted, the service rendered had been of the best.

Still standing, René waited a moment after his personal appeal for justice, but, as I have said, the Secretary did not see fit to answer. To have bluntly refused Fauchet's demand would have been his desire and decision; but as a matter of policy he must do something to disarm party criticism. With this in mind he had offered the young man a compromise; and not quite sure that he should not have dismissed him, he seemed to himself, considering all things, to have acted with moderation.

"'Then I beg to resign my position'"

De Courval, who had waited on the Secretary's silence, said at last, "I judge, sir, that you have no more to say."

"No. I am sorry that nothing you have told me changes this very painful situation."

"Then I beg to resign my position. I have many friends and time will do me justice."

The Secretary would have preferred the young vicomte to have accepted his offer. He was not assured that Carteaux's story was correct; but what else could he do? "Are you not hasty?" he said.

"No. You believe me to have lied, and my sole witness, Mr. Schmidt, is in Germany. It is he who is slandered as well as I. I shall come here no more. Here is my report on the condition of the frontier counties."

"No, Vicomte. I did not doubt your word, but only your power to prove your truth for others who do not know you."

"It amounts to the same thing," said De Courval, coldly. "Good morning."

He went to his own office, and stood a moment in the small, whitewashed room, reflecting with indignant anger on the sudden ending of a career he had enjoyed. Then he gathered his personal belongings and calling the old negro caretaker, bade him carry them to Mrs. Swanwick's.

As for the last time he went down the steps, he said to himself: "So I am thrown to the wolves of party! I knew I should be, and I said so," which was hardly just to the man he left, who would have been pleased if his compromise had been accepted.

23

Little could Randolph have imagined that the remote agency of the man he had thus thrown over
would result for himself in a situation not unlike
that which he had created for his subordinate.

"I am ruined," murmured De Courval. "Who
will believe me? and Margaret! My God! that is at
an end! And my mother!"

He walked slowly homeward, avoiding people and
choosing the alley by-ways so numerous in Penn's
city.

The hall door was usually open in the afternoon
to let the breeze pass through. He went into
Schmidt's room, and then into the garden, seeing
only Nanny and black Cicero, with whom he was a
favorite. No one was in but madame, his mother.
Mr. Girard had been to ask for him and Mr. Bingham and Mr. Wynne, and others. So it was to be
the mother first.

He was used to the quiet, unemotional welcome.
He kissed her hand and her forehead, saying, "You
look well, mother, despite the heat."

"Yes, I am well. Tell me of your journey. Ah,
but I am glad to see you! I have had but one letter.
You should have written more often." The charm
of his mother's voice, always her most gracious quality, just now affected him almost to tears.

"I did write, mother, several times. The journey
may wait. I have bad news for you."

"None is possible for me while you live, my son."

"Yes, yes," he said. "The man Carteaux, having
heard of Schmidt's absence and mine, has formally
charged me with shooting him without warning in
order to steal his despatches."

"Ah, you should have killed him. I said so."

"Yes, perhaps. The charge is clearly made on paper, attested by witnesses. He is said to be dying."

"Thank God."

"I have only my word." He told quietly of the weakness of his position, of the political aspect of the affair, of his interview and his resignation.

"Did you ask Mr. Randolph to apologize, René?"

"Oh, mother, one cannot do that with a cabinet minister."

"Why not? And is this all? You resign a little clerkship. I am surprised that it troubles you."

"Mother, it is ruin."

"Nonsense! What is there to make you talk of ruin?"

"The good word of men lost; the belief in my honor. Oh, mother, do you not see it? And it is a case where there is nothing to be done, nothing. If Randolph, after my long service, does not believe me, who will?"

She was very little moved by anything he said. She lived outside of the world of men, one of those island lives on which the ocean waves of exterior existence beat in vain. The want of sympathy painfully affected him. She had said it was of no moment, and had no helpful advice to give. The constantly recurring thought of Margaret came and went as they talked, and added to his pain. He tried to make her see both the shame and even the legal peril of his position. It was quite useless. He was for her the Vicomte de Courval, and these only common people whom a revolution had set in high places. Never before had he fully realized the quality of his mother's unassailable pride. It was a foretaste of what he might have to expect when she should learn of his engagement to Margaret; but now that, too, must end. He went away, exhausted as from a bodily struggle.

In the hall he met Margaret just come in, the joy of time-nurtured love on her face. "Oh, René!" she cried. "How I have longed for thee! Come out into the garden. The servants hear everything in the house."

They went out and sat down under the trees, she talking gaily, he silent.

"What is the matter?" she inquired at last, of a sudden anxious.

"Pearl," he said, "I am a disgraced and ruined man."

"René, what dost thou mean? Disgraced, ruined!"

He poured out this oft-repeated story of Avignon, the scene on the Bristol road, the despatch, and last, his talk with Randolph and his resignation.

"And this," she said, "was what some day I was to hear. It is terrible, but—ruined—oh, that thou art not. Think of the many who love thee! And disgraced? Thou art René de Courval."

"Yes; but, Pearl, dear Pearl, this ends my joy. How can I ask you to marry a man in my position?"

For a moment she said no word. Then she kissed him. "There is my answer, René."

"No, no. It is over. I cannot. As a gentleman, I cannot."

Again the wholesome discipline of Friends came to her assistance. It was a serious young face she saw. He it was who was weak, and she strong.

"Trouble comes to all of us in life, René. I could not expect always to escape. It has come to us in the morning of our love. Let us meet it together. It is a terrible story, this. How can I, an inexperienced girl, know how to regard it? I am sure thou hast done what was right in thine own eyes. My mother will say thou shouldst have left it to God's justice. I do not know. I am not sure. I suppose it is because I so love thee that I do not know. We shall never speak of it again, never. It is the consequences we—yes, we—have to deal with."

"There is no way to deal with them." He was in resourceless despair.

"No, no. Friend Schmidt will return. He is sure to come, and this will all be set right. Dost thou remember how the blessed waters washed away thy care? Is not love as surely good?"

"Oh, yes; but this is different. That was a trifle."

"No; it is the waiting here for Friend Schmidt that troubles me. What is there but to wait? Thou art eager to do something; that is the man's way, and the other is the woman's way. Take thy daily swim, ride, sail; the body will help the soul. It will all come right; but not marry me! Then, René de Courval, I shall marry thee."

A divine hopefulness was in her words, and for the first time he knew what a firm and noble nature had been given the woman at his side, what power to trust, what tenderness, what common sense, and, too, what insight; for he knew she was right. The contrast to his mother was strange, and in a way distressing.

"I must think it over," he said.

"Thou wilt do no such thing. Thou, indeed! As if it were thy business alone! I am a partner thou wilt please to remember. Thou must see thy friends, and, above all, write to Mr. Hamilton at once, and do as I have said. I shall speak to my mother. Hast thou—of course thou hast seen thy mother?"

"I have; and she takes it all as a matter of no moment, really of not the least importance."

"Indeed, and so must we. Now, I am to be kissed —oh, once, for the good of thy soul—I said once. Mr. Bingham has been here. See him and Mr. Wynne, and swim to-night, René, and be careful, too, of my property, thy—dear self.'

Even in this hour of mortification, and with the memory of Randolph's doubt in mind, René had some delightful sense of being taken in hand and disciplined. He had not said again that the tie which bound them together must be broken. He had tacitly accepted the joy of defeat, a little ashamed, perhaps.

Every minute of this talk had been a revelation to the man who had lived near Margaret for years. An older man could have told him that no length of life will reveal to the most observant love all the possibilities of thought or action in the woman who may for years have been his wife. There will always remain surprises of word and deed.

Although René listened and said that he could do

none of the things she urged, the woman knew that he would do all of them.

At last she started up, saying: "Why, René, thou hast not had thy dinner, and now, as we did not look for thee, it is long over. Come in at once."

"Dear Pearl," he said, "I am better let alone. I do not need anything." He wished to be left by himself to brood over the cruel wrong of the morning, and with any one but Pearl he would have shown some sense of irritation at her persistence.

The wild creatures are tamed by starvation, the animal man by good feeding. This fact is the sure possession of every kindly woman; and so it was that De Courval went meekly to the house and was fed,— as was indeed needed,—and having been fed, with the girl watching him, was better in body and happier in mind.

He went at once into Schmidt's study and wrote to Hamilton, while Margaret, sitting in her room at the eastward window, cried a little and smiled between the tears and wondered at the ways of men.

What she said to her mother may be easily guessed. The vicomtesse was as usual at the evening meal, where René exerted himself to talk of his journey to Mrs. Swanwick, less interested than was her way.

The day drew to a close. The shadows came with coolness in the air. The endless embroidery went on, the knitting needles clicked, and a little later in the dusk, Margaret smiled as René went down the garden to the river, a towel on his arm.

"I did him good," she murmured proudly.

Later in the evening they were of one mind that it was well to keep their engagement secret, above all, not to confide it to their relatives or to Miss Wynne until there was some satisfactory outcome of the serious charge which had caused Randolph to act as he had done.

XXVI

MR. HAMILTON'S reply came in five days. He would come at once. De Courval's friends, Bingham and Wynne, had heard his story, and thought he did well to resign, while Wynne advised him to come to Merion for a week or two. His other adviser would not have even the appearance of flight.

"Above all," said Margaret, "go about as usual. Thou must not avoid people, and after Mr. Hamilton comes and is gone, think of Merion if it so please thee, or I can let thee go. Aunt Gainor was here in one of her fine tempers yesterday. I am jealous of her, Monsieur de Courval. And she has her suspicions."

He took her advice, and saw too easily that he was the observed of many; for in the city he had long been a familiar personality, with his clean-shaven, handsome face and the erect figure, which showed the soldier's training. He was, moreover, a favorite, especially with the older men and women, so that not all the looks he met were either from hostile, cockaded Jacobins or from the merely curious.

Mr. Thomas Cadwalader stopped him, and said that at need he was at his service, if he desired to call out the minister or the Secretary. Mrs. Byrd, both curious and kind, would have him to come and tell her all about it, which he was little inclined to do.

He took Margaret's wholesome advice, and swam and rode, and was in a calmer state of mind, and even happy at the greetings of those in the fencing school, where were some whom, out of his slender means, he had helped. They told him gleefully how de Malerive had given up the ice-cream business for a morning to quiet for a few weeks an Irish Democrat who had said of the vicomte unpleasant things; and would he not fence? "Yes, now," he said smiling, and would use the pistol no more.

Mr. Hamilton came as he had promised. "I must return to New York," he said, "to-morrow. I have heard from Schmidt. He may not come very soon; but I wrote him fully, on hearing from you. He will be sure to come soon or late, but meanwhile I have asked General Washington to see you with me. It may, indeed, be of small present use, but I want him to hear you—your own account of this affair. So far he has had only what Mr. Randolph has been pleased to tell him. I made it a personal favor. Let us go. The cabinet meeting will be over."

René thanked him and not altogether assured that any good would result from this visit, walked away with Hamilton, the two men attracting some attention. The President at this time lived on High Street, in the former house of Robert Morris, near to Sixth Street. They were shown into the

office room on the right, which De Courval knew
well, and where Genêt, the Jacobin minister, had
been insulted by the medallions of the hapless king
and queen.

In a few minutes the President entered. He
bowed formally, and said, "Pray be seated, Vicomte. I have been asked, sir, by Mr. Hamilton to
hear you. As you are not now in the service, I am
pleased to allow myself the pleasure to do so, although I have thought it well to advise Mr. Randolph of my intention. Your case has been before
the cabinet, but as yours was a position solely in
the gift of the Secretary of State, I—or we, have
felt that his appointments should lie wholly within
his control."

"And of disappointments, also, I suppose," said
Hamilton, smiling, a privileged person.

Little open to appreciation of humor, no smile
came upon the worn face of the President. He
turned to Hamilton as he spoke, and then went on
addressing De Courval, and speaking, as was his
way, with deliberate slowness. "I have given this
matter some personal consideration because, although Mr. Secretary Randolph has acted as to him
seemed best, you have friends who, to be frank with
you, feel desirous that I should be informed by you
in person of what took place. I am willing to oblige
them. You are, it seems, unfortunate. There are
two serious charges, an assault and—pardon me—
the seizure of a despatch. May I be allowed to ask
you certain questions?"

"I shall be highly honored, sir."

"This, I am given to understand, was a personal quarrel."

"Yes, your Excellency."

"What the law may say of the matter, I do not know. What concerns us most is the despatch. In what I say I desire, sir, to be considered open to correction. When, as I am told, you followed Mr. Carteaux, intending a very irregular duel, did you know that he carried a despatch?"

"I did not until Mr. Schmidt found it. Then the man was cared for, and I delivered his papers to their destination."

"I regret, sir, to hear that of this you have no proof. Here your word suffices. Outside of these walls it has been questioned."

"I have no proof,—none of any value,—nor can I ever hope to prove that I did what my own honor and my duty to the administration required."

Hamilton listened intently while the aging, tired face of the President for a moment seemed lost in reflection. Then the large, blue eyes were lifted as he said, "At present this matter seems hopeless, sir, but time answers many questions." Upon this he turned to Hamilton. "There are two persons involved. Who, sir, is this Mr. Schmidt? I am told that he has left the country; in fact, has fled."

For a moment Hamilton was embarrassed. "I can vouch for him as my friend. He was called to Germany on a matter of moment. At present I am not at liberty to reply to you more fully. He is sure to return, and then I may,—indeed, I am sure, will be more free to answer you frankly.

"But if so, what value will his evidence have? None, I conceive, as affecting the loss of the despatch. If that charge were disproved, the political aspect of the matter would become unimportant. The affair, so far as the duel is concerned, would become less serious."

"It seems so to me," said Hamilton. "The Democrats are making the most of it, and the English Federalists are doing harm by praising my young friend for what he did not do and never would have done. They were mad enough in New York to propose a dinner to the vicomte."

The President rose. "I do not think it advisable, Mr. Hamilton, to pursue this matter further at present; nor, sir, do I apprehend that any good can result for this gentleman from my willingness to gratify your wish that I should see him."

"We shall detain your Excellency no longer."

The President was never fully at ease when speaking, and owing to a certain deliberateness in speech, was thought to be dull when in company and, perhaps through consciousness of a difficulty in expression, was given to silence, a disposition fostered, no doubt, by the statesman's long disciplined need for reticence.

After Hamilton had accepted the President's rising as a signal of their audience being over, René, seeing that the general did not at once move toward the door, waited for Hamilton. The ex-Secretary, however, knew well the ways of his friend and stood still, aware that the President was slowly considering what further he desired to say.

The pause was strange to De Courval as he stood intently watching the tall figure in black velvet, and the large features on which years of war and uneasy peace had left their mark.

Then with more than his usual animation, the President came nearer to De Courval: "I have myself, sir, often had to bide on time for full justification of my actions. While you are in pursuit of means to deal with the suspicions arising, permit me to say, from your own imprudence you will have to bear in silence what men say of you. I regret, to conclude, that I cannot interfere in this matter. I discover it to be more agreeable to say to you that personally I entirely believe you. But this you must consider as spoken 'under the rose' " —a favorite expression. De Courval flushed with joy, and could say no more than: "I thank you. You have helped me to wait."

The general bowed, and at the door, as they were passing out, said: "I shall hope to see you again in the service, and you must not think of retiring permanently from the work which you have done so well. I remind myself that I have not yet thanked you for your report. It has greatly relieved my mind." On this he put out his hand, over which René bowed in silent gratitude, and with a last look at the weary face of the man whose life had been one long sacrifice to duty, he went away, feeling the strengthening influence of a great example.

As they reached the street, René said, "How just he is, and how clear!"

"Yes. A slowly acting mind, but sure—and in

battle, in danger, swift, decisive, and reckless of
peril. Are you satisfied?"

"Yes, I am. I shall be, even though this matter
is never cleared up."

"It will be. He said so, and I have long since
learned to trust his foresight. In all my long experience of the man, I have scarcely ever heard him
speak at such length. You may live to see many
men in high places; you will never see a greater
than George Washington. I know him as few know
him."

He was silent for a moment, and then added,
"When I was young and hasty, and thought more
of Alexander Hamilton than I do to-day, he forgave
me an outburst of youthful impertinence which
would have made a vainer man desire to see no
more of me." De Courval, a less quick-tempered
character, wondered that any one should have taken
a liberty with the man they had just left.

"But now I must leave you," said Hamilton.
"If Schmidt returns, he will land in New York,
and I shall come hither with him. Have you seen
the new paper, the 'Aurora'? Mr. Bache has taken
up the task Freneau dropped—of abusing the
President."

"No, I have not seen it. I suppose now it is the
English treaty. It will interest me no longer."

"Oh, for a time, for a time. Between us, the
President has sent it to the Senate. It will leak out.
He will sign it with a reservation as concerns the
English claim to seize provisions meant for French
ports. Do not speak of it. Randolph is striving to

strengthen the President's scruples with regard to a not altogether satisfactory treaty, but, on the whole, the best we can get. It will be signed and will be of great service. Keep this to yourself, and good-by. Randolph is too French for me. I may have said to you once that if we had a navy, it is not peace that the President would desire."

De Courval hastened home to pour into the ear of Margaret so much of his interview as he felt free to speak of.

"My mother," she said, "would speak to thee of me, René." But he asked that she would wait, and his sense of satisfaction soon gave place, as was natural, to a return of depression, which for a time left him only when in the company of Margaret. Her mother, usually so calm, did most uneasily wait while the days went by, but made no effort to interfere with the lovers.

On the 9th of August, at evening, Margaret and René were seated in the garden when of a sudden René leaped up with a cry of joyous welcome, as he saw Schmidt, large, bronzed and laughing, on the porch.

"*Du Guter Himmel!*" he cried, "but I am content to be here. I have good news for you. *Ach*, let me sit down. Now listen. But first, is it all right, children?"

"May I tell him in my way, René?"

"Yes, of course; but what is your way?"

"This is my way," said Margaret, and bending over, as the German sat on the grass at her feet, she kissed him, saying, "as yet no one knows."

"I am answered, Pearl, and now listen. This morning I met Mr. Randolph and Mr. Hamilton with the President. That was best before seeing you. Mr. Randolph was silent while I told the general plainly the story of your duel. *Ach*, but he has the trick of silence! A good one, too. When I had ended, he said, 'I am to be pardoned, sir, if I ask who in turn will vouch for you as a witness?' "

"Then I said, 'With my apologies to these gentlemen, may I be allowed a brief interview alone with your Excellency, or, rather, may I ask also for Mr. Hamilton to be present?' 'With your permission, Mr. Randolph,' the President said, and showed us into a small side room. There I told him."

"Told him what?" asked Margaret.

"Your husband may tell you, my dear, when you are married. I may as well permit it, whether I like it or not. You would get it out of him."

"I should," she said; "but—it is dreadful to have to wait."

"On our return, his Excellency said, 'Mr. Randolph, I am satisfied as regards the correctness of the Vicomte de Courval's account of Mr. Carteaux's treachery and of the vicomte's ignorance of his errand. Mr. Gouverneur sends me by Mr. Schmidt a letter concerning the despatch.'

"Then Randolph asked quietly: 'Did he see it, sir?'

" 'He knows that the vicomte delivered a packet of papers to the *Jean Bart*.'

" 'And without receipt for them or other evidence?'

" 'Yes. It so seems.'

24

" 'Then I regret to say that all we have heard appears to me, sir, to leave the matter where it was.'

" 'Not quite. Mr. Fauchet is out of office and about to go home. Carteaux, as Mr. Hamilton can tell you, refused to be questioned, and has sailed for France. Adet, the new minister, will not urge the matter. You must pardon me, but, as it appears to me, an injustice has been done.'

"Randolph said testily: 'It is by no means clear to me, and until we hear of that despatch, it never will be.'

"This smileless old man said, 'I am not free to speak of what Mr. Schmidt has confided to me, but it satisfies me fully.' Then he waited to hear what Randolph would say."

"And he?" said René, impatient.

"Oh, naturally enough he was puzzled and I thought annoyed, but said, 'I presume, Mr. President, it is meant that I ought to offer this young man the position he forfeited?'

" 'That, sir,' said the President, 'is for you to decide.'

"Then Mr. Hamilton, who can be as foxy as Jefferson, said in a careless way, 'I think I should wait a little.'

"The moment he said that, I knew what would happen. Randolph said, 'Pardon me, Mr. Hamilton, I prefer to conduct the affairs of my department without aid.' They love not one another, these two. 'I am of the President's opinion. I shall write to the Vicomte de Courval.'

"Mr. Hamilton did seem to me to amuse himself. He smiled a little and said: 'A pity to be in such a hurry. Time will make it all clearer.' Randolph made no reply. You will hear from him to-morrow."

"I shall not accept," said René.

"Yes, you must. It is a full answer to all criticism, and after what the President has said, you cannot refuse."

"Mr. Schmidt is right, René," said Margaret. "Thou must take the place."

"Good, wise little counselor!" said the German. "He will write you a courteous note, René. He has had, as Hamilton says, enough differences with the chief to make him willing to oblige him in a minor matter. You must take it."

At last, it being so agreed, Schmidt went in to see Mrs. Swanwick and to relieve her as concerned a part, at least, of her troubles. The rest he would talk about later.

Even the vicomtesse was so good as to be pleased, and the evening meal was more gay than usual.

The next morning René received the following note:

DEAR SIR: My opinion in regard to the matter under discussion of late having been modified somewhat, and the President favoring my action, it gives me pleasure to offer you the chance to return to the office.

I have the honor to be,

Your obedient friend and servant,

EDMUND RANDOLPH.

Schmidt laughed as he read it. "He does not like it. The dose is bitter. He thinks you will say no. But you will write simply, and accept with pleasure."

"Yes, I see. I shall do as you say." He sent a simple note of acceptance. A visit to the office of state settled the matter, and on the day but one after receipt of the letter, René was well pleased to be once more at his desk and busy.

Meanwhile Schmidt had been occupied with long letters to Germany and his affairs in the city, but in the evening of the 12th of August, they found time for one of their old talks.

"This matter of yours, and in fact of mine, René, does not fully satisfy me. I still hear much about it, and always of that infernal despatch."

"It does not satisfy me, sir."

"Well, it seems to me that it will have to. Long ago that despatch must be in Paris; but Mr. Monroe, our minister, could learn nothing about it. And so you two young folks have arranged your affairs. I can tell you that Miss Gainor will be sorry to have had no hand in this business, and Uncle Josiah, too."

"That is droll enough. I am glad to have pleased somebody. We have thought it better not as yet to speak of it."

"Have you told your mother, René? You may be sure that she will know, or guess at the truth, and resent being left in the dark."

"That is true; but you may very well imagine that I dread what she will say of Margaret. We have never had a serious difference, and now it is to come. I shall talk to her to-morrow."

"No, now. Get it over, sir. Get it over. I must go home again soon, and I want to see you married. Go now at once and get it over."

"I suppose that will be as well."

He went slowly up the winding staircase which was so remarkable a feature of the finer Georgian houses. Suddenly he was aware in the darkness of Margaret on the landing above him.

"Don't stop me," she said.

"What is wrong?" he asked.

"Everything. I told thee thy mother would know. She sent for me. I went. She was cruel—cruel—hard."

"What, dear, did she say?"

"I shall not tell thee. She insulted me and my mother. Ah, but she said—no, I shall not tell thee, nor mother. She sent for me, and I went. I had to tell her. Oh, I said that—that—I told her—I do not know what I told her." She was on the edge of her first almost uncontrollable loss of self-government. It alarmed her pride, and at once becoming calm, she added, "I told her that it was useless to talk to me, to say that it must end, that thou wouldst obey her. I—I just laughed; yes, I did. And I told her she did not yet know her own son—and—that some day she would regret what she had said to me, and, René, of my mother. I do not care—"

"But I care, Margaret. I was this moment on my way to tell her."

"Let me pass. I hope thou art worth what I have endured for thy sake. Let me pass." He went by her, troubled and aware that he too needed to keep himself in hand. When he entered his mother's room he found her seated by the feeble candle-light, a rose of the never-finished embroidery growing under her thin, skilful fingers.

For her a disagreeable matter had been decisively dealt with and put aside; no trace of emotion betrayed her self-satisfaction at having finally settled an unpleasant but necessary business.

In the sweet, low voice which seemed so out of relation to her severity of aspect, she said: "Sit down. I have been left to learn from the young woman of this entanglement. I should have heard it from you, or never have had to hear it at all."

"Mother, I have been in very great trouble of late. That my disaster did trouble you so little has been painful to me. But this is far worse. I waited to feel at ease about the other affair before I spoke to you of my intention to marry Miss Swanwick. I was on my way just now when I met her on the stair. I desire to say, mother—"

She broke in: "It is useless to discuss this absurd business. It is over. I have said so to the young woman. That ends it. Now kiss me. I wish to go to bed."

"No," he said; "this does not end it."

"Indeed, we shall see—a quite ordinary Quaker girl and a designing mother. It is all clear enough. Neither of you with any means, not a louis of dot— a nice wife to take home. Oh, I have expressed myself fully, and it was needed. She presumed to contradict me. *Ciel!* I had to be plain."

"So it seems; but as I count for something, I beg

leave to say, *maman*, that I mean to marry Margaret Swanwick.''

''You, the Vicomte de Courval!''

He laughed bitterly. ''What are titles here, or in France, to-day? There are a dozen starving nobles in this city, exiles and homeless. As to money, I have charge of Mr. Schmidt's affairs, and shall have. I am not without business capacity.''

''Business!'' she exclaimed.

''Well, no matter, mother. I pray you to be reasonable, and to remember what these people have done for us: in health no end of kindness; in sickness—mother, I owe to them my life.''

''They were paid, I presume.''

''*Mon Dieu*, mother! how can you say such things? It is incredible.''

''René, do you really mean to disobey me?''

''I hope not to have to do so.''

''If you persist, you will have to. I shall never consent, never.''

''Then, mother,—and you force me to say it,— whether you agree to it or not, I marry Margaret You were hard to her and cruel.''

''No; I was only just and wise.''

''I do not see it; but rest assured that neither man nor woman shall part us. Oh, I have too much of you in me to be controlled in a matter where both love and honor are concerned.''

''Then you mean to make this *mésalliance* against my will.''

''I mean, and that soon, to marry the woman I think worthy of any man's love and respect.''

"She is as bad as you—two obstinate fools! I am sorry for your children."

"Mother!"

"Well, and what now?"

"It is useless to resist. It will do no good. It only hurts me. Did your people want you to marry Jean de Courval, my father?"

"No."

"You did. Was it a *mésalliance?*"

"They said so."

"You set me a good example. I shall do as you did, if, after this, her pride does not come in the way."

"Her pride, indeed! Will it be to-morrow, the marriage?"

"Ah, dear mother, why will you hurt me so?"

"I know you as if it were myself. I take the lesser of two evils." And to his amazement, she said, "Send the girl up to me."

"If she will come."

"Come? Of course she will come." He shook his head and left her, but before he was out of the room, her busy hands were again on the embroidery-frame.

"No, I will not go," said Margaret when he delivered his message.

"For my sake, dear," said René, and at last, reluctant and still angry, Margaret went up-stairs.

"Come in," said madame; "you have kept me waiting." The girl stood still at the open door.

"Do not stand there, child. Come here and sit down."

"No," said Margaret, "I shall stand."

"As you please, Mademoiselle. My son has made up his mind to an act of folly. I yield because I must. He is obstinate, as you will some day discover to your cost. I cannot say I am satisfied, but as you are to be my daughter, I shall say no more. You may kiss me. I shall feel better about it in a few years, perhaps."

Never, I suppose, was Margaret's power of self-command more sorely tried. She bent over, lifted the hand of the vicomtesse from the embroidery, and kissed it, saying, "Thou art René's mother, Madame," and, turning, left the room.

René was impatiently walking in the hall when Margaret came down the stair from this brief interview. She was flushed and still had in her eyes the light of battle. "I have done as you desired. I cannot talk any more. I have had all I can stand. No, I shall not kiss thee. My kisses are spoilt for to-night." Then she laughed as she went up the broad stairway, and, leaning over the rail, cried: "There will be two for to-morrow. They will keep. Good night."

The vicomtesse she left was no better pleased, and knew that she had had the worst of the skirmish.

"I hate it. I hate it," she said, "but that was well done of the maid. Where did she get her fine ways?" She was aware, as René had said in some wrath, that she could not insult these kind people and continue to eat their bread. The dark lady with the wan, ascetic face, as of a saint of many fasts, could abide poverty and accept bad diet, but nevertheless did like very well the things which make life pleasant, and had been more than comfortable amid the good fare and faultless cleanliness of the Quaker house.

She quite well understood that the matter could not remain in the position in which she had left it. She had given up too easily; but now she must take the consequences. Therefore it was that the next day after breakfast she said to Margaret, "I desire to talk to you a little."

"Certainly, Madame. Will the withdrawing-room answer?"

"Yes, here or there." Margaret closed the door as she followed the vicomtesse, and after the manner of her day stood while the elder woman sat very upright in the high-backed chair prophetically de-signed for her figure and the occasion."

"Pray be seated," she said. "I have had a white night, Mademoiselle, if you know what that is. I have been sleepless." If this filled Margaret with pity, I much doubt. "I have had to elect whether I quarrel with my son or with myself. I choose the latter, and shall say no more than this—I am too straightforward to avoid meeting face to face the hardships of life."

"Bless me, am I the hardship?" thought Margaret, her attitude of defiant pride somewhat modi-fied by assistant sense of the comic.

"I shall say only this: I have always liked you. Whether I shall ever love you or not, I do not know. I have never had room in my heart for more than one love. God has so made me," which the young woman thought did comfortably and oddly shift responsibility, and thus further aided to restore her good humor.

"We shall be friends, Margaret." She rose as she spoke, and setting her hands on Margaret's shoulders as she too stood, said: "You are beautiful, child, and you have very good manners. There are things to be desired, the want of which I much regret; otherwise—" She felt as if she had gone far enough. "Were these otherwise, I should have been satisfied." Then she kissed her coldly on the forehead.

Margaret said, "I shall try, Madame, to be a good daughter," and, falling back, courtesied, and left the tall woman to her meditations.

Madame de Courval and Mary Swanwick knew that soon or late what their children had settled they too must discuss. Neither woman desired it, the vicomtesse aware that she might say more than she meant to say, the Quaker matron in equal dread lest things might be said which would make the future difficult. Mary Swanwick usually went with high courage to meet the calamities of life, and just at present it is to be feared that she thus classified the stern puritan dame. But now she would wait no longer, and having so decided on Saturday, she chose Sunday morning, when—and she smiled—the vicomtesse having been to Gloria Dei and she herself to Friends' meeting, both should be in a frame of mind for what she felt might prove a trial of good temper.

Accordingly, having heard the gentle Friend Howell discourse, and bent in silent prayer for patience and charity, she came home and waited until from the window of Schmidt's room she saw the tall, black figure approach.

She went out to the hall and let in Madame de Courval, saying: "I have waited for thee. Wilt thou come into the withdrawing-room? I have that to say which may no longer be delayed."

"I myself had meant to talk with you of this unfortunate matter. It is as well to have it over." So saying she followed her hostess. Both women sat upright in the high-backed chairs, the neat, gray-clad Quaker lady, tranquil and rosy; the black figure of the Huguenot dame, sallow, with grave, unmoved features, a strange contrast.

"I shall be pleased to hear you, Madame Swanwick."

"It is simple. I have long seen that there was a growth of attachment between our children. I did not—I do not approve it."

"Indeed," said Madame de Courval, haughtily. What was this woman to sit in judgment on the Vicomte de Courval?

"I have done my best to keep them apart. I spoke to Margaret, and sent her away again and again as thou knowest. It has been in vain, and now having learned that thou hast accepted a condition of things we do neither of us like, I have thought it well to have speech of thee."

"I do not like it, and I never shall. I have, however, yielded a reluctant consent. I cannot quarrel with my only child; but I shall never like it—never."

"Never is a long day."

"I am not of those who change. There is no fitness in it, none. My son is of a class far above her. They are both poor." A sharp reply to the reference to social distinctions was on Mary Swanwick's tongue. She resisted the temptation, and said quietly:

"Margaret will not always be without means; my uncle will give her, on his death, all he has; and as to class, Madame, the good Master to whom we prayed this morning, must—"

"It is not a matter for discussion," broke in the elder woman.

"No; I agree with thee. It is not, but—were it not as well that two Christian gentlewomen should accept the inevitable without reserve and not make their children unhappy?"

"Gentlewomen!"

Mary Swanwick reddened. "I said so. We, too, are not without the pride of race you value. A poor business, but,"—and she looked straight at the vicomtesse, unable to resist the temptation to retort —"we are not given to making much of it in speech."

Madame de Courval had at times entertained Margaret with some of the grim annals of her father's people. Now, feeling the thrust, and not liking it, or that she had lost her temper, she shifted her ground, and being at heart what her hostess described as a gentlewoman, said stiffly: "I beg pardon; I spoke without thought." At this moment Margaret entered, and seeing the signals of discomposure on both faces, said: "Oh, you two dear people whom I love and want to love more and more, you are talking of me and of René. Shall I give him up, Madame, and send him about his business.''

"Do, dear," laughed her mother, relieved.

There was no mirth to be had out of it for Yvonne de Courval.

"It is not a matter for jesting," she said. "He is quite too like me to be other than obstinate, and this, like what else of the trials God has seen fit to send, is to be endured. He is too like me to change."

"Then," said Margaret, gaily, "thou must be like him."

"I suppose so," said the vicomtesse, with a note of melancholy in her tones.

"Then if thou art like him, thou wilt have to love me," cried Margaret. The mother smiled at this pretty logic, but the Huguenot dame sat up on her chair, resentful of the affectionate familiarity of the girl's gaiety.

"Your mother and I have talked, and what use is it? I shall try to care for you, and love may come. But I could have wished—"

"Oh, no!" cried Margaret. "Please to say no more. Thou will only hurt me."

"I remain of the same opinion; I am not of a nature which allows me to change without reason."

"And as for me," said Mrs. Swanwick, smiling as she rose, "I yield when I must."

"I, too," said the dark lady; "but to yield outwardly is not to give up my opinions, nor is it easy or agreeable to do so. We will speak of it another time, Madame Swanwick.'' But they never did, and so this interview ended with no very good result, except to make both women feel that further talk would be of no use, and that the matter was settled.

As the two mothers rose, Miss Gainor entered, large, smiling, fresh from Christ Church. Quick to observe, she saw that something unusual had occurred, and hesitated between curiosity and the reserve which good manners exacted.

''Good morning,'' she said. ''I heard that Mr. Schmidt had come back, and so I came at once from church to get all the news from Europe for the Penns, where I go to dine.''

''Europe is unimportant,'' cried Margaret, disregarding a warning look from her mother. ''I am engaged to be married to Monsieur de Courval—and—everybody—is pleased. Dear Aunt Gainor, I like it myself.''

''I at least am to be excepted,'' said the vicomtesse, ''as Mademoiselle knows. I beg at present to be saved further discussion. May I be excused—''

''It seems, Madame,'' returned Miss Wynne, smiling, ''to have got past the need for discussion. I congratulate you with all my heart.''

''*Mon Dieu!*'' exclaimed the vicomtesse, forgetful of her Huguenot training, and swept by Miss Gainor's most formal courtesy and was gone.

''Dear child,'' cried Mistress Wynne, as she caught Margaret in her arms, ''I am glad as never before. The vicomte has gone back to the service and—you are to marry—oh, the man of my choice. The poor vicomtesse, alas! Where is the vicomte?"

"He is out just now. We did mean to tell thee this evening."

"Ah! I am glad it came earlier, this good news. May I tell them at the governor's?"

"I may as well say yes," cried Margaret. "Thou wouldst be sure to tell."

"I should," said Gainor.

XXVII

BOTH mothers had accepted a situation which neither entirely liked; but the atmosphere was cleared, and the people most concerned were well satisfied and happy. Miss Gainor joyously distributed the news. Gay cousins called, and again the late summer afternoons saw in the garden many friends who had sturdily stood by De Courval in his day of discredit.

If Randolph was cool to him, others were not, and the office work and the treaty were interesting, while in France affairs were better, and the reign of blood had passed and gone.

The warm days of August went by, and De Courval's boat drifted on the river at evening, where he lay and talked to Margaret, or listened, a well-contented man. There were parties in the country, dinners with the Peters at Belmont, or at historic Cliveden. Schmidt, more grave than usual, avoided these festivities, and gave himself to lonely rides, or to long evenings on the river when De Courval was absent or otherwise occupied, as was commonly the case.

When late one afternoon he said to René, "I want you to lend me Margaret for an hour," she cried, laughing, "Indeed, I lend myself; and I make my lord vicomte obey, as is fitting before marriage. I have not yet promised to obey after it, and I am at thy service, Friend Schmidt."

René laughed and said, "I am not left much choice," whereupon Schmidt and Margaret went down to the shore, and soon their boat lay quiet far out on the river.

"They are talking," said the young lover. "I wonder what about."

In fact they had not exchanged even the small current coin of conventional talk; both were silent until Schmidt laid down his oars, and the boat silently drifted upward with the tide. It was the woman who spoke first.

"Ah, what a true friend thou hast been!"

"Yes, I have that way a talent. Why did you bring me out here to flatter me?"

"I did think it was thou proposed it; but I do wish to talk with thee. My mother is not well pleased because the other mother is ill pleased. I do want every one I love to feel that all is well with René and me, and that the love I give is good for him."

"It is well for you and for him, my child, and as for that grim fortress of a woman, she will live to be jealous of your mother and of René. An east wind of a woman. She will come at last to love you, Pearl."

"Ah, dost thou really think so?"

"Yes."

"And thou art pleased. We thought thou wert grave of late and less—less gay."

"I am more than pleased, Margaret. I am not sad, but only grieved over the coming loss out of my life of simple days and those I love, because soon, very soon, I go away to a life of courts and idle ceremonies, and perhaps of strife and war.''

For a moment or two neither spoke. The fading light seemed somehow to the girl to fit her sense of the gravity of this announcement of a vast loss out of life. Her eyes filled as she looked up.

''Oh, why dost thou go? Is not love and reverence and hearts that thank thee—oh, are not these enough? Why dost thou go?''

''You, dear, who know me will understand when I answer with one word—duty.''

''I am answered,'' she said, but the tears ran down her cheeks.

''René will some day tell you more, indeed, all; and you will know why I must leave you.'' Then, saying no more, he took up the oars and pulled into the shore. René drew up the boat.

''Will you go out with me now, Margaret?''

''Not this evening, René,'' she said, and went slowly up to the house.

On one of these later August days, Mr. Hammond, the English minister, at his house in the country was pleased, being about to return home, to ask the company of Mr. Wolcott of the Treasury. There were no other guests, and after dinner the minister, to add zest to his dessert, handed to Wolcott the now famous intercepted Despatch No. 10, sent back by Lord Grenville after its capture, to make still further mischief. Having been told the story of the wanderings of this fateful document, the Secretary read it with amazement, and understood at once that it was meant by Hammond to in-

jure Randolph, whose dislike of the Jay treaty and
what it yielded to England was well known in London. Much disturbed by what he gathered, Wolcott
took away the long document, agreeing to give a
certified copy to Hammond, who, having been recalled, was well pleased to wing this Parthian arrow.

The next day Wolcott showed it to his colleagues,
Pickering and the Attorney-General. As it seemed
to them serious, they sent an urgent message to the
President, which brought back the weary man from
his rest at Mount Vernon. On his return, the
President, despite Randolph's desire for further
delay, called a cabinet meeting, and with a strong
remonstrance against the provision clause which
yielded the hated rights of search, decided to ratify
the treaty with England.

The next day he was shown the long-lost, intercepted Despatch No. 10.

Greatly disturbed, he waited for several days,
and then again called together his advisers, naming
for Randolph a half-hour later.

On this, the 19th of August, De Courval, being at
his desk, was asked to see an express rider who had
come with a report of Indian outrages on the frontier. The Secretary of State having gone, as he
learned, to a cabinet meeting, De Courval made
haste to find him, being well aware of the grave
import of the news thus brought. Arriving at the
house of the President, he was shown as usual into
the drawing-room, and sat down to wait among a
gay party of little ones who were practising the
minuet with the young Custis children under the

tuition of a sad-looking, old *émigré* gentleman. The small ladies courtesied to the new-comer, the marquis bowed. The violin began again, and René sat still, amused.

Meanwhile in the room on the farther side of the hall, Washington discussed with Pickering and Oliver Wolcott the fateful, intercepted despatch. A little later Randolph entered the hall, and desiring De Courval to wait with his papers, joined the cabinet meeting.

As he entered, the President rose and said, "Mr. Randolph, a matter has been brought to my knowledge in which you are deeply concerned." He spoke with great formality, and handing him Fauchet's despatch, added, "Here is a letter which I desire you to read and make such explanation in regard to it as you choose."

Randolph, amazed, ran his eye over the long report of Fauchet to his home office, the other secretaries watching him in silence. He flushed with sudden anger as he read on, while no one spoke, and the President walked up and down the room. This is what the Secretary of State saw in Fauchet's despatch:

Mr. Randolph came to see me with an air of great eagerness just before the proclamation was made in regard to the excise insurrection, and made to me overtures of which I have given you an account in my despatches No. 6 and No. 3. Thus with some thousands of dollars the French Republic could have decided on war or peace. Thus the consciences of the pretended patriots of America have already their prices [*tarif*].

Then followed abuse of Hamilton and warm praise of Jefferson and Madison.

"The despatches No. 6 and No. 3 are not here," said the Secretary. Again he read on. Then at last, looking up, he said, "If I may be permitted to retain this letter a short time, I shall be able to answer everything in it in a satisfactory manner." He made no denial of its charges.

The President said: "Very well. You may wish at present, sir, to step into the back room and further consider the matter." He desired to do so, the President saying that he himself wished meanwhile to talk of it with his other advisers. Mr. Randolph, assenting, retired, and in half an hour returned. What passed in this interval between the chief and his secretaries no one knows, nor what went on in the mind of Washington. Mr. Randolph finally left the meeting, saying, "Your Excellency will hear from me." As he was passing the door of the parlor De Courval came forward to meet him and said, "These papers are of moment, sir. They have just come." The violin ceased, the marquis bowed. The Secretary saluted the small dames and said hastily: "I cannot consider these papers at present. I must go. Give them to the President." Upon this he went away, leaving De Courval surprised at the agitation of his manner.

In a few moments Mr. Wolcott also came out, leaving the office door open. Meanwhile De Courval waited, as he had been desired to do, until the President should be disengaged.

The violin went on, the small figures, as he

watched them, moved in the slow measures of the dance. Then during a pause one little dame courtesied to him, and the old violinist asked would Monsieur le Vicomte walk a minuet with Miss Langdon. De Courval, rising, bowed to the anticipative partner, and said, "No; the President may want me." And again the low notes of the violin set the small puppets in motion. Of a sudden, heard through the open door across the hall, came a voice resonant with anger. It was Washington who spoke. "Why, Colonel Pickering, did he say nothing of moment? He was my friend Peyton Randolph's nephew and adopted son, my aide, my Secretary. I made him Attorney-General, Secretary of State. I would have listened, sir. Never before have I allowed friendship to influence me in an appointment." The voice fell; he heard no more, but through it all the notes of the violin went on, a strange accompaniment, while the children moved in the ceremonious measures of the minuet, and René crossed the room to escape from what he was not meant to hear. A full half hour went by while De Courval sat amazed at the words he had overheard. At last the Secretary of War, entering the hall, passed out of the house.

Then De Courval asked a servant in the gray and red of the Washington livery to take the papers to the President. Hearing him, Washington, coming to the door, said: "Come in, sir. I will see you." The face De Courval saw had regained its usual serenity. "Pray be seated." He took the papers and deliberately considered them. "Yes, they are of importance. · You did well to wait. I thank you." Then smiling kindly he said, "Here has been a matter which concerns you. The despatch you were charged with taking was captured at sea by an English frigate and sent to us by Mr. Hammond, the British minister. It has been nine months on the way. I never, sir, had the least doubt of your honor, and permit me now to express my pleasure. At present this affair of the despatch must remain a secret. It will not be so very long. Permit me also to congratulate you on your new tie to this country. Mistress Wynne has told Mrs. Washington of it. Will you do me the honor to dine with us at four to-morrow? At four."

Coming out of the room with De Courval, he paused in the hall, having said his gracious words. The violin ceased. The little ladies in brocades and slippers came to the drawing-room door, a pretty dozen or so, Miss Langdon, Miss Biddle, Miss Morris, and the Custis children. They courtesied low, waiting expectant. Like most shy men, Washington was most at ease with children, loving what fate had denied him. He was now and then pleased, as they knew, to walk with one of them the slow measure of the minuet, and then to lift up and kiss his small partner in the dance. Now looking down on them from his great height he said: "No," with a sad smile at their respectful appeal—"no, not to-day, children. Not to-day. Good-by, Vicomte." As the servant held the door open, René looked back and saw the tall figure, the wreck of former vigor, go wearily up the broad staircase.

" 'Not to-day, children, not to-day' "

"What has so troubled him?" thought De Courval. "What is this that Edmund Randolph has done?" Standing on the outer step and taking off his hat, he murmured, "My God, I thank thee!" He heard faintly through the open window as he walked away the final notes of the violin and the laughter of childhood as the lesson ended.

It was only a little way, some three blocks, from the house of the President to the State Department, where, at 287 High Street, half a dozen clerks now made up the slender staff. De Courval walked slowly to the office, and setting his business in order, got leave from his immediate superior to be absent the rest of the day.

As he went out, Mr. Randolph passed in. De Courval raised his hat, and said, "Good morning, sir." The Secretary turned back. In his hour of humiliation and evident distress his natural courtesy did not desert him.

"Monsieur," he said in ready French, "the despatch which you sent on its way has returned. I desire to ask you to forget the injustice I did you." He was about to add, "My time to suffer has come." He refrained.

"I thank you," said De Courval; "you could hardly have done otherwise than you did." The two men bowed, and parted to meet no more. "What does it all mean?" thought the young man. Thus set free, he would at once have gone home to tell of the end of the troubles this wandering paper had made for him. But Margaret was at Merion for the day, and others might wait. He wished for

26

an hour to be alone, and felt as he walked eastward the exaltation which was natural to a man sensitive as to the slightest reflection on his honor. Thus surely set at ease, with the slow pace of the thoughtful, he moved along what we now call Market Street. Already at this time it had its country carts and wide market sheds, where Schmidt liked to come, pleased with the colors of the fruit and vegetables. René heard again with a smile the street-cries, "Calamus! sweet calamus!" and "Peaches ripe! ripe!" as on his first sad day in the city.

Aimlessly wandering, he turned northward into Mulberry Street, with its Doric portals, and seeing the many Friends coming out of their meeting-house, was reminded that it was Wednesday. "I should like," he thought, "to have said my thanks with them." Moving westward at Delaware Fifth Street, he entered the burial-ground of Christ Church, and for a while in serious mood read what the living had said of the dead.

"Well, René," said Schmidt, behind him, "which are to be preferred, those underneath or those above ground?"

"I do not know. You startled me. To-day, for me, those above ground."

"When a man has had both experiences he may be able to answer—or not. I once told you I liked to come here. This is my last call upon these dead, some of whom I loved. What fetched you hither?"

"Oh, I was lightly wandering with good news," and he told him of the lost Despatch No. 10, and that it was to be for the time a secret.

"At last!" said Schmidt. "I knew it would
come. The world may congratulate you. I am not
altogether grieved that you have been through this
trial. I, too, have my news. Edmund Randolph
has resigned within an hour or so. Mr. Wolcott has
just heard it from the President. Oh, the wild confusion of things! If you had not sent that despatch
on its way, Randolph would not have fallen. A
fatal paper. Let us go home, Réne."

"But how, sir, does it concern Mr. Randolph?"

"Pickering has talked of it to Bingham, whom I
have seen just now, and I am under the impression
that Fauchet's despatch charged Randolph with
asking for money. It was rather vague, as I heard
it."

"I do not believe it," said René.

"A queer story," said Schmidt. "A wild Jacobin's despatch ruins his Secretary for life, dis-
graces for a time an *émigré* noble, turns out a
cabinet minister—what fancy could have invented
a stranger tale? Come, let us leave these untroubled
dead."

Not until December of that year, 1795, did Randolph's pamphlet, known as his "Vindication," appear. This miserable business concerns us here
solely as it affected the lives of my characters. It
has excited much controversy, and even to this day,
despite Fauchet's explanations to Randolph and the
knowledge we now have of the papers mentioned as
No. 3 and No. 6, it remains in a condition to puzzle
the most astute historian. Certainly few things in
diplomatic annals are more interesting than the

adventures of Despatch No. 10. The verdict of
"not proven" has been the conclusion reached by
some writers, while despite Randolph's failure to
deny the charges at once, as he did later, it is possible that Fauchet misunderstood him or lied, although why he should have done so is difficult to
comprehend.

The despatch, as we have seen, affected more persons than the unfortunate Secretary. Dr. Chovet
left the city in haste when he heard of Schmidt's
return, and Aunt Gainor lamented as among the
not minor consequences the demise of her two gods
and the blue china mandarin. She was in some
degree comforted by the difficult business of Margaret's marriage outfit, for Schmidt, overjoyed at
the complete justification of De Courval, insisted
that there must be no delay, since he himself was
obliged to return to Germany in October.

Mrs. Swanwick would as usual accept no money
help, and the preparations should be simple, she
said, nor was it a day of vulgar extravagance in
bridal presents. Margaret, willing enough to delay,
and happy in the present, was slowly making her
way to what heart there was in the Huguenot dame.
Margaret at her joyous best was hard to resist, and
now made love to the vicomtesse, and, ingenuously
ready to serve, wooed her well and wisely in the
interest of peace.

What Madame de Courval most liked about Margaret was a voice as low and as melodious in its
changes as her own, so that, as Schmidt said, "It is
music, and what it says is of the lesser moment."

Thus one day at evening as they sat on the porch, Margaret murmured in the ear of the dark lady: "I am to be married in a few days; wilt not thou make me a little wedding gift?"

"My dear Margaret," cried René, laughing, "the jewels all went in England, and except a son of small value, what can my mother give you?"

"But, him I have already," cried Margaret. "What I want, madame has—oh, and to spare."

"Well, and what is it I am to give?" said madame, coldly.

"A little love," she whispered.

"Ah, do you say such things to René?"

"No, never. It is he who says them to me. Oh, I am waiting. A lapful I want of thee." and she held up her skirts to receive the gift.

"How saucy thou art," said Mrs. Swanwick.

"It is no affair of thine, Friend Swanwick," cried the Pearl. "I wait, Madame."

"I must borrow of my son," said the vicomtesse. "It shall be ready at thy wedding. Thou wilt have to wait."

"Ah," said René, "we can wait. Come, let us gather some peaches, Margaret," and as they went down the garden, he added: "My mother said 'thou' to you. Did you hear?"

"Yes, I heard. She was giving me what I asked, and would not say so."

"Yes, it was not like her," said the vicomte, well pleased.

The September days went by, and to all outward appearance Madame de Courval accepted with no further protest what it was out of her power to control. Uncle Josiah insisted on settling upon Margaret a modest income, and found it the harder to do so because, except Mistress Gainor Wynne, no one was disposed to differ with him. That lady told him it was shabby. To which he replied that there would be the more when he died.

"Get a permanent ground-rent on your grave," said Gainor, "or never will you lie at rest."

"It is our last ride," said Schmidt, on October the first, of this, the last year of my story. They rode out through the busy Red City and up the Ridge Road, along which General Green led the left wing of the army to the fight at Germantown, and so to the Wissahickon Creek, where, leaving their horses at an inn, they walked up the stream.

"*Ach, lieber Himmel,* this is well," said Schmidt as they sat down on a bed of moss above the water. "Tell me," he said, "more about the President. Oh, more; you were too brief." He insisted eagerly. "I like him with the little ones. And, ah, that tragedy of fallen ambition and all the while the violin music and the dance. It is said that sometimes he is pleased to walk a minuet with one of these small maids. and then will kiss the fortunate little partner."

"He did not that day; he told them he could not. He was sad about Randolph."

"When they are old, they will tell of it, René." And, indeed, two of these children lived to be great-grandmothers, and kissing their grandchildren's children, two of whom live to-day in the Red City, bade them remember that the lips which kissed them had often been kissed by Washington.

"It is a good sign of a man to love these little ones," said Schmidt. "What think you, René? Was Randolph guilty?"

"I do not think so, sir. Fauchet was a quite irresponsible person; but what that silent old man, Washington, finally believed, I should like to know. I fear that he thought Randolph had been anything but loyal to his chief."

For a little while the German seemed lost in thought. Then he said: "You will have my horses and books and the pistols and my rapier. My life will, I hope, need them no more. I mean the weapons; but who can be sure of that? Your own life will find a use for them, if I be not mistaken. When I am gone, Mr. Justice Wilson will call on you, and do not let the Pearl refuse what I shall leave for her. I have lived two lives. One of my lives ends here in this free land. Mr. Wilson has, as it were, my will. In Germany I shall have far more than I shall ever need. Keep my secret. There are, there were, good reasons for it."

"It is safe with me."

"Ah, the dear life I have had here, the freedom of the wilderness, the loves, the simple joys!" As he spoke, he gathered and let fall the autumn leaves strewn thickly on the forest floor. "We shall meet no more on earth, René, and I have loved you as few men love." Again he was long silent.

"I go from these wonder woods to the autumn of a life with duties and, alas! naught else. Sometimes I shall write to you; and, René, you will speak of me to your children.''

The younger man said little in reply. He, too, was deeply moved, and sorrowful as never before. As they sat, Schmidt put his hand on René's shoulder. "May the good God bless and keep you and yours through length of honorable days! Let us go. Never before did the autumn woodlands seem to me sad. Let us go.'' He cast down as he rose the last handful of the red and gold leaves of the maple.

They walked down the creek, still beautiful to-day, and rode home in silence amid the slow down-drift of the early days of the fall.

In the house Margaret met them joyous. "Oh, René, a letter of congratulation to me! Think of it—to me, sir, from General Washington! And one to thee!'' These letters were to decide in far-away after days a famous French law-suit.

THE sun shone bright on the little party which passed among the graves into the modest Gloria Dei, the church of the Swedes. Here were the many kinsfolk; and Washington's secretary, Colonel Lear, Alexander Hamilton and Gouverneur Morris, with Binghams and Morrises; Whartons and Biddles, the forefathers of many lines of men since famous in our annals, whether of war or peace. Women there were also. Mistress Gainor in the front pew with Mrs. Swanwick and Lady Washington, as many called her, and the gay Federalist dames, who smiled approval of Margaret in her radiant loveliness.

Schmidt, grave and stately in dark velvet, gave

away the bride, and the good Swedish rector, the Reverend Nicholas Cullin, read the service of the church.

Then at last they passed into the vestry, and, as Margaret decreed, all must sign the marriage-certificate after the manner of Friends. De Courval wrote his name, and the Pearl, "Margaret Swanwick," whereat arose merriment and an erasure when, blushing, she wrote, "De Courval." Next came Schmidt. He hesitated a moment, and then wrote "Johan Graf von Ehrenstein," to the surprise of the curious many who followed, signing with laughter and chatter of young tongues. Meanwhile the German gentleman, unnoticed, passed out of the vestry, and thus out of my story.

"What with all these signatures, it does look, Vicomte," said young Mr. Morris, "like the famous Declaration of Independence."

"Humph!" growled Josiah Langstroth, "if thee thinks, young man, that it is a declaration of independence, thee is very much mistaken."

"Not I," said René, laughing; and they went out to where Mistress Gainor's landau was waiting, and so home to the mother's house.

Here was a note from Schmidt.

DEAR CHILDREN,
     To say good-by is more than I will to bear. God bless you both! I go at once.
                    JOHAN GRAF VON EHRENSTEIN.

There were tears in the Pearl's eyes.

"He told me he would not say good-by. And is

that his real name, René? No, it is not; I know that
much.''

René smiled. ''Some day,'' he said, ''I shall tell
you.''

In a few minutes came his honor, Mr. Justice
Wilson, saying: ''I feared to be late. Madame,'' to
Margaret, ''here is a remembrance for you from our
friend.''

''Oh, open it!'' she cried. ''Ah, if only he were
here!''

There was a card. It said, ''Within is my kiss of
parting,'' and as she stood in her bridal dress, René
fastened the necklace of great pearls about her neck,
while Madame de Courval looked on in wonder at
the princely gift.

Then the Judge, taking them aside into Schmidt's
room, said: ''I am to give you, Vicomte, these papers
which make you for your wife the trustee of our
friend's estate, a large one, as you may know. My
congratulations, Vicomtesse.''

''He told me!'' said Margaret. ''He told me,
René.'' She was too moved to say more.

In an hour, for this was not a time of wedding
breakfasts, they were on their way to Cliveden, which
Chief-Justice Chew had lent for their honeymoon.

So ends my story, and thus I part with these, the
children of my mind. Many of them lived, and
have left their names in our history; others, perhaps
even more real to me, I dismiss with regret, to become for me, as time runs on, but remembered phan-
toms of the shadow world of fiction.

L'envoi

BEFORE De Courval and his wife returned to France, the Directory had come and gone, the greatest of soldiers had taken on the rule, and the grave Huguenot mother had gone to her grave in Christ Church yard.

Mrs. Swanwick firmly refused to leave her country. "Better, far better," she said, "Margaret, that thou shouldst be without me. I shall live to see thee again and the children."

In after years in Penn's City men read of Napoleon's soldier, General the Comte de Courval and of the American beauty at the Emperor's court, while over their Madeira the older men talked of the German gentleman who had been so long among them, and passed so mysteriously out of the knowledge of all.

Pictures Cameras
Dec. 29 - 1908
"Vara" and "Olda."